Praise for *Will's Surreal Per*

"What a wonderful read! It's a fascinating premise that proves a beautiful canvas for musings on creativity, sexual politics, and food. It makes you want to drop what you're doing and listen more closely to what the universe is trying to tell you. And even if you took everything out of the novel other than the descriptions of food and drink, you'd still have a tremendous read—in fact, after finishing *Will's Surreal Period*, all I wanted to do was cook!"

—GLENN GERMAN, screenwriter and producer of films including *At Middleton* and *Racing for Time*

"A Jiu-Jitsu master of literary plotting, Robert Steven Goldstein flips the script on a dysfunctional family comprised of two emasculated adult sons and their cantankerous wealthy father, who, with petulant vagary, reallocates their respective inheritances at the fulcrum of his paternal control. Marvel and chuckle as these fraught men each succumb to the grace of separate lovers, the serendipity of which amalgamates into a late-in-life chance to rebind the strands of their frayed familial relationships."

—MICHAEL ROSE, author of *The Sorting Room*

"*Will's Surreal Period* proves why works of fiction are high art, hitching us to a wild ride with an ensemble of engaging and eccentric characters brought together by a maladjusted family—some we may love and others we may scorn—but all seductively propel us into their psyches. Robert Steven Goldstein deftly converts our raw human foibles into emotive entertainment and, as he does, reminds us, sometimes painfully, sometimes hilariously, who we are."

—MICHAEL J. COFFINO, award winning author of *Truth Is in the House.*

"The ups and downs of dysfunctional family life are on full, fascinating display in Robert Steven Goldstein's well-imagined novel, *Will's Surreal Period*. Full of twists, turns, and the familiar boorish behavior that we seem to reserve specially for family, follow protagonist Will Wozniak as he grapples with a brain tumor, infidelity, and an unexpected career shift, a journey that is at times both hilarious and deeply poignant. Strap in for a ripping good ride with this entertaining read."

—MADELEINE JONES, author of the
forthcoming novel *The Witchhammer*

"*Will's Surreal Period* is a witty, engaging romp. Cantankerous Arthur Wozniak wants to control his adult sons who are each struggling to find their place in the world. Hidden passions ignite, suppressed talents emerge, and the Wozniaks reluctantly evolve into the family they were meant to be."

—CARLA DAMRON, author of the forthcoming novel
The Orchid Tattoo, The Stone Necklace (winner of the WFWA
Star award) and the Caleb Knowles mystery series

"In a sly take on Ovid's *Metamorphosis*, Will, a mediocre painter, suffers a brain tumour that transmogrifies him into an uninhibited creative genius. His quarrelsome family members are deftly portrayed with considerable literary merit. There is an unerring eye for multi-ethnic mores (especially involving food) and American material culture, as well as a strong sense of time and locality. A well-crafted and provocative read."

—DAVID JENKINS, Formerly Professor of Arts Education,
University of Warwick, UK, and author of the
satirical chess-themed novel *Spurious Games*

WILL'S SURREAL PERIOD

WILL'S SURREAL PERIOD

A Novel

ROBERT STEVEN GOLDSTEIN

spark
press

Published by SparkPress, a BookSparks imprint,
A division of SparkPoint Studio, LLC
Phoenix, Arizona, USA, 85007
www.gosparkpress.com

Published 2022
Printed in the United States of America
Print ISBN: 978-1-68463-143-8
E-ISBN: 978-1-68463-144-5

Library of Congress Control Number: 2022901399

Formatting by Kiran Spees

For Sandy, my eternal love,

Although I conquer all the earth,
yet for me there is only one city.
In that city there is for me only one house;
and in that house, one room only;
and in that room, a bed.
And one woman sleeps there,
the shining joy and jewel of all my kingdom.

(Sanskrit)

CHAPTER 1

*T*HE canopies along the expansive row of outdoor stalls were worn and frayed. Standing inside his narrow booth, William Wozniak carefully layered a dozen framed paintings and pen-and-ink drawings into a large, soft-sided case. He zippered it shut slowly, making certain not to snag an edge of canvas.

You only sold two damn paintings today?

The shrill, imagined voice shattered his reverie. But he pushed it aside, and made certain the canvases were secure.

He hauled the case in one hand and his folding table and chair in the other as he trudged back up the hill to the dusty auxiliary parking lot. The paved lot was closer, but the old dirt lot was a good deal cheaper.

I bet they bargained you down to like ten or fifteen dollars each, right?

He meticulously piled everything into the back of his old van. He climbed in, started the engine, and merged cautiously into the throng of vehicles exiting the San Jose flea market.

He'd rewired the van's old stereo box just that week and it was working well now. The audio book resumed where he'd left off. It was a library rental—a scholarly biography of Leonardo da Vinci. It would be good company on the hour-and-a-half drive back to San Francisco.

This is really getting ridiculous, you spending every Sunday down there. For this? You need to get a real job.

Yes, the uninvited comments hurtling through his brain were negative. But that was only logical. The mind enumerates the more likely possibilities first.

He acknowledged, though, that he could be wrong. Perhaps he'd find Rosemary in a cheerful mood, cooking some exotic, aromatic stew to serve over pasta or rice. Maybe she'd be obsessing joyfully over spices and herbs, and have cocktails prepared. Perhaps she would have already started sipping on one.

That alternative was less likely, but not inconceivable.

The traffic began thinning. Highway 101 was the more direct route, but William opted for highway 280, which for years had boasted signs proclaiming it "The World's Most Beautiful Freeway." Those signs were gone, but the road's wide lanes still wound through magnificent rolling hills covered with lush foliage. And the detour only added fifteen or twenty minutes to the ride home.

That would afford him a bit of extra time to gird himself for whatever Rosemary might have in store for him.

Arthur Wozniak insisted that his house in Scarsdale be impeccably maintained. Its old outer walls were built of a solid red brick that contrasted artfully with the property's green lawn and boxwood hedges in spring and summer, and with the white snow that blanketed the front yard in winter. In autumn, when the two large maple trees shed their gold and crimson leaves, Arthur had his son Bertram sweep them off the paved paths onto the lawn, where they crackled under Arthur's feet if he walked on them.

"Bertram!" Arthur yelled from the brown leather recliner in his study.

He heard no response.

"Bertram!" Arthur screamed once more, just a few moments later—louder this time, and with exaggerated irritation. "Bertram! Where the hell are you?"

His son was slightly out of breath when he finally reached the study.

"Goddamn it, Bertram! Where were you? I've been calling you for ten minutes."

"You haven't been calling me for ten minutes," he said, grimacing. "That's ridiculous. It's probably been a minute and a half, if that. Just calm down, for God's sake."

"Well, what were you doing?" Arthur demanded.

"I was in the middle of putting together a pot roast for dinner tonight, damn it. I had to shut the burner off and wash my hands when I heard you call. Jesus!"

"Why the hell are you out of breath? You're not even forty years old. A man your age should be able to run up that staircase without a problem. I could do it at your age. You're not taking care of yourself. If you're not around, where the hell is that going to leave *me*?"

"Don't worry about *my* health," Bertram said. "I'll be here for a long time after you're gone."

"Let's hope so."

"And speaking of health"—Bertram shook his head—"why the hell aren't you doing those exercises the physical therapist gave you? You had a goddamn hip replacement. You need to do 'em. You wouldn't have to scream for me to come running every time you drop something if you could move better."

With that, he bent down and picked up a pad and pencil that had fallen from Arthur's desk onto the rug beneath it.

"I move just fine. I didn't call you here to pick that up. I can pick that up myself. I just didn't get to it yet."

"You'd move better if you did the exercises."

"I get enough damn exercise. Those physical therapists are out of their minds. No sane person is going to do all those things. It's idiocy."

"So? What's so urgent that you called me up here?"

"I want to see a copy of the will. Where the hell did you put it?"

"I didn't put it *anywhere*," Bertram said, his voice shrill with exasperation. "*You* put it somewhere. You must have filed it in one of the drawers here in the study. Did you look?"

"I looked . . . I didn't see it," Arthur mumbled sheepishly, turning away and glancing down.

"You didn't look at all." Bertram started yanking desk drawers open and rummaging through their contents.

"Be careful with those papers," Arthur shouted, his voice reclaiming its contentious timbre.

"What the hell do you want with the will, anyway?" Bertram asked. "We just changed it again, a few months ago."

"What did we change it to?"

"Seventy-five/twenty-five," Bertram replied quickly. "Why, Dad?" His tone had abruptly modulated and now had a calm, solicitous quality. "Did you want to change it again?"

"Maybe. I might be willing to up your share to 80 percent if you had a better attitude and spent more time here at the house."

"More time here at the house? I *live* here."

"You're out a lot," Arthur grumbled.

"I need to have at least a little bit of a social life, Dad," Bertram pleaded. "And I have a job, for God's sake."

"A job?" Arthur chuckled. "Who are you trying to kid? You don't have a job."

"I'm a real estate broker."

Arthur laughed loudly. "Right. And how many properties did you move last year? Two? Three? I bet you didn't even move three. You're my caregiver. That's what you do. You're not great at it but at least you're here, which is more than I can say for your deadbeat brother in San Francisco who thinks he's a painter and lives off his wife."

"That's right!" Bertram said, seizing on his father's last remark, his demeanor turning more upbeat. He raised his right arm and shook his index finger in his father's face for emphasis. "If William had stayed here in New York, he could be helping us with some of this. And *you'd* be better taken care of." He scrutinized Arthur's countenance, and his posture relaxed slightly. "I'll find the will," he said, now searching much more calmly and methodically. "We can move it to eighty/twenty. You'll be happy with how I take care of you."

The aromas in the small kitchen were pervasive and exhilarating. Rosemary was immersed in preparation. Lidded pots simmered on three burners. She leaned down and sniffed the uncovered saucepan on the fourth flame as she gently stirred its contents.

And something wonderful and sweet was percolating in the oven.

On the far end of the counter, a tall aluminum cocktail shaker, moist with condensation, stood alongside a number of reamed lemon halves, with an open bottle of vodka just a few inches away. A partly filled stemmed glass holding cloudy liquid with a twist of lemon rind hugging the bottom sat near the stove.

When Rosemary turned and greeted William with a broad smile and a warm "Hi, honey!" he realized that she was working on at least her second drink of the evening.

This was the best domestic tableau he could have hoped for.

"Hi," he said, "let me throw this stuff in my studio, and I'll be right back to join you."

It was a modest two-bedroom flat. His art studio, the smaller of the two bedrooms at the end of the hall, was crammed with canvases of all sizes. Brushes, tubes of paint, inkbottles, and cans of turpentine and linseed oil were strewn upon shelves and the floor. There were two easels, an old chair on rollers, and a drafting table, above which stood a projector mounted on a tripod that could cast a photograph or other image onto a canvas for tracing. William dropped his soft-sided case, folding table, and chair in the doorway and raced back to the kitchen. He thought for a moment of stopping to urinate, but quickly dismissed the thought; it was such good fortune to find Rosemary so engaged and ebullient, he did not want to keep her waiting and risk triggering impatience or anger.

He gave her a quick kiss when he walked in. "That lemon drop looks good," he said.

"Pour yourself one, honey. I chilled a glass for you. It's in the freezer."

William fetched his glass.

"Shake before you pour it," Rosemary said.

He obliged, then brought his glass over to toast before taking a sip.

"Where's your twist of lemon rind?" she demanded. "I left one for you, right there next to the shaker. Go back, rub it on the rim of the glass, and then twist it and drop it in. What's the point in my making a perfect cocktail if you don't treat it properly?"

"I just couldn't wait to dig in, I guess," he said apologetically. He took his drink and garnished it as instructed, and was back a moment later.

"Much better," she said. "Cheers!"

"Cheers," he replied, and they clinked glasses.

William downed about half the drink with a couple of large gulps. "What are you cooking?" he asked. "It smells great in here."

She turned to him and smiled. "Oh, does it?" Her blue eyes

widened and her grin grew broad—she had a childlike proclivity for excitement and enthusiasm. Her short stature, slender, boyish figure, and pixie haircut added to her youthfulness. "I'll tell you all about it in a minute, but I have to season this first."

William smiled, then gulped down the rest of his lemon drop. "Wow, that went down easy," he said. "I think I'll pour myself another."

"Top off mine too while you're at it," she said as she dropped pinches of herbs into the saucepan before her.

When he returned with the two full glasses, she was consulting a food-stained sheet of paper, one of several strewn upon the counter beside the stove—printouts of recipes she'd gleaned from the internet. She lifted the lid on a small pot.

"Ah, you made rice too." The tip of William's tongue made an almost imperceptible sweep of his lower lip.

"It's actually a pilaf," she said, tasting a few grains. "Fantastic!" she cried. "Here, taste!" She held the spoon up to his mouth and cupped her hand under to catch anything he dripped.

"Oh, so good!" he said. "What are the flavors I taste?"

"Onion, garlic, and a touch of cumin. Everything tonight is going to be from Turkey, Afghanistan, Persia—you know, those kinds of places."

"What's in the other pots?"

"Well, this is Afghani eggplant stew with turmeric and cayenne," she said, pointing to the saucepan she'd been stirring. "That's Turkish butter beans with oregano, harissa, and cumin. And in the back, next to the pilaf, is a Middle Eastern vegetable stew; it has green beans, zucchini, tomatoes, onions, carrots, and celery." She looked up, clearly seeking approval.

"Sounds wonderful! I can't wait." William gazed down at her warmly. "And do I smell something in the oven?"

"Persian apple cake with rose water and raisins!"

"Wow!" he exclaimed. "Your food is always great, but you've really outdone yourself tonight!"

She giggled and gave him a hug. "I really should cook every weekend," she said. "It's invigorating. I feel so alive when I do it."

"You should," he agreed.

"It's just hard to get started sometimes, you know? After being on my feet all week at the dentist's office—leaning over people's mouths, scraping tartar—I usually just want to veg out on the couch."

"Well, here's to a great meal tonight! All thanks to you!" He held out his glass, and they toasted.

"Okay, honey," Rosemary said after a couple of gulps, "I've had a bit to drink now. Dare I ask if you sold any paintings today?"

"I sold two pieces," he said. "One painting and one pen-and-ink drawing."

"Who bought them?"

"Oh, the usual: parents who thought they'd be nice in a kid's room."

"So, then, you didn't get much for them?" she probed.

"Well," he said hesitantly. "Thirty-five for the pen-and-ink. Fifty for the painting."

"Well, that's something, I guess."

William finished his drink. "I'll mix up another round."

"Thanks," Rosemary said. "You know, honey—you don't make lemon drops nearly as spectacularly as I do. But I guess with all I've had already, it won't really matter." She smirked at him as if he'd find that funny.

He didn't, but refrained from reacting. He took the shaker to the freezer and piled in some more ice.

"Did anybody who was seriously into art look at your stuff today?" Rosemary asked.

"Actually," he said, "a couple of snothead assholes did. They showed up together—I think they might have been a couple. One claimed he worked at a museum here in the Bay. The other said he was an art professor."

"And what did they say about your stuff?"

"Oh, the usual shit. They said my work was stiff and rigid—like it couldn't decide if it was a photograph or a comic book."

Rosemary's eyes narrowed. "What did you say to them?"

"I thanked them and smiled," William said.

"Thanked them and smiled? They were insulting you!"

"Well, in a way, what they said had some element of truth to it. My paintings and ink drawings are all about fine, exacting detail. In my best ones, the lines and shading are indistinguishable from a photograph. But the creatures that inhabit them! Ah!" He smiled. "They don't exist other than in my imagination. And the feats they perform are impossible for human beings."

"But they were mocking you!"

"Yes."

He downed some more of the lemon drop, and looked at Rosemary. She appeared distressed.

"But I had the last laugh," he assured her. "They assumed I was actually taking their words as compliments—like I was some sort of idiot who was incapable of discerning their intent. But the joke was on *them*. I knew *exactly* what they were saying, whereas *they* had no clue as to *my* comprehension of the situation."

She looked up at him sadly. "I think you need to get a real job, honey," she said softly, her hand lightly fondling his chest. "And maybe think about painting in a different style."

William set his drink down on the counter. "I'm sorry, babe, you need to excuse me for a moment—I have to pee." His shoulders dropped as he traipsed dejectedly toward the bathroom.

Chapter 2

*I*T had been brisk and foggy in San Francisco when they set out. But here in San Leandro, just south of Oakland on the east side of the Bay, it was sunny and warm. Rosemary loved the expansive farmers market that materialized there every Saturday morning at nine. She always insisted they get there early, before the crowds, so she'd have time to wander through the myriad folding tables piled high with fresh offerings—each stand protected from the bright sun by a cloth awning strung on tall plastic poles.

She used the market to stock up on pretty much everything she'd need for the week. Today, she noted to William, the eggplant and peppers looked especially luscious, and there were fresh brown eggs, soft, fragrant goat cheeses, and crusty loaves of country-style sourdough bread. The local, organic fare was precisely the quality Rosemary coveted, and cost a fraction of what it would in San Francisco's trendy markets.

William slogged along close behind her, constantly fighting the urge to saunter off and examine alluring or exotic tidbits. He lost his focus for a moment and was drawn to a table of strange, aromatic, prickly Asian fruits with iridescent skins ranging in shades from orange to green. A young Filipino woman was fondling and sniffing the fruit. She wore a skintight polka-dot halter top, and cutoff jeans so skimpy that their white pocket linings dipped lower on her thighs than did the frayed bottoms of the shorts themselves.

"William! Get back here!" Rosemary yelled just before he reached the array.

He returned obediently and resumed his silent vigil at her side.

"How many times have I told you not to wander off?" she chastised him. "Stay with me. I need you here. I can't keep looking for you when you go wandering off."

He watched as she sampled and selected produce with great care, squeezing, prodding, smelling, and shaking the various edibles to assess their suitability. He glanced back quickly at the Filipino woman, and took a moment to conceptualize the distinction. Rosemary's examination of produce was efficient, pragmatic, and direct, whereas the young woman's was sensuous and playful. But perhaps when he had watched Rosemary inspect fruit for the first time years earlier, he had found her modus operandi sensuous and playful then too.

His musings were interrupted abruptly as Rosemary thrust another parcel into his backpack, jarring him forward just a bit. Although she insisted that William carry the paper bags containing eggs, tomatoes, and other delicate items in his hands so they wouldn't be crushed, the hardier fare was stuffed unceremoniously into the large backpack she had him wear.

By the time they were ready to load the van and head home, William's backpack was bulging and he was awkwardly juggling multiple paper sacks in each of his arms.

William had never been adept at athletics. He was much taller than Rosemary—big boned, yet not imposing—and although he wasn't fat, there was a droopy softness about his frame and posture.

He was relieved when he was finally able to load the groceries into the back of the van. Moments later, he was seated comfortably behind the wheel, sliding the transmission into reverse, ready to start the drive home. Rosemary clambered into the passenger seat, and he slowly backed out of the parking spot and exited the lot.

He flipped on the radio. An NPR program was playing a segment about efforts to retrieve art stolen by the Nazis during World War II.

It had only been on for a minute or two when Rosemary reached over and switched the radio to another station. "Let's hear some music instead," she said.

The blaring volume of the jazz improvisation caused William to wince momentarily, but Rosemary quickly lowered it a bit.

What he'd heard of the story about Nazi stolen art had been intriguing, and he would have preferred to keep listening to that. But the music was all right—and Rosemary was clearly enjoying it, her eyes closed, head bobbing to the rhythms. He relaxed and turned onto the road leading to the freeway.

They were nearly to the Bay Bridge when William's cell phone rang. He took it out of his pocket to see who was calling, but Rosemary plucked it out of his hand before he could glance at it.

"Don't look at that while you're driving!" she admonished, already studying the screen. "Oh! It's your father. I'll put it on speaker."

William didn't feel like talking to his father, and he started to tell her so, but she'd already answered and switched the phone into speaker mode, so he snapped his mouth shut.

She held the phone up to his face; he said nothing.

"Hello? Hello?" cried Arthur on the other end. "Who's there? Why the hell don't I hear anything?"

William intentionally waited silently for a few more moments before finally responding.

"Hi, Dad. It's William," he said flatly. "I'm here with Rosemary."

"What's going on? Why did it take you so damn long to answer the phone? Where the hell are you?"

"We're in the van. We're on our way home from the farmers market."

"Farmers market? Don't you two ever shop in a supermarket like normal people?"

William glanced at Rosemary and rolled his eyes. "How have you been, Dad?"

"Fine. Fine. Listen, I have something to discuss with you. Do you have a few minutes?"

"Sure. What's up?"

"I changed the will," Arthur said.

"Okay."

"Listen, I want you to hear this. I changed the percentages again."

"Okay."

"Don't you want to know what your new share is?"

"Sure."

"I changed the will to eighty/twenty. Eighty percent to Bertram. Twenty percent to you." Arthur waited for a response.

"Okay, that's fine," William said calmly.

"I don't think you heard me! I reduced your share to twenty percent."

"I heard you, Dad. That's fine."

"Do you understand what I'm saying? You're down to twenty percent. Bertram's here helping me. He deserves it. Do you hear what I'm saying?"

"I hear you, Dad, and it's fine. It's your money. You can do whatever you please with it. It's fine with me. If you leave me anything at all I'll certainly appreciate it, but I'm not planning on it, and I don't need it. So any way you choose to do it is fine."

"Goddamnit! Are you even listening? I cut your damn share to twenty percent."

"Hey, I'm getting near the house now, and I have to find a place to park. I need to go. Thanks for the call. Be well."

"I'm not done!" Arthur screamed.

"Sorry, Dad. I've got to go. Be well. Say hi to Bert for me." With that, Arthur turned to Rosemary and silently mouthed, "HANG UP."

Rosemary complied, then shoved the phone into one of the van's cup wells. William recognized her exasperated glare and hyperbolic exhalation as a precursor to an oncoming verbal tirade.

It materialized almost immediately, just as he pulled alongside an available parking spot.

"Why do you keep saying 'fine'?" she snapped. "What's the matter with you? He's cutting you out of his will—bit by bit, but it's clear where it's going. First it was sixty/forty. Then it was sixty-five/thirty-five. And on and on. This is like the fifth time he's done it. You're going to get *nothing*! This is your *life*. This is *our* life. How can you be so blasé? Why don't you stand up for yourself?"

"To what end, exactly?" William replied, calmly but firmly. "Do you honestly think he's going to change his mind? The will is what it is. It doesn't matter what I say. It's all based on the fact that I left New York and, in his mind, abandoned my family responsibilities. And I don't regret that decision for a moment. I had to get away from that insanity. I have a right to live my own life. And I never would have met you if I hadn't."

"But we *need* that money. Why do keep telling him we don't?"

"The money we get or *don't* get is whatever it's going to be, Rosemary. But what *he's* after is seeing me grovel. *That's* what he wants. He already controls the money; I can't change that. But I certainly can deny him the pleasure of seeing me beg and squirm. That he'll *never* get. And he wants it. Didn't you hear how frustrated he got when I kept saying fine?"

"But we *do* need the money, Will. Renting a crummy little flat like ours may be fine for you, but I want a house. And we'll never be able to buy a house in the Bay Area if you don't get a job."

"Maybe my art will start to sell."

"Please, Will, get a job in the meantime. Why won't you listen to reason? We're never—"

The blare of angry horns startled them both. The van still sat alongside the empty parking spot. William's quick glance in the rearview mirror revealed three cars queued up impatiently behind him, drivers screaming and gesticulating. He raised his right hand apologetically and backed slowly into the space, ignoring the procession of middle fingers thrust in his direction as the cars sped by.

CHAPTER 3

So dour and aloof was the customary demeanor of Dr. Judith Feigenbaum that many of her fellow faculty members at the medical center speculated she might fall somewhere on the autistic spectrum. Though the term "Asperger syndrome" had been eliminated as an official medical diagnosis several years prior, older physicians often referred to Dr. Feigenbaum as "Mrs. Asperger" in snide whispered conversations.

Dr. Feigenbaum rarely engaged in social interaction with her peers. Any verbal remarks she uttered were almost always limited to staff meetings, where her comments were reliably succinct, occasionally surprisingly insightful, and without exception painfully humorless.

Despite all that, none of her fellow physicians could deny that she was a uniquely brilliant neurosurgeon. And by all accounts, she was a relatively effective teacher to the third- and fourth-year medical students with whom she regularly interacted.

Like her colleagues, Judith Feigenbaum published scientific papers in medical journals.

But unlike her colleagues, she also wrote books for the lay public. And what her peers found nearly impossible to comprehend was that these books all became bestsellers and were universally applauded for their conversational tone, cordial sensibility, and human perspective.

Some fellow faculty members were not merely baffled but also infuriated by this. If Judith Feigenbaum was capable of relating to ordinary people so personably in print, why the hell couldn't she wish a fellow physician good morning when they passed one another in the hallway?

Due to her busy schedule and awkwardness with crowds and social situations, Dr. Feigenbaum's publisher and agent scrupulously shielded her from book signings or public readings. But they'd discovered that Dr. Feigenbaum, for some reason that no one could quite explain, sounded warm and friendly, even maternal, on the radio. So periodic radio interviews to promote her books were arranged, each carefully scripted and organized logistically such that Feigenbaum could participate by phone while sitting alone in her office, door locked and shade drawn.

Every interview adhered to the same pattern: a few scrupulously scripted questions and answers were followed by Feigenbaum reading an excerpt from her book—her disembodied voice uncannily mellifluous and reassuring over the airwaves.

William was in his van one Sunday morning, driving down to the flea market in San Jose, when he first heard Dr. Feigenbaum. His radio was tuned to San Francisco's National Public Radio station, and she had just been introduced for a brief interview.

After a few perfunctory questions were posed and answered, Dr. Feigenbaum read this short excerpt from her most recent book:

"The human brain weighs about three pounds. It is an extraordinarily fragile organ.

"The mistaken notion that the brain is firm and rubbery is due to the fact that brains viewed outside the body have been preserved in chemicals such as formaldehyde, which harden the organs so that they can be handled and dissected. A living brain is actually the consistency of an overripe avocado. It is so soft that it must float in cerebrospinal fluid to remain undamaged. Were it to actually rest on bone within the skull, it would eventually be crushed by its own weight.

"But the capabilities of this pulpy, convoluted mass are remarkable. Despite centuries of research, scientists know relatively little about how the brain accomplishes its feats of logic, memory, computation, and analysis. Its mechanisms exhibit some aspects of digital technology and some of analog, yet much of its modus operandi remains completely unexplained.

"The human brain is frequently compared to a computer. While there are some similarities, the two are not at all the same.

"It took scientists decades of work to program a computer to consistently defeat human grandmasters in chess. But those computers cannot find joy in chess, or ponder the subtle analogies between chess and life. Nor can those computers decide that they have played enough chess for today, and think instead about what they might want for dinner. They cannot then go to the grocery store and discover unexpected produce, ripe and in season, and decide, on a whim, that an impromptu menu adjustment would make for a delectable surprise. And those computers cannot then go home and cook dinner, open a carefully selected bottle of wine, and appreciate the poetic nuance of the pairing."

William found Dr. Feigenbaum's ideas mesmerizing and her voice—intoxicating.

Brokerage offices occupied the bulk of the thirty-five-story brick building in lower Manhattan. In the restroom on the fifteenth floor, Dag Odegaard stopped momentarily at the mirror to fuss with his hair. It lay flawlessly, but he nudged a couple of strands nonetheless.

Dag's three-piece suit was tailored to fit his trim torso snugly—his tie was knotted into a perfect isosceles triangle.

He quickly moved over to the bank of five urinals and set up at the one at the far end. It was mounted lower on the wall than the other four, and better accommodated his short stature.

As he pulled down his zipper, he heard the men's room door open; looking over his shoulder, he saw the IT repair guy stroll in.

Dag closed his eyes and emitted a barely audible sigh.

The fifteenth floor was occupied solely by brokers, but desktop PCs malfunctioned often and the itinerant IT guy was therefore a frequent visitor. Dag disliked him not because he was gay—Dag was gay too—but because he flaunted his sexuality so flagrantly. Dag cringed when the IT guy strolled among the cubicles, sashaying ludicrously. A stud earring, or even two, might have been tasteful, but the IT guy insisted on large hoops and colorful baubles that dangled ostentatiously from each ear. His feminine vocal inflection was so exaggerated and shrill that Dag was sure it must cause physical damage to the eardrums of those who were too frequently subjected to it.

As Dag expected, the IT guy stationed himself at the urinal right next to the one he was using, even though the rest of the bank of five were clearly available.

He was a tall, slender fellow, and towered nearly a foot above Dag. With him standing so close, Dag was unnerved to the point that he couldn't get his urine stream going. He forced himself to relax and breathe deeply.

Finally, a slow trickle emerged.

They were silent for a few moments, but Dag recoiled imperceptibly as soon as he heard the strident voice snark, "So, girlfriend, you had asparagus for lunch!"

"What?" Dag said indignantly, staring tensely at his own urine stream, refusing to make eye contact.

"You had asparagus for lunch!" the IT guy repeated, and smirked. "It's obvious. I can smell it. What cuisine was it? Chinese?"

"What do you mean you can smell it?" Dag said, turning his head to glare.

"I can smell it. Your urine reeks of asparagus. Are you telling me you can't smell that?" The IT guy finished and zipped up.

"My urine does not smell! Just leave me alone, you jerk." He paused for just a moment, then added, "And I am certainly *not* your girlfriend!"

"My god! You're such a self-important old queen," the IT guy taunted before prancing out the door.

Dag finished urinating, jiggled and tapped scrupulously until the dripping stopped, and zipped up. He hated in general when young men approached the urinal while he was midstream yet finished long before he did. In this particular case, it was even more annoying.

He washed his hands and bristled as he replayed what the IT guy had said as he left.

Dag didn't especially mind being called self-important or a queen. It was rude to verbalize, but both of those were arguably true. However, he hated being called *old*. He'd just turned fifty-one. And he had no trouble keeping up with his boyfriend who was in his late thirties. They were supposed to see one another tonight—perhaps it would be a good idea to feel him out about the age difference and get some reassurance that fifty-one was just an arbitrary number.

He also made a mental note for the future: *When you have lunch at that Chinese hole-in-the-wall you love and order your usual beef and asparagus with black bean sauce—urinate in a private stall for the rest of the day.*

Arthur was sitting in his study, gazing at charts on his computer, when Bert walked in.

"Ah, Bertram," Arthur said. "Come take a look at this. I just sold a bunch of shares in a gas company. It's done well for us for the past few months, but I think it's plateaued. So, I'm looking to buy something new. See this?" He pointed to the screen. "*This* company produces corrugated cardboard boxes. Among other things. But the *boxes*, you know, everybody buys online now and everything's delivered in *boxes*. Can you imagine how many of them get delivered and then thrown out, every day? Look at this sales graph, Bert, and this list of customers. They're a small company, but growing."

"So you're investing?"

"Oh yes, I'm buying shares. Quite a few. This is going to be a good investment. I can feel it."

"That's great, Dad. You always seem to be right about these things."

"Damn straight. How do you think we got this beautiful house, two pieces of rental property, and a nice nest egg of stock? How many people do you know who could build a little empire like this just sitting in front of a computer screen all day, researching companies and trading?"

Bert had heard Arthur extoll his own financial acumen many times before.

"Well, I came up to let you know that I'm going to be gone for a few hours."

"Where are you going?" Arthur demanded.

"I'm meeting a friend for drinks, in the city. I'll probably stay for dinner. I left you a plate of roast beef with mashed potatoes and broccoli. You just have to put it in the microwave—it's ready to go. And there's some salad from last night if you want that too."

"All right. You go ahead and have fun with your friend. I'll be fine, I suppose. Sitting here alone. Eating by myself."

Bert had determined long ago that ignoring Arthur's self-pity was his only plausible strategy. Even so, it invariably rankled him. "You'll be fine, Dad," he said. "Call me if you need me."

"Did you boil the broccoli till it's soft?" Arthur called out as Burt jogged down the stairs. "You know I can't stand it unless it's soft."

"It's soft!" Bert yelled back, then raced out the front door and shut it firmly behind him before Arthur had a chance to complain about anything else.

Ten minutes later, he pulled into the railroad station's parking lot, raced up to the platform, and slipped onto the express headed into Manhattan just as it was shutting its doors.

The hotel was only a few blocks from Grand Central Station—it took Bert less than five minutes to walk over. The lobby bar's low tables, plush couches, and upholstered chairs were framed by mirrored walls and a tall ceiling. Arresting glass chandeliers dangled down on golden chains. The gestalt hovered precariously between tasteful and ostentatious. Bert spotted Dag sipping on a vodka martini.

They met here often.

Dag rose as Bert approached. Bert hinged his knees and hunched over for a perfunctory hug before they both sat down.

Dag raised his hand to catch the waitress's attention.

"Same as him," Bert said as the waitress set down a napkin and a complimentary ramekin full of very salty nuts.

Dag produced a glistening silver case from the breast pocket of his suit coat and opened it as Bert fished through the ramekin for a filbert.

"Bertie, I have a new business card!" Dag said. "I want you see it."

"A new card? Did you get a new position?"

"No, no," Dag said. "I changed the spelling of my name."

"What do you mean?"

Dag handed him a card.

DAG ØDEGAARD

ACCOUNT EXECUTIVE

Bert's eyes and cheeks scrunched uncomfortably, then he looked back to Dag. "You didn't actually change the spelling of your name. You just put a slash through the 'O' in Odegaard. Where on earth did you come up with *that?*"

"I didn't *come up* with it," Dag grumbled. "That's the traditional spelling of my family's name."

Bert laughed. "Maybe in Norway. Not in fucking Manhattan."

"It looks classy. It'll help attract clients."

"It might. On the other hand, it might look a little pretentious."

"Pretentious! It's not pretentious!" Dag squealed indignantly.

"Some people might think it is. I mean, you're not from Norway, for God's sake. You were born in Bay Ridge. In *Brooklyn*."

"This is how my family originally spelled it. Maybe it looks pretentious to *you*, but to the kind of people I'm trying to sell to, it looks classy."

"What does *that* mean? You wouldn't want to sell to *me?*"

"Well, Bertie, you have no money."

"But I will. When my Dad's estate turns over, I'll have lots of money. More than you."

"Well, that's exactly it, Bertie. You have the *potential* for money, but right now you actually don't *have* any money. I sell to people who *have* money *now*. And maybe when you *have* money in the future, you won't find a business card like this quite so *pretentious*."

Bert laughed until his shoulders shook. "Oh, I'll still find it pretentious," he said. "Really pretentious. But if *you* like it, sweetie, that's all that matters. And I wish you good luck with it. Here's to many good sales."

"Well! I'll drink to that."

They clinked glasses.

They enjoyed a second round and then caught a taxi uptown, where they took an elevator up to Dag's spacious tenth-floor co-op. While Dag mixed another pitcher of martinis in the kitchen Bert sat quietly in the living room, gazing out the picture window. It stretched nearly across the entire far wall and had a grand view of Central Park.

They sipped and cuddled and shared a few tokes on a joint, and as the sun began to set over the park meadow, they slipped into the bedroom, kissing passionately as they made their way to the bed.

They made love in their customary manner: Bert topping, Dag on all fours. Dag always insisted that even if he didn't ejaculate, he experienced a sort of extended prostate orgasm, much as he imagined a woman would—oscillating, with ebbs and flows.

Even so, on some nights Bert reached down just as he came and finished Dag by hand. He did so this evening. Despite his habitual protestations that Bert's extra ministrations were unnecessary, Dag predictably rolled over into an especially blissful stupor when he finished.

Tonight, though, Dag's ejaculation also appeared to make him reflective and, after a few minutes, eager to share.

"You don't mind that I'm always the bottom, do you Bertie?"

"Not at all. That's just who you are."

"You're right. I'm such a bottom." Dag smiled broadly. "I could never be with a woman. But I know *you* have, Bertie. You said it was just a couple of times, but you managed it. I could never do that."

"Well, I was thinking about *guys* while I did it," Bert said with a shy smirk.

"And it doesn't bother you that I never let you be the bottom with us?"

Bert pondered exactly how to respond.

"Actually," he whispered hesitantly, "I don't think my anus could handle it even if I wanted to."

Dag propped himself up on one arm and looked down at Bert. "Why's that?"

"I guess I never told you about the . . . problem I had when I was born."

"No, Bertie." Dag stroked his arm. "What happened?"

"You know, I never even knew about it until a couple of years ago. I went in for my annual checkup. I had just gotten a new doctor, and he made a comment that my anus was abnormally small. He was surprised that nobody else had ever pointed it out to me. He said it was about a third of normal size, and it had some scarring. So, I go home and ask my father if he knows anything about it. And Arthur tells me this story that he's never shared before, never even mentioned. He tells me that when I was first born I couldn't shit. He says he and my mother had to force their fingers in and pull out tiny bits. So they finally took me to the doctor, and apparently, I barely had any opening at all. So the doctors had to do a surgery to open me up. I mean, it works okay now, but it's still not close to normal size."

"Oh God!" Dag winced. "That's a big deal, Bertie. And your father never thought to mention it?"

"You know, I asked him about that. Here's what he said . . . " Bert snickered and affected a deep, hoarse whisper and a heavy New York accent as he imitated Arthur: "Hell! You don't even remember it. So what's the big deal? And the doctor said you were lucky. Back when people *my* age were kids, they just laid you on your belly and reamed you open. Didn't bother with anesthetic."

Dag gasped. "Jesus, Bertie!" Then he thought for a moment and chuckled. "So within the first few weeks of your life you were totally full of shit—and then you had your dick circumcised, and your ass reamed. No wonder you're fucked up."

"Yeah, we make a good pair that way." Bert nudged him with his elbow. "At least I have an excuse."Dag squeezed closer and rested his head on Bert's chest. Dag liked that Bert's torso was taut and solid. Bert had been a star athlete in school, a pitcher on the baseball team. He didn't work out that much anymore, but his physique had endured well nevertheless.

"How do you feel about our age difference, Bertie?" Dag asked softly, glad that Bert couldn't see his face as he posed the question; he was sure his uncertainty was discernable.

"It's not an issue for me."

"You're sure?"

"Absolutely."

"So, you think I keep up with you okay?"

"You keep up with me just fine." Bert kissed the top of his head.

"Then why won't you move in with me?"

"Dag, we've talked about this. I can't right now. My father needs me."

"Okay, I understand that your father needs you to help him out. But why can't I come and visit you there, at your Dad's house, once in a while? Stay over some nights?"

"That won't work."

"Why?"

"It's just not feasible."

"Why? You always say it's not feasible. *Why* is it not feasible?"

Bert hesitated before answering. Finally, he took a deep breath and mumbled tentatively, "My father doesn't know I'm gay, Dag. Nobody does, really. Outside of the little circle of friends that you've introduced me to."

"Are you kidding me?" Dag yelled, bolting up and sitting erect on the bed. "You never told me that!"

"Well, I'm telling you now. You're my first guy. I never even acknowledged my sexuality to *myself* till now."

"You need to come out, Bertie! It's the twenty-first century. Gay marriage is legal. What's stopping you?"

"He's not ready for it."

"Who's not ready?"

"My father," Bert said. "He's a throwback."

"Why the hell do you put up with that?"

"I don't want to mess with it—you know, the inheritance and all. I'm ashamed to say it—it's embarrassing—but it's the truth. I don't want to mess with the inheritance." Bert grimaced and his body squirmed.

"You've got it all wrong, Bertie!" Dag exclaimed, grabbing Bert's left hand with both of his.

He loved Bert's hands. Each of Bert's palms was large enough to engulf both of his, fingers and all.

"You have to examine the power dynamic here. Take a moment and look at it. Your father *needs* you. He needs you to take care of him. *You* have the power."

"No." Bert sighed. "He holds the money in the will over my head."

"You can't let him do that! You could make a *fine* living if you didn't feel beholden to him." Dag relaxed and set his head back down on Bert's chest. "And if you moved in with *me*," he whispered, "I'd take care of you. A whole lot better than your dad does. Look at this beautiful place I have, right off Central Park. But it's so empty without you, Bertie. I need you here. I'd take care of you, I really would."

CHAPTER 4

WHEN Rosemary dashed in, William was at his easel, working on a large canvas. Molly, their housecat, was curled on the floor at William's feet, sleeping peacefully. She'd unknowingly served as inspiration for the scene upon which William now toiled meticulously.

The alien creature in the painting's center stood upright and had a powerful body cloaked in studded, leather-like armor. Its humanoid torso incongruously but proudly sported Molly's head, reproduced nearly photographically, but with the addition of two tall antennae emanating from its pate and an ornate pair of electronic goggles covering its eyes. The figure held some sort of laser sword, poised threateningly. The alien's golden, saucer-shaped ship sat in the background. A crowd of earthlings gaped at the creature. These humans, also rendered in scrupulous detail, were smaller than the creature and cowered before him.

William stopped what he was doing—painstakingly populating the hills in the background of his colossal canvas with tall stalks of grass, each blade slotted in individually with a quick upward thrust of a narrow-pointed brush—and acknowledged Rosemary when she appeared.

He was a bit surprised. He'd heard her unlock the front door, but generally when she arrived home from work she spent a few minutes in the kitchen and the bedroom before sauntering into his studio. Today she raced in immediately, holding her cell phone, grinning broadly between heaves of breath. She'd evidently run up the stairs to the flat.

"Yay!" she cried, giggling. "Yay, yay, yay! Will! I'm so excited. I think I found you a job!"

William's eyes narrowed and his brow furrowed. He opened his mouth with the intent of saying something but aborted the endeavor, leaving his lips awkwardly agape.

Rosemary continued with exuberance. "My patient, Joyce Miller, came in for her cleaning this morning. I've told you about Joyce—she accumulates tartar really fast so I have her come in every four months instead of six? She runs the senior home in Mill Valley?"

William squinted and cocked his head. "I don't recall you mentioning her."

"Well, I have, many times," Rosemary said, slightly annoyed. "Joyce Miller! You just don't pay attention. Your mind is always on your next painting. But I've told you about her." Rosemary seemed to realize she was digressing. Her features softened and she resumed with enthusiasm, "She manages the senior home, Will. She's had a guy there for years running her art program, doing painting and drawing and clay sculpture with the residents . . ."

William didn't like the sound of this, but he said nothing.

". . . and he just quit," Rosemary exclaimed. "He's moving to Arizona to teach in a small college. So she needs someone to replace him. And I told her about you!"

"Me?" William asked in a whimper.

"Yes! She's very excited to meet you. She just texted me. She talked to the owners, and they think you'd be a perfect replacement. And it's only twenty hours a week, Will, so you'll still have lots of time for your own painting! It's perfect, don't you think? She wants to interview you tomorrow at one."

"Tomorrow?" William blanched. "I can't do it tomorrow. I'm not prepared. I'm just hearing about it now."

"Oh, you can do it, honey." Rosemary walked nearer and stroked the back of his neck. "I already told her a lot about you, so she's already pretty sold."

William pulled away. "I'd have to put together a portfolio of work to show her. That takes time, Rosemary."

"Oh god!" Rosemary threw up her hands. "You're doing it again. Procrastinating. Avoiding. This is what you always do! Just throw a few damn paintings into your bag and take them over with you. What difference does it make? Whatever you show her will prove you're an artist. That's all she needs to see."

"What I take to show her *matters*, Rosemary. It will define me as an artist in her eyes. I need time to put it together."

Rosemary's face reddened with anger. She stomped out of the room, yelling as she did, "I should have known. You just don't want to do it. You're refusing to work. Like you always do."

She had reached the bedroom now, but he could still hear her clearly.

Her voice grew shriller. "How can you stand yourself? Living off your wife like a parasite! Maybe I should just move out and go live with my mother. See how you'd do then!" The bedroom door slammed so hard that the floor in the studio vibrated. Molly, who'd awakened when the shouting began but hadn't moved, now rose and stretched and sauntered into the kitchen, where she curled up near the heat vent.

William turned back to his canvas and flicked in three more blades of grass—then grimaced, sighed heavily, and laid his brush down carefully on the edge of the easel. He walked slowly across the hall to the bedroom and knocked softly.

Through the door he heard, "I don't want to talk to you!"

He turned the knob gently and took a step into the room.

Rosemary was face down on the bed, her forehead buried hard into a pillow. She turned her head slightly, revealing one eye and the edge of her mouth. She was still seething.

"I don't want to talk to you! Get out!" she cried.

"I'm sorry," he said softly. "You're right. I need the job. And the paintings in the portfolio don't really matter. I can put a decent set together before tomorrow afternoon. I think you just caught me off-guard, and I responded like an idiot. I'll go on the interview. I'll take the job if Joyce Miller offers it. I love you. I'm sorry."

The enraged expression on her half-buried face gradually softened. She rolled over and looked at him full on. "You will?"

"I absolutely will. I'm sorry."

"You really will? You're not just saying it?"

"I promise. I'll call her first thing tomorrow and confirm the appointment."

"At one. In the afternoon. Right?"

"At one."

Rosemary smiled broadly and relaxed her shoulders. She leaned forward and opened her arms wide. "Come here, sweetie, let me give you a hug."

William sat down close to her on the bed and they embraced.

"I'm so glad you're doing this," she whispered. "You'll be great at it and it will really help with our budget." She pulled him closer and kissed him, first with gentle affection, then more passionately.

Her mouth opened, her tongue began probing feverishly.

Her lips moved close to his ear.

"I want to celebrate," she cooed.

Arthur sat at the big polished wood table in the dining room and peered over the top of his laptop as he bellowed, "So tell me again. Who is this guy you're insisting on inviting over for dinner?" His raspy voice projected through the dining room, past the ledge of the small bar with its three high stools, and into the open kitchen, where Bert was finishing work on an elaborate dinner.

"Dag," Bert called back. "His name is Dag."

"And he's your friend?"

Bert walked to the bar and looked at his father. "Yes, he's my friend. I thought you might like to meet him. He's a stock broker, and *you* trade stocks all day, so you two may have a lot to talk about."

"I don't need any advice," Arthur mumbled.

"That's fine," Bert said, "you can talk about other things."

"You said his name is Dag?"

"Yes. Dag."

"What the hell kind of name is that? Is he white?"

Bert paused, not wishing to dignify the statement with an answer, but finally—he did need to keep Arthur in a civil mood for the dinner—forced himself to reply, "It's a Norwegian name."

"He's a foreigner? I don't want a foreigner here."

"He's not a foreigner. He was born in Brooklyn. Bay Ridge."

"Brooklyn? Who the hell names a kid Dag who's born in Brooklyn? What the hell kind of parents name a kid that?"

Bert struggled to keep his composure. "Like I said, it's a Norwegian name. It's part of their heritage. Maybe they named him after a grandfather or something. What difference does it make?"

"What's his last name?"

"What do you care?"

"Just tell me his last name."

"Odegaard."

"Spell it."

Bert sighed heavily but obliged, choosing to omit the optional slash through the "O." Then he went back to working on dinner.

Arthur said nothing for a moment. He was busy typing on his laptop and jabbing his finger along the mouse pad. Suddenly he was heaving with laughter, trying but failing to say something.

Finally, he calmed down enough to spurt it out between cackles: "Do you know what Odegaard means in Norwegian?"

"I have no idea."

"Deserted farm." Arthur laughed hysterically and typed some more. "Not just any farm—some rotting, deserted farm! What the hell kind of name is that? And look here. Dag means 'day.' So your friend works the dayshift on a smelly, rotting, deserted farm. Maybe they named his brother 'nightshift.' And his sister 'weekend.'" Arthur's eyes began to tear as he rocked forward and back with laughter.

"I'm glad you're finding yourself so amusing," Bert muttered as he finished tossing a big bowl of salad. He strode back over to the ledge of the bar and warned Arthur sternly, "He's my friend, Dad. Just be nice to him."

"Your friend the deserted, rotting, decomposing farm worker!" Arthur croaked, nearly asphyxiating on his own laughter, his face now candy apple red, his shoulders convulsing like spasmodic jumping beans.

Bert's cell phone chimed. He grabbed it from the counter, perused the text message, then placed the phone in his pocket. "Okay, he just got to the train station. I'm going to pick him up. When we get back here, I want you to be nice to him."

Bert grabbed his car keys and was off. Arthur was still howling when Bert closed the front door behind him.

William was driving to Mill Valley for his job interview at the senior home when he heard Dr. Judith Feigenbaum interviewed again. His van's radio was tuned to a smaller NPR station that broadcast from the North Bay. William preferred the station's more edgy and eclectic programming to the bigger NPR station in San Francisco, but found that his van's old radio couldn't quite lock in on the station clearly until he'd crossed the Golden Gate Bridge and driven north into Marin County.

As he listened, William found himself wondering whether the station's esoteric content was due more to its small budget or to a conscious editorial predilection. He decided it was some fortuitous combination of the two.

It was at that moment that Dr. Feigenbaum was introduced on the program.

Following the scripted questions and answers, the doctor was asked to read a passage. William fully expected to hear the same segment he'd heard on the other show, but was surprised to be presented with one that was completely different. Although it was from the same book, its subject matter was not something William had ever before considered. He found it especially intriguing.

Dr. Feigenbaum's soothing, mellifluous voice began:

"Is it possible that cooked food, as opposed to raw food, is responsible for the remarkable powers of the human brain?

"At first this seems like an absurd question. But some scientists actually believe it is possible that our genetic predisposition had no contribution whatever to the fact that the human brain developed such greater power and nuance than that of any other known species.

They posit that it was primitive humans' mastery of fire, and the eventual use of fire to cook food, that was responsible.

"The argument is most persuasive when comparing the brains of humans to those of our closest relatives, the great apes.

"Apes eat a mostly raw and herbivorous diet, chock full of leaves and greens, which take a great deal of time to chew and digest. If you have ever cooked a big pot of raw spinach, you know how dramatically it diminishes in volume as it is heated. This not only makes the food much quicker and easier to ingest, but it also creates a more nutrient-dense commodity. And some of those nutrients actually need to be broken down with heat in order to be fully absorbed by the stomach and intestines.

"Some researchers hypothesize that over time, because humans cooked their food, their bodies no longer needed such large digestive tracts, and smaller ones evolved that could absorb nutrients faster and much more efficiently. As a result, the body did not need to fuel the work of digestion nearly as much, and a far greater percentage of the body's fuel could now feed the brain, which, in turn, grew bigger and more complex. And by spending less time eating, we could engage in more stimulating activities, further developing our intellectual capacity.

"So, according to this theory, human mastery of fire provided us with an insurmountable advantage in the evolutionary growth and development of the brain. The raw diets of our simian relatives could not possibly provide sufficient calories or nutrients for their brains to compete."

Dr. Feigenbaum paused for an extra beat before delivering a postscript:

"But as interesting as this argument may be, it does not present any sort of explanation as to what afforded humans the capacity to tame and exploit fire, and begin cooking food in the first place, when no other animal was capable of making that leap. So, something special was clearly going on with our brains long before any of this food-related evolution could have transpired."

The doctor's intelligence, the musicality of her voice, and the hint of snarkiness in her concluding repudiation formed a gestalt that William found intoxicating. It threw him into an unexpectedly calm and cheerful demeanor as he pulled up to the senior home, grabbed the portfolio of paintings he had carefully assembled, and walked into the building for his job interview.

When Bert and Dag got back to the house, the downstairs rooms were deserted.

Bert walked to the foot of the stairs and shouted, "Dad! Are you up there?"

After a few moments of silence, Arthur yelled back, "Yeah, I'm here." There was another pause; then he said, "I couldn't just sit around and wait for you. I have work to do."

Bert turned to Dag and said softly, "I can't believe he went all the way back upstairs. Steps are hard for him since his hip replacement. He's not fully recovered."

"I heard that!" Arthur screamed. "You're full of crap. I can walk up and down perfectly well."

"Well, then come back down," Bert shouted. "I want you to meet Dag."

"I'm doing some research on stocks," Arthur yelled back. "I'll be down when I'm done."

"I'm going to mix a pitcher of martinis," Bert screamed. "Come down if you want one."

"Bring mine up here."

Bert's head drooped in disgust as he trudged into the kitchen.

Bert and Dag preferred vodka martinis, but Arthur considered a martini made with anything but gin a wimpy abomination, and Bert and Dag had agreed to acquiesce tonight to his predilection. While Bert mixed the cocktails, Dag ambled into the living room, where he observed the plush furnishings and the bookcases. He quickly surveyed the novels on the top shelves, curious to see how many he'd read, but soon became fixated on the lower half of the third bookcase, where he found a collection of musical CDs, cassette tapes, and, most remarkably, long rows of old vinyl record albums. These then led him to seek out what turned out to be a magnificent old turntable sitting among the other stereo components on the far side of the room.

He gently raised the lid and studied the impeccable workmanship.

Bert appeared holding a martini. "I'm going to take this up to him," he whispered, "and then I'll be back down to toast, and we can have some hors d'oeuvres." He began to walk away, then returned and whispered even more softly, "Finish up with the turntable before he gets down. He doesn't like anybody touching it."

Dag grinned and nodded, and Bert glanced warily up the staircase. When he'd ascertained without doubt that it was vacant, he gave Dag a quick peck on the lips and then headed upstairs.

Bert set the martini down on a coaster next to Arthur's computer. "Here's your drink. Why don't you take a couple of sips and then come down and be sociable?"

"I have work to finish," Arthur said without looking up. "Go entertain your friend. I'll be down when I'm ready."

"You've been working on this stuff all day. Why do you have to do this now?"

"Just go down and leave me alone. I said I'll be there when I'm ready."

Bert returned downstairs.

He and Dag had just finished their second round of martinis when Arthur finally appeared, plodding down the staircase half a step at a time, one hand cautiously gripping the banister, the other holding an empty cocktail glass.

"I need a refill," he announced as he joined them in the living room and plopped down on his favorite black leather recliner.

Bert and Dag were sitting together on the couch. The appetizer plates arrayed upon the coffee table had only a few morsels left.

Bert was about to make introductions but before he could, Dag bounced over to Arthur and extended his hand. "Dag Odegaard," he announced. "Pleased to meet you."

Arthur's right hand held his empty glass, and he made no effort to move it.

Bert walked over and took the glass. "I'll make refills for all of us," he said. "In the meantime, say hi to Dag."

Arthur did not rise; he extended his right hand lethargically and withdrew it before the grasp fully finalized. "You're shorter than I thought you'd be," he muttered, scrutinizing Dag. "And your hair is brown. I thought Scandinavians were tall with blond hair."

"I guess we're not all that lucky," Dag said cheerfully. He returned to the couch.

Bert had momentarily postponed tending to the beverage refills, hovering instead to make sure nothing too untoward occurred between Arthur and Dag during their initial encounter. He scanned the tableau: Dag was seated comfortably back on the couch, and things seemed relatively copacetic for now.

It occurred to Bert that additional alcoholic lubrication might serve to maintain this uneasy tranquility, so he traipsed into the kitchen to mix another pitcher of drinks.

"So, Mr. Wozniak," Dag ventured. "May I call you Arthur?"

"If you must," Arthur droned.

Bert, monitoring the conversation from the kitchen, mixed the gin, vermouth, and ice as quickly as he could, strewing a few ice cubes onto the floor in his haste. He left them there to melt on the tile as he raced back into the living room to moderate.

"I understand you dabble with stock trading," Dag said, leaning forward and smiling indulgently.

"I don't dabble! I do it for a living. And as you can see, I've done very well. I'm good at it."

"Do you have an overarching philosophy?" Dag asked.

Bert found that inquiry comforting. An open-ended question like that could get Arthur talking, help him to relax a bit. It seemed like a good time to refill everyone's glasses.

Bert ran into the kitchen to grab the glass cocktail pitcher and secure a few more blue-cheese-stuffed olives for garnish. The martinis were now well chilled. When he returned to the living room, Arthur was still pondering Dag's question.

Bert poured the drinks and proposed a toast: "To friends."

Bert and Dag clinked glasses. Arthur raised his glass halfheartedly from the recliner. Bert and Dag started to rise to walk over to toast with him but he was already gulping down his drink, so they retreated.

Arthur finished half his martini before he spoke again. He looked at Dag. "You know, I'm thinking about your question about an overarching philosophy," he said, singsonging the phrase 'overarching philosophy' to make it sound prissy and contrived. "And now I realize why I can't answer it. Because it's a damn stupid question. People who try to impose a philosophy on stock trading are just afraid of trusting their own gut. It's not rocket science, for God's sakes. You do the research, and when you find a company that looks like it's onto something, you buy it. And if a company you own looks like it's screwing up, you sell it. It takes a lot of time and effort. And you have to trust your own intelligence. Your own instincts. There's no other way to do it."

"You're taking a big risk, Arthur," Dag said. "You should consider trusting at least some portion of your portfolio to a professional. We stockbrokers understand market trends, and we get information that laymen aren't privy to."

Arthur finished his drink and thrust his glass in Bert's direction. Bert obligingly rose and took it. As he refilled it, Arthur said, "You big-shot professionals. What the hell do *you* know? You make money on every trade whether the stocks go up or down. Why the hell do you even care if you make money for anybody?"

"People wouldn't stay with us if they were unhappy with our results."

"People are idiots. They don't want to take the time to do the research so they trust big shots like you. You don't know *anything*. Did you make money in 2008?"

"Nobody made money in 2008, Arthur."

"I did! I pulled out of most everything and focused on a few small companies that weren't playing games with mortgages or bank loans. I made money that year. I make money every year."

Dag shook his head. "You're comparing apples and oranges, Arthur. I'm a professional stockbroker. I invest for hundreds of people. That's tens of millions of dollars. You can't put tens of millions of dollars into tiny, hole-in-the-wall companies!"

Using the term "hole-in-the-wall" made Dag think, for a moment, of the little Chinese place near work that he loved so much, and the lout who'd taunted him a few weeks earlier about the asparagus aroma in his urine.

Arthur gulped down the rest of his drink and chewed loudly on one of his cheese-filled olives as he shouted his response, snapping Dag's attention back to the conversation at hand.

"I make a good living doing this. And I've done it for years. I don't need some charlatan like you telling me what to do!"

Bert raised his hands and spoke gently. "This is getting a little heated, guys. Why don't we talk about something else?"

"Because this schmuck thinks I'm an amateur!" Arthur yelled. "He thinks I'm a gambler. I make a good living, and I'm not full of myself like he is. He's insulting me! I should throw him out!"

"You can't throw him out, Dad. He's our guest. Let's just take a deep breath and change the subject."

"It's *my* house, and I can throw him out if I want to! He's a condescending snob."

"He's my friend, Dad."

"I don't care if he's your friend, he's insulting me," Arthur shot back, his voice loud and agitated. "Big-shot corporate underling. I want him out of my house!"

"Dad, please. Stop this. I want you to treat Dag nicely. He's more than a friend to me."

"What the hell does *that* mean—'more than a friend'? What the hell *is* he? Your broker? Are you trading behind my back?"

"Look," Bert pleaded. "I just want you two to talk, work it out. You two can get along. I know it."

"*What do you mean* he's 'more than a friend'? What *is* he?"

Bert said nothing.

"Answer my question!" Arthur yelled.

"He's, um, well . . . How do I say this? Dag is my partner."

"What do you mean your 'partner'? You two opened a business?"

"Not that kind of partner."

"What the hell kind of partner?"

Bert hesitated and looked at Dag, who nodded, then back at Arthur. "I'm gay, Dad," he stammered. "I'm with Dag. We're a couple." There was a long silence. Arthur's mouth hung open. His eyes grew wide, their upper lids quivering against his plunging eyebrows.

"You're a fag?" he finally screamed, leaning forward so far that he nearly slipped off the recliner. "A fag? What the hell is *this*, now? You're thirty-eight years old, and you suddenly decide to become a faggot? What the hell is wrong with you?"

Arthur glared at Bert, who said nothing but inched closer to Dag on the couch.

"Why?" Arthur demanded at the top of his lungs. "Because you can't find a girlfriend? I guess it's chic and trendy now to be fag in New York City. Is that it? What a fucking loser."

"That's ridiculous, Dad," Bert whined. "What you're saying is ridiculous."

"Oh really? So when the hell did you decide to become a fag?"

Dag had struggled till now to keep silent, but he couldn't any longer. He leaped up, pointed at Arthur, and, trembling slightly, said loudly, "He didn't *decide*, you idiot. He's always been gay. This is not a decision. It's how you're wired, biologically. No one in their right mind would *choose* this with all the bullshit attached to it. Especially from people like you. What century are you living in, for God's sake?"

"You!" Arthur screamed, rising and gesturing at Dag. "You! You're a bad influence. You get the hell out of my house, you goddamn troublemaker!"

"If you throw him out I'm going too," Bert said hesitantly as he got off the couch and stood alongside Dag.

"Fine," Arthur said. "I don't want either of you here. You two can go play house somewhere, you goddamn perverts. I don't need you. I can do just fine without you."

"Oh yeah?" Bert shot back. "Let's see how well you do without me."

"Get the hell out! That's all! This conversation is over!" Arthur plopped back down into his recliner, dug the remaining olive out of the bottom of his glass, and popped it into his mouth.

Bert said quietly to Dag, "Come with me."

The two began walking upstairs.

"Where the hell are you going?" Arthur shrieked. "I said to get out!"

"I'm just going to my room to pack up a few things," Bert said calmly. "Then I'm leaving."

"Well hurry up. And good riddance!"

Bert and Dag made their way slowly upstairs and into Bert's room. Bert grabbed some underwear and shirts and threw them into his gym bag.

"He'll change his mind," Dag whispered. "He'll see how much he needs you."

"I'm not so sure," Bert mumbled as he collected a pair of sneakers and a pile of random socks. He stopped packing for a moment and turned toward Dag. His face was ashen. "I think I may have made a mistake, Dag. A big mistake."

CHAPTER 5

*T*HE space had been cleared the night prior for a poorly attended square-dance activity, so William had to drag all fifteen easels out of the storage closet and set up each one, trying to duplicate, as closely as he could recall, the art room's customary configuration. The placement of the easels themselves, spaced uniformly in rows, was not the challenge. It was the height to which each was raised—and the type of seat, if any, to place before it—that he couldn't quite remember. A few of the usual resident attendees painted standing up; most of the others were fine with tall stools, but a few preferred lower chairs, and a couple of his most avid pupils navigated with electric wheelchairs, which required that the easel sit not only at a specific height but also angled so it thrust forward a bit from its tripod mounting.

William's apron was stained with paint from the past few classes. He could certainly have had it laundered by the institution's staff, but he preferred it this way. It was far more effective than a nametag in identifying him as the senior home's art teacher. And in a more artistic sense, although he personally eschewed abstract expressionism, the chaotic splashes of color on the apron seemed to him particularly appropriate given the experience into which each of his class sessions eventually devolved.

Early on, after he'd first gotten the job, he'd imagined himself painting a picture of the room during a class, depicting each of his students at an easel—the painting's orientation such that you could catch both the expression on each painter's face as well as snippets of what was on the canvas. But that fanciful notion supposed a quiet classroom of studious, self-sufficient artists who would silently go about their business as William sketched the scene in a leisurely fashion from the chamber's far corner. Such was never the case. He was busy every moment of class and was frequently harried. It occurred to him, though, as he continued to adjust easels and chairs, that if he'd had the time to complete such a grand painting, he'd be able to consult it now and allay his confusion.

He checked his watch. Only ten minutes till class started, and he still had much to do. He'd spent far too long trying to arrange, then rearrange, the room to conform to his memory of where each student worked. He'd have to leave it as it was now, and resign himself to the inevitable whining and complaining from certain pupils that their space was not set up correctly.

He prepared dozens of paper cups for class, filling each partway with acrylic paint he'd watered down into a consistency that would be easier for older arthritic hands to apply. Next to each easel he situated a small folding stand—these had been stacked in the closet as well. Three brushes were set upon each stand: a small and a medium round brush, and a broad flat one. He had more in reserve for specific applications, but for most purposes these three sufficed. A sketching pencil, a water jar, and a couple of rags for each painter were laid out as well.

He retrieved fresh canvases from the closet. He had spent hours thoroughly coating them with gesso to prime their surfaces and enable them to accept the acrylic paint cleanly, with good adhesion and no seepage into the weave. When he first started teaching the class, he'd tried to make the students gesso their own canvases, but they'd complained bitterly to Joyce Miller that the new teacher was making them do stupid things and not allowing them to paint.

William recollected, as he placed a canvas on each easel, how wonderful Joyce had been when she gently reprimanded him after listening to the residents' protests, and how she'd steered him toward preparing the canvases himself. He'd argued that he wasn't having his pupils gesso the canvases out of laziness but because that was part of what an artist did, and he was trying to teach them to be artists. Joyce had laughed softly, touched him lightly on the shoulder, and complimented him on such a noble and admirable sentiment before explaining how sadly misplaced such an approach was with a room of very old people looking for an activity to help fill one of many days where boredom hung as their existential threat.

She'd used precisely that term, "existential threat," but whispered it so gently, clearly appreciating the irony of employing so fiery a phrase in conjunction with something as seemingly innocuous as eldercare ennui. And then she'd smiled and touched him again.

That encounter had entirely changed the way he viewed Joyce. She was at least ten or fifteen years older than he, but ever since that incident, he'd ascribed to her a sensuality and allure he'd not previously appreciated. Prior to that, he'd seen her just as his boss, and had been wary of her.

He might have taken the fantasy a bit further at this moment, but his students started filtering in. "Sorry," he said, "the room was dismantled and I had to set it up from scratch, so forgive me if the seats are out of place or your easel needs a height adjustment." He repeated this several times.

Most of the students were patient with him, but Mrs. Liebman, who was always crabby and depressed anyway, immediately began carping, "You're wasting our time. The old art teacher never had this problem! You know I can't sit on a stool. Get me a chair. Or is this your way of telling me you don't want me here at all!?"

"Oh, I definitely want you here Mrs. Liebman," William assured her in his most patronizing monotone. "I'm really very sorry." He swapped out her stool for a folding chair and readjusted the height of her easel.

As he did so, he noticed his gifted star student, Alice, softly chuckling in the back row. Though she rarely left her scooter, she was unfailingly positive and upbeat, and almost clairvoyantly tuned in to the nuances of interactions going on around her.

He walked over to her station and adjusted her easel. "I'm sorry, Alice," he whispered, leaning in close. "My memory just wasn't good enough to reconstruct the room in my head."

Alice tugged at his elbow and smiled coyly. "If you think your memory's bad now, Willie dear," she murmured, "just wait till you're my age."

He chuckled. "You always make me laugh, no matter what else is going on."

He returned to the front of the room and scanned the workstations. "Is everybody okay now and ready to paint?" A few people were still fiddling and fidgeting with their easels and chairs. "Why don't we get started," he implored. "Once we're painting I can always fine-tune your easel height if it needs it."

In previous classes he'd used fruits and flowers as models, but he wanted to try something different today. He held up a brightly colored wood sculpture of a parrot perched on a branch. "The other day I visited the room of one of our own students, Alice, to help her hang a very lovely painting she did here last week—and while I was there I saw this parrot sculpture in her room. I thought it would be a really fun thing to draw and paint, and Alice was kind enough to give us permission to borrow it."

In the front of the room sat an old folding tripod, its stem stretched to its limit. William carefully positioned the model atop it at a height where everybody could see it clearly.

"Red, yellow, blue, and white are the primary pigments you'll need if you stick to what you see," he announced. "I've mixed a bunch of those for you already; let's get them distributed now." He started to deliver the paper cups to some of the students, while others stepped forward to retrieve their own. "I also have a few greens and purples and browns, too, if you want to get a little creative and abstract. Just let me know if you want those, or any other color that I can mix for you."

As was always the case, his more confident pupils starting sketching immediately. Others wanted help, and many insisted that William sketch the entire scene on their canvas so they could just color it in.

Before he went to individual workstations to offer assistance, he strode over to the large whiteboard on the side of the room, picked up a marker, and, using basic shapes, drew a segmented outline of the perched parrot and its prominent wing and tail feathers. "If you're having trouble sketching freehand," he said, "try starting with simple geometric shapes like these, and go from there. It makes it much easier."

He raced from pupil to pupil, helping as he could, encouraging everybody to try to finish as much of the sketch as they were able to without his intervention.

He could sense cranky Mrs. Liebman glaring at him impatiently as he assisted a couple of other pupils. When he finally reached her workstation, she was in no mood for pleasantries. "Draw it for me!" she demanded. "You've made me wait long enough!"

"Don't you want to try to at least outline the parrot yourself, Mrs. Liebman, following the sample I drew on the board?"

"Just draw it. I don't have time for this."

"I know you can do some of it yourself," he said. "I've seen you draw. You're a lot more talented than you give yourself credit for."

"I want you to do it for me."

"Why?" he pushed. "Why won't you try?"

Mrs. Liebman's features curled into an expression that could have been a precursor to either rage or tears. "Why won't I try?" she yelled. "Why? I'll ask *you* why. Why do you keep insisting that I do it? So I can fail at it like I did at everything else in my rotten life?" Her eyes teared up.

"Come now, Mrs. Liebman," he said softly. "That's not true. I've seen your daughters here visiting, and they're wonderful people. So you obviously did a good job with them. And I know you worked for the city for many years; I'll bet you were good at that too."

She sniffed. "Don't you get tired of trying to be nice to me?"

"Evidently not." He smiled. "Here, take the pencil. I'll stay right here and guide you, and if you start to go wrong I'll help."

"Oh, good lord!" she cried. "Give me the damn pencil. I'll do it just to make you stop. You're a terrible bully, you know."

William chuckled. "Yes, I'm cruel and fearsome."

Mrs. Liebman sketched the outline of a fine head, and a very promising body.

"That's excellent," William said. "Both the head and the body are very well formed. But look at them closely. You see how the head is just a little small in comparison to the body? You need to erase the head and make it just a little bigger."

"Good grief." She sighed. "I told you I'm no good. I want *you* to do it."

"You're doing very, very well. It's no big deal to have to redo something. Good artists fine-tune their sketches constantly. Nobody ever gets it perfect the first try. *I* certainly don't. That's why pencils all have erasers on them. Do it exactly as you had. Just a little bigger."

She moaned, then re-sketched the head. After she did so, she leaned back in her chair and gazed at the canvas. She smiled broadly. "I'm actually not bad at this," she tittered.

From the back row, Alice, who had already finished a professional-looking sketch and started applying paint when William had passed by her easel a few moments earlier, gasped and cried for William's help. When he turned she was pointing at Ira, the quiet old man who always sat in a low chair to her left. Ira never wanted any help, and his paintings always turned out eerily interesting while bearing no resemblance whatsoever to the model William had put up.

Ira had mixed a rich concoction of colors, thoroughly saturating his paper-plate palette, and had then promptly keeled over and fallen asleep. His head was now soaking serenely in the polychromatic amalgam.

It was a cool, foggy Friday evening in San Francisco. Rosemary had mixed a big pitcher of rye manhattans. The cocktail was a superb vehicle for showcasing the basket of perfectly ripe sour cherries she'd scored at the farmers market the weekend before. She'd brandied the fruit in a mix of rye whiskey and Amaro liqueur, along with a sweet syrup she'd concocted using demerara sugar with bits of cinnamon and nutmeg.

There were no pots on the stove tonight. Rosemary and William were treating themselves to a stuffed Chicago-style pizza, which they were waiting to be delivered along with a couple of Greek salads. Friday night takeout was the sort of nicety on which they could splurge now, with William drawing a regular salary.

Molly, their cat, had made a brief appearance early in the evening, but disappeared soon after into the back of the house to nap.

William gulped his drink quickly, then fished out the two sumptuous cherries at the bottom of his stemmed glass. As he chomped on them, Rosemary dumped two more cherries in his empty glass and poured him a second round. She had a bit of trouble holding the pitcher steady—the story William was relating had her shaking with laughter.

"So I'm staring at Ira," William continued. "His face is covered in paint. It's just soaking there, in a huge palette full of every color you can imagine. And the guy's sound asleep. Snoring! So, I'm thinking, what the hell do I do now?"

Rosemary's eyes were tearing from laughter. "What *did* you do, honey?"

"Well, thank goodness for Alice. She's always so levelheaded. I grabbed a rag and was going to try to clean him up, but Alice insisted that I call a nurse or an aide. She said they know how to do it without tearing skin or anything. And listen to what she said . . ." He took a few more sips of his second round and tightened his vocal chords to affect a tremulous falsetto. "Skin gets very thin and fragile as you get old, Willie dear, and I'm quite sure Ira doesn't use moisturizer."

"Moisturizer?" Rosemary guffawed. "The guy's face is lying in a plateful of paint, and she's wondering if he uses moisturizer?"

"That's right!" William said. "Dear, dear Alice! She's such a hoot! Really sweet, but such a hoot."

Their gaiety was abruptly fractured by the jarring peal of William's cell phone.

"Better check it, honey," Rosemary said. "Could be the delivery guy."

William leaned slightly to the side to yank his cell phone out of his pants pocket. He glanced at its screen, and his features puckered into an unsettled scowl. "It's my father."

"Arthur?" Rosemary wheezed. "At this hour? It's past ten in New York. Why on earth would he be calling now?"

"I have no idea," William said hesitantly. "I guess I ought to answer."

Rosemary nodded affirmatively and William switched the call to speaker.

"Hello, Dad," he proffered in a tepid monotone.

"Hello? Hello? William? Is that you?"

"Yes, it's me, Dad. What's up? Why are you calling so late? Is everything okay?"

"Yes. Everything's fine. What did you think? That I'm dead? I wouldn't be calling you if I was dead."

"I'm glad you're not dead, Dad. And that everything's okay. So . . . why are you calling at this hour?"

"I'm coming out to live with you two. I'm going to buy a nice house that we can all live in. Somewhere near San Francisco."

William's face froze into a mixture of incredulity and shock. He gazed at Rosemary, who appeared equally astonished.

"What?" he cried.

"I'm coming to live with you two," Arthur repeated.

"What the hell is going on with you?" William demanded. "You go from cutting me out of the will to telling me you're moving in with me three months later? This is insane. And who says I want to live with you, anyway? Where the hell is Bert? I want to talk to him."

"Leave Bertram out of this. I'm coming to live with the two of *you*. Like I said, I'll get a nice house. A whole lot nicer than that little shithole flat you live in now. Your *wife* will like it. We'll get a house with a big yard. A garden. She'll like that."

Rosemary dangled her jaw, hoisted her shoulders and raised her palms in disbelief. She tried to contain herself but couldn't. She leaped to her feet. "You've never even been to this flat!" she screamed into the phone. "How the hell do you know if it's a shithole?" Arthur started laughing. "Oh god, Rosemary. I didn't know you were there. You're a spunky one. I get a kick out of you! Don't you remember? You described your flat in great detail, Rosemary, when you visited a couple of years ago and got drunk in my living room. I have a clear picture of it in my head. You used that very term."

Rosemary leaned her head back and expelled a harrowing sigh.

"Anyway, I'm coming," Arthur said. "That's all there is to it. There's nothing—"

"What's going on between you and Bert?" William interjected.

"I'm done with Bertram."

"You're 'done' with him? You've been telling me for years that he's the good son who takes care of you and I'm a useless piece of shit."

"I never used that kind of language."

"You need to make up with Bert. What you're saying about moving out here is insane."

"I'm done with Bertram. He's queer."

"Listen, Dad, Bert's always been a bit odd. All of us are. Mom was the only sane one in the family. So he's a little strange, who—"

"No! You're not following. Bert is *queer*! He's a fairy. A fag."

"What?" William exclaimed. He paused for an extended moment, mind swirling, then said, "Are you saying Bert is *gay*?"

"That's right. Gay. That's how you people refer to it now. He's god-damn gay. Gay used to mean happy, but you can't even use that damn word that way now because it's been hijacked by queers. Yeah. He's gay."

Rosemary and William stared at each other in disbelief.

"Are you sure?" William asked.

"He told me so. He brought his little boyfriend around."

"It's hard to believe," William said, half to himself. "I never suspected. I knew he was shy around women—I assumed that was why he didn't have many girlfriends—but I never thought he was gay."

"He's a fairy, and I'm done with him," Arthur said matter-of-factly. "I contacted a realtor out where you are. She's going to start looking for a nice place for us. Maybe in the Sonoma Valley. I want you two to work with her. I'll give you her number. You get this going. I'll be out in a few weeks to join you."

William was about to argue, but Rosemary grabbed his arm and enthusiastically nodded yes. *Say yes*, she mouthed exaggeratedly. *Say yes! Yes! Yes!*

William's confusion rendered him transfixed and speechless for a long, long moment. Staring at him, Rosemary reiterated her silent entreaty in an even more desperate and hyperbolic pantomime.

"All right," William finally muttered into the phone. "Give me the information for the realtor . . . for now. I'm still not absolutely sure about this." He glanced at Rosemary. "But I'll go with it for now."

It's amazing. I'm living with a hot young stud.

That sentiment had been ricocheting through Dag's consciousness all morning, reanimating each time he spied Bert, wearing only a T-shirt and workout shorts, gamboling about the kitchen.

When Dag finally sat down at the breakfast table, he was dressed for work, attired impeccably in a three-piece suit with a tie and pocket square that played off each other in what Dag assessed as a striking yet dignified fusion. Had Dag been nearly in underwear as Bert was, he would have felt puny and unworthy by comparison, but sumptuously tailored as he was, he was confident he could hold his own.

Dag was accustomed to dashing out of the house and grabbing a pastry and latte at the coffee shop in the lobby of the building where he worked. But ever since Bert had moved in three days earlier, a new tradition had emerged: Bert careening about the kitchen, searing eggs in cast iron pans, microwaving bacon between wads of paper towels, and buttering slices of whole-grain toast while Dag showered, shaved, and dressed.

The table was set with wicker placemats, blue cloth napkins, and fine silverware that felt heavy when you picked it up. Bert laid down two plates of steaming hot food and filled each of their mugs with freshly brewed coffee before sitting down and joining Dag.

Dag's enthusiastic assertions were garbled a bit, emitted through teeth chomping joyfully upon softly scrambled eggs scented with the barest hint of fresh dill and tarragon. "Wonderful breakfast, Bertie. This is so lovely, having breakfast before I leave for work."

"Yes, it's nice," Bert said. "I'm so glad you like it."

"Are you all moved in yet, Bertie?"

"No. I'm picking up my stuff a little at a time. I make a couple of trips a day, there and back, while you're at work. I should be done by Sunday."

"Bits and drabs, eh? Do you and your father talk when you go over?"

"He's civil, and he'll answer a question if I ask it directly, but it's terse. The minimal interaction required. It's hard for me."

"Why don't you just say that the two of you need to talk about this?"

"I have, Dag. He says there's nothing to talk about."

"Well, tell him there is."

Bertram took a few moments to sip on his coffee and frame his response. "You can't bully him, Dag," he said softly. "He's the expert at bullying. The world champion. You can't out-bully the world-champion bully." He took another sip of coffee. "And who'd want to, anyway? But if I keep going over to get my stuff a little bit at a time, maybe he'll warm back up to me."

"That's being passive, Bertie. You need to stand up to him. He'll respect that."

"Frankly, I don't know if he'll ever respect me again."

There was silence for a while as the two ate. The isolated sounds of masticating and swallowing resounded in Dag's head and unnerved him. He felt the need to resurrect the conversation.

"So what's his next move, do you think?" Dag asked. "Is he getting someone in there to help him?"

"You won't believe this," Bert muttered. "He says he's going to move to the San Francisco Bay Area. Buy a house and live with Will and his wife."

"What?" Dag cried, expelling tiny morsels of egg and toast from his lips onto the napkin in his lap. "I thought he hates Will."

"He's been bitching for years that Will left New York and abandoned the family. But I guess for him being a deserter isn't nearly as bad as being a pervert." Bertram's eyes started to tear up, but he blinked rapidly and nipped the display before it went any further.

"You're not a pervert," Dag said firmly. "*He's* one for thinking that way."

"He just makes me feel like shit."

They were quiet for a time. Bert refilled Dag's cup with hot coffee.

Dag looked up and offered an idea: "Hey, maybe he'd let you handle selling the house when he moves. That would be a good listing to get you going again in real estate. Now that you're out of his house you should start getting back into that."

"I thought of that. I asked him. He says he's not selling it."

"He's not selling? Well, then maybe he's really not moving. Maybe he's just saying it to get into your head."

"Oh, he's moving. But he says he's going to turn the Scarsdale house into a rental property. He's going to use the same property management guy he uses for the other rentals he owns."

Dag pondered that. "That's actually pretty smart. I hate to say it, Bertie, but it is. Arthur gets to keep the property in case California doesn't work out. Meanwhile, it appreciates in value. Plus he gets monthly income. It's smart."

"And I suppose he also can use it as collateral for his new mortgage. Trading stocks on your personal computer isn't exactly what a loan broker wants to see as a stable primary profession."

"True. But, you know, he's done well at it for years. I don't know many people who could pull that off. I don't think I could. Arthur's a smart guy. A total asshole. But a smart guy."

"More of an asshole, I think." Bert snorted.

"So, what *are* you going to do now to get back into the real estate flow?" Dag asked.

Bert shifted in his chair. "What the hell, Dag? I just started living here. I'm not even all moved in yet!" He raised his eyes to meet Dag's—and his exasperation morphed into dejection. "Look at us. Here. Now. This is nice, just sitting and having breakfast together. It's so goddamn nice. But you can't just let it be, Dag. You have to go and ruin it, trying to push me to make money. Shit."

"Bertie! I love you, and I love having you here. But some additional income would be nice—for us, but more so for *you*. For *your* self-esteem. Your whole persona. I care about that. You need to have self-respect to be happy."

Bert sighed and lowered his head. "I suppose you're right, Dag. Jesus. I'd have to find clients. I don't know how the hell I'd do that. I've never been any good at it."

"You should come with me to some of the networking events I go to in the evenings," Dag said, pointing his fork in Bert's direction for emphasis as he spoke.

Bert leaned back and put his cup down. "Speaking of networking events . . . Jesus, I didn't realize you go to those things almost every fucking night."

"Why? Do you mind?"

"Well, it would be nice to have you around once in a while. Have dinner with you."

"I understand," Dag said apologetically. "I do tend to eat at those things. There's always a whole lot of food laid out. I tend to just hang around and graze."

"Well, now you have someone at home who's a damn good cook and who would like your company."

"You're right, Bertie. I shouldn't eat there. You know, I don't need to stay *that* late—and I suppose I could cut down on the grazing and save my appetite. We could have late dinners. I'll try to get home a little earlier than I have been."

"Why do you have to go so often?" Bert complained. "I really didn't picture myself being alone here every night."

"Well, how do you think I get clients? You know I make a good living. A damn good living." Dag waved his fork in the air. "Look at this place I have. It's not by magic. It's because I have clients. You should come with me. Drum up real estate clients while I'm drumming up my investment clients. We could munch on appetizers *together* out there."

"Oh god! I'd rather starve than spend an evening in a clusterfuck like that."

"You're in sales, for god's sake! That's what real estate is. Sales. How the hell do you think it works? You can't sell anything unless you have people to sell to. You should come. At least to a few. Why don't you start with the Rotary Club? I can sponsor you as a member."

"Oh shit! The Rotary Club?" Bert ran his hand through his hair. "A bunch of old white Republicans? Jesus!"

"They're not like that so much anymore. A couple of decades ago they had to open up to women and gays. It's different now. New York doesn't have one yet, but San Francisco just opened the first LGBTQ+ Rotary Club in the United States, and the club I go to here is very cool. Everyone there knows I'm gay. I'd be happy to take you to a meeting with me."

"The whole thing sounds dreadful."

"It's good. You meet people. And we do good work for the community."

"Come on, Dag, you're there for leads to get new clients and make money. The charity stuff is a front, at least for you. And didn't you tell me they open with a prayer? And a patriotic song? How the fuck do you sit through that?"

"Because I'm interested in making money and getting clients, asshole. And you should be too. We *all* have to sit through some tedious shit sometimes. And believe me, it's a whole lot more tolerable than the years of shit *you* took from your asshole father. And that was for money too. Wasn't it? For the goddamn inheritance."

"God, Dag! Stop! I don't want to fight. I love being with you. I don't want to ruin it." Bert lowered his head dejectedly. "You're right. I need to get out there and be a real estate broker. I mean, I have my license, but really, I've never done anything with it other than help with a few houses for some friends and a couple of my cousins. Oh, and one aunt and uncle. I need to do it. I'm just really bad in crowds, Dag."

"You'll be with me. I'll introduce you around. I know everyone. You'll start making connections. You might even have fun."

"All right. Sign me up for the Rotary Club." Bert sighed. "God!" he muttered softly. "Why do I suddenly feel like pouring a shot of vodka into my coffee?"

CHAPTER 6

*C**LASS* had concluded hours earlier.

Upon each easel sat an unfinished painting awaiting completion at the next session in a couple of days. William had checked—the room was not scheduled for any other use till then, so leaving the paintings out was fine.

A drawing pad with heavy textured sheets rested on his lap. He had made a series of sketches depicting the art room with its easels and chairs from several different perspectives, based on a few photographs he had taken with his cell phone during the most recent class. These sketches were studies that he hoped would eventually materialize into that painting of the class at work—the one he had envisioned since he started this job.

He was a bit startled when the door opened.

"Oh, Willie dear," Alice said. "What a nice surprise. I didn't expect to see you here. Why are you still around?"

"Hey Alice. Nice to see you. I'm just hanging out, doing some sketches."

"Shouldn't you be home with your wife? It's after seven."

"Oh, she's out with a realtor, looking at houses."

"Are you two moving?"

"Actually, my father's coming out to live here. He's buying a house, and my wife and I will probably move in with him, help take care of things."

"Then shouldn't *you* be looking at the houses too?"

William laughed. "Yes, I probably should. But I went out with them the first couple of times and my wife said I was really no help at all. I guess an introverted artist like me can be happy living anywhere. I liked everything I saw, even if my wife and the realtor found them awful."

"Well, I think it's nice that you're so accepting."

"You always see the bright side, Alice." William chuckled. "What brings you to the art room?"

"Well, dear, I just came by to look at the painting I was working on today. I had some thoughts about what I might do with it next class."

"It's really coming along beautifully, Alice. I'll be sketching for a while. If you want I can mix up some paints for you, and you can work on it while I'm here."

"Oh, that's so sweet of you, dear. But no, I'm meeting my usual bunch of friends for dinner in a few minutes. I just wanted to take a look and think about some possibilities."

"You know, Alice, your stuff is so good. I think people would buy some of your paintings if we framed them up nicely. I don't know if I ever mentioned it to you, but I have a stall at the San Jose flea market every Sunday where I try to sell my paintings. If you want to come with me some Sunday, you can display your stuff with mine. Maybe you'll sell some. Anyway, it's a nice way to spend a day—you meet people, chat. It might be good for you. To get out a bit."

"Oh, I'd love to, Willie. But I don't know if Joyce would approve my joining you like that. She's protective—very by the book, if you know what I mean."

"I tell you what, I'll check with Joyce. See if we can talk her into it."

"Thanks, Willie. That's very sweet of you." Alice glanced up at the big clock on the wall. "Oh dear, my friends must be waiting for me in the dining room. I better run. It's roast beef and mashed potatoes tonight. One of my favorites here. See you soon, dear."

"Bye, Alice."

After she left, William sketched for a few more minutes and then walked over to Joyce Miller's office. He knew she sometimes worked late, so he knocked.

"Come in," she called.

He opened her door and found her standing near a bookshelf, an open book in her hand. She nodded and motioned for him to come in as she read just a moment longer. She replaced the book and turned to William as he walked toward her.

"Well, hello William," she said, smiling. "You're here late tonight. What can I do for you?"

He set out his idea about taking Alice with him, some Sunday, to the San Jose flea market. He tried to make his presentation thorough, upbeat, and reassuring as to safety concerns.

"It's so nice to see you taking a personal interest in your art students," Joyce said.

"I'm interested in all of them," William replied. "But Alice is special. She's a wonderful, positive person. And she really is extremely talented. It's a shame that she didn't pursue her art when she was younger. But think how exciting it would be for her if she sold a piece now."

"It certainly would be nice," Joyce said. "But I can't just send her out with you for the day. She uses a wheelchair. There are liability issues."

"Can we work around them?"

Joyce cocked her head and raised her eyebrows, and her lips curled into a coy pout. "I see you really want to make this happen. So I'll do two things for you: I'll mention it to our attorney when I see him next week, and if he gives the go-ahead I'll ask Alice's daughter if she'll grant her approval. She might want to meet you first."

"I actually met Alice's daughter briefly a couple of months ago. But I'd be happy to chat with her again if it would help."

Joyce stepped closer and laid her hand softly on William's shoulder. "All right, William. We'll do that, and see where it takes us. Thanks for coming in and asking. I think you're doing a wonderful job."

"I appreciate that, Joyce," William said. He waited, expecting her to remove her hand and step back. But she didn't stir, and as the seconds passed, her hold on his shoulder felt increasingly sensual. Her gaze seemed imploring. Their faces were now just inches apart.

William leaned forward and tried to kiss her on the lips.

Just before their skin touched, Joyce gasped, pushed him away, and leaped back, her features contorted into a scowl.

"My God!" she cried. "What the hell are you doing?"

William's jaw grew slack. He fumbled for words but found none. He trembled noticeably.

Joyce gave him a hard stare. "Perhaps it would be best if you resigned."

"Oh god, please, no," he bleated. "I'm so sorry, Joyce. Really. I can't believe I just did that."

"What on earth possessed you?"

"Please, believe me, Joyce, I'm so sorry. Please don't fire me. I love this job. I'd never impose myself on anyone like that if I didn't . . ." He swallowed. "I thought you were sending signals. Honestly. The way you were touching me. And looking at me. I'm so sorry."

"I'm quite certain I did nothing to lead you on," she asserted, her tone firm and resolute. "Have you no respect for me?"

"I respect you a great deal, Joyce. I really do. And I love working for you. I'm so sorry I misinterpreted the situation. I think sometimes it's very hard for a man to know what kind of signals he's getting. And I'm especially bad at it."

"You're married, William. And your wife works for my dentist and cleans my teeth regularly. Think for a minute. Did coming on to me in my office really seem like a good plan to you?"

"No. Not at all. I screwed up. I'm really sorry."

"You should be."

"Please don't fire me, Joyce. I really need this job. I'll never approach you that way again. I love working here. You won't have a problem with me again, ever. I promise."

"All right," she said flatly. "I'll let it pass. But you make absolutely sure to be the perfect gentleman around me in the future."

"Yes ma'am, I promise. Thank you. Thank you so much."

"All right then," Joyce said.

William turned to leave.

Just as he started to walk through the door he heard Joyce say, "And William, despite this mishap just now, I *will* talk to our attorney about whether Alice can spend the day with you in San Jose."

He turned back to look at her. "Thank you, Joyce. That's very kind of you. Thank you. You're a good person."

He shut the door behind him and headed home. On the drive back to San Francisco, he berated himself unceasingly.

A pervasive sense of mortification plagued him for days.

Every Wednesday night, Joyce Miller and her old friend Sybil Harrington met for drinks and a late supper after work. They invariably dined at a small family-run Chinese restaurant in Mill Valley called House of Cheung. They affectionately referred to it as "House of Same," because they'd never deviated from that spot even once during the nearly ten years they'd been meeting. It was a dark, cozy place with good food and a few spicy dishes that Joyce especially loved. They drank tea from tiny porcelain cups as they ate and chatted.

But they always rendezvoused for cocktails first at a seedy dive bar just down the block from the restaurant. The tavern was run by a couple of lesbians, and though there were always male patrons there too, most of the clients were women, and many of them were gay. Joyce and Sybil were not, but they felt safe and comfortable in a place where so many other women were drinking together without male escorts.

They were in their customary little corner nook, which was almost always empty when they arrived because most everybody else sat at the bar. Sybil had just returned from the counter, where she'd picked up their second round of pomegranate cosmopolitans. She set the two cocktails onto the rough wooden table and sat down on the bench across from Joyce.

They'd been ordering cosmopolitans here for years, but a few months ago the bar had run out of cranberry juice just before they arrived and one of the owners had offered them a version with pomegranate juice, on the house. They'd been hooked ever since.

Joyce was halfway through her second drink before she worked up the courage to bring up the incident with William.

"He made a pass at me," she said. "Right there in my office. He tried to kiss me on the lips."

"Goodness. How old is he?"

"Early forties."

"My God! You're a cougar! You have over ten years on him."

"Closer to fifteen, I'm afraid." Joyce blushed.

"Just out of blue?" Sybil asked. "He just came on to you with no warning?"

An embarrassed chuckle spewed out of Joyce's mouth as she

shielded it with her fingers. She took a few more sips of her drink before admitting, "Oh, I've been flirting with him for months. I have my hands on him all the time. I was right in his face when he made the pass."

"Well! He must be cute if you're paying that much attention to him."

"He is—tall, broad shoulders, not muscular but definitely on the leaner side. Handsome. And he's very sweet. But I was such a bitch. I pretended to be infuriated. I absolutely denied that I was flirting. And I threatened to fire him."

"Oh God, you didn't!"

Both women started giggling.

"Why on earth did you do that to the poor man?"

"Oh, at first I think I was afraid I'd just gotten myself in over my head and it was a way to back out. But then I really started to enjoy it. I mean, here was this young stud, apologizing and groveling and begging me not to fire him. It was such a power trip, you know?" She took another sip. "I really am a raging bitch, aren't I?"

Sybil laughed. "Well, men play with women's feelings all the time, so I guess you're entitled to take a shot at it once in a while, honey."

Joyce chuckled. "Maybe so!"

"What will you do if he tries it again?" Sybil asked.

"Oh, he won't," Joyce assured her. "I put the fear of God in him. You should have seen that poor boy trembling. But in a way, I wish he *would* try again. I'd love for him to fuck my brains out."

"You're such a nasty girl, Joyce!" Sybil howled, trying to keep her laughter at a reasonable decibel level. "But you wouldn't really do it, would you?"

"No. He's married. And he works for me. I may be a raging bitch, but I'm not stupid—and I'm certainly not a homewrecker."

Rosemary studied the realtor closely as they interacted. So much about her was intriguing.

For one, she was obese, and years of carrying excess weight had evidently worn down her knees and made walking difficult. The ungainly struggle she endured entering and exiting her new Mercedes, in which she ferried Rosemary from house to house, was painful to watch and occasionally caused Rosemary to turn away in discomfort.

The woman also chatted incessantly.

Arthur had hired Laurel as his realtor using only the Internet and the telephone; he hadn't left his sanctuary in Scarsdale, or consulted with Rosemary or William, when he did it. But she wasn't a bad choice. Laurel had over thirty years' experience and boasted excellent credentials.

What Rosemary was most curious about was what Laurel might have been up to *prior* to her career in real estate. Her long, unstyled grey hair, beaded earrings, flouncy, ankle-length dresses, and the laidback insouciance with which she prosecuted her sales chatter suggested that she might have been a flower child in the Haight Ashbury for some period of time in the sixties or seventies. The corporate image in her professional online photo bore little resemblance to the person with whom Rosemary interacted during these house-hunting expeditions.

Rosemary didn't mention this little irony to anyone, but it amused her greatly every time she imagined Arthur unwittingly conducting business with someone who in person would surely detonate a shell in his explosive stack of prejudices.

It was their fifth trip out. Now that Laurel had a better idea of exactly what Rosemary was looking for, she'd abandoned searching in Marin and was focused farther north, in Sonoma County, where small castles could be had on relatively isolated lots within the price range Arthur had stipulated.

They'd seen several nice properties today, but the last one they'd inspected had seemed to Rosemary especially promising. They were heading home now, and Rosemary decided to call Arthur on her cell phone as Laurel drove.

It rang several times before he picked up.

"Hello? Hello? Who is this? Hello! Are you there?"

She waited for him to exhaust his usual histrionics before she responded, "Hi, Arthur. It's Rosemary. How are you?"

"It's late. Why are you calling so late?"

"I know you asked me not to call after eleven your time, and it's a little past that. I'm sorry, but I thought you'd want to know about this place we just saw. It's a really nice property, Arthur. You may want to jump on it and put a bid down."

"Are you driving? I don't want to talk to you if you're driving."

"No. Laurel's driving."

"Laurel?"

"You remember—Laurel, the realtor you hired."

"Right. Right. I didn't remember her first name. Who the hell remembers first names?" He paused a moment. "So, you say the house is nice? Did William like it?"

"Will didn't come with us this time. It's just me and Laurel here."

"William's not with you? What—he can't find time to look at houses with you? It's too big a sacrifice for him and his busy life?"

"Just between you and me, Arthur, I told him not to come. He's really not much help. Everything looks fine to him. All he does is imagine where his art studio would be."

"He's always been that way. He doesn't know how to be pragmatic. I'm better off dealing with you."

"I'll take that as a begrudging compliment."

"What? What did you say? What kind of compliment?"

"Never mind about that, Arthur. Do you have your computer up? I took a bunch of photos of this place, and I want to send them to you. I think you'll like them."

"It's late. I shut everything off. I'll look at them tomorrow morning."

"All right, but look at them early. Before breakfast. This place is really nice. People are going to jump on it."

"All right."

"It has land around it. And a separate cottage. You said it would be nice if you could have a separate space to work. The cottage would be perfect for that."

"A separate cottage?" Arthur repeated with a hint of muted enthusiasm.

"Yes. A separate cottage. Just about fifty yards away from the main house. And the property's a little bit isolated. Like you said you wanted."

"How the hell far up in Sonoma is this place? I don't want to be in the middle of goddamn nowhere."

"It's in a nice town. Five minutes off the freeway. Ten minutes to Petaluma, which is a fairly small city. Half an hour to Santa Rosa— that's a somewhat bigger city. And an hour north of San Francisco or Berkeley."

"Don't talk to me about Berkeley. It's a place for lunatics."

"You don't have to go to Berkeley, Arthur."

"All right. It's late. I want to go to sleep. I'll look at it in the morning."

"Remember. It has a separate cottage."

"I like the separate cottage. I'll look in the morning. Bye."

"Bye." Rosemary clicked off her cell phone and closed her eyes briefly. "And you're welcome," she muttered under her breath.

CHAPTER 7

D^{*AG*} was at work.

Bert sat hunched in an upholstered leather swivel chair in front of his computer. His lower jaw sagged dejectedly.

He had five browser windows open on his screen, each containing a different article on the same subject: how to "work a room." He also had a Kindle book open on the topic—he'd just finished skimming several chapters of it. The number of disparate sources he consulted didn't matter. They all said exactly the same thing: keep moving from person to person, spend no more than three minutes with any individual, repeat your well-rehearsed two-minute pitch, look for things to differentiate yourself, ask a few open-ended questions, don't get into anything controversial.

Bert could hardly think of a more horrific way to spend an evening—but, after being harangued relentlessly by Dag, he'd agreed to do it. He had dutifully attended two Rotary Club meetings, but had stuck close by Dag at each one and said little to anyone. Dag was now convinced that Bert needed to try something on his own, and had identified a large networking event in a hotel ballroom in Midtown Manhattan that he thought Bert should attend. It was to be held this evening.

At six, Bert made a final check in the full-length mirror of their bedroom. He had on tan slacks, a light blue shirt, a navy blazer, and a multicolored tie with paisley shapes that looked, at least to him, like copulating paramecia. He ran downstairs, jumped on the subway, and was waiting in front of Dag's office building at six thirty as Dag popped through the revolving door.

Dag made a point of walking him over to the hotel and taking him inside. There, Bert paid his admission fee and secured his nametag. Only then did Dag say good-bye and head off to his own event a few blocks away.

Dag had insisted that he was seeing Bert off this way to wish him luck and buoy his spirits. But Bert suspected that he'd really done it to be sure that Bert actually showed up and participated.

Bertram grabbed a glass of white wine from the long table in the front of the ballroom, tapped his jacket pocket to make certain his stack of business cards was easily accessible, and took a deep breath before joining the fray.

Each encounter went pretty much the same way. The people he shook hands with had evidently read the same books and articles that he had, but seemed a bit more facile with the process and jumped into their prepared speeches before Bert could get to his. By the time it was Bert's turn, the virtual three-minute timer was running out, whomever he was talking to was already getting antsy and eyeing their next target, and poor Bert was rushing perfunctorily through his spiel. Then they'd do the obligatory business card exchange, and Bert would compliantly move on.

Bert allowed himself a few swallows of wine between each awkward rendezvous, but the alcohol had little salutary effect in girding him for the next face-off.

He'd been courageously slogging through for about forty-five minutes when he came upon a short, cheerful fellow wearing a jaunty fedora that Bert assumed was at least in part to conceal a receding hairline. The man looked to be about thirty-five and was just a bit paunchy.

They shook hands and exchanged names. His was Miguel.

In direct contrast to how things had proceded thus far that evening, Miguel waited politely for Bert to start his pitch.

Bert's lips had just begun to form the opening salvo of his well-rehearsed patter when he stopped, sighed, and said softly, "I'm sorry, I just can't. I've been at this for nearly an hour, and I just don't have it in me to go through this inane prattle again. I'm terrible at this. And I hate doing it. I'm really sorry." Bert glanced about and located the exit. "I think I'm going to leave and find the hotel bar and have a couple of drinks."

"God, I hate it too," Miguel said. "This is my first mixer like this and honestly, man, I don't know how these people do it. It's soul numbing. You mind if I join you for that drink?"

Bert laughed heartily. "Oh man, please! Let's get the hell out of here!"

The hotel bar one floor down from the ballroom struck both men as sterile and oppressive. They froze in the entryway and went no further.

"I know a bar a couple of blocks from here," Miguel said. "It's a nice place. They have a piano player. He keeps it soft and mellow."

"Okay," Bert said, nodding his head.

They set off. Miguel's frenzied pace upon the crosstown sidewalks was that of a Manhattan native. Having been raised in Scarsdale, Bert's gait was by nature a bit more leisurely, but he scurried to keep up.

There was something about Miguel's energy that he liked.

The bar was exactly as Miguel had described. They found a table in a quiet corner, on the opposite wall from the piano player.

Bert ordered a vodka martini.

"That sounds good," Miguel said to the waitress. "I'll try one too."

The drinks arrived quickly. The two men toasted and started drinking.

"So." Miguel grinned. "If you'd actually gone ahead with your pitch back there, what would it have been?"

"Oh," Bert chuckled. "Real estate." He took a few hearty gulps of his martini. "Yeah. I sell real estate. Or at least, that's what I do on paper. To tell you the truth, I don't really sell much. I never have. I don't know if my heart's in it."

"Then how do you make a living?" Miguel probed.

Bert guzzled what was left of his drink and signaled the waitress to bring another round for both of them. "I actually lived with my dad until just a few months ago," he acknowledged. "Pretty sad, huh? Now I live with my boyfriend."

"Oh, you're gay," Miguel observed genially. "I'm straight. A wife and one kid. But we work with lots of gay people, have lots of gay friends," he added hastily. "Anyway. You seem like a good guy. I'm sorry you don't like real estate, man."

The second round arrived. Miguel downed the small amount remaining in his first so the waitress could take the glass away. He smiled as he handed it to her. "Didn't want you to have to make another trip!"

"Thanks, that's nice of you," she said before walking off with the glasses.

"And what were *you* intending to pitch back there?" Bert asked.

"I'm trying to get a gig going as a personal chef," Miguel said.

"Really? A personal chef. That sounds interesting." Bert leaned forward. "What exactly does that entail?"

"Finding clients who want you to come to their homes and cook a meal now and then. You buy the groceries, prepare the food, serve, and clean up. It's an interesting gig because different people like different kinds of dishes, so you're always cooking something new."

"So, you're a chef?"

"Well, kind of. I've been cooking in restaurant kitchens for years. I got this gig now in a French place downtown where I do line cooking three nights a week and fill in for the chef the two nights a week he's off. So I'm kind of the sous-chef. But it's a really small place, so they don't call me that."

"Is your wife a chef too?"

"No. She waits tables. She has a good gig now at a Caribbean place up in Spanish Harlem. She likes it there. And her mom lives up there and watches our kid every night while we're at work."

"That's nice. Did you meet your wife in a restaurant?"

"Yeah. We were both working at a really cool Italian place in midtown. That was years ago, man. The placed closed though. Too bad, because the food was damn good. The rent just got ridiculous."

"It's a tough business, restaurants," Bert said. "I know an incredible number fold in the first year."

"A lot. But a lot hang in for a year or two, even though it's tough, and *then* throw in the towel, 'cause they just can't keep it going. It's hard work, man."

"So you wouldn't want to open your own restaurant?"

"You know"—Miguel smiled—"it's something my wife and I used to talk about all the time. We'd always say, someday we're gonna do it. Open our own place. But hell, then we saw how tough it really was for the folks we worked for. Even if you make a decent living, the hours you put in are brutal."

"And how did you come up with the idea of being a personal chef?"

"I know some guys who cook in restaurants but do the personal chef thing once in a while on their nights off. One night, one of the guys couldn't make his gig, and he asked me if I could fill in for him. I wasn't working that night so I said sure. He told me what the clients liked and where I should pick up the groceries, all that stuff—and it was a blast, man! The couple I was cooking for really loved my food, and they recommended me to a few other people. So now I do it once in a while—if someone wants me and I have a night off and my wife's okay with it. Usually she is, because we can use the money."

Bert sipped on his drink and pondered. "I love to cook," he said. "I always have. I cooked for my dad for years. Now I cook for my boyfriend. I mean, I'm not trained or anything, but I've probably watched more cooking shows than anyone on the planet. And I'm always buying cookbooks. I think I'm pretty good. But I'd love to know what a real chef like you thinks of my food."

"Hey, I got a great idea!" Miguel's eyes widened. "My wife and I promised to cook her mom a big, fancy dinner next week at her house. You know, to thank her for watching our kid all the time. My wife was gonna help me make it, but she'd just love it if I had a different assistant and she could relax with her mom and the kid. You wanna come up to Spanish Harlem and cook with me? I love cooking with friends. Then you can join us for dinner. Get to know the family."

"I'd like that very much," Bert held up his glass for another toast.

Rosemary would have been finished with her patient by a quarter to three, but he was one of those rare people who retain all of their wisdom teeth, and they were difficult for him to reach with a toothbrush. Scaling tartar on patients like this became something akin to a religious mission for Rosemary—only when every surface in the remote crannies of their mouths finally felt smooth and unblemished could she make herself stop.

So it was 2:55 p.m. by the time the patient was out of the chair, regaled with the requisite niceties and farewells, supplied with a complementary toothbrush and pack of floss, and hustled out to the receptionist to pay for the cleaning and schedule his next appointment. Which left Rosemary just five minutes to run to the ladies' room and apply the slightest hint of blush and a wisp of pink lip-gloss.

Her features were delicate and a tad boyish—too much makeup made her look tawdry—but small amounts, applied judiciously, elicited an unspoken but clearly palpable reaction from Moe.

Moe's given name was Mahmoud. He'd come to the United States years ago from Iran on a student visa and had majored in chemistry at Stanford. He wound up completing dental school there as well, became a US citizen soon after, and opened his own dental practice, of which Rosemary was a longtime employee. Photos of his wife and three children adorned the desk and walls of his office. At fifty, his temples had turned gray and his formerly athletic physique was now more burly than chiseled, but he was still a formidable specimen.

Moe identified ethnically as Persian to anyone who asked, and he refused to utter the word "Iranian." Despite coming from a devout Muslim family, he denied having any religious affiliation at all; he insisted he was a secular, agnostic humanist.

To Rosemary he had always seemed dashing and alluring—and though his diction evinced only the slightest Farsi inflection, for her his accented baritone inexplicably augmented his already commanding manner.

Moe smiled when they met at the door to the larger of the two exam rooms at 3:00 p.m. sharp. They entered together. Rosemary locked the door and made certain the blinds were drawn.

Moe stripped naked. Rosemary did as well, but as was Moe's preference, she then unlocked the bottom drawer of the instrument case and withdrew a bright red baby doll negligee. It fit her snugly, and she knew Moe loved watching her slither into it.

From the same drawer, Rosemary pulled out half a dozen thick black leather straps. She worked at fastening Moe to the reclining exam chair with the same meticulous focus she brought to the most clinical aspects of her job. When she was done, Moe was bound tightly to the chair and practically immobilized. His hands and feet were helpless to intervene no matter what Rosemary chose to do. His penis was by now engorged and throbbing.

Rosemary returned to the bottom drawer and retrieved the pièce de résistance: a ring gag, a fist-size hoop of hard black plastic with wide leather straps attached at opposite ends. Rosemary disinfected it with alcohol, then wedged it into Moe's mouth, forcing his jaw wide open and giving her full and unimpeded access to his teeth and gums. She buckled the straps securely behind Moe's head, smiled coyly, and stroked his chest.

"Let's begin your cleaning, honey," she purred.

She laid out a fine assortment of sharp-tipped probes, scalers, and curettes. She added a few cotton swabs and carefully set down a small porcelain vessel, into which she poured a shallow reservoir of hydrogen peroxide.

"Let's see what's going on in here," she whispered as she picked up a probe and explored around his gum line for areas that seemed vulnerable. "Ah, you need some work here, honey," she cooed.

As she reached for a curette, Moe recoiled, strained against his straps, and suppressed a gasp. But he was powerless to stop her. She entered, impaled his gum, and slowly increased pressure until the trickle of blood grew from irregular to copious, at which point she withdrew the tool, dipped a cotton swab into the puddle of hydrogen peroxide, and dabbed the wound. Moe stifled a scream; the bleeding slowly subsided, and Rosemary watched the area turn white and bubble a bit as it did.

She rubbed his chest sensually. "Oh, that wasn't so bad," she assured him. "We have lots more to go."

He tried to say something in response. It came out as an unintelligible groan with a hint of resigned desperation.

She repeated the sadistic procedure in various areas of Moe's mouth with a wide assortment of instruments, in some cases twiddling the tool a bit to exacerbate the pain she was inflicting. Rosemary also made sure to have her arm casually brush Moe's penis from time to time as she entered or withdrew, causing the bulging member to quiver and gurgle for an instant before it reverted to rigid immobility.

Their play went on for quite some time, with Rosemary periodically catching furtive glimpses of the wall clock to be certain they managed their time judiciously.

Moe's gums were checkered with puffy white wounds when she finally said, "You've been a very good boy. Your cleaning is done. I think you've earned a big red lollipop."

She climbed on top and carefully lowered herself onto him. She started slowly, but was soon riding him with abandon.

At about the same time that Rosemary and Moe shared an orgasm and tried their best to muffle their ecstatic cries, Joyce Miller's Uber car pulled up outside the building. Joyce thanked the driver, got out, and walked up the stairs to the dentist's suite, where she checked in for her regularly scheduled cleaning. From her vantage point at the receptionist's desk she could see down the short hallway where the exam rooms were. It didn't seem that anyone was around, but then she heard the rattle of a door-lock and watched as Rosemary slunk out of the larger of the two exam rooms with flushed cheeks and a furtive demeanor, her lips curled into the barest suggestion of a mischievous grin. She raced down the hall to the chamber at the far end, reserved for cleanings, and moments later Joyce's dentist emerged from the same room she'd just vacated, hiking up his pants and buttoning his white robe. He closed the door behind him and rushed off.

No patient was anywhere to be seen.

Joyce understood immediately.

Dag was in his underwear, reclining awkwardly on the living room sofa, when Bert finally got home. An open bottle of bourbon sat on the coffee table beside the couch, and from what little was left in it, Bert surmised that he had been drinking for a while. His large flat-screen television droned on about financial markets, but the volume was turned low and Dag didn't seem to be paying attention to it.

Dag's face was an indignant red. His lips curled inward and quivered spitefully as if he was preparing to form words but couldn't quite decide on what to spew out. He had the semblance of a grenade about to detonate.

"Hello, Dag," Bert ventured cautiously.

"Where the hell have you been?" Dag screeched. "Your networking event closed down two hours ago. I know it did. I called the hotel to check."

"I made a contact," Bert said. "I was talking to him. We got to know each other a bit. We had a couple of drinks." Bert's tone was defensive, but also an attempt to de-escalate.

"Did you ever think of calling me? Or texting? Just to let me know you're alive and not lying dead on some subway platform?"

Now Bert grew agitated. He marched over to the sofa where Dag lay and glared at him. "How many goddamn nights have *you* been out? Wooing customers or God knows what? Did you ever call *me*? Did I ever fucking complain about it?"

Dag seemed taken aback by Bert's aggressive tone, or perhaps by the sight of his large, sinewy frame towering just above him. He stammered for a moment—"Well, um, I . . ."

Bert leaned down, his face now flared crimson too. "Well?" he shouted. "Did I ever fucking complain? Answer me!"

Dag lifted his hands in a gesture of surrender. "Mea culpa. Mea culpa. I'm sorry, Bertie." He sat up a bit, and Bert retreated a couple of steps. "I really was worried about you. But I shouldn't have come at you that way. I'm sorry."

"Well, okay," Bert grumbled.

"Here," Dag said, starting to stand up, "let me get you a glass and you can have some bourbon with me."

"I've been drinking vodka all night. I don't want bourbon. You know I don't like to mix liquors."

"Okay," Dag said, already scampering into the kitchen. "Let me whip you up a quick martini."

"Just pour me some vodka on ice," Bert called.

Dag was back quickly with the drink. "I want to toast to this contact you made. I'm so proud of you! Scoring at a networking event. I want to hear all about him. What kind of real estate is he in the market for?"

Bert swished his vodka in the ice to chill it, then took a sip. "He's not in the market for real estate," he said quietly.

"Oh!" Dag said. "I'm sorry, I shouldn't have jumped to that conclusion. Is he part of a real estate firm you might join?"

"Goddamn it, Dag! This has nothing to do with real estate. Get real estate off your mind. I was just *talking* to a guy."

Dag's tone hardened and the contrite furrows on his cheekbones faded. "What do you mean it has nothing to do with real estate? That's the whole reason you went to this networking thing! To drum up real estate business. If that's not what you were doing, what *were* you doing?"

Bert walked slowly to the leather recliner. He plopped into it, holding his glass aloft, then took a few pensive swallows. Dag returned to the sofa and leaned back with his drink while he waited for him to say something.

Finally, Bert said, "He's a personal chef."

"A personal chef?" Dag replied, looking puzzled. "What on earth does *that* have to do with anything?"

"I'm going to cook with him next week. At his mother-in-law's place in Spanish Harlem. Just to see what it's like. I don't know, it might be an interesting thing to do."

"Spanish fucking Harlem?" Dag cried, jerking forward on the sofa. "Are you crazy? White people get killed up there!"

"I'll be fine. Miguel's a good dude."

"Is this guy gay?"

"No. He's straight. He's married. They have a kid."

Dag's eyes closed and his head shook incredulously. "I'm sorry, Bertie. What am I missing here? How is this helping your real estate career?"

"I hate real estate, Dag. I've always hated it. I try to tell you that, but you don't listen. Or maybe you listen but you pretend not to hear it. I think I'd be good at being a personal chef. And I think I might like it."

Dag bolted to his feet, his mouth agape. He raised his shoulders and turned his palms outward in a gesture of disbelief. "A personal chef? Really. A personal chef. Of all my clients, I don't have a single one who's a personal chef. You know why, Bertie? Because they don't have any money to invest. Why in hell would you throw away a career in real estate to make pennies cooking for other people? It makes no sense."

"I just told you. I hate real estate. Or were you not listening that time too?"

"Jesus! You're like a little kid. Today you want to be a personal chef. Maybe tomorrow you'll want to be a fireman. And the next day an astronaut. Damn it, Bertie, be realistic."

"Fuck you." Bert rose and started walking toward the bedroom. "You can be such a little *shit*! If I wanted to have conversations like this, I could have kept living with my asshole father."

CHAPTER 8

*A*RTHUR had only been on an airplane a couple of times before. Those flights were years earlier, and both his wife and young Bertram had accompanied him then. He'd never realized how much he'd depended on the two of them to shepherd him around the airports until now.

This morning he'd called a taxi, which had transported him from Scarsdale to La Guardia without incident. But from there it was like stumbling through a giant maze with rude and dismissive gremlins stationed at each turn. When he finally arrived at the proper gate, it was just moments prior to the boarding cutoff. Perspiration soaked his clothing and shimmered on his face.

He trudged unsteadily through the narrow, claustrophobic jet bridge. His briefcase was stuffed with papers and his old, heavy laptop. The exertion of lugging that, along with his ungainly carryon suitcase with rickety wheels, had exhausted him and left him stressed.

His hip ached and he was out of breath when he finally reached the apex of the gangway's gradient. But seeing the plane's boarding door just a few steps away encouraged him to take a deep, slow breath. As he did, he felt his anger and frustration begin to subside.

A polite voice somewhere off to the side rang out. "Excuse me, sir, we're going to have to check that bag."

Arthur turned his head. It was a young gentleman whose airline uniform clung impeccably to his lithe frame without a single visible wrinkle or gather. Given how his own sweat-soaked shirt had pulled up out of his trousers and the waistband of his pants now slunk lower onto his hips with each plodding painful stride up the jetway, Arthur found the fellow's crisp appearance annoying.

The man was pointing to Arthur's suitcase with its squeaking, compromised wheels.

"You're wrong," Arthur shot back. "I measured this bag last night, and checked your website. It meets your airline's regulations exactly. So, stop giving me a bunch of idiotic crap and let me get on the damn plane."

"I'm sorry, sir," the young man replied with what appeared to Arthur an insincere and cloying smile. "The overhead bins are all full. And that piece is too big to fit under your seat, which is where your briefcase needs to go anyway. So I have no choice but to check it. You can retrieve it at baggage claim when you land in California. I'm sorry for any inconvenience, sir."

Arthur glanced toward the jet's door, where a pilot and a couple of flight attendants were glaring at him. Only two other passengers had not yet boarded—they stood behind him waiting, and he caught one of them rolling her eyes when he peeked back.

"Oh, all right, for God's sake!" he cried, shoving the suitcase toward the obnoxiously courteous young man.

"Here's your claim ticket," the man said.

A flight attendant showed Arthur to his row near the back of the plane and pointed to his seat. It was one of the few remaining unoccupied spots, a middle seat wedged between a man on the window side and woman on the aisle. Arthur immediately noticed that the armrest between his seat and the one nearer to the window had been pulled up. The obese fellow sitting near the window was the obvious culprit—the copious flesh upon his thighs, buttocks, and hips sprawled like ectoplasm over into Arthur's space.

"Tell this guy to put his armrest down!" Arthur yelled, pointing to the rotund gentleman, who was curled up against the window with a small paperback book held nearly against his face. "I want my whole seat!"

The man lowered the book and turned his head slowly, his eyelids quivering painfully as if he was reliving an oft-repeated episode of indignity. He made a halfhearted attempt to force the armrest down, but it was clearly impossible for the armrest and his body to occupy that same space simultaneously. "I'm really sorry," he pleaded. His face shriveled in mortification. "It's a glandular condition."

"Glandular, my ass!" Arthur grumbled without making eye contact. "You're a pig—you eat too much," he muttered as he stumbled past the young woman in the aisle seat, who hadn't bothered to rise.

Arthur's foot caught on something and he lost his balance, but he was just a step from his seat and he managed to plummet sideways into it. The flight attendant, a middle-aged blond woman sporting a disgusted scowl, waited a moment for Arthur to right himself, then ordered him to stow his briefcase in the space beneath the seat in front of him.

It took a bit of ungainly wrestling, but Arthur did manage to jam most of it in.

When the flight attendant was satisfied that Arthur had done what he could, she saw to it that he buckled his seatbelt and then she headed back to the front of the plane—where, as chief attendant, she was due to narrate the safety instructions. Along the way, she passed the attendant responsible for the rear of the plane, who was seating the final two passengers. "Keep an eye on the old fart in the middle seat back there," she whispered to her colleague. "He's going to be trouble."

A short time after takeoff, as the plane was heading west over Pennsylvania, the beverage cart finally came by. Arthur secured three tiny plastic bottles of Jack Daniel's, which he began to suck down with a can of club soda. The bulbous gentleman beside him drank only a Diet Coke, which caused Arthur to snicker, especially as he watched the fellow first chomp down his free bag of pretzels seemingly in a single inhalation.

"Do you want mine too?" Arthur asked the man, holding up his unopened bag. "They're too salty for me."

The man looked at Arthur warily, but as Arthur expected, he couldn't resist. "Thanks," he mumbled, then grabbed the bag and turned toward the window to consume them.

Arthur smirked and sipped on his bourbon.

He eyed the slim young woman seated to his right. She wore a starched white blouse. Her complexion was pale. Her long hair was straight and hung down past her shoulders and was the exact same shade of black as her snug but professional-looking skirt. She'd been reviewing some sort of PowerPoint presentation on a tablet as she drank a vodka with cranberry juice, but now she slipped the tablet back into her oversize purse, pulled out a set of ear buds, and a tiny music device, reclined her seat, and closed her eyes.

As she fell asleep, her body shifted and the top of her blouse opened noticeably. Arthur wasn't quite sure whether she'd left her top buttons open intentionally or through an oversight, but either way, he now had an unobstructed view of her frilly white demi-bra, and the creamy tops of her breasts rising and falling gently with each breath.

He became fixated.

Arthur drank all three bottles of Jack Daniel's while watching her. He averted his gaze only to open and pour each incremental serving into his ice-filled plastic cup.

Suddenly, without warning, some sort of commotion alongside his row shattered the silence of his leering stupor. An old woman in the aisle seat across from him had summoned the flight attendant, and was now gesticulating and screaming.

"That man is harassing that poor woman!" she cried. "He's staring at her while she's sleeping! He opened her blouse, or it opened by itself, I don't know. But what he's doing is disgusting! I can't stand watching it anymore. Please! Do something!"

That passionate rant awakened the young woman next to Arthur, who bolted up. "What's going on?" she asked.

"That man's been ogling you!" the old woman yelled. "He's staring down your blouse."

The young woman glanced down at her blouse, gasped, and buttoned it up with exaggerated indignation. "My God, how long has he been doing it?" she pleaded, looking at the flight attendant and the older, agitated passenger.

"It's been going on for over an hour," the old woman said.

The flight attendant, attempting to defuse the situation, raised her hands and said, "We've barely been in the air for thirty minutes, ma'am."

The young woman turned angrily toward Arthur. "And what's *your* problem? What kind of pervert gets off spying on sleeping women?"

"Don't flatter yourself, honey," Arthur snapped back. "You're all skin and bones. There's nothing there worth looking at."

"My, my, we're judgmental about body size in all sorts of ways," observed the obese fellow in the window seat from behind his paper-back book.

The young woman now turned back to the flight attendant. "I need to change my seat," she said. "I can't sit next to this man."

"I understand," the flight attendant said, "but the plane is full, honey. There isn't a single empty seat. Just hold on though. Let me see if I can find someone who's willing to trade seats with you." With that, she shot a withering sneer at Arthur and stalked off.

She returned just a couple of minutes later, accompanied by a brawny man in military garb who displayed a stern demeanor and carried a small satchel. From the angled stripes on his uniform, Arthur inferred that the man was a sergeant of some sort—and judging by his carriage and demeanor, probably a sadistic, overbearing drill instructor.

"This gentleman has agreed to trade seats with you," the flight attendant said to the young woman, who quickly gathered her things and disappeared. As the sergeant sat down and stowed his carryon bag, the flight attendant gestured toward Arthur and said, "Let me know if the gentleman in the middle seat gives you any trouble, sir."

"Oh, I don't think I'll have a problem with *this* guy, ma'am," the sergeant retorted in a crisp, growling baritone. His lips curled into a self-assured grin and he shot a condescending glance in Arthur's direction.

"You really helped me out here, sir." The flight attendant placed a hand lightly on his upper arm. "My offer of a free meal is still good if you want it." She smiled and turned to walk away, but looked back for a moment to add, "And thank you so much for your service to our country."

The drill sergeant nodded politely.

The corpulent passenger to Arthur's left chuckled, curled back toward the window, and buried his face back in his tiny paperback book.

"Close up your pigments and get your jacket on," Rosemary exhorted, poking her head into William's painting studio. "I want to leave for the airport!"

"Now?" William whined. "It's too early. If we leave now we'll be waiting there for over half an hour. We don't need to leave yet. We have lots of time."

"I don't want to keep your father waiting under any circumstances," Rosemary insisted. "He's *always* cranky, and after a long plane flight he'll be worse. If we're late and he has to wait for us he'll be impossible. Don't argue with me. Let's just go."

"It takes twenty-five minutes to get to the airport," William persisted. "Why do we have to leave *now*?"

"What if there's an accident? Or they're doing roadwork? You can't be sure there won't be delays."

"It's Sunday morning. Traffic is so light that we'd get by any impediment without a problem."

"You can't be positive. I don't want to risk it. Stop giving me trouble. Let's go! Now!"

Rosemary roared out that last directive with such fuming authority that as she stomped away, William closed his eyes, exhaled, and dropped his head. He knew further resistance would be counterproductive. He hastily capped his tubes of paint and open cans of turpentine and linseed oil. He inverted an old plastic bowl over his palette, hoping to keep it fresh, and slung on his jacket.

There was, in fact, a fender bender on the opposite side of the freeway that caused traffic to slow for gawking, but it only delayed them five or six minutes. Rosemary gloated just a bit when they first encountered the slowdown, but grew quiet when they cruised past it with so little difficulty.

"We still have over half an hour to kill," William muttered as they pulled into the airport's short-term parking lot.

"Let's get a couple of lattes while we wait," Rosemary chirped. "You like the lattes at that coffee shop upstairs."

William recalled an especially creamy latte he'd had at that same shop a year or two earlier and flashed her a grin. "I guess I *am* in the mood for a latte."

They savored their coffees unhurriedly then took the escalator down to the baggage claim area and parked themselves next to the drivers holding up cardboard signs with the names of the passengers they were meeting. William found it interesting that a couple of drivers had converted from cardboard to electronic tablets.

Rosemary spotted Arthur first. "There he is," she said, pointing to a disheveled figure trudging toward them lugging a bulging leather briefcase. Countless wrinkled papers poked chaotically from the case's back pouch.

When Arthur reached them, he shared an unenthusiastic hand-shake with his son, then Rosemary slipped between the two men and threw her arms around him. He did not resist, but he did not actively reciprocate.

"How was your flight?" Rosemary inquired cheerfully.

"Uneventful," Arthur said.

"Here"—Rosemary reached for Arthur's briefcase—"let William carry that for you."

Arthur tugged the case closer to him. "I can carry it myself." He looked around. "Where's the bathroom? I need to go. That tiny crap-box in the plane was disgusting."

They waited for Arthur outside the men's room. He took an inordinately long time, but appeared in somewhat better spirits when he finally emerged. "I'm hungry," he announced. "Let's go up and see what they have to eat."

"We ought to get to the baggage carousel first," Rosemary said. "If we don't pick up your luggage, someone might walk off with it."

"Damn," Arthur muttered, nearly inaudibly, and shuffled after them as they walked slowly to the carousel.

They waited there for fifteen minutes, along with a huge throng of passengers. Arthur said nothing but his irritation grew noticeably more pronounced as each moment passed.

"I'm hungry, damn it!" he finally shouted. He thought for a moment, as if trying to picture something in his mind. "When I was walking from the gate up there I saw a place that had a sandwich that looked good," he said. His eyes edged to the corner of his sockets as he tried to recall. "Right! A Brie and prosciutto sandwich on a ciabatta roll. Bertram used to make me something like that for lunch sometimes. I wanna get one of those."

"All right," Rosemary said. "I'll run up and get the sandwich. You wait here with William to identify your bags when they come out."

"No!" Arthur said. "I need to go and make sure they make it the way I want."

"Let's just go get it now," William said.

"I'm worried about his luggage," Rosemary warned.

"For God's sakes, I'm not gonna sit down and *eat* it there!" Arthur said. "I'll take it in the car."

"We should wait here for the luggage first," Rosemary pleaded.

"No!" Arthur screamed. "This luggage is taking forever. I want the goddamn sandwich *now!*"

William groaned. "Let him get the sandwich, please."

Rosemary's eyes closed as her head drooped in frustration. "Okay," she whispered.

They took the escalator up and found the food court just a few steps from where the moving stairway deposited them. Arthur ordered the sandwich, which was methodically assembled under his intense scrutiny, wrapped neatly in brown parchment, and then wedged into a small white paper bag. As Arthur fumbled with some cash, Rosemary unceremoniously grabbed the food and raced back toward the escalator. William and Arthur trudged dutifully behind her.

Arthur leaned his head closer to his son's and chuckled. "Still a spitfire, isn't she?"

When they reached the carousel, the space around it was deserted. Rosemary stared at them, scowling.

One old brown suitcase was the lone squatter on the slowly circling belt. Apart from the conveyor's barely audible rumble, the area was silent.

William grabbed the bag.

A few minutes later, the trio was in the airport garage and William was loading Arthur's suitcase into the back of the van. Two other pieces of luggage, one belonging to William and the other to Rosemary, were already stowed in the van's rear, along with a small satchel full of toiletries.

The plan, which Arthur had insisted upon a few days earlier, was to avoid William's and Rosemary's San Francisco flat entirely. Instead, the three of them would drive directly from the airport to Sonoma County, where they'd meet the realtor, Laurel, and she'd show Arthur the house Rosemary had found so promising. If Arthur liked it, Laurel would start the purchase negotiations immediately—if not, there was still a good deal of time left in the day for the four of them to look at other properties. In any event, Arthur had reserved them adjoining rooms in a nice Petaluma hotel, and he, William, and Rosemary would stay up there for the night after having dinner at a nice Italian place in Healdsburg.

When the car first rolled up, Bert could not quite make sense of how tiny the thing was. It seemed more a toy than a bona fide vehicle—a red metal box on wheels that you could grab and plop into a bathtub and still have room to squeeze in beside it and take a soak.

For a few awkward moments, he stood motionless on the curb, failing to signal a greeting or make any effort to reach for the passenger door's handle. A bemused, embarrassed glare had seized his features. He sensed it, and knew it was due to how wrong, and perhaps stereotypical, his assumptions had been. For the past few days, he had been trying to imagine what sort of car Miguel might be driving, and had narrowed it down to either a vintage convertible with fins and big round headlights or a knocked-up pickup truck, maybe a Ford or a Chevy.

Certainly not this.

Finally, Bertram gave his head a quick shake to clear its fog and opened the passenger door. "Hey, good to see you. I've been looking forward to tonight."

"Me too," Miguel said cheerfully. "From the look on your face I guess you never rode in a Smart car before, huh man?" He smiled broadly. "Get in, buddy. It's a little snug but it won't bite."

Bert glanced at the bag of groceries perched on the passenger seat and then back at Miguel.

"Oh, sorry about that," Miguel said. "I have three paper sacks stuffed with food in the trunk, and that's all that'll fit. Can you hold this bag on your lap or maybe set it down between your legs? We'll be up there in just a few minutes."

"Sure thing," Bert assured him as he slid into the passenger seat and eased the bag down onto the floor.

Initially, he'd planned to drive up to Spanish Harlem himself. But when Miguel offered to pick him up, he'd reluctantly agreed. It was the way Miguel had gently posited the strategy as they finalized the arrangements over the phone: "It's your first time in Spanish Harlem, Bert . . . you don't know your way around . . . it's different from the neighborhoods you're used to . . . let me pick you up at your condo, man."

As soon as Bert snapped on his seat belt, Miguel pulled the car out and headed uptown.

"So, you feel safe driving this thing in New York traffic?"

"Oh, I hold my own." Miguel chuckled. "And I'll tell you, man, there's not a street in the city I can't find a parking space on."

"Well, there's sure as hell something to be said for *that*!" Bert declared with a laugh.

Miguel was wearing the same tan fedora he'd had on the night they met. He drove aggressively, his soapbox car slithering between taxis, buses, and other behemoths on Manhattan's crowded streets. He got on the FDR Drive and took it north as far as Ninety-sixth Street, where he exited and switched to First Avenue.

The traffic was relatively light heading into East Harlem. Miguel wound around to East 118th Street and slowed down, looking for a parking spot. As promised, he soon found a tiny patch of curb between a car and a motorcycle—a spot into which only a vehicle like his could wriggle.

As Miguel maneuvered into the spot, Bert spied a dozen young Hispanic men just twenty feet farther up the block. One sat on a stoop, a few others leaned menacingly against the brick wall of the small apartment house, and the rest stood on the sidewalk. They'd been chatting, but now they were eyeing the Smart car as it nestled into its space.

Bert turned to Miguel and whispered, "Those guys loitering up there . . . they look a bit unsavory. Are we okay?"

Miguel chuckled. "You mean they look like a Puerto Rican street gang? Like in *West Side Story*?"

"I just want to be sure it's safe."

Miguel patted Bert on the thigh. "My wife grew up with these guys. My mother-in-law's known them since they were kids. She bakes cookies for them and makes them lunch now and then. They're more like her personal bodyguards than gang bangers. I think you'll make it upstairs in one piece."

Bert and Miguel grabbed two grocery bags each and headed to the front door of the apartment house up the block. To get there, they had to pass through the gauntlet of young men. Bert kept his head down and walked close to Miguel.

"Hey Miguel," one of the guys shouted as they approached, "those empanadas you gave us to try last week—that was tasty shit, man. You make us some more?"

Miguel smiled broadly. "I'm glad you liked 'em. Me and my friend Bert here are actually gonna fry up a bunch more of 'em tonight for Connie and her mom. We'll make an extra dozen or two and bring 'em down to you."

"Thanks man."

A husky young man leaning against the brick wall looked at Bert. "Where you from, Bert?"

"Oh, right here in the city," Bert said, suddenly a lot less nervous. "I just met Miguel a few weeks ago. We both like to cook so we're going to give it a try together."

"Cool, man."

Miguel led Bert a few doors farther up the street to a narrow five-story brownstone, where he fumbled for his key to the heavy metal door. They climbed the stone stairs to the top floor. "*You'll* bring the empanadas down to them later," Miguel said. "They'll associate you with the food, see you as a friend too. That way, when you come up to visit again, they won't hassle you."

Bert laughed. "You're a psychologist as well as a chef, eh?"

Miguel's wife, Consuelo, heard them on the landing and opened the apartment door. Bert observed her closely as she chirped, "Hi honey," and gave Miguel a quick kiss on the lips.

She was young, and very pretty. She wore tight jeans and a clingy white sweater. Bert would not have imagined a woman that beautiful would be married to a paunchy, unassuming guy like Miguel, but somehow he'd snared her. Bert recalled that he'd liked Miguel the moment he met him, but now he wondered if perhaps there was more to the man than he'd fathomed.

"Bert, this is my wife, Connie," Miguel said.

"I've heard all about you," Consuelo announced with a gleaming smile. "Welcome to El Barrio!" She ran over and gave Bert a brief hug, which he was unable to reciprocate because he still held a heavy sack of groceries in each hand.

They entered the apartment and dropped the bags off in the kitchen. Then they headed into the living room to greet Consuelo's mother.

A full-figured woman with long dark hair and bright eyes, she was sitting on the couch and playing with a baby who rested on her lap.

"Mom, this is our friend, Bert," Consuelo said.

Miguel's mother-in-law did not say anything or get up, but she flashed a warm smile and held out her right hand, palm down, her wrist just limp enough to appear beckoning and sultry.

Bert gently took hold of the woman's hand but didn't quite know what to do with it. On impulse, he bent over and kissed the back of it. "Nice to meet you, ma'am," he stammered.

The woman laughed. "Such a gentleman you brought to our home," she kidded in a heavy Puerto Rican accent. She glanced at Bert and winked. "And don't call me ma'am, you sweet thing! That's for old ladies. You call me Luisa."

"Nice to meet you, Luisa," he said, grinning.

"Enough flirting, Ma!" Miguel said with a wink. "Bert and me are going to unpack the groceries and mix up a big pitcher of piña coladas for everyone, and then we're going to cook a great dinner, special for you two pretty ladies."

"You bring Bert over and cook for me every week from now on!" Luisa teased, as the two men headed back to the kitchen.

"Okay," Miguel said as he laid out two large wooden cutting boards on the counter, "you're going to be my sous-chef. You'll do a lot of the prep and some cooking too. You up for this?"

Bert nodded quickly. "Absolutely."

"All right. First a quick quiz, so I know what I'm dealing with. D'ya know the difference between sautéing and sweating?"

"Pretty much the same, really," Bert said, a bit surprised to be grilled this way. "When I sweat vegetables, I use a little lower heat and I don't let them brown."

"Very good! And if I say chop, you know, or dice, or mince, you know what I want?"

Bert smiled with a surge of confidence. "By chop, you mean a rough chop. A dice is smaller, minced smaller still."

"And you can do all that?"

"Just give me a French chef's knife or a cleaver and I'm your man."

"All right!" Miguel put his hand up for a high-five, and Bert slapped it.

Miguel cocked his head. "You know how to mix piña coladas?"

"You got me there," Bert admitted. "Martinis and manhattans, I'm an expert, but I've never made a piña colada. Not sure I've even ever drunk one."

"Well, come over here and learn." Miguel fished around in the grocery sacks for the bottle of rum and cans of pineapple juice and coconut cream, then grabbed a lime from the dish on the counter. "First, we wash our hands. Always that first." As he soaped up under the kitchen sink's hot running water, he said, "You know, if you want to be a personal chef, you gotta know how to make people's favorite cocktails. It's important. I have a bunch memorized, but I always carry my little bartender cheater book with me when I work a gig, too. Some people want some pretty strange drinks!"

After throwing the piña colada ingredients in the blender with some ice, Miguel poured the concoction into festive glasses and he and Bert delivered them to the living room, where everyone toasted.

"Okay," Miguel said to Bert after his first sip. "Time to fry up empanadas."

Back in the kitchen, Miguel fished a huge yellow onion out of one of the bags and tossed it to Bert, who was startled but managed to catch it.

"Good catch!" Miguel exclaimed. "I thought for sure you'd drop it."

"I played baseball in college."

"Really?"

"What? You think gay guys can't play baseball?"

"No, I just didn't think *you* could play baseball!" Miguel shot back, laughing. "Now dice the onion. Here's another." He tossed a second onion.

This one Bert caught with one hand, snapping his arm at it and snagging it gracefully, palm down.

"Oh man, now you're just showing off!" Miguel crowed. "All right, dice 'em both and start 'em sautéing in olive oil."

As Bert diced the onions, Miguel unloaded ground beef, a small jar of sofrito, a plastic tub of olives, two heads of garlic, a can of tomato sauce, and some Puerto Rican cheese. "We're taking a couple of shortcuts tonight, he explained. "We're not making the sofrito or the tomato sauce from scratch, and I bought empanada wrappers. Otherwise these can take hours. And once you fry 'em up they taste just as good this way anyhow."

They wrapped and fried the empanadas in batches, laying them on paper towels to drain and sipping on their drinks as they went. Bert brought a few hot empanadas out to the women, along with refills on the piña coladas, once the first batch was ready, and then came out again with a second pitcher twenty minutes after that.

By then, Consuelo and Luisa had put on music and were dancing. Consuelo was holding the baby and rocking her to the beat. Luisa motioned for Bert to put down the pitcher, then grabbed his arm, pulled him toward her, and whirled in circles under their clasped hands.

When Bert returned to the kitchen, Miguel had piled about twenty empanadas onto a fancy silver-plated platter. "Here," he said, "bring these down to the guys on the street."

"On *that* platter?" Bert exclaimed.

"They'll take good care of it," Miguel said. "And they'll bring it back. You watch and see."

When Bert returned, Miguel was busy prepping a soup.

"It's *asopao*," Miguel said. "It's like a gumbo—rice, shellfish, chicken, chorizo, lots of good stuff. Start mincing some garlic. We go heavy on the garlic in this house."

Bert broke off half a dozen cloves of garlic from the bulb and pounded each with the side of his French chef's knife just hard enough to slide off the skin. Then he began smashing each one flat in preparation for mincing. He glanced over at Miguel and grinned mischievously. "Do you ever take off that damn hat?" he asked as the side of his knife pulverized a garlic clove with a resounding thud.

Miguel chuckled. "Yeah, man. When I shower, sleep, and make love. So I guess you'll never see the top of my beautiful head . . . you asshole."

"I'll make damn sure I don't!" Bert replied with a laugh. He perused the varied ingredients strewn about on the counter. "So, what else is on the menu tonight?"

"*Arroz con gandules y lechón* is the main dish. It's yellow rice and pigeon peas with roasted pork. Kinda like Puerto Rico's national dish. Then a dessert you're gonna love: guava *pastelitos*. It's like a stuffed pastry. It looks so beautiful, man, like it took hours to make, but we'll whip it up in twenty minutes."

Dinner was wonderful, and by the third pitcher of piña coladas, Bert had lost track of time. It was after midnight when Miguel offered to drive Bert home.

"I don't want to put you out," Bert said. "And you've been drinking. I'll get an Uber."

Miguel walked Bert to the door. "I'm impressed with your skills," he said. "You can do this, man. You got the talent and the feel for it. I mean, Puerto Rican food isn't your specialty, I'm sure, but you took to it like you've been doing it all your life."

"So you think I'm ready for culinary school?"

"Fuck culinary school, man. You're ready to work."

When Miguel opened the apartment door, Bert saw the now empty empanada platter sitting on the landing.

CHAPTER 9

*I*T was a foggy Wednesday night in Mill Valley when Joyce and Sybil rendezvoused for their accustomed midweek supper. They each had three pomegranate cosmopolitans at their favorite dive bar, their conversation flitting impetuously from topic to topic. Then they staggered down the block, arm in arm, to the House of Same.

After soup and spring rolls, the main dishes arrived. Joyce had her customary extra spicy Kung Pao beef, while Sybil opted for chicken with black mushrooms, water chestnuts, and bamboo shoots. As Joyce utilized her chopsticks to pick gingerly through the fiery mélange before her, she at last opted to share thoughts that had been smoldering inside her all evening: "Sybil, do you remember that handsome younger man I told you about who made a pass at me in my office at the senior home?"

"You mean the sexy art teacher you'd been seducing for months, who you then mercilessly tormented once he succumbed to your feminine wiles?"

Joyce tried to stifle a laugh but failed, and the pulverized amalgam of beef, peanuts, and spicy pepper that had already slithered halfway down her esophagus lurched back into her throat, where she inadvertently inhaled just enough of it to send her into a fit of spasmodic coughing. She hacked ignobly into her napkin for half a minute, then finally took a couple of gulps of jasmine tea from her tiny porcelain cup, at which point she felt relieved enough to speak.

"Yes," she said, chuckling and coughing. "*That* guy."

"Well, what about him?" Sybil prodded.

"Oh, I just had some new ideas about what to do with him."

"New ideas? Do you plan to put the poor boy in thumbscrews and leg irons and have him kneel under your desk and lick your feet while you work?"

Joyce giggled playfully. "As pleasant as that might be, I had something else in mind. Dare I say it?" Joyce took another sip of tea and mustered her courage. "I actually want to lure him into my office after-hours some evening and have him fuck my brains out."

"What the hell is the matter with you?" Sybil practically screamed. She glanced about furtively and modulated her voice as she continued, "You know you shouldn't fraternize with employees like that. And you yourself said he's married, and you're not a homewrecker."

"I might actually be helping him in that regard."

"Helping him? How on earth would you be helping him?"

"His wife is having an affair. I don't think he knows."

"And how in hell do *you* know?"

"His wife is my dental hygienist. The last cleaning I went for, I saw her and the dentist come out of a locked exam room with no patient in there with them."

"That doesn't mean anything, Joyce. They could have been doing any number of things in that room. Maybe a performance evaluation. You don't know."

"I know that the dentist was hiking up his pants and buttoning his white coat when he walked out. And I know that both of them had that look on their face. *You* know that look, Sybil."

"Well, yes," she admitted, "I do know that look."

"So, I'm thinking that if I had an affair with William, it might actually be *good* for their marriage."

"Good? How in God's name would it be good, Joyce?"

"I mean, if she's cheating on him, then *him* cheating with me would add symmetry to the whole thing."

"Symmetry?"

"Well if one of them ever finds out, then it's not as if either one is guiltless, you know? Since they both did it, they might agree to forgive and forget, and live happily ever after."

Sybil considered this assertion as she swallowed a mouthful of chicken. Then she sighed and shook her head. "Your logic is utterly depraved, dear. But I wish you and the boy the best of luck."

"You take the front seat, Arthur," Rosemary said. She was trying to be gracious, but it was clear that Arthur never had any intention of sitting anywhere else. He was already tugging on the front passenger door's handle as the words left her mouth.

She gently took his arm to help him climb up into the van's high passenger seat, but he yanked his arm away indignantly.

"What? You think I'm some old fart who can't get into a car by himself?" he demanded.

"It's a really high seat," Rosemary said in the most deferential tone she could muster.

It did provide her just a bit of vengeful pleasure as she watched him strain and stumble his way up into the seat; he even pummeled his shin on the door's lower ledge before finally heaving himself inside.

William was already behind the wheel and shifting the van into reverse as Rosemary scrambled into the backseat. She positioned herself in the middle of the rear bench so she could see the road ahead over the van's wide console and keep an eye on both William and Arthur.

William backed out and cautiously wound his way out of the airport's parking lot. Arthur made no offer to pay the nominal fee as they exited. They headed north toward the Golden Gate Bridge and Sonoma County.

"How old is this damn jalopy?" Arthur squawked as they merged onto the freeway. "It's gonna make mincemeat out of my kidneys!" He waited for a response, but when none was forthcoming, he groaned and turned back toward Rosemary. "You still got that sandwich I bought?"

Rosemary retrieved the Brie and prosciutto on ciabatta roll from where she'd stuffed it unceremoniously into her oversized purse.

"You just shoved it in there?" Arthur growled. "You crushed the damn thing."

"It's perfectly fine, Arthur." Rosemary attempted to inconspicuously massage it back into its original shape as she handed it to him.

Arthur tore voraciously at the sandwich's wrapper and immediately began chomping away. Rosemary watched silently as crumbs fell on Arthur's lap, the car seat, and the floor mat beneath him. She seethed but forced herself to refrain from commenting.

"This is a damn good sandwich," Arthur mumbled, expectorating bits of meat, cheese, and bread onto his shirtfront as he decimated a huge chunk between his molars. "This ciabatta roll—it's just as good as the ones we get in New York. You know, Bertram used to make me sandwiches like this. He wasn't a bad cook. I guess faggots are good at that kind of thing."

At first, no one responded. Then William said gently, "Dad, you have to stop talking like that. This is the twenty-first century. Gay marriage is legal. Your doctor or dentist could be gay. Your grandkid's teacher could be gay. Here in the Bay Area, half the people you deal with are going to be gay."

"God help us," Arthur growled as he swallowed the last bit of his lunch. "And I don't have any grandkids." He crumpled the white wrapper into a ball and glanced about. "You got a garbage bag in this clunker?"

"Here, I'll take it." Rosemary grabbed the wad and deposited it in her purse, observing how Arthur was part cranky old man and part scruffy, impatient child.

They drove in silence over the Golden Gate Bridge and north through Marin county. They were at the lower edge of Sonoma when they hit some traffic.

"How far from San Francisco *is* this godforsaken place?" Arthur demanded.

No one said a word.

Finally, a few minutes later, William said, "I can't be sure, but I bet this house is actually closer to San Francisco than your house in Scarsdale is to Manhattan." He glanced toward his father, expecting some sort of response, but Arthur had fallen asleep.

He remained so until they pulled into the hotel parking lot in Petaluma, where Laurel was waiting in her car.

William and Rosemary exited the van first. It took Arthur a bit longer to ease himself from the high passenger seat down to the black asphalt of the hotel lot. His descent was spasmodic, and his feet hit the ground with an awkward thud. Rosemary made no effort to assist him.

When Laurel recognized her clients, she opened the driver's door of her Mercedes, shifted slowly around, and swung her heavy legs into the aperture. She extricated herself painfully, through a series of plodding, ungainly lurches, and then wobbled unsteadily on her feet for a moment before establishing her equilibrium and shuffling over to greet them.

Perfunctory niceties were exchanged. Laurel offered Rosemary and William hugs. When she turned to Arthur and spread her arms, Rosemary fully expected him to bristle and stiffen in response, but Arthur startled her by reciprocating Laurel's embrace warmly and pressing his cheek affectionately against hers.

"We need to check in and store our bags in our rooms," Rosemary proclaimed in the tone of a camp counselor corralling unruly teenagers. "Then we'll be able to go look at the house!"

A couple of days had passed since Bert and Dag had argued about Bert's choice to become a personal chef. They had spoken little in the interim, exchanging only perfunctory grunts and mumbles when they passed each other in the condo. Bert had spent his nights in the small spare bedroom, and hadn't emerged in the mornings until after Dag left for work. That left Dag with no one to cook him breakfast, and he'd reverted to his old habit of picking up a pastry and latte at the coffee shop in the lobby of the building where he worked. But he sorely missed the buttered toast, steaming eggs, and crisp bacon slices that Bert had dispensed each morning prior to their fight. And he missed Bert's semi-clad athletic body darting about the kitchen and pouring him fresh coffee and orange juice even more.

He understood that some sort of apology on his part was now required. But what exactly to say? And what tone to adopt? All through the day, at his desk between meetings and client calls, he obsessively pondered possible approaches.

At four in the afternoon, he returned from his weekly sales meeting, closed his office door, and plopped dejectedly into his upholstered swivel chair. He still didn't have an answer to the problem with Bert. But he was determined to figure it out before he left work.

He lifted his phone receiver to his ear so that anyone peering through the glass walls of his office would assume he was talking to a client. But he didn't press a button to activate a line. Instead, he spoke sternly to himself, trying methodically to work aloud through the tangle of issues. He vowed not to put the phone down until he had a plan of action.

"I need to apologize. Okay, that's a given. He'll break up with me if I don't.

"But he can't leave for a while—he doesn't have any money and he doesn't have a place to go. So I have some leverage. For now. But the sooner I apologize, the less damage. So I might as well do it now.

"I do love him, I guess. I absolutely love the sex. And the breakfasts maybe even more than the sex. So I have to apologize. That's a given.

"But I'm not *wrong*, for God fucking sakes! Giving up a career in real estate to cook meals for people? It's idiocy. Like choosing to be a housemaid if you could be a CEO. Who does that? You have to be a moron. And it's selfish. I mean, I make a lot of money. I don't need his income. But he doesn't even give a shit about it.

"Okay. Stop, damnit. Think. You have to apologize. You have to. It's a given. So, you have to find a way to do it.

"But I can't say to him that I'm wrong. I'm not wrong, for God's sake. I'm right. But I can't say that. It's a delicate balance. He has to believe it's sincere.

"And I can make it sincere. But only if I don't say too much.

"And flowers. Right! Flowers. Flowers are good. He set the table with flowers the first time he ever cooked dinner for me. He likes flowers. So, give him flowers. Lots of them. Expensive ones. He associates flowers with food. With cooking and setting the table. Even better. So, flowers, for sure.

"And keep it short. Don't go into the whole damn thing. The more you say, the more you'll put your foot in it. He'll just get pissed off, and we'll be right back to where we are: sleeping in separate rooms and not talking to each other. So just say you're sorry. And leave it at that. And that he can cook if he wants.

"Okay. Flowers. And keep it short and simple. That's it. Flowers. Short and simple. Kiss and make up."

Dag slammed down the phone.

Uncharacteristically, Dag dashed out of his office at five o'clock sharp. He went directly to the flower shop in the lobby of the building a couple of doors down, where he had the proprietor assemble a huge, elaborate bouquet. Dag had no idea what kind they were—he wasn't well versed in the names of flowers. But some of them looked like the fake flowers he and friends had made as kids, using a couple of white facial tissues and a bobby pin for each one.

The subway got him home in less than half an hour. Before taking the elevator upstairs, he checked himself in the lobby mirror. His suit lay impeccably—his tie and coordinated pocket-square were flawlessly configured. He coaxed a few stray hairs into place atop his head, then entered the condo.

He found Bert in a T-shirt and shorts, curled up on the sofa with a cookbook. He put down his briefcase, held up the flowers, and spoke softly.

"I want to apologize, Bertie. I don't want to fight anymore. I love you, and I want to be with you." He gazed at Bert, hoping for some sort of response. There wasn't any, so he went on. "You're a great cook. I love that you cook for me—it makes me happy. So if you want to cook for other people and make *them* happy, and maybe do some catering, that's cool. I'm not gonna fight with you about it. If you bring in some money, that's fine; and if not, that's okay, I make enough for both of us. Can we kiss and make up?"

Bert put down his cookbook and eyed Dag warily. "And no more talk about real estate? Or networking events?"

"I'll never mention those things again," Dag said. "I promise." He paused for an uncomfortable moment. "What do you think of the flowers?"

"I suppose they're beautiful," Bert said haltingly as he rose slowly from the couch. He walked over, took the flowers, and examined them closely.

Dag marveled at how much shorter the stems looked in Bert's enormous hands.

"They'd make a great centerpiece for the table if I cooked dinner for us tonight," Bert ventured with the hint of a smile.

"Oh, I'd love that, Bertie." Dag said. "I've missed your cooking so much."

Bert leaned down. The two men embraced and kissed.

"I'll take it!" Arthur declared triumphantly after examining the big house and its adjacent cottage for just over half an hour.

He strutted back and forth through the large entry area just beyond the home's front door as the others stood facing him. His feet made loud shuffling sounds on the polished hardwood floor. Behind the group, a grand curved stairway rose on the right. On the other side was a spacious sitting room, and then a hallway that dipped behind the stairs and led to the kitchen, dining room, pantry, and living room, all of them huge and ornate. There were six bedrooms on the floor above them, and above that a capacious attic with a sloping ceiling and redwood beams the size of logs.

"You three did a good job finding this place!" Arthur exclaimed. "It's an old castle! And that's what I need in my old age. To be king of my castle!"

Laurel had been her customarily chatty self during the extended inspection of the house. But now that Arthur had agreed to purchase it, she just stood silent for a moment, grinning proudly and taking in the group's exhilaration.

Arthur gazed about and did a full turn, staggering just a bit on his artificial hip as he came full circle. "We'll share the *house*," he cautioned with a bit of a laugh, looking in William and Rosemary's direction and pointing at them, "but that cottage is all mine. You two stay out. I'll set up my office and my computer in there. No trespassing!" He paused a moment. "Well, Rosemary, you can come in once a week to clean."

Rosemary stifled a snarl and then sustained a blink long enough to conceal her eyes rolling contemptuously. It was worth the indignity, though, she reasoned, to live in a huge house like this. And after a few weeks, she'd get everyone to agree to bring a housekeeper in twice a month. Arthur would have fallen in love with her cooking and cocktails by then, and if she told him she needed someone to help clean every two weeks, he'd surely acquiesce.

"I'll have the papers drawn up by tomorrow afternoon," Laurel said. "With what you told me you're willing to pay, Arthur, there's no doubt we'll get it—but I'll negotiate the best price I can for you."

"Make 'em squirm a little," Arthur instructed, smirking archly.

"I will," Laurel replied with a chuckle. "And congratulations. It's a beautiful place. You're all going to love it here. What a sensational house!"

William hadn't spoken during the entire tour, but now he smiled broadly and proclaimed, "Well I guess there's nothing left to do this evening other than a celebratory dinner!"

Rosemary noticed the slightly unfocused look in his eyes and immediately realized that what he was thinking about was not dinner but the cavernous room in the back of the garage with unfinished walls, which everyone had agreed would be his painting studio. It was at least five times bigger than his art room in their San Francisco flat.

"Yes! Dinner!" Rosemary exclaimed, then added, "With lots of champagne!" She thrust her fist in the air for emphasis.

Arthur turned to Laurel. "You're the one who found this great house. You should join us for dinner! We're having Italian."

Laurel smiled. "Well, I'd love to, Arthur, but I was going to head back to San Francisco and start the negotiations. There are lots of documents to get going on too, you know."

"You can do that tomorrow, damn it," Arthur replied with a shrewd grin. "I'm flying back to New York Tuesday morning anyway. We can do all the paperwork online. You got that electronic signature gizmo stuff in your office, right?"

"Oh, we certainly do," Laurel assured him. "In that case, I'll make a quick call to put in our bid, and then I'd love to join you all. Thank you so much. And Italian food sounds especially nice. It's one of my favorite cuisines. All those pastas and sauces. And the bread; they have wonderful bread, don't you think? And wine. Oh, the wine. All of it! It's just all wonderful."

Rosemary wondered morosely why Arthur had felt empowered to invite "lavishly loquacious Laurel" to intrude on their family dinner without checking with anyone first. (Rosemary had just privately assigned Laurel that alliterative sobriquet during the recently concluded walk-through.) She also took a moment to silently note that, given Laurel's girth, it did not appear that there were many cuisines Laurel *didn't* consider one of her favorites.

The restaurant, in the small downtown center of Healdsburg, was lovely and dark, with upholstered seats, white tablecloths, and napkins so crisply starched that if you tried to fold them their edges retained the classic curves of ancient Roman columns. Rosemary ordered a bottle of champagne for the table, but before the waiter could dash off, Arthur bellowed, "You wimps can celebrate with bubbly if you want—I'm celebrating with a couple of stiff martinis."

Much to Rosemary's surprise, William opted to join his father in the cocktails, so Laurel and Rosemary had the bottle of champagne entirely to themselves.

By the time the first course was delivered, everyone was a bit tipsy.

The more Laurel drank, the more she babbled. Phrases like "cool," "groovy," and "right on" slinked stealthily into her commentary. Even in Rosemary's inebriated state, she picked up on this immediately and took it as a quiet victory and vindication. It confirmed her long-held suspicion that Laurel had been a Haight Ashbury hippie before going corporate. She was curious to see if Arthur would notice and, if so, how he might react. She gazed at Laurel, and a satisfying wave of schadenfreude overtook her. She had imbibed too much at that point to feel at all guilty about the sentiment.

Though a couple of bottles of chianti were also drained at dinner, William didn't partake in any of the wine, nor had he finished all of his second martini, so by the time everyone had their coffee and dessert, he felt fine to be the designated driver back to the hotel. During the ride, it occurred to Rosemary that Arthur had paid for dinner without a murmur of complaint. That surprised her, but she figured he'd really had no choice.

They parked in the hotel lot. Everyone got out, and Laurel began making the rounds with good-bye hugs.

"Hold on!" Arthur shouted to Laurel. "With all you've had to drink you can't drive all the way back to San Francisco. What's the hell's the matter with you? You have to stay here at the hotel."

"Well, I could see if they have a room . . ." Laurel giggled.

Arthur stepped toward her. "Why don't you stay in *my* room?"

Rosemary's jaw went slack.

"Actually," Laurel said with a coy cock of her head, "I'd like that very much."

"I always pack a couple of extra toothbrushes," Arthur assured her in a lascivious stage whisper, shoddily reminiscent of Groucho Marx.

Laurel chuckled.

About ten minutes later, just down the hall from the room Arthur and Laurel were now sharing, William and Rosemary sat beside each other in utter silence on their hotel bed. Neither had washed or taken off any of their clothes. It felt as if they'd been there for half an hour.

Finally, Rosemary pierced their stupor. "What planet am I living on, Will? Did your father just score with our real estate agent?"

"I believe so," he stammered. "I'm still processing it. It's kind of hard to fathom."

"My god, Will, she was a hippie. You told me he hated hippies."

"Well they haven't started talking politics yet," he said. "But I think there's a higher priority for him here."

"What's that? He likes women who never shut the fuck up?"

"No, not that. Laurel . . . looks a lot like my mom did."

Rosemary's eyes flared momentarily and her lips parted. "Ah!" she whispered. "I hadn't thought of that. I guess your mom *was* very fat before she died. But I didn't know her when she was young. Was she fat when Arthur married her?"

William thought about it. "You know, it's interesting. They never had any photos out from back then. I think my mother was embarrassed about how she looked. But Bert and I found their wedding photos in an old album up in the attic once. She was very heavy then too. I imagine she always was."

"So Arthur's attracted to obese women?"

"That would appear to be the case. Maybe that's why he picked Laurel in the first place. Just by looking at her face in her website picture, you can tell she's heavy."

"That's right!" Rosemary exclaimed, nodding her head and patting his thigh. "So, Arthur knew. I bet you're right." She laughed softly. "It's strange though—I could swear I've heard Arthur mock fat people a whole bunch of times."

William pondered that for a few moments. "Actually," he said, "I know I've seen him making fun of overweight *men* on many occasions. But for the life of me, I can't recall him ever once making fun of a fat *woman*."

Rosemary lowered her head and sighed loudly. "God, Will, what fucking planet am I living on?"

William leaned over and slowly began kissing Rosemary—first softly, on her neck and cheek, then with twitches of his tongue just above her eyelids. Rosemary turned toward him, grabbed his face with both her hands, and kissed him hard on the mouth.

Hotels had always turned William on. For Rosemary, the thought of soon living in an enormous castle was even more of an aphrodisiac. But overarchingly for both, they were not going to be outdone by the two misfits in the room down the hall.

William and Rosemary tore each other's clothes off frantically, and made passionate love.

CHAPTER 10

*T*HE San Francisco flat now felt oppressive and small. Many of their belongings had already been packed—boxes piled three or four high sat crammed between pieces of furniture in the living room and bedroom.

William and Rosemary were impatient to get out, but they had no choice but to wait for Arthur and Laurel to finish filing their paperwork, and for Arthur to get his things shipped across country. It was a slow, tedious process.

And day-to-day responsibilities remained. In fact, Rosemary was currently gathering her purse and coat, preparing to leave for work. Her shift started in less than an hour.

She'd already tendered her resignation to Moe, and was now finishing out her last couple of weeks. She had feared that he might be disappointed or resistant to her leaving, but he seemed as relieved as she was to be presented with an amiable pretext for ending their liaison.

As soon as Rosemary kissed William good-bye and left for work, the house grew quiet. William wasn't due at the senior home for his art class until late in the afternoon. In his small studio in the rear of the flat, he'd begun sketching a picture on a new canvas. The imagined scene was vivid in his mind—he was anxious to see its outline materialize. Yet despite his determination to focus fully on that task, he could not. For a reason he couldn't quite fathom, the melodious voice and intriguing perspectives of Dr. Judith Feigenbaum kept encroaching, uninvited, into his thoughts.

Finally, he surrendered. He threw down his charcoal stick, dashed into the living room, and squeezed around some boxes to access their aging computer, which sat atop a small desk in the far corner. He was very careful to open a private window, so that if Rosemary scanned the browser's history (as she often did), no trace of his search would appear.

He found a couple of photographs of Dr. Feigenbaum, each portraying a modest but not unattractive woman with pulled-back hair and a stern demeanor. He searched but could find no picture of her smiling.

Background information on the doctor was no more extensive than what he'd heard in the radio introductions.

But the real discovery was a cache of podcasts—radio interviews from stations around the country. These seemed to him a treasure. Now he could listen to her whenever he wished (as long as he was in the house alone).

He pulled one up. It was another excerpt from her latest book, a segment he hadn't heard. She began speaking:

"Why is it that we know so little about the human brain? The organ's innate complexity accounts for at least a part of it. But in fact, the brain is a very difficult entity to study.

"Many factors contribute to make this so.

"Traditionally, when a brain is removed from a cadaver for examination, it is preserved and hardened in order to be handled. Scientists have used chemicals, such as formaldehyde, for this purpose for over a century, but such agents cannot be depended upon to perfectly maintain the organ's minute structures.

"Some innovative neuroscientists have employed a different tack. They've placed a soft, unpreserved brain in a blender and whirled it into a liquid whose chemical makeup can be studied and analyzed. Such a process stops short of destroying the nuclei of cells, and has proven to be a remarkably efficient way of counting the number of neurons and other types of cells that enable the brain to do its work.

"Ultimately though, this kind of brain soup has its limits in terms of usefulness. That's because specific areas of the brain are responsible for distinct and different functions, and they therefore need to be studied separately. Inevitably, of course, in an apparatus as complex as the human brain, there is always some degree of interdependency and redundancy, but for the most part, each area of the brain has its own assigned duties. So, in order to truly understand how the brain works, a mechanism must be established to access and isolate individual portions for observation.

"But trying to do this can be very challenging, especially on a living, working brain.

"Researchers can attach electrodes to the scalp to measure activity in particular areas of the brain. Scientists will also sometimes insert needle-shaped electrodes directly into brain tissue, but due to the potential for serious injury and long-term damage, this sort of experimentation is more often done on animals.

"Remarkably, though, it turns out that unexpected and uncontrollable events often prove most propitious.

"Historically, injuries to a discrete area of the brain have provided scientists with situations they could never ethically create in a laboratory setting, but which offered rich opportunities for inquiry. Perhaps the earliest and most famous example of this was an incident that has come to be known as the 'American Crowbar Case.' In 1848 an explosion caused a cylindrical tamping iron more than a yard long and just over an inch in diameter to propel completely through the head of a railroad foreman named Phineas Gage, entering at his left cheek and exiting through the top of his skull. Although the injury destroyed much of the left frontal lobe of his brain, Gage survived. In fact, in the accident's immediate aftermath, Gage neither lost consciousness nor became incoherent while interacting with doctors. Although there were some long-term physical ramifications, the most notable changes to Gage had to do with his personality. Many who knew him described him as a completely different person following the incident.

"The natural presumption would be that the injury itself caused an area of the brain to behave differently or cease to operate at all, or that trauma related to the incident had a lingering psychological effect.

"But it is also possible that when one region of the brain ceases to operate, another region, formerly reticent and insecure, suddenly feels free to assert itself and takes over the tasks previously handled by the injured domain. What emerges in terms of judgment and perspective can be vastly different from what has been experienced before. And because the area of the brain that has now taken on new responsibility has been isolated and suppressed for so long, it can manifest itself in a vigorous, and even primitive, manner."

It was this last sentence that William found especially beguiling. He'd read in college about Jung's belief that suppressed aspects of the personality, when finally unfettered, could manifest in a primitive way. But the idea that physical areas of the brain could do the same seemed to William an entirely different proposition, and one ripe for all sorts of conjecture.

He closed the computer's window, checked again that his browsing had left no record, then shut the machine down.

Molly was curled up asleep on a window ledge in the living room, where a slice of warm sun had finally broken through the morning fog. She opened her eyes briefly when William rose to leave the room. The cat yawned, stretched, then curled up again and went back to sleep. William trod lightly as he exited, so as not to disturb her.

He had intended to do some more work on his canvas, but when he reached the end of the hallway he instead turned abruptly into the bedroom, where he lay down and masturbated, fantasizing that Dr. Judith Feigenbaum had pulled up her lab coat and mounted him from above, taking him at her leisure, never once relaxing the stern demeanor on her face as she rode him.

"I am so proud of everyone in this class," William announced as he opened a tattered cardboard box and pulled from it a plastic figure. "You've all really made terrific strides in your art. And I'm not just saying this to make you feel good. Every one of you is painting on a level so much higher than when we all started together a few months ago."

William held up a large plastic replica of a pink flamingo.

"Look!" he exclaimed. "It's a flamingo. This is going to be a really challenging—but a really rewarding project. It may take us a few classes to complete. Before we start, though, listen up—we're going to focus on something a little more nuanced today."

"What the hell is *nuanced*?" Ira growled from his seat next to Alice.

"Ira's right," Mrs. Liebman whined, "don't use words we don't know and try to confuse us. It's insulting." Mrs. Liebman still started every class predictably cranky and depressed, but William had coaxed a good deal of latent talent out of her, and more often than not she wound up pleased, and even enthusiastic, about the paintings she produced.

"My apologies," William said, unfazed. "I'm sorry. Let me be specific. I'm talking about shading. We've done mostly straight coloring, with the colors I've mixed for you. And you've done great stuff with that. You know how I often give you a slightly darker and lighter version of the same color, and when we put them on different sides of the same object it causes it to look at little three-dimensional? Well, shading just takes that one step further. It's what will make you real artists."

William reached for two paintings. Just before class, he had hastily mounted them in pleasing but inexpensive wooden frames. "Some of you have already been doing this kind of shading for a while. I want you to look at these two beautiful paintings here." He held them up. "The one in my right hand was done a few weeks ago by Alice. The one in my left hand, Mrs. Liebman completed just last week. Look at how, in both, they didn't just stick with the darker and lighter shades of the colors I gave them. They did a little more mixing, and made a bunch of subtle shades in between. You see how the shading makes things leap off the canvas? Like the difference between making something look like a flat circle versus making it look like a real, round ball? You see that?"

William paraded the paintings around the class for a couple of minutes, pointing out the areas on each painting where shading had created the illusion of depth.

"Okay," he said, returning to the front of the room and putting down the paintings. "Now look at this flamingo." He held the plastic bird aloft. "It's all pink. That's it. Just one shade of pink. Remember back when we painted the parrot? It had a bunch of different colors. Now we're painting a bird that's all one color. But if you paint it like it's all one color, then it's going to look like a flat cartoon, no matter how well you draw it. Now watch this."

William propped the bird up on top of the tripod. Then he

dimmed the overhead lights a bit and shined a spotlight he'd brought from home onto one side of the flamingo.

"Okay, now look. Really closely. With the very bright spotlight, all the shadows here are exaggerated. So, look closely. Suddenly it's not all the same color pink. You see that? Look here, right on the side where the light's hitting it first. It's a really bright, light pink." He raced to the other side. "Now, look at this side, directly opposite, where very little light is hitting. It's a much darker, duller pink. Almost purple, or purplish-red. Right? You see that?"

He heard mumbles of acknowledgment from the class. That encouraged him.

"Now, how do you get from the light, bright pink over there to the dark almost-purple over here? It's not like there's a line where one stops and the other begins. Right? It's gradual. It gets darker as it goes across. You see that? Follow my finger. Bright here. Getting a little darker here. A tiny bit brighter where this thing sticks out a little and catches some light. Then darker again, and even darker here at the end. You can see that, right? And the gradations aren't along straight lines—they follow the curves of the animal. See?" His finger traced a particularly obvious ridge of color change. "So, if you can see it, and if you really focus on what you see, then you can paint it."

"That seems really hard," Ira moaned.

Ira wasn't going to paint anything even remotely resembling a flamingo anyway, so his posing this particular lament was somewhat pointless. But William used it to his advantage.

"Actually, it's not that hard, Ira—to paint what you see, I mean. You can see it—you can see where it gets lighter and darker—and you can just paint what you see. The tricky part, actually, is mixing the colors so you get the shades that resemble what you're seeing. Now, I've already mixed a range of a few shades for you and put them on your palettes, but I also put some white, red, yellow, and blue on your palettes, because I want you to feel free to take a little of any shade I gave you, drag it to a different spot on your palette, and change it just a little with one or more of those other colors. If you need help, just call me over. Mixing colors is a little counter-intuitive at first"—he saw several pairs of lips pursing in preparation for a salvo and quickly rescued himself—"by counter-intuitive I just mean that it can be hard to look at a shade of color, and then figure out exactly what colors you need to mix in order to match that shade, unless you've done it a lot before. Its's not like you intuitively know how to do it. But like I said, I can help you with that. Mixing colors is actually one of the most fun things you can do in painting. And once you start doing it, you'll pick it up really fast."

William glanced at the faces in the room. Quite a few seemed to him surprisingly eager. No one, aside from Ira, seemed overly dejected or morose.

"Okay!" he said. "Then we're ready to go. As always, I'll ask you to try to sketch the outline of the flamingo on your canvas to start. You can do it directly from the model up on the tripod, or you can use geometric shapes and follow the sketch I'm going to do right now on the whiteboard. Either way, give it a try, and if you need help I'll come around. And as always, if you really need me to, I'll sketch it on your canvas for you, no problem at all."

The class was generally quiet whenever William did his quick sketches on the whiteboard that hung on the side of the room. And that was the case today—at first. But slowly, as he drew, a buzz of whispers swelled. Then there were a couple of muffled gasps, and finally laughter just as he finished.

William spun around to see what was going on. "What's so funny?" he demanded.

For a few moments, no one spoke. Then Alice pulled her hand away from her mouth, where it had been politely masking her giggles. "Why, it's you, Willie dear! The way you drew that!"

"What do you mean, the way I drew it?"

"Your bird! Look at it, Willie. It's so different from how you usually draw."

"I drew it just like always, no different," William said, gazing quizzically at her.

"No, Willie," she cried. "Please! Just look at the picture."

"For God's sake, look at the damn picture!" Mrs. Liebman cackled uproariously. It was the first time William had ever seen her laugh that hard.

Finally, he turned around and studied his drawing.

At first, he wasn't certain what he was looking at. He stepped closer, and squinted. The whole thing first went a bit blurry, but then he brought it back into focus. And that's when he saw. His face froze, his eyes fixed themselves on the image. His mouth stretched into a flustered grimace.

The flamingo was distorted, as if pieces of it had melted slightly and then buckled before they reformed. Each of William's usually precise lines had veered off playfully and meandered a bit before finding its terminus. His geometric shapes were malformed—subtly, but enough to be immediately apparent.

"Oh my god!" he exclaimed, gazing incredulously at his sketch. "It's a bit surreal, isn't it? How on earth did that happen? I didn't intend to do that." He took a step back and cocked his head to get a different angle, his back still to the class. "I *never* draw that way. Wow, that's so weird." He turned back to the group and grinned sheepishly. "My mind must have been on something else."

"Maybe it was on Salvador Dalí," Ira croaked between guffaws.

In the foyer of Dag's condo, just off the master bedroom, sat a narrow closet that housed a stackable washer and dryer. Bert appreciated the convenience of having the appliances so near to the bedroom, where they kept the hamper, but because the machines were small, multiple loads were always necessary. Today he'd been at it for a couple of hours. Each time the machines started whirring through their next cycle, he migrated into the living room, where he sat cross-legged on the rug and immersed himself in the pile of cookbooks he'd stacked on the floor.

His mind wandered as he examined a Portuguese eggplant recipe, and he momentarily thought back to his father's home, twenty-five miles north, in Scarsdale. It had much bigger appliances, but the washer and dryer were in the basement and laundry had to be lugged down two flights of stairs and then back up when it was done. Bert wondered how Arthur could possibly manage such a thing now, alone, with his bad hip. Should he have at least offered to come by once a week to do his father's laundry?

But then Bert recalled the circumstances of his leaving, and tried to let the thought go. He knew his father would soon move out of the house anyway. Still, though, the image of Arthur struggling with a basket of laundry on the narrow staircase—unsteady on his feet—would not easily melt away.

Bert heard the machines stop. He got up, unloaded the dryer, shoved in the wet clothes, and packed the final load of the day into the washer.

Just as he started the cycle going, his cell phone rang.

He glanced at the display. The call was from Miguel. Bert perked up. He was scheduled to shadow Miguel this evening on a personal chef gig—their first together. It was exciting to get going on this new chapter.

"Hey, Miguel, how're you doing?"

"I'm good, man. How are you?"

"I'm psyched for tonight. What time are we getting together?"

"Hey, listen, man. Slight change of plans. I'm really sorry about this, but the head chef in the restaurant where I work called in sick, so they need me to fill in. I gotta do it, man—can't say no to my boss."

"Oh, shit," Bert mumbled. "So our gig is off? I was really looking forward to being there with you tonight. You know—so I could see what you do, and get started on learning how to do it myself. I understand, though. How's your client taking you canceling on 'em?"

"I'm not canceling, man. I don't want to let these people down. They've used me a lot, and it's good money. So, I told 'em I'd send someone in my place. Somebody good."

"Who are you sending?"

"*You*, Bert."

"What?" Bert screamed. "I have no idea what to do! Are you out of your fucking mind? You can't just throw me into this and hope I don't implode! What the hell are you thinking?"

"Look, man, I could give it to someone else. There are people I know. But I thought you and me—we were going kinda partners on this. I wanted to keep it in the family, you know?"

"Well that would be great if we'd done it together once or twice, and I had some goddamn idea of what to do so I don't make a fucking ass out of myself."

"Hey, I wouldn't ask you if I wasn't totally sure you could handle it. You did great with me and my family up in the Barrio. This'll be a no-brainer. The woman is full of herself—thinks she's like a beauty queen or something. Her husband works like a dog—I don't know exactly what he does, he don't say much, but I guess he does very well and, you know, she buys herself lots of clothes and fancy makeup and goes out all the time. So I guess that's why she keeps the guy around—I mean, he's kind of a schlub, you know? And she's pretty hot. But she don't like to cook. They usually go out—there are all kindsa neighborhood restaurants on the Upper East Side where they live. But now and then she wants to stay in and have a personal chef cook for them." He chuckled. "She tried making her husband cook, but he's a waste case for that. They said they wanted Italian tonight. Italian's easy, right? You said you cooked lots of Italian for your pop when you lived with him."

"Well I *am* pretty good with Italian dishes," Bert acknowledged reluctantly.

"See? And I'll tell you exactly what they like, where to shop for it, everything. Piece a cake!"

Bert was silent for a while. Miguel waited and said nothing.

"Okay," Bert said haltingly, "I think maybe I can give it a shot. You tell me exactly what they want to eat and what I need to get—and I assume they have seasonings and oil and stuff like that in the house, right?"

"I'll go through everything with you, man. It'll be easy."

"All right, Miguel. I'll do it."

"Great, man. And like we agreed, if you get a gig off me, I get ten percent of what they pay you, right?"

"Yeah, okay."

"Fantastic. You can write me a check after they pay you."

Bert paused and thought for a few moments. "So," he said slowly, "one of these days, when you get a gig off *me*, then I get ten percent too, right?"

Miguel laughed, hard and long. "Jesus Christ, listen to this fucking big shot! You never even cooked for nobody professionally in your life, and you're already negotiating your cut. You got *cojones,* man!"

Bert flushed a little. "Well, if it works one way, it works the other."

"Yeah, yeah, no problem, man. It's good that you're doin' this tonight. Good for both of us. Now, let's put together the menu . . ."

It had really amounted to just a bit of laughter and teasing. But when the tittering finally subsided, William's somewhat surreal depiction of the pink flamingo on the whiteboard had the strange ensuing effect of dampening the inhibitions in the room and galvanizing his pupils' collective motivation.

Everyone got to work quickly, except for Ira and Mrs. Liebman, who continued to hurl a few jocular taunts at William as he returned to the whiteboard, determined to rein in the meandering lines and geometric shapes he'd errantly set down. He found he needed to concentrate inordinately hard to make the appropriate revisions, and had to, at times, grip the marker so tightly that his fingers were sore and cramped when he finished. He attributed these difficulties to nerves and embarrassment.

He remained equally focused and deliberate as he sketched the outline of the bird on the canvases of the students who requested his assistance. There were far fewer in need of his help than before; with William's encouragement over the past months, many pupils had grown comfortable doing their own sketches.

For most of the folks in the room, this was their first attempt at a relatively sophisticated painting technique, and in general they acquitted themselves surprisingly well. Alice, who had been employing this sort of color mixing and shading progression in her work for some time, completed about half the flamingo during the session, and it looked fabulous.

When the class ended, the students put their brushes down and started filing out, but stopped momentarily to listen as William called after them. He was ebullient as he said, "You all did a really fine job here today, folks. I'm so proud of everyone. We'll continue to work on these pieces for the next few sessions. I think we're going to have some very impressive paintings at the end. Thank you. And keep up the great work."

As her classmates left, Alice waited patiently. When the room was empty, she got up from her scooter, walked slowly to William's desk in the front of the room, and sat down in the chair alongside it. "Time for a quick chat, Willie dear?" she asked.

"Sure!" William answered with a warm smile. He sat back down at his desk. "Your work today was especially good. I didn't want to go on about it in front of everyone else, but truly, it's terrific."

"Oh, thanks so much, Willie. I think you've brought the whole class along so well. You're really *teaching* us things. The old instructor just gave us outlines to color."

"Thank you," William said. "That means a lot to me." He waited a few moments but when she remained silent, he said, "Was there something specific that you wanted to talk to me about?"

"Oh, yes, yes!" she said, giggling. "Something very exciting. Goodness, my mind wanders sometimes. I wanted to tell you that I met yesterday with Joyce Miller. My daughter came for the meeting too. If you can believe it, Willie—I'm cleared to go with you to the San Jose flea market some Sunday, if you're still willing!"

Alice's face scrunched into a childlike smile, her eyes stretched wide with elation.

"Wow, that's great! What fantastic news, Alice!" William leaped up and darted the couple of steps to her chair, where he leaned down and gave her a quick hug and kiss. When he stood back up, he paused and thought for a moment. "That must be what Joyce wanted to talk to me about. She asked me to stay after I clean up. She wants to meet in her office around five. Oh, this is wonderful—you're going to love it, Alice."

"Oh, I know I will. I'm so excited."

"So, Alice," he said, "to prepare for this, you should gather together your best ten or twelve paintings from the ones we've done. If you're not sure, I'll be happy to go through them with you. We need to get them framed nicely and make sure they're signed before we go."

"I've already started, Willie dear! Do you think I'll sell one?"

William pondered that as he sat back down behind his desk. "You know, Alice, what I've found is that some days are better than others for sales. But I'll tell you this: if we go down there a few times, I'm sure you'll sell at least one, maybe more." (He was already plotting that if they tried a couple of times and she didn't sell any, he'd arrange on the third go-round for a few of his friends to drop by, pretending to be strangers, and make a purchase.)

Alice beamed. "Thank you so much for making this happen, Willie, dear. You're such a sweet man." With that, she rose, walked slowly to his chair, and kissed him on the cheek, then promptly dragged her thumb along her tongue just enough to moisten its tip and used it to wipe the lipstick smudge from his face.

This little ritual struck William as archaic and shockingly unsanitary—but it was Alice, and she was from another era, and so endearingly sweet, so he said nothing and did his best to neither wince nor flinch. (He did, however, make a mental note to wash his face as soon as she was gone.)

William made certain that Alice's scooter had vacated the area before dashing to the men's room and scrubbing his face, being particularly vigilant in scouring the saliva-smeared segment of his cheek. After that, William cleaned up the art studio. When he finished, he still had about fifty minutes before his meeting with Joyce, which gave him ample time to settle in with the Stephen King novel he'd just borrowed from the library. William's ritual in this regard never wavered—the moment he learned about the publication of a new Stephen King novel, he put his name on the waiting list for it at his local library branch. It often took months before he received the auto-generated text indicating that the book ready for him, but he pounced on it as soon as it was.

One hour later, William knocked on Joyce's office door and she told him to come in.

"Hello, William!" she said with an exuberant grin. "Thank you for coming by. Have a seat please."

He sat down in one of the three guest chairs in front of Joyce's large mahogany desk. Though the two had shared a few benign interactions since his ill-conceived and nearly catastrophic sexual advance, he was still nervous around her and careful to project his most professional and gentlemanly persona whenever they were in the same space.

"Well, I have wonderful news," Joyce said. "Everything's been cleared for you to take Alice down to the San Jose flea market with you."

"Thank you so much for making this happen, Joyce," William said, beaming. "I can't tell you how much I appreciate it. Actually, Alice just shared the news with me after our art class today, so I already knew. But I was so excited to hear it, and I'm excited to hear you confirm it now."

"I think it's a win all around, William. Our attorney is working up a special agreement about having Alice in your care, and driving the company van—you'll need it for her wheelchair—and so on. Everything should be drawn up and the two of you should be ready to go by Sunday after next. Can you do it then?"

William winced. "Oh, gee, you picked the one Sunday all year that I can't, Joyce. Really, I go down almost every Sunday. But, you know, Rosemary and I are moving up to Sonoma, and we need to clear out the flat, and we're doing it the weekend after next. But I can definitely do it the Sunday after that. I hope that's not a problem."

"We're drawing up the agreement to cover as many as half-a-dozen Sunday excursions after the date it's executed, so it's perfectly okay. In fact, the extra week will give our attorney a little additional time to get everything in order; he did tell me that he'd be a bit rushed to get it done by the date I suggested, but Alice seemed so excited that I wanted to get it done sooner than later."

"Well, thanks again," William said as he rose from his chair, preparing to leave. "It's going to work out great!"

Joyce got up quickly and intercepted him as he began to stroll toward the door. She put her hand on his shoulder and faced him. He barely moved his head, but could glimpse her fingers out of the corner of his eye. The angle and proximity made the image blurry, but her slender digits and their long crimson nails resting on his light tan shirt were frighteningly evident. His torso stiffened nervously. He drew a deep breath.

"William," Joyce whispered, "I want you to know what a terrific job I think you've been doing. And what an exceptionally wonderful thing you're doing right here for Alice. She glowed like a little girl with a new toy when I told her we could do this."

"She deserves it," William said softly, stammering almost imperceptibly. "Alice is incredibly talented. But she never really believed that about herself. She was so wound up in the roles of wife and mother—or, rather, the version of those roles that used to be so prevalent. You know?"

Joyce removed her hand from William's shoulder and stepped back. William immediately felt relieved—his body relaxed into its usual, comfortable slouch. But his ease turned to confusion as Joyce slunk over to her office door, locked it, and pulled the shade down over the window.

She moved back to William, and his confusion morphed quickly into panic as she slid her hands around his neck, pulled him toward her, and began kissing him passionately, her tongue pushing apart his lips and probing inside his mouth.

He neither resisted nor reciprocated. He waited and allowed it to happen, but as soon as Joyce took a breath he leaned his head back and looked at her. "What's going on here, Joyce?" he implored in a gentle, noncommittal whisper. "You read me the riot act and nearly fired me when I tried to kiss you that one time. I don't want any trouble. I like my job."

"Think of how much *more* you'll like the job if you're cozy with your boss," she said in a sultry whisper before pulling him toward her and kissing him again. She unbuttoned his shirt and pulled it open, exposing his chest, which she stroked sensuously with the palms of her hands.

William stood motionless, doing nothing.

"Oh, don't be like that," she implored girlishly. "Listen to me, you hunk. I'm really sorry for the way I treated you last time. That's on me. You came on to me when I wasn't expecting it. You caught me off-guard and I overreacted. Let me show you how sweet I can really be."

The smile she flashed was a mix of vulnerability and surrender. It melted him.

The buttons of her silky blouse came undone beneath his frantic fingers. Joyce had on a lacy black demi-bra, which immediately made William suspect that her sexual salvo was not entirely impromptu, and also excited him. He had always enjoyed fondling breasts through a pretty bra—it presented more tactile options than bare breasts did.

When she lead him to the couch and pushed him down, he leaned back and watched as she unbuckled his belt and pulled his jeans down to his ankles.

"Lie down," she whispered as she shed her skirt and panties.

The couch was narrow. He was still fidgeting a bit when she wedged in above him, her knees outside his thighs. She took his erect penis in her hands and guided it inside her as she gazed down from above him.

Her stare made him uneasy. For an instant, he feared he was about to go limp. But when he closed his eyes, his subconscious mind astonished him by spontaneously conjuring up the image of a stern Dr. Judith Feigenbaum atop him, her clinical robe hanging open, flapping reliably with each unhesitating thrust.

He clung steadfastly to that vision till the end. It was glorious.

CHAPTER 11

*I*T was close to midnight when Bert squeezed quietly through the
front door of Dag's condo. He was exhausted, but elation was
coursing through him. The cloth bag he lugged was filled with the
staples that Miguel had advised him to bring from his own pantry—
two bottles of extra virgin olive oil (one for sautéing, and a more
expensive variety for dressing salads and drizzling on top of just-
plated hot dishes), three different types of salt (Miguel had just said
salt, but Bert loved playing with the subtle differences in taste and
texture among coarse kosher salt, fine sea salt, and occasionally
even pricey pink Himalayan), black peppercorns in a huge wooden
grinder, an assortment of dried and fresh herbs and spices in small
glass jars, and what was left of a stick of unsalted butter.

Bert was surprised to see Dag, in jeans and a sweater, asleep on
the living room couch, an open hardcover novel splayed face down
on his chest. He closed the door to the apartment gently, so as not to
wake him, but the sound of the deadbolt latching caused Dag to open
his eyes and turn his head.

"Hey, Bertie, you're home," he mumbled, glancing at the clock.
"My god, it's almost midnight!" He sat up, cleared his head with a
quick shake, and leaned forward excitedly. "So tell me all about it.
How did your first gig as a professional chef go?"

Bert chuckled. "Let me put these things away and mix myself a quick martini. Then I'll come in and tell you all about it. It was a blast!"

"Mix one for me too, while you're at it. I want to hear everything about your adventure."

"Are you sure? You have to be at work tomorrow morning."

"I'll be fine. I wanna hear."

When Bert returned, he handed Dag his drink and they clinked glasses. Then he plopped onto the easy chair across from the sofa, took a long swig, and laughed.

"The woman's name was Gina. She flirted with me all night, Dag. I didn't have the heart to tell her I was gay."

"Well, she has good taste in men, anyway."

Bert snickered. "Gina—what a piece of work. She had on this really tight, clingy top. Wore it off her shoulders, down her biceps, you know. Jesus, half her tits were showing, and she kept leaning over when she talked to me to show me more of 'em."

"Wasn't her husband there?"

"Pathetic, paunchy guy. Just skulked around. Never really said much. Gina talked to *me* all night. I kinda see now why Miguel gets such a kick out of going there."

"Is she a good-looking woman?"

"Pretty hot, actually. You know, in a kind of 'refined slutty' way?"

"So that's the couple, huh? And they live on the Upper East Side?"

"Yeah, a really nice apartment. Maybe it's a co-op and they own it. I don't know. Beautiful furniture. You know, when I envisioned this personal chef thing, I figured it would be pretty high-class people."

"And they paid, right?" Dag probed, appearing momentarily agitated.

"Oh yeah. The guy paid, no problem. Here's the check." Bert retrieved it from his shirt pocket, unfolded it, and held it up.

Dag walked over, took the check, and examined it. "Hey, Bertie! That's not bad for a night's work. Pretty damn good!"

Bert blushed and grinned.

"What did you cook for them?"

"Main dish was veal Milanese and fettucine alfredo. They loved it. I started the meal with a little minestrone, a little salad. Then a platter of braised zucchini. You know, lots of courses, spread out over the evening, makes it fancier. They liked my martinis so much they wanted me to just keep pouring them all night. They never got to the wine. They were sloshed, totally. I brought cannoli shells for dessert and stuffed them with ricotta, whipped cream, sugar, cinnamon, allspice, and chocolate chips just before they ate 'em. They think I'm like a television chef!"

"This is great, Bertie!" Dag cried, still holding the check and gazing at it. "You're a professional chef! Let's toast again. To you and your new career!"

Bert was in the middle of saying "I'll drink to that" when his cell phone rang.

"Oh, hey, it's Miguel. Let me just take this. It'll be quick."

Bertram switched the phone to speaker mode so he could rest it on his chest as he reclined into the leather chair. "Hello?"

"Hey, man, it's Miguel. How ya doin'?"

"I'm great, how are you?"

"I just now finished my shift, man. The restaurant was crankin' tonight. But I want to hear about your gig with Gina and her old man. How did it go?"

"Went great. No problems. They loved it."

"So the pointers I gave you worked out?"

"Really smooth. I appreciate everything, Miguel."

"Fantastic, man! I'm proud of you, I knew you could do it!"

"Thanks so much for your confidence in me." Bert chuckled contritely. "Look, I know I totally freaked out when you first proposed it, but I'm glad you stuck with me. I think this is what I'm meant to do. I'm looking forward to my next gig."

"Terrific, man, glad to hear it. Have a good night. Oh, and hey, don't forget to write me a check when you get a chance."

"Don't worry, I won't forget. I appreciate the opportunity. It means a lot to me. Take care, man. And send my love to your beautiful wife."

"Thanks, Bert. Chau."

Bert clicked off the phone.

"Look at you!" Dag exclaimed. "A working chef. With a partner." He raised his martini glass. "To your new success!"

Bert smiled and raised his glass.

"Yeah, I'm really grateful to Miguel for turning me on to this. This is something I can do and enjoy."

Dag held up the check. "So, you give him a cut of this?"

"Ten percent."

"Ten percent," Dag repeated, mulling the amount over in his mind. "I guess that sounds fair. You two are in business together now. So I assume he gives you ten percent of *his* jobs?"

"It depends who found the clients. These are *his* clients. I'm filling in for him, so he gets a cut. If I find clients, and he needs to bail *me* out some evening, then I get a cut."

"Ah. Well, Bertie . . . then you need to find some clients! Do you want to come to another Rotary Club meeting?"

"God, Dag! No! No more of those meetings. I can't take them, really. Please don't suggest that. Look, I'll find clients. My own way. Let's not complicate the evening here. I just want to have a drink and celebrate my first professional chef gig."

"Don't worry, sweetie, I'll ask around for you. Between all my clients at work, and the Rotary Club, and networking events, I'll find you tons of hungry folks. You'll be collecting cuts from your buddy in no time."

That all felt a bit too fast for Bert, but he said nothing—just lifted his glass in Dag's direction and took some big swallows.

The weekend they'd designated for the move was three days away.

Rosemary and William had nearly finished packing. There were just a few random items remaining—things they needed access to every day—but these could be thrown into boxes just prior to leaving.

They'd already filled and sealed the tall pile of uniform cardboard moving containers with room designations that Arthur had bought for them, but they needed a few more boxes. Luckily, a friend of Rosemary's was happy to part with some flattened cartons in her coat closet from a move a few months earlier. Rosemary ran over to pick them up, and when she got back, she set them down in the foyer and went looking for William.

She found him in his painting studio at the end of the hall, and was about to say hi, but his demeanor and body language dissuaded her. He was motionless, standing several feet from his canvas, staring at it pensively. The picture was fully sketched, but no paint had as yet been applied. Rosemary couldn't be certain, but it seemed to her that despite his stoic demeanor, her husband was quite distraught.

She studied the canvas. Her eyes widened and she smiled enthusiastically. "I really like it!" she exclaimed. "It's different from the stuff you've been doing. It looks kind of surreal. Everything's a little wobbly. That makes it really interesting, honey. I like this direction you're taking."

She hoped her encouragement would cheer him up.

"Surreal," he muttered, barely audibly. "Right. Surreal." He turned to her and spoke a bit more distinctly. "The same thing happened at my art class at the senior home, Rosemary. The stuff I drew came out looking surreal. What the hell's going on with me?"

"What do you mean? It's great!"

"Are you listening to me? This wasn't intentional. Not this time— and not last time. It just came out this way. I didn't even realize it till I stepped back and really looked. It's just kind of happening on its own!"

"Wow, that's strange." She studied the image. "Do you think that on some level you knew you needed to change your style to find buyers, and your subconscious mind drove the change?"

"What?" he cried. "Is that even possible? I have no fucking idea, Rosemary. It's scary. Damn scary. My hands are not listening to my brain."

Rosemary stepped closer, hugged him, and laid her head tenderly upon his chest. "Oh, don't worry, honey. Maybe it's the move. I mean, our whole existence is about to change. It's very stressful. Really, who knows what living in Sonoma will be like? And who the hell knows what living with your insane father is going to be like? It's enough to throw anybody off! Really, I wouldn't worry about it. Once we settle in up there, we'll get used to it and figure everything out, and things will calm down. In the meantime, I think you should try painting the canvas the way you sketched it. It might come out really good. Why don't you just try that?"

He said nothing.

She took his hand. "Come on, baby. Let's go to the bedroom. You need a break from this."

Molly the cat was on the bed, but when she saw them come into the bedroom, she leaped off and curled up on the hassock in the corner.

Rosemary led William to the edge of the bed and sat him down, then began kissing him softly. She opened his shirt and stroked his belly as she kissed him about the neck and chest. After a few minutes of numb stillness he began to respond, and soon he was reciprocating with passion.

Although William became highly aroused, he did not allow that to shift his focus: he attended relentlessly to Rosemary's needs, while stubbornly deferring his own. His motivation was illogical, but he feared that any deviation from this approach might inadvertently cause his wife to suspect that something was amiss.

After all, he'd had sex with Joyce Miller (while fantasizing about Dr. Judith Feigenbaum) just the day prior. He'd showered, of course, and scrubbed his genitals fervidly, but it still felt to him as if some trace of Joyce clung inexorably to him—and might be detectable. Perhaps it was all more psychological than physical. Regardless, tending selflessly to Rosemary's pleasure while disregarding his own seemed to him tonight's only unimpeded path to consummation.

The heavy and bulky items were hauled on Saturday—furniture, several cartons of books, cookware and dishes, and a huge stash of William's painting equipment and canvases.

With stairs to negotiate at both ends, it was an exhausting venture. William had prevailed upon a couple of old college friends to help. The three men started early in the morning and made two trips to Sonoma before nightfall.

During their second trip up, Rosemary, cocooned now in the eerily denuded San Francisco flat, grew pensive, and sat down on the bare wood of the living room floor. Molly was curled up on the window sill across the room. The cat occasionally appeared to doze, but she periodically opened her eyes to check on Rosemary, who was leaning back against the wall, knees hinged in front of her, legs entwined and extended together to her left.

"Come, Molly," Rosemary cajoled in the most alluring tone she could muster. "Come sit on my lap."

As was invariably the case, Molly declined the invitation.

"All right, then," Rosemary said. "I'll talk to you from here. I have a lot to tell you."

Molly yawned and arched her back into what looked to Rosemary like an advanced yoga pose. After a few moments, she hunkered back down and fixed her gaze intently upon Rosemary.

"Well, it's really happening," Rosemary said. "Tomorrow we'll be in a new house in Sonoma. I think you'll like it there. It's a big place, with lots of rooms for you to explore." She sighed. The corners of her mouth raised in the slightest suggestion of a grin. "I'm so ready. I really had to work my contacts up there to wangle my new dental hygienist position. But, you know—there was no way I was going to commute all the way back down to San Francisco every day."

Rosemary paused, leaned her head back and closed her eyes. "Really, though, Molly, you know what's more important? This move gave me a gracious way to end the affair with my boss. I really needed to do that. I've been thinking about ending it for a while now. And Moe—he was so nice about it. I think, actually, he was as relieved as I was to be done with it." She shook her head. "I never should have done it in the first place—the affair, I mean. God, it went on for a long time, didn't it? He was so cute before he put on weight. I knew it was wrong, of course—all along I knew it—but it really was exciting for a while."

She smiled wistfully. "And the stuff he was into—good god! The bondage and the pain. I'd never even thought about that kind of thing before. It was really all *his* thing, you know. I mean, I was playing the dominatrix, but really I was just doing what he said he liked. You know, to please *him*. I don't think I'd ever do those kind of things on my own—with Will I mean." She pondered that for a moment. "I don't know, though—now that I've tried it—maybe a little?" She winked playfully at Molly, then grew ruminative again.

"I'm just so horribly guilty about the whole thing now—that's the truth, Molly. I should never have done that to Will. But I'll make it up to him. You'll see. My love for him is rekindled now. I'm really working hard on that—I want it to happen. This whole thing with the house in Sonoma—it's a clean start, a total new beginning. It's like we're being reborn. Together. We're going to be living in a big, beautiful house." She exhaled loudly. "I don't think Will ever really understood how much I hated living in this tiny flat all these years. All my friends bought houses over the years, Molly. That's why I stopped having them over. It was mortifying for me. Does that sound stupid and shallow?" She lowered her head and spoke softly. "Probably. But that's how I felt. I couldn't help it."

She chuckled. "But now, look at us! We're moving to an enormous house—and Will has a job. He's bringing in money. Granted, it's not a lot, but I'm so relieved that he's finally bringing in *something*. I think maybe that was part of why I cheated on him, you know? I hate to say it—but I think it's true." She pursed her lips, then relaxed them. "But it's all good now. Because we'll be living in the Sonoma house rent free! Did you hear that, Molly? Rent free! So between what Will brings in and my salary, we'll be doing really well. And the kitchen up there! God! I can't wait to start cooking in that huge, gorgeous kitchen."

Rosemary was quiet for a while. She closed her eyes and began thinking about a meal she might prepare, but soon fell asleep there on the floor.

A couple of hours later, Rosemary was awakened by voices on the staircase just outside the flat's front door. A moment after that, William and his two friends loped in and announced gleefully that the day's moving was done, that nothing had been damaged, and that they were exhausted and famished. Rosemary hopped up, and the four of them walked over to a little Italian place a couple of blocks away and gorged themselves on huge portions of pepperoni pizza and pitchers of Hefeweizen beer.

William paid the bill using his newly issued credit card. He and Rosemary then bid their two friends good night and thanked them heartily for their help.

Back at their small flat, memories radiated palpably from the walls as they prepared to spend their final night in San Francisco. Their bed had already been moved to the Sonoma house, so they rolled out sleeping bags, and slumbered contentedly, side by side, on the living room floor.

It was Sunday night, just past eight. It had taken another two trips for Rosemary and William to transport all the odds and ends remaining. On the final drive up to Sonoma, they brought Molly in her travel crate. Corralling her had been much easier than usual—she'd had no furniture to dart under.

They hauled all the boxes into a temporary holding area just inside the entryway, hastily loaded the refrigerator with any perishable food, and made certain their new front door was shut tight before they let Molly out of the crate. As soon as they did, the cat began racing about. She seemed amazed at the vast expanse now comprising her territory, and immediately disappeared into the labyrinth.

William and Rosemary, meanwhile, trudged upstairs and plopped down, exhausted, atop their unmade mattress—alone at last in their new, castle-like bedroom.

They were both very hungry.

"I'm willing to do pizza and beer again," William said softly. "It's easy. Comfort food, you know?"

"I want comfort food too, but something more exotic," Rosemary said. "It's our first night in our new house, Will. I want something special."

A cool breeze wafted in from the open window. The star-filled Sonoma night glimmered outside. It was oddly quiet—no city traffic or street noise.

"Mexican?" William asked.

"Oh yes!" Rosemary exclaimed, bolting up. "Remember that little place in Petaluma with the huge icy margaritas we went to a year or two ago?"

"Oh yeah," William said. "Great idea. Let's go now. If I lie here much longer I'll never want to get up again."

The restaurant was quiet. They were seated at a lovely table near a picture window with a view of moonlit vineyards. The food was served on enormous platters—ample mounds of seasoned rice, shredded lettuce salad, and refried beans sat aside each main course. Rosemary ordered spicy chicken enchiladas. William opted for chiles rellenos, which oozed creamy queso asadero into the plate's brown gravy when he sliced into them.

But most striking were the majestic margaritas, blended with ice into a near slurry state and served in oversize stemmed glasses with bowl-shaped tops decorated with gaudy paintings of Mexican flowers and fruits.

As the evening wore on, they ordered three margaritas each. Rosemary drank most of William's last one, though—he was trying to remain sufficiently awake and sober to drive home.

They were too full and exhausted for sex when they got back to the house, and in no mood to search through boxes for sheets and blankets to make the bed. However, their two sleeping bags were near at hand, so they laid them out atop the bare mattress and squeezed inside. Rolled-up jackets served as makeshift pillows.

They slept soundly.

They awoke early to a cool but sunny Monday morning. Rosemary had seen to it that her new job didn't start till the following week, and William didn't have an art class to teach at the senior home until the next day, so Monday had been designated for unpacking and settling in.

Rosemary was anxious to try out her massive new kitchen, and she got their day started with a festive breakfast of soft-scrambled eggs, home-fried potatoes with caramelized onions, sourdough toast topped with fresh strawberry jam, and a pot of steaming Earl Grey tea.

Then they got to work.

When they finally came across the box with linen and pillows, it was late afternoon. They made the bed together, William following Rosemary's detailed and precise instructions dutifully so that his side matched hers exactly. But just moments later, she tugged him onto the bed, and the two of them proceeded to mangle the immaculately ironed sheets and tight hospital corners with spontaneous and tumultuous lovemaking.

For William, the Joyce Miller/Dr. Feigenbaum incident seemed a bit more remote now—almost phantasmagoric in his mind. Rosemary's enthusiasm and newly found passion lured him into the moment and cleared his mind of the emotional detritus that had been stubbornly lingering.

Most everything was unpacked by seven. To celebrate, Rosemary started to prepare a shaker of vodka gimlets. It occurred to William that his paints and other art supplies still lay piled in boxes in his new art room—he hadn't wanted to risk upsetting Rosemary, who surely felt that other tasks took priority. He considered tending to the paints now, but thought better of it. He'd get to them over the next couple of days. Rosemary was in a great mood. He didn't want to tinker with that.

Instead, while she mixed the cocktails, he checked email on his phone.

"Hey honey," he shouted. "You won't believe this. My father just sent an email. He's not going to be here tomorrow like he planned."

"What? Why?" Rosemary asked excitedly.

William laughed. "Wow! At the last minute he decided he didn't want to fly. He already hired a guy, you remember? To drive his car out here? So now that guy's going to take my father in the backseat, and follow the fucking moving van all the way to California." He looked at Rosemary and grinned. "Imagine it, Rosemary. This poor schmuck is going to drive three thousand miles on Highway 80, alone in a goddamn car with Arthur Wozniak. Jesus! It's great for *us*, though—my father won't be here till the weekend at the earliest."

"Yay!" Rosemary clapped her hands and jumped up and down. "We have the whole castle to ourselves for nearly a week! Now we *really* have something to toast!"

Rosemary shook the gimlets with preternatural enthusiasm and poured them into chilled martini glasses. "To us!" she cried. "Together in our new place!"

They toasted. She had added a little extra simple syrup to the concoction to make it more festive—the drinks were sweet and delicious.

After a couple of rounds, they decided to have Chinese food delivered. They weren't expecting it to be anywhere near as good as the stuff they got in the city from Chinatown, but it surprised them—it was rich, spicy, and very filling.

They made love again before going to sleep. After a bit of initial hugging and kissing, Rosemary retreated slightly and whispered, "I have a special treat for you, baby—your reward for being so focused and steadfast about getting everything unpacked and put away." With that, she made her way down his body, kissing his torso at progressively lower points, until she reached his erect penis, which she took into her mouth.

It immediately occurred to William that his decision to leave his paints for another day had been an especially good one.

She kept at it a long time, passionately and energetically. For William it was ecstatic, but also almost spiritually peaceful and hypnotic—so much so that at one point he was lulled into a reverie so deep that he softened just a little.

With her mouth still on his member, Rosemary reached up, grabbed his nipples, and squeezed and twisted them mercilessly for a few moments; then she yanked her fingertips sharply down and away.

"Hoo!" William exclaimed as his eyes shot open. "Wow! Honey! You've never done that to me before!"

She took her mouth off him and lifted her head. "Oh, just thought I'd try something new. Did you like it?"

"Actually, I did."

Rosemary darted up and took one of his nipples in her mouth, biting it hard but through lip-enfolded teeth, so as not to tear his skin. She kept at it, tugging at his captive flesh.

William moaned and squirmed, and his penis grow rock hard against her. She lowered herself and took him in her mouth once again. As she did, she raked her sharp fingernails along his belly, leaving red track marks in her wake.

William grew so excited as Rosemary continued to work on him that there were several points at which he had to strain to withhold his orgasm and prolong their intimacy.

He had developed a specific technique for this that was profoundly reliable: he conjured up a mental image of a baseball player sliding into third base. It took his mind off the proceedings just enough to defer his ejaculation.

William seemed to recall some distant connection between this tack and a line he'd once heard in a Woody Allen movie—but the precise recollection had long since faded away.

CHAPTER 12

*B*ERT was antsy. It was three in the afternoon, too early to start cooking dinner for Dag and himself—Dag was attending a networking event after work, and wouldn't be home until eight—but there really wasn't anything else Bert felt like doing.

Then it occurred to him. A stovetop beef stew—it would be the perfect solution. Dag loved that dish. And because it slow cooked for hours, starting now would be exactly right. Bert checked the refrigerator, and his recollection was correct: he had a big chuck steak in there, and it needed to be cooked anyway or it would go bad. He especially enjoyed working with underappreciated cuts like chuck; the fat and gristle gave it great flavor, but unless it was cooked properly, it was far too tough.

He was about to pull the chuck out of the meat bin when his cell phone rang. The name that displayed was surprising. He clicked his phone on.

"Hello?" Bert ventured warily.

"Hi! It's Gina. You remember—you cooked dinner for me and my husband the other night."

Of course Bertram remembered. It was his grand premiere as a personal chef. And so far, his lone gig.

"Sure, I remember," he said. "Veal Milanese and fettucine alfredo. And quite a few martinis."

"We just loved it! We want you to come cook for us again tomorrow night. Are you available?"

"Tomorrow night?" Bert stammered. "Oh, Gina, you know, Miguel's off tomorrow night, and you're really *his* customer. So I think you ought to call *him*. I was just filling in for him—it wouldn't be right."

"No!" Gina cried. "I want *you*. You cook better food."

That made Bert smile and ponder for a moment—but it was still Miguel's gig. "Look," he said, "that's really flattering for you to say. But Miguel's a super good cook. I mean, he's the chef at a French place now, and he's cooked at Italian places and Mexican places before. You know—the guy's a pro. And like I said, you're really *his* customer. It wouldn't be right, Gina."

"That's bullshit, man!" she replied—in an oddly cheerful tone, given the phrase she'd just uttered. "Look, sweetie, I paid Miguel well when he cooked for me. That's how it worked: he cooked, I paid. It was that kind of thing, you know? There was no long-term contract. So now I have no obligation to use him over anybody else—see what I mean, sweetie? And your food is *better*. It's just flat-out better. And your cocktails are *really* better. And you're a whole lot cuter."

"Okay, look," he said cautiously, "I'd love to cook for you and your husband again, but I've got to talk to Miguel about it first, all right? Can I call you back after I talk to him?"

"Of course, sweetie, I'll wait to hear from you. I'm really looking forward to you cooking for me again. Don't disappoint me now, you big hunk. Bye bye."

The call clicked off.

Bert closed his eyes, took a deep breath, and shook his head. "Jesus!" he cried.

Then he called Dag at work and explained the situation to him.

"Just take the gig!" Dag exclaimed. "You don't owe Miguel anything."

"What do you mean I don't owe him anything?" Bert shot back. "He helped me get into this whole thing. Of course I owe him something. I have to at least *tell* him."

"Fine, then," Dag acquiesced. "So tell him. Call him and tell him."

"No," Bert said, forming his words slowly as he thought through his tack. "No. I think I'll go down to the restaurant and talk to him in person. I can get there on the subway in ten minutes. I've got to do this face to face."

Dag chuckled. "You're too nice sometimes, Bertie. But I guess that's why I love you. Sure. Go. Just be careful."

The bar at the French restaurant opened at five, with dinner seating at five thirty. It was around four when Bert arrived.

It was not difficult to locate Miguel, who was up front reviewing the night's specials with the line cooks. Most of the cooks were taller than Miguel, but his tan fedora was unmistakable. Bert wondered for a moment if he'd actually recognize his friend bareheaded if he passed him on the street.

"Bert!" Miguel called when he spotted him. "What a surprise. Nice to see you, man. Let me finish up here and I'll be right with you."

Bert waited near the front door. A minute or two later, Miguel joined him and gave him a hug.

"What are you doing here, man? Just in the neighborhood and wanted to say hi?"

"I wish it were just to say hi," Bert said. "We have a problem, and I need to talk to you about it."

"Okay. What's the problem?"

Bert looked around. People were racing about—setting up tables, cleaning the bar, mopping the floor. "Any chance you can take a quick break and step outside? What I want to talk about is kind of sensitive."

"Sure," Miguel said. "Let's go in the alley out back."

Bert followed him through the kitchen and out to a small yard with a narrow alley leading to the street. The backs of old brick buildings formed a wall around them. Huge, dented garbage cans stood nearby and dozens of cigarette butts were strewn about on the cracked asphalt. The stench of rancid grease that had been used for deep frying permeated the air.

"So, what's up?" Miguel inquired.

Bert looked away. "I feel really uncomfortable about this, but . . . I just got a call from Gina. She wants me to cook for her tomorrow night. I told her she should call you, she's *your* customer. And I said you're off tomorrow and you could do it. But she insisted she wanted *me*. I really don't know what to do."

"Jesus!" Miguel cried, flinging his head back and stomping his foot. "That bitch. You know what this is about? She wants to fuck you, man. I called her the morning after you cooked for her—you know, just to check in and make sure she was happy with you. Know what she kept tellin' me? How fuckin' hot you are. What a whore."

Bert waited a moment, then said softly, "She said she liked my cooking, Miguel."

Miguel laughed. "She wants to fuck you, man, don't you see that? And flirt with you in front of her husband. She's sick. Did you tell her you were gay?"

Bert stiffened. "That's none of her business."

"Oh, so you're playin' along?" Miguel said, raising his voice. "Just tell her you're gay. That'll stop it."

"Look, Miguel, I think you're a great chef. And a good guy. But I have to be honest. She said she liked my cooking better than yours."

"Of course she said that," Miguel cried. "What do you think she'd say? 'I want you because I want to fuck you'? Just tell her you're gay and she'll back off."

"I'm not going to tell her that because it's none of her business. And that's not what this is about!" Bert's tone grew firmer. "What is it with you? You think it's impossible that someone might like my cooking better than yours? Why is that impossible? I mean, you're scoffing at it like it's out of the question."

"Because I'm a fucking professional, and you're a home-cook novice. And I'm trying to be a nice guy and give you a break to get started. And what do I get in return? You're already trying to steal my fucking customers." He moved toward Bert and glared at him. "Your first goddamn gig! I got it for you—and you're stealing already!" Miguel's face grew red. "You're just a fucked-up piece of shit, man." He shoved Bert in the chest, and then took a step closer to him as Bert stumbled backward.

Bert set his feet. "Back off, asshole!" he shouted, his eyes wide, his jaw set, and his eyebrows dipping ominously. "I may be gay, but I can kick the living shit out of a little twerp like you. So just back . . . the hell . . . off."

Miguel took a breath and gazed up at Bert. He exhaled slowly and said, "All right. Sorry, man." He took a couple of steps back. "I shouldn't have done that. My bad. I'm really sorry. I've just got a temper, you know? And I'm pissed as shit at that bitch. It's not your fault. I'll tell you what. Let me call her. I'll talk some sense into her. I can't do it right now—I gotta get back to work. But I'll call her tonight. All right?"

Bert frowned. "You gonna tell her I'm gay? I'd rather you didn't."

Miguel raised his hands as if in surrender. "I get it, I swear. I won't tell her."

"Thank you. And listen, I don't want to steal your customers. Really. That's the whole reason I came here to talk to you—you understand that, right? I'm grateful for your help. I'm not the bad guy here."

"I know, man. I'm sorry. I'm just a fucking hothead. My wife always says so. I do know you're a good guy." He extended his hand. "Still friends?"

Bert slapped his hand away and pulled him in for a tight, affectionate bear hug.

"Holy shit!" Miguel chuckled. "You *are* strong! Thank god I didn't try to fight you."

Bert laughed. "Okay. You talk to Gina and work all this out. I'll be really relieved once it's settled."

By the time Bert got back home it was past five, and he rushed to get to work on the stew. He cut the chuck steak into pieces and began browning the meat in small batches in his cast-iron Dutch oven. Soon he had all the browned beef sitting in an aluminum bowl on the counter. He added more olive oil to the pot, along with some butter, and began sautéing onions, garlic, carrots, and celery. His preference was to season each aromatic vegetable separately as he added it, so he sprinkled salt and fresh-ground pepper into the pot in waves, along with dried rosemary, thyme, marjoram, and paprika. The small Yukon Gold potatoes didn't need peeling, but he scrubbed and halved them before he threw them in. He cleared a hot spot in the pot for a bit of tomato paste to come to temperature before he added the beef stock and meat and mixed it all with a few sprinkles of Worcestershire sauce and a couple of bay leaves. Then he opened a bottle of good zinfandel and poured in a hearty dose, and poured a big glass for himself as well.

He checked the clock when he'd finally brought the pot to a boil and covered it for its long simmer. It was already six. Dag would be home right around eight—two hours wouldn't be enough cooking time. As Bert finished his glass of zinfandel, he decided that if he greeted Dag with a shaker of martinis and an appetizer plate of fresh figs stuffed with goat cheese and walnuts with a reduced balsamic honey syrup over top, Dag would be a happy boy while the stew got another hour or so to cook. When it was time to serve, as long as the meat was tender, he could thicken the stew with a quick cornstarch slurry if he needed to.

Dag was a bit late getting in. That was fine. It gave the beef a little more time to get tender, and Bert was already working on his second martini, so he was in a fine mood.

"Wow!" Dag exclaimed the moment he entered the condo. "It smells fantastic in here! I actually started smelling it out in the hall as soon as I got off the elevator, and I was hoping it was coming from our kitchen. What is it?"

"Beef stew," Bert said as he rose from the sofa.

"Sounds great, Bertie!"

Dag gave him a big hug and kiss. While he put his things down, Bert went into the kitchen and poured a martini for him. He also grabbed the silver tray holding the stuffed figs he'd made and brought both into the living room.

Dag was undoing his tie when he spied the figs. "And what have we here?"

"Fresh figs stuffed with goat cheese and walnuts."

Dag grabbed one and gobbled it right down. "Fantastic! What's the syrup?"

"Reduced balsamic vinegar and honey."

"You are a master, sir!"

Bert put down the tray and handed Dag his martini. He then grabbed his own, and the men toasted.

"To the chef I love!" Dag exclaimed as they clinked glasses.

Dag took a few sips and sat down on the sofa. Bert sat across from him on an easy chair.

"So, did you get it all worked out with your man Miguel?" Dag asked.

"I think so," Bert said. "He told me that he was going to—"

His cell phone rang, and he checked the screen.

"Oh shit, it's that woman Gina again. What the fuck is going on now?"

"Put it on speaker," Dag said. "I want to hear this."

Bert complied, and answered the call. "Hello?"

"Hi sweetie! It's Gina. How are you doing tonight?"

"Fine, thanks. Did you talk to Miguel?"

"Yeah, I talked to him. What an asshole! He said I only wanted you to cook for me, because I thought you were sexy. Well, you *are* sexy, sweetie, but I'm not a totally shallow bitch. I want you to cook for me because you're a better cook. And I told him so."

"You told him that?"

"Hell yeah. Then you know what that asshole did? He tried to tell me you were gay—he thought that would turn me off to you. I don't give a shit if you're gay, sweetie. Rock Hudson was gay. I'd let him cook for me any time—if he could cook, that is. Hell, you know what I mean. I don't give a shit if you're gay or if he just said you were. I want you to cook for me. And I told him that. He doesn't own me. I told him to fuck off. So, will I see you tomorrow night, sweetie?"

Bert looked to Dag who nodded his head affirmatively.

"I guess so," Bert said. "And Gina . . ." He paused a moment and glanced at Dag. "I *am* gay, by the way. But you're right. It doesn't matter. I'll be happy to cook for you tomorrow night. What do you want me to make?"

"Surprise us! As long as it's Italian. I trust you totally, sweetie. And hey, your martinis were to die for—can you make manhattans just as good?"

"Oh yeah. I make them with rye, not bourbon. They're much better that way. You game for that?"

"Absolutely, sweetie, I'm game. Get a nice bottle of rye for us. Bye now."

Bert clicked off his phone.

"Well, *sweetie*," Dag teased, "looks like you have your first client. And no ten percent cut to pay."

"Looks like it," Bertram whispered, as he momentarily gazed up at the ceiling and sighed. "And I suppose I'm done with Miguel," he muttered sadly. "I feel funny about how all this went down, Dag."

"Fuck Miguel," Dag shouted. "Like the lady said, he doesn't own these people. And he sure as hell doesn't own *you*. The guy just can't handle the fact that you're a better cook than he is. Besides, he outed you. So fuck him. You're going to be a big success at this, Bertie!" Dag held up his glass in Bert's direction, took another hearty swig, and reached for a couple of stuffed figs.

The drive to the senior home in Mill Valley felt interminable.

Just yesterday, when he and Rosemary were unpacking, making love, and gulping down their first taste of Sonoma's Chinese takeout, everything had seemed fresh and unfettered. William had pictured himself spending time with Rosemary in the evenings, and in his new art studio during the day, sketching and painting for hours at a time. But now, the reality of driving from their location in Sonoma all the way to the senior home—and the thought of repeating the drive there and back three times a week—seemed crushing.

Rosemary had opted to change jobs rather than commute to the city—maybe she had it right. William hadn't thought so before. Usually he didn't mind driving—it relaxed him. So why did this now feel so oppressive?

He thought about the senior home and his students—especially Alice—and his commitment to take her to the San Jose flea market. That was important. Even if he were going to reconsider working at the senior home, he certainly wouldn't make a change until he and Alice had spent a few Sundays together in San Jose. That was a promise he would not break.

He wanted to clear his head. As he drove south on Highway 101, he fiddled with the car radio. Some music or talk would surely take his mind off these concerns. But nothing interested him; he kept sampling new stations, but each was more boring than the last.

Finally, he turned the radio off. As soon as he did, it occurred to him that his long-planned adventure with Alice at the flea market was just five days away. Starting to consider logistics made sense. That would be a healthy thing to think about as he drove. And then he'd have some ideas to talk through with Alice when he saw her later today.

He pictured her—he imagined the excitement on her face—for a moment making her look like a young woman again. Yes, he'd focus on those logistics.

But the more he tried to think about the flea market, the more his mind wandered back to this seemingly endless commute, and how much farther Sunday trips to San Jose would now be. An hour south of San Francisco! Good god! Maybe he could find another flea market, somewhere in Sonoma. But he'd promised Alice the San Jose flea market—and he was familiar with that one—so no, he wouldn't make a change till he'd fulfilled his commitment.

Maybe Joyce would consider allowing him to teach just two classes a week instead of three. He could make each class half an hour longer. He wondered if he should ask her. But as he tried to formulate how he might put it, an image of Joyce took over his mind—hovering over him, fondling and kissing him.

The sex with Joyce—that couldn't last. It would blow up at some point. And with Rosemary excited about moving to the new house and suddenly so sexually ardent with him, the idea of an affair with Joyce, which just a short time ago seemed titillating and subversive, now felt like a burden. But if he tried to stop it, she'd undoubtedly fire him—throw him out on his ass right then and there.

Which actually would be okay.

But not until he'd fulfilled his commitment to Alice.

Maybe that was the way to play it. Take Alice to the flea market three or four times, make certain she'd sold a few paintings (one way or another), and then break it off with Joyce. And if Joyce didn't fire him, he could quit. He'd be free. Rosemary would be fine with it. They didn't really need the money now.

When he finally pulled into a space in the senior home's parking lot, he was drained. He closed his eyes and took a few deep breaths. He needed to summon some strength—his students deserved the best of him.

Inside the home, William set up the art room and prepared everyone's paints. He made an effort to greet his students cheerfully as they trickled in.

At five minutes past the hour, nearly everyone was in place. But one easel still had no one sitting by it.

"Alice isn't here yet," William observed aloud. "Does anyone know where she is? She's never late."

"She had some kind of medical issue," Mrs. Liebman said.

"I think they took her to the infirmary," Ira added.

"Do you know what's wrong with her?" William inquired, his brow furrowed, his voice urgent.

People shook their heads no and looked to one another throughout the room to see if anyone had more information. No one did.

"Oh, god, I hope she's all right," William said softly. He looked around the room and wondered exactly how to proceed. "Well," he finally said, "I suppose there's nothing we can do about it right now. So I guess we'll move ahead with the class, if that's okay with everyone. And we'll try to get an update on Alice's condition when we can. Any objections?"

There was silence, with a few heads nodding affirmatively. William searched the faces of his students to see if could detect concern or fear. But nobody seemed any different than usual.

Today's class was the final session devoted to the pink flamingo. Most of his pupils had done incredibly well with this study of shading and color gradation, which made William think that he could move the class along to even more sophisticated challenges—perhaps dealing with linear perspective, or the illusion of light.

William was prowling about the room, helping people put final touches on their canvases, when Joyce knocked on the door and poked her head in.

"May I see you at five in my office, William?" she asked.

He offered the barest hint of a smile. "I'll be there," he said, as he girded himself for another sexual encounter. His feelings about the prospect were mixed and confused.

When William knocked on Joyce's door, she called for him to come in. As he stepped into the room, he noticed the shade was already drawn. He closed the door behind him.

Joyce was behind her desk, in her oversize leather chair. "Have a seat, William," she said. "We need to talk."

William sat down across from her. "Is everything okay?" he asked. "Do you have an update about Alice?"

"That's precisely what I need to talk to you about, dear," she said solemnly. Her lips rolled inward—pursed into a thin strip. She sat motionless for a moment. Then she continued, softly, "Alice just passed away, dear. A massive stroke. I know she was your favorite student. I wanted you to hear it from me before any public announcement was made."

"What? She's dead? Alice? Dead? No! No!"

William began to hyperventilate. Tears welled up in his eyes. He leaped up from his chair, his chest and shoulders oscillated frantically as he began to sob. "She never got to go to the flea market, Joyce! She never got to go! I put her off a week and she missed her life's dream! One goddamn weekend the whole year I couldn't go—and *this* happens! How can I live with myself? This was her dream. Jesus Christ! How can I live with myself?"

Joyce gazed up at him from her chair. Firmly, but with compassion and reassurance, she said, "William, listen to me. The important thing for Alice was knowing that you thought she was worthy of going and selling her paintings. *That* made the difference for her. Actually going, sitting for hours in the hot sun, maybe not selling anything—that wasn't the thing, William. The thing was *you*—a real artist, someone she respected, someone who sells his work—believing in her, believing she was worthy. And you gave her that. Think about it, who knows what would have happened down there? If she would have sold anything? What *you* gave her—that changed everything for her. I saw it in her face. You gave her that dream."

William's sobs became uncontrollable—he could not respond

to what Joyce said, and just remaining upright was becoming difficult.

Joyce walked around her desk, stood before him, and opened her arms. "Come here, baby," she said softly.

He melted into her, and she held him tightly until he stopped crying. It took several minutes.

"Are you okay now, honey?" she asked gently when his sobs subsided, taking a step back but keeping her hands on his shoulders.

"Yeah, I think so," William whispered. "Thank you."

Joyce offered a warm smile—she was very pretty when she smiled.

He watched as she ambled to the door and locked it, then came back to where he stood.

She embraced him. Her lips pressed against his, forcing his mouth open. He could feel her tongue crawling like a serpent along his palate.

For a few moments, he allowed it to happen. He tried to yield to her advances. But it was impossible. Finally, he pushed her away— not violently, but with a sense of resolve—and held her arms.

"Damn it, Joyce," he whispered, his voice breaking. "Alice just died. You want to make love here on your couch like nothing happened? I can't do that. I'm sorry. I just can't."

Joyce's brow crinkled sympathetically. Her eyelids widened with sadness and compassion. "William, honey," she said, her timbre solicitous but still somehow sultry, "this is a senior home. People die. All the time. In your art class you've been lucky—you have just a small group of students, and fortunately you haven't had to experience this till now. But if you stay long enough, you will. Over and over. I don't want to seem heartless, but this is the business we're in. The longer you stay, the more death you'll see. I'm so sorry dear, but it just doesn't affect me the way it used to—I can't allow it to. It's the same for me as with doctors and nurses: if we let the patients who die affect us emotionally, we can't do our jobs."

"Well, I'm not like that. And I don't *want* to be like that. Especially about Alice." He let go of Joyce's arms and took a moment to silently compose his next sentence before saying it aloud. "And frankly, Joyce, this thing between us—it just seems wrong in so many ways. I think we need to stop."

"We just started, honey," Joyce said softly, but with an upbeat and encouraging inflection. "Don't let one incident cloud your mind. Go home and sleep on it." She stepped closer to him and caressed his face with both her hands. "I was wrong to want to do it today. I forgot that you're new to all this. And what a sweet, sensitive man you are. But what we have here, you and me—long term, I think you'll see that it's a good thing."

William gently removed her hands from his cheeks, and let them drop to her sides. "I really don't think I can keep doing it, Joyce." He paused, then started to speak, then paused again. Finally he blurted it out in a hoarse whisper, tears about to well up again: "Maybe I shouldn't work here either. I think I have to quit, Joyce. I'm sorry. I don't think I can come back. It's gotten too complicated."

Joyce stared into William's eyes; she seemed to be pondering something. "You don't have to quit," she eventually said. "Please, honey, don't jump to a conclusion based on emotions. Take some time and think about it."

At that particular moment Joyce seemed to William authentic and caring—and consummately luscious in her snug black blouse, tweed skirt, and stiletto heels. He was growing more confused. He knew for certain, though, that he didn't want to prolong this encounter, and he didn't want to fight with her. He needed to get away and have time to figure out what to do.

"You're right," he said. "I need to think about it. I really like you, Joyce. I think you're a beautiful woman. And nice. I just don't know if this is right for me now. I'll have to let you know."

"All right then, honey," Joyce said. "I'll wait to hear from you."

As soon as William turned toward the door and Joyce was no longer in his field of vision, he suddenly became a bit more certain he wasn't coming back. And if he was indeed leaving, it would be far easier to just send an email later than to have it out in person like this.

He returned to his art room and packed up his personal belongings, just in case.

On his way home it occurred to William that Rosemary had changed dentist offices—she'd never see Joyce again. So he could tell her anything about why he quit, and she'd never have occasion to check it out. He wouldn't have to mention the affair. He could simply explain to her that she was right about the commute—it was just too long to be workable. He could look for a part-time job up in Sonoma. And maybe he'd sell more art up there—different tastes and such.

When he pulled into the garage at the Sonoma house, it was early evening. It didn't feel as if he'd been on the road long at all.

Over dinner, William explained to Rosemary that between Alice's death and the length of the commute, he was leaning toward resigning from the home. To his surprise, Rosemary not only thought it was a great idea, she told him she'd secretly predicted that he'd do exactly that within a week of moving. When he offered to look for another part-time job in Sonoma, she astonished him again by saying, "You know, that new surreal style you're experimenting with is so interesting—why don't you just focus on your painting for now?

We really only need one income up here. And with just the van, it's so much easier if only one of us works."

He submitted his resignation to Joyce via email that night.

CHAPTER 13

$\mathscr{A}$T five in the morning on Thursday, William and Rosemary were awakened by the ringing of William's cell phone. He staggered to the bureau, where it sat charging. In his ungainly struggle to unplug it, the phone smashed twice onto the top of the bureau before he finally corralled it.

"It's my father," he whispered to Rosemary, who was sitting up in bed, her semi-conscious face suffused with the dull orange glow of the tiny nightlight they had plugged into the baseboard socket.

"Put it on speaker," she groaned. "I want to hear why this lunatic is calling us in the middle of the night."

He complied, then mumbled, "Hello, Dad."

"What the hell took you so long to answer?" Arthur snapped. "It must have rung ten times. What's going on there?"

"It's five in the morning, Dad. We were asleep."

"Oh, right, the time thing. It's eight out here. I figured you'd be up by eight. What's the difference—forget about it. Listen. I changed my plans."

"What do mean you changed your plans?" William asked.

"These idiots from the moving van company didn't tell me that the truck has two drivers and a sleep compartment. They never stop the damn thing. Well, maybe a couple of minutes here and there to go to the bathroom and pick up some sandwiches. But for *my* damn car,

I got one scrawny kid driving me. We can't keep up with the damn moving van. Jesus! I need to stop for decent meals and a goddamn night's sleep."

Rosemary rolled her eyes.

William grinned but suppressed a laugh. "So why don't you fly?"

"I don't like the way they treat me. Airlines used to have some class. Now they're a bunch of goddamn cattle cars."

"You could fly first class . . ."

"What—you don't think I thought of that? First class and business class are booked up for weeks. It's a goddamn racket they're running. I'm not gonna be part of that bullshit."

"So when will you be here?"

"I'll get there when I get there. A week or two, maybe. But the moving van is going to be there this weekend."

"So you want *us* to decide where to put everything?"

"It's not rocket science, for God's sakes. Put the stuff marked "living room" in the living room. Put the stuff marked "dining room" in the dining room. Anything marked "Arthur's bedroom" goes in the big master bedroom. That's where *I'll* sleep—don't even think of sleeping in there. Anything labeled "Bertram's bedroom"—put that in one of the guest rooms, or, if you want it for yourself, put in your own bedroom; it's probably better than the junk you have in your bedroom now, anyway."

Rosemary scowled and stared at the ceiling.

"Okay, we can do that," William said. "But Rosemary and I already have some of our own stuff in the living room."

"Move that secondhand shit out. Have the movers put it in one of the guest rooms if you want to keep it. I don't want your cheap crap in my living room."

Rosemary grabbed William's pillow and shoved it against her face to mute the screaming epithets she was hurling in the direction of Arthur's disembodied voice. When her head reemerged, her face was bright crimson and her bottom teeth were jutting forward, giving her a menacing, lupine look.

"Don't worry, Dad, we'll take care of it," William assured his father. "Rosemary has wonderful fashion sense, she'll figure out where things need to go. She's happy to work with you on this." He grinned at Rosemary and his chest and shoulders oscillated slightly—the hint of a silent chuckle.

Rosemary cocked her head and raised her eyebrows sardonically, conveying to William, in no uncertain terms, that the gloating he was displaying over his tidbit of ironic humor was not impressing her.

"All right, I gotta go," Arthur snarled. "I hope I can find some half-decent hotels in these godforsaken hick towns we're gonna stop in. Jesus only knows what kind of low-lifes have slept in those beds."

Before William hung up, Arthur sent one last proclamation over the air waves: "And don't fuck it up with the movers!"

The Sonoma house was beginning to feel a bit less like an austere castle.

Arthur's furniture had been set down in the appropriate rooms by the movers, but Rosemary had then insisted that William help her resituate the pieces multiple times in the ensuing days, until she felt the layout was exactly right. She had chosen the precise spots for William to hang the paintings Arthur had shipped, and had William position Arthur's many small statues and knickknacks as her eye dictated—from their appearance, she surmised that William's mother had probably bought most of them, and they'd remained in the Scarsdale house after she'd passed away.

The kitchen was now stocked with an amazing array of cooking equipment, which Arthur owned but which Bert had clearly selected and utilized over the course of many years before he moved out. The pots and pans were gorgeous, gleaming specimens—each with a core of heat-conductive copper sandwiched between immaculate layers of stainless steel. Rosemary found them irresistible. She began using them the moment they arrived and had so far produced a week's worth of utterly delectable feasts.

With furniture now in so many rooms, Molly had myriad surfaces upon which to climb, and countless nooks and corners in which to relish solitude. William and Rosemary rarely saw her. The food they put out got consumed and the two litter boxes in the house filled up, but Molly was rarely spotted in conjunction with either.

Rosemary arrived home from work that evening a bit later than expected. She found William in his enormous art studio, which was now fully appointed. The painting he'd been working on was finished, and he was standing across the room, gazing at his creation.

It was that same large painting he'd sketched the beginnings of in San Francisco. Its surreal demeanor had distressed him then. But to Rosemary the sketch was so striking, she'd insisted that he complete it.

"Wow—it's fantastic, honey!" she exclaimed the moment she entered the room. "*Super* fantastic! I think this is the best thing you've ever painted!"

William smiled and stared at his work. "Thanks, babe. I have to admit, I really like it too. Now that I've gotten used to it." He turned back to Rosemary. "When did you get home? I never hear you come in anymore."

Rosemary chuckled. "This house is so big, you can't hear things from one part to another. But this painting! Wow! I mean, what did it feel like, painting this?"

"Honestly? It was fascinating, but kind of frightening at the same time."

"Frightening?"

"Yeah. Well, you remember—the sketch was weird, you know, kind of surreal. So when I started the actual painting, I wasn't really sure how to go about it. So I just tried to do what I always do. But it didn't come out that way. I mean, every time I stepped back to get some perspective on how it was going, it just blew me away. I thought I was blending colors the same as always, but . . . you know how the lines of the sketch kinda went their own way? Well, the colors really did the same thing too. Like they had a life of their own. Look at it, babe. This isn't how I paint. But I guess it's how I paint *now*."

Rosemary studied the canvas. William's color blending had become jagged and arresting. Surfaces melted into each other and overflowed onto whatever was next to them. It was vibrant and exciting—even a bit unnerving. She was transfixed.

"I have absolutely no idea how it's happening," he said. "But the more I paint, the less it scares me."

"It's just beautiful, honey. Keep it up. You can sell paintings like this—I mean, *really*. Maybe for a lot."

"The reason for it, though . . ." William mused aloud. "It's like everything I've always done just suddenly morphed into something so different. I've been trying to figure out *why* this is happening, and I just don't know." He looked upward and took a breath. "I think I may finally have a clue, though."

"Yeah?"

"I think it has something to do with our move here to Sonoma, like you've been saying. Everything's so different now. You and me especially—we've clicked again. It's so great. And even with my father; it's like we're going to be trying to rekindle that relationship too. Of course, we'll have to see what happens when he finally gets out here—you know, whether it works or not. But I think it's like a grand new beginning—and it's freed up something inside me. It was probably always there, but it couldn't come out till now. I think that has to be it. I mean, what other explanation could there possibly be?"

"I think you're right, honey. And I love it." Rosemary trotted over to him and kissed him passionately. When they drew apart again, she said, "I have so much to tell you about work, but I want to put something up for dinner first. God, I love those pots and pans Arthur shipped out. You know, after a day like today at the office, if we were still back in San Francisco, I wouldn't feel like cooking at all. But up here, with the new kitchen, I'm up for making a little something."

"That's great, babe. I'm looking forward to it."

"Are you done here? I was thinking maybe you could mix us a couple of martinis and sit with me in the kitchen while I cook."

"That sounds great," he said. "Let me just put away a couple of things and I'll be right in."

By the time William got to the kitchen, Rosemary had a line of ingredients laid out on the counter: a big purple eggplant, a couple of small yellow onions, a few garlic cloves, the cup or so of white wine left in the bottle they'd had with dinner the previous night, a can of San Marzano tomatoes, and various herbs and spices.

Olive oil was heating in a skillet. A big pot of water with a pasta sleeve inside it sat on the opposite burner over a low flame.

Rosemary was rummaging through the vegetable bin in the enormous refrigerator that came with the house.

"I think a simple salad tonight," she said, seemingly to herself but with the clear intent of drawing William in. "Some nice Bibb lettuce with a balsamic vinaigrette? Maybe crumbles of goat cheese? How about on top a few toasted pine nuts, and some chopped Kalamata olives?"

"Sounds great," William said distractedly as he stood right next to her, focused on the ice dispenser built into the tall door on the freezer side of the unit. The first couple of times he'd fiddled with it, ice had sprayed onto the floor and a couple of pieces had even hit him in the groin, so his approach now was cautious and deliberate.

To his relief, he successfully filled his large aluminum shaker to the brim without spilling a cube. He loaded some of the ice into the two martini glasses he had set down next to the sink, and added water to help the glasses chill. Then he came back to the ice dispenser to top off the shaker; his second attempt went as flawlessly as the first.

Rosemary had moved back to the stove, where onion slices were already sautéing. William noticed the eggplant was gone from the counter too—he glimpsed the two long halves face down on an oiled baking sheet Rosemary was just now slipping into the oven. She had a mitt on, so she must have preheated the oven before he came in.

William filled the shaker with gin and added a splash of dry vermouth. He made sure the cover was wedged on tight, and waited until Rosemary looked in his direction before starting to shake. To make the visual a bit more entertaining for her, he held the shaker high and accompanied its vigorous agitation with what he thought were deft hip rotations.

She laughed and then, raising her voice just a bit to be heard over the rattling of the ice, said, "I'm just going to throw together a quick pasta—kind of my take on pasta alla Norma. You know, roasted eggplant and a light tomato sauce."

"Sounds great," William said as he put the shaker back down on the counter. "I think the pasta's out in the pantry. You want me to grab a package? What do you want? Rigatoni? Ziti?"

"No," she said. "I'm in the mood for something long." She glanced at William's crotch, giggled, and looked him in the eyes. "Well, we'll have that too, but later. For now, I was thinking like spaghetti or linguini? I know we have one or the other in there."

When William got back with the package of pasta, he didn't pour the martinis just yet. Rosemary preferred to let them to sit on the ice for at least three or four minutes, and then be shaken again. She felt the small amount of ice that melted into the drink smoothed out the gin's rough edges.

While he waited, William emptied the glasses of their ice baths, and grabbed a jar of pimento-stuffed green olives from the refrigerator.

The onions had grown translucent and sweetly redolent. Rosemary added minced garlic to the pan and stirred it with a few pinches of herbs. She glanced over at William, who was fishing olives out of the jar and plopping them into the empty martini glasses.

"Oh, honey," she said, her eyes suddenly wide, her lips curling into a broad smile, "I have a great idea. Pluck those pimento pieces out of the olives. I have goat cheese out on the counter for the salad. Why don't you stuff the olives with a little of that instead? It'll make the drinks really special."

William fetched a couple of toothpicks and began plowing through the painstaking olive-innards-transplantation process. As Rosemary started to talk about her day at the office, he looked up.

"Oh, sorry, babe, I want to hear all about your day at work, but I forgot—Arthur called a few hours ago, and I wanted to give you the update first. You won't believe this. He's still in Nebraska. But he says he'll be back on the road soon."

"Still in Nebraska? He was there when he called a week ago!

I thought he'd be here by now for sure. Why the hell is he still in Nebraska?"

William erupted in laughter, which caused him to push a dollop of goat cheese too hard—he watched as his finger split the olive in two. He popped the disarticulated pieces into his mouth, grabbed an intact replacement from the jar, and continued his tale amid guffaws and more cheese-cramming—"Yeah, well, he decided that he didn't like being in the car more than five hours a day."

"Five hours a day!" Rosemary exclaimed. "It'll take him forever to get across the country that way."

"Exactly. And that didn't sit well at all with the guy he hired as his driver. I mean, the poor kid had negotiated a fixed price for the job, and he needed to be back to New York for another gig. So they fought for a few days, then Arthur finally agreed to pay him off and they parted ways somewhere in Nebraska. My father said it took him nearly a week to find a new driver and negotiate an agreement, and then another couple of days before the guy was ready to start. So he's still four or five days out. Maybe more."

"*Wow* is all I have to say to that," Rosemary sputtered, laughing uproariously along with William. When she was done, she leaned over and sniffed the mélange sautéing atop the stove. The onions and garlic were just beginning to caramelize. She poured in the white wine that was left in the bottle, and stirred and scraped to deglaze. Then she raised the flame as high as it would go to begin reducing the liquid.

"All right," William said, "enough about my father, the lunatic. We'll have more of him than we can stand in a week or so. Tell me about your day at work—you're just starting your second week, so you must have a pretty good feel for it now."

"You know, honey, I've really been thinking a lot about this new job. I can't believe how much more I like working at this dental office than I did the one down in San Francisco."

"What do you like about it?" William asked as he grabbed the shaker for a final jiggle and pour.

"The dentist up here was a hygienist herself for years before she went back to school for her DDS, so she knows what I do, and how hard it is."

"That's really nice." William handed Rosemary her martini. They clinked glasses and each took a sip.

"Oh! Good job, honey," Rosemary purred. "You're learning!"

"To us, babe," William said. "So . . . are you getting along with the other people there?"

"I think really well," Rosemary said, as she lowered the flame on the pan and added a few of the canned plum tomatoes, squeezing each one into a mushy mass before carefully setting it into the liquid, which had by now reduced down to a syrup. "You know, my first week went so well—I think people saw right away that I'm good at what I do. It's like a family. I felt a part of it after just a few days. You know what's interesting: it's a small office, just four people—the dentist, me, the dental assistant, and the receptionist—and we're all female. The whole vibe there is so much more welcoming and supportive than the San Francisco office's was—you know I spent years down there and it still seemed sort of cold and sterile to me. I've never worked for a woman before. I like it."

William was about to say that good and bad bosses came in both genders—and was about to cite Joyce Miller as an example of a bad boss—but he considered for a moment where that conversation might lead, and took a few sips of his martini instead.

"I'll tell you," Rosemary continued, "I feel less tired now after a day of work. It must be psychological and emotional, you know?

Like today, a couple of patients were scheduled for minor procedures and then cleanings to follow, and the procedures both ran long, so I wound up working later than I was supposed to. After a day like that back in San Francisco, I'd just want to get home and veg out on the couch and be pissed off. But here, I'm up for cooking." She stirred her sauce and added another crushed tomato. "Maybe it's this cooking equipment, too. It's fantastic stuff. Super high-end."

"You really did a beautiful job organizing the house," William said as he finished his martini and poured himself another. He walked over and topped off Rosemary's as well. "I was thinking about it; it's kind of funny, I mean, *I'm* the artist, and I can lay out a canvas—but you're so much better at laying out a house."

She walked over and kissed him. "I'd do you right now," she said, "but I'm cooking. Save that thought for after dinner!" She went back to the stove and lowered the flame to simmer. "You know," she said as she stirred the sauce, "classically, pasta alla Norma has the eggplant cubed, but for this one I'm roasting it like I would for baba ghanoush, and I'm going to mash it into the sauce that way. It's my invention."

"Sounds cool, babe."

Rosemary turned the flame up under the pasta water. "Can you get the salad spinner down from the cabinet?" she asked as she started washing the leaves of butter lettuce for the salad.

By the time she finished the salad and dressed it, the martini shaker was empty, as were both their glasses.

"Put the spaghetti in the water and keep an eye on it," she said. "You have to stir it now and then."

William had boiled pasta many times; he knew how to do it. But all he said was, "Sure."

Rosemary put on her oven mitt and slid the eggplant out. Rather than allowing it to sit and cool for a few minutes, she somehow managed to scrape the pulp out of the skins right away (though not without periodically jerking her hands away and screeching "ouch!").

She added the mashed eggplant pulp to the sauce and sprinkled in salt, crushed red chili peppers, and pinches of various spices.

"You put all the seasoning in at the end?" William asked.

"No—every layer's gotten it, you haven't been paying attention. I need to keep you in the kitchen with me more often when I cook!"

When the pasta was al dente, she added it to the sauce and grated in a healthy dose of Pecorino Romano.

Dinner was delicious. They had a second round of martinis instead of wine with the meal and then went directly upstairs to wash up and frolic in bed.

At about three in the afternoon, William took a break from the new canvas he was sketching and wandered into the kitchen to grab a snack. He poured a couple of dozen cashew nuts into a small bowl, and was on his way back to his studio, when he heard the doorbell ring. He assumed it was a package, but when he opened the door he was astonished to see their real estate agent Laurel, with a small suitcase on rollers standing beside her.

He stared at her blankly, his mouth slightly agape.

"Will!" she exclaimed. "So nice to see you again. Let me give you a little hug." She embraced him without waiting for a response, her bulbous bosom engulfing his torso, and he reluctantly reciprocated, his arms wound loosely about her as he struggled to keep his bowl of cashews from spilling.

When she finally withdrew she noticed the nuts in his hand. "Oh! Cashews!" she cried. "I love them. Do you mind if I have a couple?" She posed it as a question but her fingers were already reaching for the bowl.

"Here"—he handed it to her—"take the whole bowl. I'll get myself another."

"Thanks!" She grabbed it without hesitation and started munching.

"What exactly can I help you with?" William inquired.

"Oh, didn't your dad tell you? He's arriving tonight and he wanted me to be here. We've talked on the phone for, like, hours every day. I'm really excited to see him again. What a trip he had! Do you know about the snafu in Nebraska?"

"Yes, he told us about that," William said. "But we haven't heard from him since."

"Well, we'll all be together again tonight! Isn't it exciting? I better go up and unpack. You just go back to whatever you were doing—I suspect you've been sketching, I see charcoal dust on your fingers. I should have been a detective, right?"

He glanced down at his fingers. "Yes, seems that way."

"No need to worry about me," Laurel assured him, "I'll just head up to the master bedroom; I know exactly where it is—I *found* this house for you, after all!" She giggled a bit at that last observation as she grabbed her suitcase and wheeled it into the house.

William was still too dumbfounded to say much in response—but he did recall the effort it had taken her just to get in and out of her car when they were house-hunting a couple of months ago, so he hesitantly asked, "Would you like me to carry that suitcase upstairs for you?"

"Oh, you're such a dear!" she cried as she let go of her suitcase's handle. She caressed his cheek with her free hand and gave him a light peck on the lips.

William blinked at the unexpected intimacy, then lifted the bag and started climbing the staircase. After he placed the bag in the doorway of the master bedroom, he returned to the top of the stairs and found that Laurel was still only halfway up, her huge body twisting and leaning with each arduous step. Her absurdly large purse dangled precariously from her shoulder; one of her hands gripped the banister tightly; and the other held her bowl of cashews, careful to keep it upright.

She paused briefly and popped a couple of nuts into her mouth. She chewed for a moment, then glanced up at him where he stood on the second-floor landing. "These cashews aren't roasted or salted, are they?"

"No," William said with a faint sigh. "Rosemary buys all her nuts raw."

"Well, we'll fix that!" Laurel said with a chuckle.

A sour surge that could have been adrenaline or stomach acid shot through William's gut, debilitating him momentarily and causing his torso to tighten and lurch forward involuntarily. "Okay, then," he stammered as his posture slowly resumed its habitual slouch, "I guess I'll go back to my sketch now . . . uh . . . if you need anything, just give me a shout."

"All right, dear," she said, breathing heavily. "Thanks so much for your help." She'd finally reached the top of the steps.

William rushed back to his studio, pulled out his cell phone, and began frantically typing a text message to Rosemary. In it, he laid out exactly what had just transpired, vigilant to include every detail. He realized that she probably wouldn't see the message until the top of the hour, when she had a few moments between patients—but he nonetheless felt the need to transmit it without delay.

He took a deep breath, trudged back into the kitchen to fill another bowl with raw cashews, and took the nuts back to his studio, where he tried to resume work on his sketch—but he was now too preoccupied to focus.

At exactly four, his cell phone beeped.

The response from Rosemary was a text comprised solely of one emoji—a face with its eyes rolling upward and to the left, its mouth twisted into a writhing, asymmetric scowl.

Rosemary pulled the van into the driveway around five thirty. She sat motionless in the driver's seat for a couple of minutes before exiting, trying desperately to gird herself for the incessant chatter and intrusive energy she knew awaited her inside the house.

She turned the tumbler in the deadbolt deliberately, and then slowly opened the front door. She glimpsed Laurel immediately, sitting on a couch in the living room, reading a book, and sipping on a glass of red wine.

As soon as Rosemary shut the door, Laurel turned her head and their eyes made contact.

"Rosemary!" she cried. "Oh, hi, sweetheart. It's so nice to see you again!"

Discerning no alternative, Rosemary traipsed into the living room and leaned down slightly to affect something resembling an unenthusiastic hug. It was clear to her that Laurel had no intention of rising to greet her.

She sat down in an easy chair across the room.

"Oh my god!" Laurel exclaimed with rousing enthusiasm. "I've been walking all over the house—I just love what you've done with it, honey. The way you've laid out Arthur's furniture, and the placement of the paintings and all . . . It's just beautiful. The place looks so homey. It's really just gorgeous. William assured me it was all your doing."

Rosemary felt her body relax a bit, and she couldn't suppress the sheepish grin that crawled across her features. "Well, thanks!" she said. "I really like it too."

William had heard their voices while working in his studio, and he now entered the living room from the opposite direction, rubbing charcoal off his fingers with a yellow rag, and ambled over to where Rosemary sat. He put a hand on her shoulder as he hinged his knees to give her a quick kiss on the forehead, then glanced over toward Laurel and proclaimed, "She really does have a great eye for home decorating."

There was a brief, awkward silence, but Laurel's voice quickly permeated the void. "I've been talking to Arthur for hours every day," she reiterated. "I know he's so excited to finally get here. The house looks really beautiful, but I haven't been out to the little cottage— that's going to be his office, isn't it? Is it all furnished and decorated like in here?"

"Oh yes," Rosemary assured her. "We put everything from his office in Scarsdale in there. I think I arranged it in a way he'll find very comfortable. He has this old-fashioned mahogany computer desk—a big, beautiful thing, you know, L-shaped—with a huge leather chair that swivels from the computer over to a big, long credenza for writing and documents. And it has a ton of drawer space. I made that the center of the setup—I figured that's where he'll spend most of his time."

"It sounds like you got that exactly right!" Laurel said. "He was complaining to me how some of the motels they stayed in along the way had lousy Wi-Fi—it kills him if he can't get online and look at those stocks he's always investing in."

"It's kind of remarkable how well he's done with that," William said. "I mean, he's completely self-taught."

"And he sure as hell won't take advice from anyone," Rosemary added snippily.

William started laughing, which prompted Rosemary to join him. Laurel smiled politely.

The doorbell rang.

Rosemary answered the bell, with William close behind her. In the doorway stood Arthur—his face exhibiting no discernable expression. Alongside him was his driver, a burly African American man who appeared to be in his late forties.

"Hello! Welcome!" Rosemary shouted, her mouth wide and smiling. She stepped toward Arthur, as if to initiate a warm hug, but when Arthur stepped backward, she quickly aborted the attempt.

William knew better. He accepted Arthur's quick, perfunctory handshake.

Laurel finally reached the doorway. She laid a hand lightly on Rosemary's left shoulder and another on William's right, and gently pushed the two apart to carve a quick path to Arthur.

Her hug with him was passionate and prolonged.

"I'll go grab the suitcases," the driver mumbled.

"I'll help you with that," William offered.

Arthur disengaged from Laurel as the two men returned with his bags. "Rosemary," he barked, "show this guy where the master bedroom is."

"No need," William interjected quickly as he watched Rosemary start to seethe. "I have one of the suitcases—I'll go up there with him." Moving deftly around the driver and taking the lead, he added, "I'll make sure the bags get where they need to be."

"The master bedroom!" Arthur bellowed. "Make sure they get in *there*. Nowhere else."

William and the driver climbed the steps and deposited the suitcases alongside the walk-in closet in the master bedroom.

"Are you his son?" the driver whispered.

"Yeah, I am," William whispered in response. "And I'm sure he was a handful on the road. I'm sorry if he put you through a bunch of shit."

The driver smiled. "He sure as hell did. And on top of that, he's a damn racist. You know that, right?"

"I know it," William said dejectedly. "I'm really sorry." He paused and grinned. "If it's any consolation—you should know he's just as fucking nasty to me and my wife as he was to you."

The driver laughed and extended his hand. William reciprocated with a firm, warm handshake.

"You're all right with me!" the driver announced. He was still laughing as he added, "Good luck, man. You're sure as hell gonna need it."

When William got back inside from seeing the driver out, things were not going well. Arthur was gesticulating angrily, and Rosemary, uncharacteristically silent, looked furious.

"I don't like the way this is sitting here," Arthur groused, pointing at the living room sofa. "And these pictures are hung all wrong. That's not the way I had 'em." He glanced around. "And the loveseat, and the easy chair. Jesus! I'm going to need rearrange everything. This layout you got here is a bunch of crap."

Rosemary's features tightened even further, and her face morphed slowly from its normal pale hue to a bright crimson. Finally, she exploded.

"I worked hard on this! Really hard! Give it a goddamn chance before you come in here like a crazy man and undo everything I worked so hard on!"

"You can't talk to me like that!" Arthur shot back. "Who the hell do you think you are? This is *my* goddamn house. I'll throw you the hell out if you talk to me like that. This place looks like shit."

To William's great surprise, Laurel—using a gentle yet authoritative tone he had not heard her employ before—chimed in. "Arthur," she said, "I think the house looks beautiful. And I do houses for a living. I believe Rosemary's absolutely right. You need to give it a chance, honey. It's gorgeous. I'm quite sure it'll grow on you if you give it a chance."

Arthur said nothing but his shoulders went limp, his eyelids drooped, and his jaw slackened. "Oh, what the hell," he muttered. "All right . . . Jesus . . . Everybody makes such a big deal out of everything. I'll try to get used to it."

Rosemary shot William a quick glance. He recognized it immediately—that nearly imperceptible, momentary smirk she flashed when feeling victorious.

Laurel took a step toward Arthur and touched his shoulder. "And *you*, Arthur Wozniak, why don't you go upstairs to the bathroom and freshen up, then get your ass back down here and take us all to dinner. I made a reservation at the steakhouse in Petaluma. We'll get there early and have cocktails. Their bar is pure redwood—a lovely antique piece with a brass top. You'll love it."

Arthur dutifully complied.

CHAPTER 14

W/HEN his cell phone rang, Bert was on the living room couch, wallowing in a morose stupor.

He'd acquired a bevy of new personal-chef clients—all conscripted by Dag, who'd cajoled and coerced some of his brokerage customers, as well as a number of ardent Rotarians, to give his services a try. Bert had not asked him to do this, and although the gigs produced income, none of them were the type of people Bert especially wanted to work with. He resented Dag's having foisted these clients upon him, leaving him no way to extricate himself from the commitments.

But his mood perked up immediately when he saw that the call on his cell phone was from Gina.

"Gina!" he exclaimed. "Hi! I haven't heard from you in a while. I thought maybe you'd given up on me."

"On *you*, sweetie? No way! Didn't I tell you? We were on vacation for a few weeks."

"Oh, that's nice. Where did you go?"

"The Bahamas."

"Wow, the Bahamas—that's cool." An image of Gina in a bikini, sipping on a piña colada, popped into his mind. "Well," he said, laughing, "I guess you've had your fill of rum drinks for a while! I'll have to come up with something else for you."

Gina chuckled. "You're right about that. But you make the best cocktails, sweetie—and I love the way you match them to the cuisine. My husband and I are still talking about those margaritas you blended up for us when you cooked Mexican. The best we've ever had."

"Thanks, Gina. That was the last time I was at your place, right? That must have been nearly a month ago."

"Well, we just got back, and we were hoping you could cook for us tomorrow night."

"Tomorrow night? Sure. I'm open. I'd love to. What kind of food are you up for?"

"How about something French, but kind of earthy? You've never cooked French for us, sweetie. Do you do French?"

"Oh, I can whip you up a French country pot pie to die for. I'll build a whole menu around it for you. It'll be fun!"

"Wonderful! What kind of cocktails go with a country pot pie?"

Bert pondered that for a moment. "Do you like sidecars?"

Gina's started giggling. "Sidecars? Aren't they, like, frumpy old things from, like, ancient Humphrey Bogart movies? Does anybody really drink those things anymore?"

That made Bert laugh, and he had to catch his breath before responding. "Actually, they're very good. And they're even better if you don't mind springing for some good French Cognac and a bottle of Cointreau."

"Great! Let's do it, sweetie. Get the high-end stuff. See you tomorrow night."

A sense of renewed vigor infused Bert's spirit the moment he hung up the phone. Soon he was sitting cross-legged on the rug—furiously penning menu ideas into his notebook, open cookbooks strewn around him on the floor.

Bert was still at it a couple of hours later when Dag entered through the front door.

Bert looked up from where he sat. "Hey," he said excitedly. "I'm putting together a menu for a gig tomorrow night."

Dag smiled as he set his briefcase down. "Who's it with?"

"It's Gina and her husband. I was afraid that maybe they weren't using me anymore, or maybe they went back to Miguel. But it turns out they were on vacation. And they're back now. So that's great."

"Well, you have other clients too now, Bertie—thanks to me. So even if you lost Gina, you'd still be doing fine."

Bert thought a moment about whether he should respond. He opted not to. He rose up off the floor and started to walk into the kitchen to make cocktails. But then he stopped and turned back to look at Dag. He couldn't restrain himself. "You know," he said hesitantly, "I appreciate the clients you've drummed up for me. I really do. It's just that . . . I like cooking for Gina because it's more inventive. I mean, they trust me to concoct all sorts of menus for them. That's fun for me—you know, creative. The clients you got me pretty much want steak or roasts and potatoes . . . you know, salad, bread, a green vegetable. That's fine . . . but . . . it can get boring."

Dag's features tightened. "That's called *work*, Bertie," he said, his voice suddenly high-pitched and a bit quivery. "For God's sake, don't you get it? Work! It's not *supposed* to be fun. Do you think everything I do with people's investments is fun? No! But that's my job. You have a job now. You're not living off your father anymore. And—for your own self-respect—you really shouldn't be living off me either. So work is important. You need to embrace that. It's work—not fun."

"Okay, I'm sorry I said it," Bert acquiesced—more because he didn't feel like fighting than because he thought Dag was right. "Let me make us a couple of cocktails and whip up something for dinner." He moved closer to Dag. "Please, honey . . . forget what I said . . . I shouldn't have opened my mouth."

He gave Dag a quick kiss before turning back and heading toward the kitchen.

Gina's husband was not yet home from work.

Bert had arrived a bit earlier than usual. He wanted to get the pot pie and the soup going, ensuring that the courses would flow gracefully throughout the evening.

Gina insisted that he join her in a cocktail to start—and then he could sip while he cooked.

"Actually, that's a great idea," Bert said, "because I wanted to make two versions of the sidecar for you to taste. You can have the one you like better—I'll have the other."

Gina fluttered her eyelashes at him. "You're such a sweetie."

"Both France and Great Britain claim they invented the sidecar— Paris and London, to be exact," he expounded as he started unloading his cocktail paraphernalia. He put a couple of cocktail glasses into the freezer to chill. "But the best version is made with Cognac, which is French—so I think we're on solid ground having it tonight."

"Just Cognac? You mean there's no actual liquor in it?" Gina asked, appearing a bit disappointed.

"Well . . . there's Cognac," Bert stammered.

"Isn't that wine?"

"Ah!" he exclaimed, smiling. "I see what you mean. Cognac starts its young life out as wine, yes. But then it's distilled, just like whiskey. It's forty proof by the time it's done."

"Oh, goody!" Gina purred.

"So, classically, a sidecar is just three ingredients," Bert said, as he ladled a couple of teaspoons of Demerara sugar into a cup and added a small amount of water. "Two parts Cognac to about one part Cointreau and one part or a little less lemon juice." He put the cup in the microwave and set it for one minute. "But these days, a lot of people prefer it with just a splash of simple syrup added. So I'm going to make it both ways for you. See which one you like."

When Bert removed the simple syrup from the microwave a minute later, the crystals had dissolved and the liquid glistened. He put it in the refrigerator to cool a bit. "I made the syrup with Demerara sugar," he told Gina. "That's high-end stuff. It's sweet like regular sugar, but also has just a hint of caramel or toffee. Not many people use it, but it's really great for this cocktail."

"You should have a cooking show on TV, sweetie."

Bert had brought two cocktail shakers with him. He made the sweeter version in one and the classic version in the other. Gina tasted both.

"Oh!" she cried, "this one, absolutely!"

As Bert suspected, she liked the sweeter version. He was happy to sip on the other. They clinked glasses, then he went to work on the dinner while she went into the living room and called a friend. Bert heard them chatting about clothing and shoes as he started sorting out the ingredients he'd brought with him.

He was cheating, just slightly, on two items. He needed puff pastry for the pie—but concocting puff pastry from scratch was a grueling and time-consuming ordeal, so he'd bought a very good frozen version that he'd used before with good results. He'd also brought a jar of beef stock from his refrigerator at home—he'd made it a few days earlier for a dinner with Dag—that would serve well as the base for the French onion soup.

As was his habit, he laid the ingredients out on the long counter, divided in groups representing each of the courses. A few things, like onions and garlic, would be in more than one dish; those he put at the very front, so he could prep them first and use them as needed. Once everything was laid out as he wanted it, he got to work.

Gina brought her husband into the kitchen when he arrived home. Bert started explaining about the two versions of the sidecar, but she stopped him abruptly.

"He'll have it the way I'm having it," she said with a regal inflection Bert had never heard her employ.

"Sure," Bert said, and poured the man's cocktail into a chilled glass.

"All right, come along now." Gina tugged her husband back out into the living room.

Bert prepared another round of drinks, and served them with an appetizer of lightly steamed asparagus drizzled with melted butter, salt, pepper, and a hint of fresh lemon juice.

He'd bought a thin, small French baguette, most of which he planned to put on the table with a tub of softened butter just prior to the soup course. But he took four slices now, toasted them, and converted them into large, buttery Gruyere croutons. Then he served the dark, rich soup, redolent with the aroma of caramelized onion, in small porcelain bowls, each topped with two of the large croutons wedged tightly together.

Bert asked if they'd like him to open a bottle of wine to accompany the main course, but as he suspected, they opted for a fourth round of the sidecars.

He brought the savory French country pie to the table in individual porcelain bowls—larger matching versions of those he'd used for the soup. Gina's eyes widened, and she smiled excitedly as her fork cracked through the puff pastry that sealed the top. She was greeted with chicken, melted Havarti cheese, potatoes, peas, carrots, onions, and leeks swimming in a thick gravy of chicken stock, heavy cream, and a bouquet of herbs. She inhaled the aromas and savored them before taking her first bite.

"You've outdone yourself, sweetie," she exclaimed after her first mouthful. "This is the best." She glanced at her husband. "Isn't it the best?"

He nodded agreeably but made no sound.

Bert returned to the kitchen to get a head start on cleaning up while they ate.

Both Gina and her husband were quite full after the main course, so Bert waited a while before serving the small canisters of chilled crème brûlée and coffee he'd prepared for dessert.

At the table, he affected an exaggerated flourish as he browned the tops of the desserts with his small blowtorch.

He really was pretty good at this.

Bert noticed that his fingers were trembling slightly as he punched in Miguel's number. It was early enough to catch him before dinner prep started at the restaurant—he just hoped he would pick up.

"Hello."

It was indeed Miguel's voice. The intonation was curt, cold, perhaps even angry. But at least he'd answered.

"Hey, Miguel, thanks for taking my call. I appreciate it."

"What do you want, man?"

"Listen, I'm so, so sorry about how things went down with us. It still really bothers me." Bert paused for an instant, gathered himself, and continued, "I, um, I've been doing the personal chef thing. It's been going okay. Anyway, I, um, I got double-booked. Stupid thing on my part. It's next Thursday. I remembered that you used to be off from the restaurant on Thursdays, and I thought that maybe, uh, I could give you one of the gigs. If you aren't already booked, you know? Kinda like a peace offering."

Miguel's tone grew harsher. "You know what? Go fuck yourself."

Bert moved the cell phone away from his ear to soften the impact.

"I don't need your goddamn handouts, man! Don't call me no more."

The connection terminated.

Dag would be hungry when he got home. The evening eating pattern that had evolved over the past couple of months pointed to that. On those evenings that Bert had a personal chef engagement, Dag grazed extensively at whatever networking function he attended and Bert had a snack before he left for his gig. Then he and Dag shared a light supper when he finally got home, if it wasn't too late. But on nights Bert was not working, he made an elaborate dinner for Dag, who saved his appetite.

He knew Dag would prefer it if he took more gigs and generated more income, but having a private chef in-house a few days a week was a difficult thing to complain about, and he took pains to make sure Dag understood that.

Tonight's meal materialized in Bert's mind as soon as he set foot in the kitchen. He knew that one of Dag's guiltiest pleasures was a dinner that started with a big bowl of Italian meatball soup and ended with a main-course duo of old-fashioned eggplant parmigiana oozing with melted mozzarella cheese alongside a succulent pile of pesto linguini. Dag generally opted for more elegant fare, especially if they were socializing, but that earthy mélange had

been a weekly special at a neighborhood Italian restaurant in Bay
Ridge, Brooklyn, just a block from where Dag had grown up, and
for years his family had savored that very meal together a couple
of times each month.

Bert had always found this fact about Dag endearing—and he
knew he'd appreciate him recreating the meal for him.

He had everything he needed; he dug in.

Bert waited until dinner was nearly finished before he broached the
subject. Dag had, at that point, been cajoled into downing three manhattans and was working on his second glass of Chianti, which had
been the house wine at his boyhood restaurant.

"Dag," Bert stammered, "I have an issue I could use your help on."

"What's that?"

Bert knew that Dag enjoyed offering advice, so he'd try to frame it
that way—at least initially.

"I did a kind of a stupid thing: I somehow got myself double-booked
for a dinner gig next Thursday. I'm going to need to cancel—or at
least move the day—for one of the couples you got me. They're clients
of yours at work—I'm really sorry. I thought maybe you could help
me figure out how to talk to them about it?"

Dag stopped chewing abruptly. His features tightened and his
eyes narrowed. He still had a bit of food in his mouth as he said,
"How the hell did you get double-booked?"

"Like I said, it was a stupid thing. Kind of an oversight."

"Who was booked first?"

"The couple you turned me on to."

"Then you should bump the other people."

"I can't do that. Can you help me out with this?"

"Who's the other couple?"

Bert gazed at Dag and said nothing for a moment. Then he looked down at the table and mumbled, "Gina and her husband."

Dag's eyes widened. He swallowed what was left in his mouth—his lips squeezed into a taut crease—then opened to reveal his teeth. "Oh, your favorite—hot, slutty Gina." His hands rose to form air quotes as his tone grew shrill and sardonic. "Oh, Dag, you know how much I love her creative menus." He stared at Bert silently for a moment, then resumed his tirade. "And now you're suddenly double-booked? By an oversight? It's not a goddamned oversight. You just got this booking and you like cooking for them better, so you're choosing them. That's not right, Bertie! You can't do business that way. How many times have you cooked for these people I got for you?"

"Just once."

"Jesus! They're new. Goddamnit, Bert, you need to woo them for a while to make them regulars. You can't just fuck 'em over like this."

"Look, I know it's awkward. I'm sorry. But it's Gina's anniversary, and they're my best clients. I have to do it. It's a lot more money in the long run. So please, help me with this."

"So now it's on *me*? I have to go through the humiliation of apologizing to my clients on *your* behalf? I recommended you to them, I got you the gig, and now it's *my* reputation you're fucking with—for some slut that calls you *sweetie*. Jesus, Bertie. I'm really disappointed in you." Dag shot up from his chair and marched out of the dining room.

Bert heard him scream "Fucking shit!" just before the door to the master bedroom slammed shut.

Bert sat silently at the table for a while. He didn't eat any more food, but he sipped slowly on the rest of the Chianti in his glass, then poured himself another, which he nursed for nearly half an hour. The trance into which he eventually sank enabled him to clean the kitchen and put away the leftovers with no recollection of having done so. Finally, a bit after eleven, he trudged, zombielike, into the small guest bedroom and began to undress.

His cell phone rang. He had no idea who'd call him so late. He yanked the phone out of his pocket and was astonished to see that the caller was Miguel.

"Hey, Miguel. Hi."

"Hey, man. I wanted to call you back and talk a little more about this."

"Okay. What's up?"

"After my shift, I called my wife. She thinks I should take the gig you offered."

"Oh, man. That would really help me out!"

"Look, I know I'm a hothead—but I was still mad at you for stealing Gina. I told my wife that. She said it wasn't your fault—it was on Gina. I said it wasn't—that you coulda just told Gina 'no.' But my wife said you really couldn't. And she said I woulda done the same thing you did . . . and when I thought about it, I realized I probably would've."

"You're wife's a smart lady."

"Yeah, I know. So, okay, tell me how you got double-booked. Who are you keeping and who are you pawning off on me?"

"Well, as you probably already figured out, the couple I'm going to do the gig with is Gina and her husband."

"Jesus, man!"

"Look, it's their anniversary. They asked me to do a special deal for them. But the other couple—they actually booked first, and Dag is pissed as shit at me for bailing on them, 'cause they're clients of his. Anyway, they'll be easy. They're old meat-and-potatoes people—for them something really special is a lobster tail that you shell for them and serve alongside a steak."

"Surf and turf, huh? Yeah, that's easy. How many times have you cooked for these old geezers?"

"Only once, actually. This would be the second time."

Miguel chuckled. "So maybe they'll like me and *I'll* steal them from *you!*"

Bert laughed too. "That would only be fair. You're welcome to them. Truly. It would make me feel better if it worked out that way. And no ten percent split for me on this one—it's all yours."

"Look man, you and me, we had something pretty good," Miguel said, his voice a bit more relaxed now. "I'm willing to give it another try. I want you to understand, though, this don't mean we're buddy-buddy again—not yet. I'm still a little pissed off. But if things like this come up, we can do business. And maybe, who knows, someday I might invite you back up to the Barrio to cook with me. My wife and my mother-in-law think you're cute—they want to see you again. But it's gonna take me a while to get there. We'll keep it business for now."

"Okay," Bert said. "That's still a lot better than it was. Thank you for taking this gig—I really appreciate it. I'll text you the info."

"All right. Later, man."

"Bye, Miguel."

Bert took a moment to ponder what had just happened, and then he walked across the hallway and knocked on the door of the master bedroom. There was no response.

Bert opened the door anyway.

Dag stared at Bert blankly, saying nothing, when he entered the room.

"Hey," Bert said gently, "I wanted to let you know, I just talked to Miguel. He'll cook for your clients on Thursday. The guy's a professional—he can do surf and turf way better than me anyway. So we don't need to cancel or move your clients. I'll just let them know that Miguel will be coming in my place. It's all fixed."

Dag was completely unresponsive for what seemed like half a minute. He was still seething—still unwilling to acquiesce to a solution.

Finally he blinked, grimaced, and whined, "Why am I busting my balls to get clients for that Puerto Rican hothead? Jesus, Bertie—you can't just give away clients I get for you!"

"I'm sorry," Bert said calmly. "But listen, this was a special situation, and I found a solution. So you don't have to go to your client now and fix things up—I already fixed it. Maybe these people will stay with me, maybe they won't. Can we just accept it and move on? I really don't want to fight anymore."

Dag gazed at the tall, handsome, half-naked man standing in his bedroom doorway. Not for the first time, he realized this wasn't something he should take for granted. He'd pushed enough. "Oh, all right, Bertie. I know you're trying your best, and I do love you. Just come to bed."

Bert walked toward his nightstand. "Hey, listen," he added softly, "how about you don't get me any more clients for a while, okay? I'm still learning to juggle what I have. And I'm sure that I'll wind up getting some more clients by word-of-mouth in the next few months, anyway. I appreciate what you've done, but let's slow it down for now. All right?"

Dag sighed, but he was too exhausted to engage. "Okay, honey," he whispered. "Come to bed."

CHAPTER 15

WILLIAM glanced up from the painting on which he'd been working. The wall clock in his studio showed that it was already one in the afternoon. Evidently, another artistic reverie had engulfed him—when he'd last checked the clock, it hadn't yet been ten in the morning.

He hastily put down his brush, wiped his hands with a rag, and scurried out to the small cottage next to the house. As he entered, he braced himself for an especially rude and cranky encounter. Arthur preferred his lunch at precisely twelve noon.

Maybe he could mitigate the situation with a preemptive apology.

"Sorry I'm a little late, Dad," he began. "I got caught up in my painting again."

Arthur said nothing. He sat motionless, staring at his computer screen.

"I'm going to heat up something for lunch now," William continued steadfastly. "Rosemary put some leftovers away for us—you know, from the roast we had for dinner last night? You want me to bring some out here for you? Or you can join me in the house if you like."

Arthur remained silent and still. As William waited for a response, he thought about how this little lunch ritual had evolved into something so unvarying during the three weeks since his father arrived.

William would come out to inform him what was for lunch—usually it was leftovers from dinner, but if there were none, Rosemary would have made sandwiches that morning while she prepped her own lunch for the day—and then William would politely invite his father to join him in the house, but Arthur would always opt to dine alone in the cottage. William would then dutifully fix a tray and bring it out to him. An hour or two later, he would come back to collect the remains.

"Come here," Arthur finally mumbled, still staring intently at his computer screen. He hadn't moved his head or made eye contact since William entered the room. "You're an artist. Take a look at this stuff."

Standing behind Arthur's cushy leather chair, William had to crouch a bit to see the screen clearly. Arthur scanned through several web pages of paintings. All of them were nature scenes, a few with an exaggerated illusion of light. Some were dense with naturalistic detail, others a bit more suggestive.

"What do you think of this art?" Arthur asked.

"Well . . . it's inoffensive," William offered, trying to be cautious so as not to provoke his father.

Arthur chuckled. "But it's schlock, right?"

William grinned and stood up. "Yes. I suppose. I can't believe you're thinking of buying some of these. You have better taste than that."

Arthur, laughing softly, swiveled his chair to face his son. "You're damn right I do. No, I'm not buying any of these paintings. I'm investing in the company."

"Really?"

"I just spent over a month of my life staying in god-awful hotel rooms in half the shithole states between here and New York. Every

damn one of 'em had paintings like these. So does every office building I've ever gone into. And every doctor, and dentist. This shit is
everywhere. Precisely because of what you just said. It's inoffensive.
So I found information on this company here. They have a ton of
independent painters who sell work through 'em. Come here. Look
at these profits over the past twelve quarters."

Arthur switched to another computer window, this one with
graphs.

William wasn't able to decipher precisely what he was looking
at. But the general direction of all the graphs was, without a doubt,
steadily upward.

"Well"—William sighed—"I won't argue with you. You're a genius
at this stuff. You put both your sons through college on your profits."
He paused, hoping his father might respond. But Arthur was silent,
his facial expression unmoving—he appeared to be admiring one
graph in particular with palpable self-assurance.

"Do you want to join me in the house for lunch?" William asked
again. "Or I can bring it out here."

"No, I'll come in and eat with you."

For a moment, William stood motionless, too dumbfounded to
respond or even generate a coherent thought. "Oh," he finally peeped.
"That's great, Dad. That's nice. Come on in."

Inside the house, Arthur started veering toward the large dining
room, but William stopped him. "You know, when it's just me for
lunch, I eat at the little table in the kitchen. It's easier—you know, it's
right next to the microwave and the fridge. Do you mind?"

"Fine with me," Arthur said, and followed his son into the kitchen.

The small table in the corner was lightly polished oak. There were
two matching chairs.

William rinsed his hands. From the refrigerator, he dug out the meat, the vegetable mixture topped with mushroom gravy, and the roasted potatoes. He dished them onto a large platter for reheating. "You want a beer?" he asked, still a bit confounded by Arthur's good humor.

"Sure, why the hell not."

William retrieved a couple of bottles of the locally produced Hefeweizen he'd recently discovered at their nearby market, pried off the caps, and set them on the table. Soon, the microwave beeped.

"I love your wife's food," Arthur announced as William dished out two portions. "She's as good as Bert was, and he was a damn good cook—I gotta give him that—even though he turned out to be a faggot."

"Dad, really, you shouldn't use that term," William said, shaking his head. "He's gay."

"Jesus!" Arthur groused. "Our women aren't around, can't we talk like men at least when we're alone? What the hell happened to you? You used to be a normal guy."

"I *am* a normal guy! I guess living in the Bay Area happened to me—I mean, you can't really live here without the whole sense of tolerance and compassion rubbing off on you. It's good shit, actually, Dad. You should give it a shot."

Sudden heaves of laughter caused Arthur to curl his body into a spasming ball. His face turned red and he started coughing, but continued to laugh. William jumped up to slap his father's back and wound up catching him as he nearly toppled off his chair.

As he set his father upright, William found himself joining him in uncontrollable guffaws.

"What the hell's gotten into you?" William sputtered.

"Jesus Christ, son!" Arthur wheezed, still convulsing with laughter.

"What the hell do you think—that you're going to change me at *this* age? I'm a cranky old bastard! And I'm damn well gonna stay this way."

"Well, I thought it was worth a shot. Hell, if I don't, between Laurel and Rosemary somebody's gonna get to you!"

"Let 'em try. I don't like their chances!" Arthur composed himself sufficiently to stuff his mouth with a thick piece of meat and a couple of small roasted red potatoes. "Damn!" he proclaimed while chewing manically. "This food is so good. I'm gonna gain a ton of weight here!"

William got up to grab a bottle of ketchup for his potatoes. Rosemary invariably grew incensed if he even *looked* at a bottle of ketchup when she served her potatoes hot out of the oven—but these were leftovers, and she was safely at work.

"You have paint all over your hands," Arthur observed when William sat back down. "How the hell can you eat like that?"

"Believe me, Dad, I wash my hands before I eat. The paint only comes off if I use turpentine or thinner, and I don't like to do that until I quit for the day."

"What the hell are you painting these days, anyway? I hope it's better than those paintings you showed me years ago. You remember—you wanted me to buy some and hang 'em in my office?"

William winced. "I remember. You told me they were shit. '*Shit!*' That was the exact word you used."

"Well, they were! Jesus—sugarcoating things doesn't help a kid grow up or improve."

"I was already grown up. And you could have used a kinder word."

"Well, is your stuff any better now? I sure as hell hope so."

"Interesting you should ask," William replied cautiously. "Just in the last few months my painting style has changed. Drastically. I mean, *super* drastically. It looks completely different. And it kind of

just flows now. It's um . . . oh . . . god . . . I can't conjure up the word .
. . the kind of stuff Dalí painted . . ."

"Surreal?"

"Yeah, that's it, surreal. It just comes out. Spontaneously. I produce
so many more paintings now than I used to. I'm goddamned prolific.
I'm about ready to find a flea market to start trying to sell some of
this new crop. I got a shit-ton of paintings in this new style now."

"So, you really think they're good?" Arthur seemed genuinely
interested.

"Well, Rosemary thinks so, and she's always been tough on me.
Not as tough as you, of course."

They both chuckled.

"Anybody else think they're good?"

"Well, your girlfriend," William said. "Um . . . oh Jesus . . . um . . .
I'm sorry, Dad, I forgot her name now . . ."

"Laurel? She's here every goddamned night. How the hell can you
forget her name?"

"I don't know. I'm really sorry. I'm forgetting words lately. I think
because I'm falling into these painting trances and everything else
leaves my head. Anyway, she likes them too."

"All right," Arthur said, "when we're finished eating, let me take a
look at some of 'em. I have a pretty good eye for art, you know."

After lunch, the two men walked together into William's studio.

"It's kind of weird," William said, "you've lived here now for nearly
a month and this is the first time you've been in this room."

Arthur's face froze—eyes wide and mouth agape—as he scanned
the paintings around the room. He turned in a slow circle, taking
them all in, and then did two more turns, deliberately and silently.

"Jesus Christ, these are terrific!" he finally cried. "When the fuck did you learn to paint like this?" He looked William in the eye. "For God's sake, don't waste your time on some shithole flea market, son. You can get real money for these."

"You think?"

"Take some pictures of 'em and email 'em to me. I know a couple guys in New York—art dealers, I used to buy paintings from 'em once in a while. They'll tell me how much these can sell for. I mean it. Get me the photos today. There's fucking money here."

For the past few months, each day Dag spent at the office had been identical to the last—a loitering muddle of boredom and frustration. Though he'd certainly been losing clients to online do-it-yourself trading sites for the past number of years, he'd been able to keep up his numbers by relentlessly corralling new clients to replace the ones he'd lost. But that equilibrium was proving harder to maintain, and to make things worse, many of the new clients he'd garnered were steady, cautious types: they held what they had and rarely traded shares.

Although this had become terribly worrisome, Dag had not mentioned anything about it to Bert. He insisted to himself it was to spare Bert from needless concern—but he knew full well it was because he feared he'd lose face in Bert's eyes if he admitted that business wasn't good, and that Bert would be less likely to stay with him if financial security was not part of the package.

He decided to craft an email targeting a list of clients he hadn't heard from in at least six months. He was going over and over the wording—a frank reminder that fluctuating market conditions necessitated revisiting their portfolios, along with a recommendation that they contact him to explore rebalancing for better growth and protection from catastrophic loss. He wanted to get the tone exactly right—something that would instill sufficient fear to motivate taking action, balanced with a hint of the exuberance inherent in new opportunity.

As he was finalizing the note, a call came in. From the phone's readout, Dag could see it was Mason Reinbart, one of his wealthiest clients. His portfolio with Dag was quite substantial. His mood perked up.

"Mason, good to hear from you," Dag declared, his enthusiasm impeccably professional. "How have you been?"

"Very well, very well, Dag. How about yourself?"

"Oh, I can't complain, Mason. Life is good. What can I do for you today?"

"I want to sell a few shares—you can tell me best where from. I need some money to buy a couple of paintings; the cost is more than I usually keep in my checking account."

"Art, eh? Well, I know you're a collector, Mason. If you're buying for the love of it, that's fine. But if you're looking at this as an investment, I have to advise you—the stock market inevitably outperforms art over time, unless you're a genius at assessing new artists."

"Well, I think in this case it's a bit of both. It's this new artist out in California. Amazing stuff. It's creating a real buzz among us collectors. You need to look at this stuff, Dag. You haven't seen anything quite like it. How does one describe it? It's surreal—exalted, baroque comic-book frames on LSD. God, I'm not doing justice to it. Are you near a computer?"

"Sure, right here."

"I'll email you a link. You can bring up the online gallery where he's showing—it's an exclusive gallery for collectors. Who knows—you might want to buy some of his work yourself. It's damn exciting to see a new American artist burst onto the scene like this."

Dag stormed into the house just a few minutes after five.

Bert was bewildered and unnerved. He hadn't expected him home till eight or so, after his networking event concluded.

Bert had managed to wrangle only one professional chef engagement so far this week, and just two the week before. He knew Dag was growing angry and impatient with his slow progress, so he'd planned an extravagant Friday night dinner with exotic cocktails and an elaborate Greek theme. He'd planned to dress in a suit and ask Dag to keep his on, and serve kolokithokeftedes—pan-fried Greek zucchini fritters—with the cocktails.

But Dag's appearing nearly three hours early threw everything into shambles. Bert was still dressed in sweats. The zucchini for the fritters had not yet been grated. The chicken for the avgolemono soup sat raw on a plate. And the ingredients for the lamb dinner to follow hadn't even left the refrigerator.

Perhaps most critically, cocktails were not made.

But Dag didn't appear to care about any of that.

"Bertie!" he cried, his voice high-pitched, his body language frenetic. "Bertie, you gotta see this!" He grabbed Bert's arm with a frenzied urgency and dragged him to the computer in the small room off the kitchen they used as an office.

Dag's fingers were slamming upon the keyboard so frantically that he repeatedly hit the wrong keys and had to delete and start again. Instead of causing him to slow down, these mishits just provoked him to attack the keys more ferociously.

The site that finally materialized was that of an exclusive online art gallery. To Bert's amazement, the first page of the showing featured a large photograph of his older brother, along with a brief biography.

It was followed by pages of bizarre paintings, none of them like anything Bert had ever seen before.

"This is Will's stuff?" Bert stammered. "He's never painted like this. He's actually never painted anything that was all that great." Bert shifted his position and leaned in to get a closer look. "I mean, he was more talented than the average person—but nothing like this. Where the hell did this *come* from?"

"If you read the notes," Dag said impatiently, "it says he completed all the pieces on here in, like, six to eight weeks. Do you see how many fucking paintings there are?" Dag's voice grew shrill and even louder. "And do you see what they're selling for? My god! At this rate, he'll bring in tens of millions by the end of the year. Look at this!"

The two of them scrolled through the pages of paintings for several minutes. When they reached the end, Bert rose from his crouch. "Let me go and mix us a couple of cocktails. I have special ones planned— they're Greek. Then we can sit and I'll tell you everything I know about my brother and his history with painting."

While Bert prepared the drinks, Dag returned to the beginning of the exhibit and scrolled hyperactively from painting to painting a second time, his eyes jumping to each one's asking price before glancing perfunctorily at the work itself and moving on. He noticed that some of the paintings apparently had multiple people trying to purchase them, and those people were now immersed in a bidding process that was raising the paintings' prices even higher.

Dag did not drag himself away from the website until Bert yelled from the living room that the drinks were chilled and poured, at which point he closed down the computer, joined Bert for a toast, and took a few sips standing before plopping down in his accustomed recliner.

"We gotta get in on this, Bertie," he said excitedly.

"Do you like the cocktails?" Bert asked.

"Oh. Yeah. They're great. But we gotta get in on this."

"In on what? What are you talking about?"

"The paintings."

"The paintings? How would we do that?"

"Bertie, I want a piece of this. And you should want that for me too. He's your brother, we have an *in*."

"An in on what? These are *his* paintings. It's *his* money. What do you want me to do? Steal his money? Beg him for a handout? I don't know what you're suggesting."

"No, no, no—for God's sake, Bertie, not that. Don't you see? I can manage his money for him. He suddenly has all this cash coming in. People don't know what to do when that happens. I can manage his portfolio. Invest it for him. Help it grow."

"My father's probably already doing that. You know he's living with them out there. Don't you think he's taking care of that?"

"Your brother can't trust all his money to an old geezer like your father—who's a fucked-up madman, by the way. You need to go out to California, Bertie. Visit them. Talk to your brother. I'm sure he knows what kind of a lunatic your dad is. And listen, I don't even want *all* of it. Your father can have some. Just convince your brother that it's prudent to diversify. He could put *half* with me. I'm not greedy. And I have clients who are art dealers—tell him that. If I can get your brother to use them, I'll get a cut of that too. And why the hell is your brother selling his paintings online? These people I know run the best galleries in Manhattan. Real galleries—brick and mortar."

Bert set his drink down and rubbed his temples. "Listen, even if I thought it was a good idea to go to California, which I don't, my father would never even let me in the house. We parted on really bad terms. I'm sure you remember that, Dag. You were there that night. You're the one who convinced me to come out as gay."

"Well of course you had to come out, Bertie. For God fucking sakes, you're almost forty years old. Were you going to stay in the closet your whole goddamned life? Don't change the subject with this nonsense. You need to go out there and talk to your brother. It's not like you're working too much to get away." He couldn't help but sneak in that last jab.

"There is no way my father is going to let me in that house, Dag. And I'm not going to subject myself to that. So what do you want me to do? Go out to California and stay in a hotel and invite my brother to lunch? Jesus. William and I barely talk. Birthday cards, maybe a text message to say hi once or twice a year. There's no way I'm going out there."

Dag, growing exasperated, raised his voice. "Do you know what's going on with me, Bertie? Do you have any fucking idea what I'm going through at work? Why do you think I bust my balls at networking meetings and with the goddamn Rotary Club all the time? People don't use stockbrokers anymore, Bertie. Everybody thinks they can do it on the internet. They're choking me—I'm slowly dying in front of your eyes. And now I'm asking for some goddamn help. Do you know the commission I can make off a portfolio like your brother's? Jesus, we're a family here, Bertie. Now's a chance for you to pull your weight."

Bertram closed his eyes and heaved an exhausted sigh. "God, Dag, you don't make it easy." He paused and looked down, then back at Dag. "Okay, look—I can't go out there, but I can try to give him a call."

It was late morning when William's mobile phone rang, but he was so deeply immersed in his painting reverie that at first the tones didn't register. He was assailing a huge canvas, larger than anything he'd previously attempted, and he was enthralled with how beautifully the work was unfolding before him.

By the time William became aware of the sounds, his first instinct was to ignore them. But when he glanced at the small table where the phone sat and noticed that the call was from his brother, he changed his mind. Bert called so rarely—perhaps something was wrong. William put down his brush, wiped his hands hastily with a rag, and caught the call just before it rolled over to voicemail.

"Hey, Bert, how you doing? Is something wrong?"

"No, no," Bert assured him. "Things are good here. How are you?"

"I'm fine."

"I'm actually calling to congratulate you. I saw your gallery show online. That's fucking amazing, man. When on earth did you start painting like that?"

"It's really the strangest thing, Bert. It wasn't even a conscious decision I made. It just happened—like, spontaneously, from inside me. All of a sudden I was drawing and painting in this, uh, you know, uh—shit—I'm forgetting words lately—that style that Salvador Dalí painted in . . ."

"Surreal?"

"Right. Right. Surreal. Yeah, just kind of happened. And now I'm churning out paintings like a motherfucker. And like you said, I got a gallery show."

"Yeah, about the gallery show. Dag and I were wondering—oh, by the way, Dag says hi . . ."

"That's nice. Tell him hi back."

"Yeah, thanks. Uh . . . so . . . Dag and I were wondering, exactly why are you doing a gallery show online? Dag knows art dealers with brick-and-mortar galleries here in New York. He could get you fixed up."

"Oh, you know, Arthur took care of all that. He knows art dealers in New York too. Three of 'em called me after they saw the stuff Arthur sent 'em. Jesus, I was about to try to sell these things at a . . . shit . . . uh, you know, an open place outdoors where people sell stuff out of booths?"

"A flea market?"

"Right, right, a flea market. Yeah, I was going to try to sell the paintings that way. But I talked to the dealers and according to all three of them, those um . . . what do you call 'em when the galleries are actually there on the street—you know, you just said it?"

"Brick and mortar?"

"Right, right. So, according to all three of the guys Arthur turned me on to, brick-and-mortar galleries are kind of passé—you know, like everything else now that isn't online. It actually makes some sense. They told me, 'You know, if your stuff is showing in a gallery in Manhattan, what, maybe a few hundred people see your stuff? Online it can be tens of thousands.' And they were right, 'cause now I've got people bidding against each other. It gets intense, man."

"So you have money coming in. Who's handling all that for you?"

"Arthur. Who'd ya think?"

"You're letting Dad handle all the money for you? Jesus, Will. How can you trust him with that? He's a little *off*—don't you think?"

William laughed explosively. It was contagious—soon Bert was howling along.

"A *little* off?" William panted between guffaws. "You think? He's fucking *out there*, Bert. How the hell you managed to put up with him all those years by yourself is hard to imagine."

"So why are you are giving all your money to him?"

"Look, Bert, I'd never say Arthur is a sane individual. We both know he's far from it. But he's a fucking genius with stocks. He supported our whole family doing it all our lives growing up. He put you and me through college, for God's sake. And, besides, he'd be pissed as shit at me if I gave any portion of it to your boyfriend . . . uh . . . sorry . . . what's his name again?"

"Dag," Bert said plaintively.

"Dag. Right, right. Dag." William shook his head. "I'm not even going to tell you what Arthur calls Dag. It's not pretty."

"I'm sure it's not," Bert acknowledged softly.

"Oh, and get this. You know, ever since we got here, Rosemary's wanted someone to come in every week or two to clean the house. It's, like, a really big place. So we've been walking on eggshells, trying to catch the right moment to get Arthur's permission. But now the paintings are bringing in so much money—Rosemary and I said what the hell, and we just hired some people. What the fuck can he say?"

"Well, it's been so nice to catch up, Will," Bert said unenthusiastically. "Congratulations again. I think what you're doing is great. I wish you all the best. Let's try to talk a little more often."

"Sounds good, Bert. Bye now."

CHAPTER *16*

THEIR plans changed at the last moment.

Originally, William was going to drive the van. But at the last minute, he came down with another of those piercing headaches that had been plaguing him of late, and he insisted he couldn't do it.

Rosemary had never loved driving; she'd deal with it for the short trips she needed to but the trek from Sonoma to San Francisco, punctuated by navigating city traffic downtown once they arrived, was not something she wished to undertake.

So they found themselves in Laurel's roomy black Mercedes instead. Laurel was driving; Arthur was next to her in the front passenger seat; and Rosemary and William were side by side in the rear.

"Can I have another one of your Valiums?" William whispered to Rosemary.

The medication had been prescribed to her to address back spasms that sometimes erupted after she spent hours on her feet, constantly bending over to work inside people's mouths. For the past few weeks, however, she'd been sharing an occasional pill with William when his headaches didn't respond to over-the-counter analgesics.

She pulled one out of her purse and gave it to him. "Here, take this." She pulled a bottle of spring water out of her bag and passed that to him too. "You need to be pain free at your showing."

"Thanks," William said as he popped the pill in his mouth and took a few sips of water.

"But when this exhibit is over, you really need to see a doctor," Rosemary said with some urgency. "You've been forgetting words left and right for months. That's gotten worse, and now you're getting headaches. You've never gotten headaches in your life. You need to get it checked out, honey."

"You really do," Laurel added from the driver's seat. "Just to be safe, Will, you really do."

"It could be all psychological," William said. "You know, with everything happening so fast. The crazy thing is, I never feel any pain while I'm painting all day—only before and after. Maybe it's just stress. This is all so new to me. You know, just six months ago I was teaching art in an old-age home and selling pieces for forty bucks at, uh . . ."

"A flea market," Rosemary added reflexively. "Still, honey," she pressed, "getting it checked is the prudent thing to do."

"All right. All right. I'll do it. Once the exhibit's over, I'll make an appointment. I promise."

"Good!" both Rosemary and Laurel shouted, nearly in unison.

Rosemary slipped her hand inside William's upper arm and leaned against him. She was concerned about his health, but even more so, she was terrified of the way Laurel drove. Unlike William, who habitually settled into the right lane and proceeded placidly, Laurel swerved and changed lanes wildly, racing far faster than the cars around her. Whenever a bottleneck prevented her from making headway, she'd slide to the left lane and belligerently trail inches from the rear bumper of the car ahead of her until it reluctantly moved right and allowed her to hurtle forward.

What Rosemary found especially perplexing was how different

this *personal* driving style of Laurel's was from her professional real estate agent mode. Back when she was showing homes to Rosemary, she'd been unceasingly meek and steadfast on the road, no matter how many hours they spent together.

Their destination was San Francisco's Museum of Modern Art, tucked in the northeast corner of the city, a few blocks from the bay. Although most of William's paintings had already been sold, his dealer had agreed to a one-week showing of about thirty pieces before the paintings were packed and shipped to their buyers. The museum wanted very much to display the works of this new American phenom (who was a local, after all) and William's dealer thought the publicity and exposure would be validating for him, not to mention excellent for future sales.

After exiting from the Golden Gate bridge, Laurel made her way pugnaciously across town, along the Marina and the Embarcadero into downtown.

Rosemary breathed a sigh of relief as they pulled into a huge parking lot south of Market Street, a few blocks from the museum.

"So, William," Arthur said as he got out of the car, "you said they call this neighborhood SoMa?"

"Right. For south of Market."

"And they call the museum MoMa?" Arthur continued.

"Right," Laurel said. "For the Museum of Modern Art."

"So, then," Arthur exclaimed, chuckling, "it's goddamn MoMa in SoMa. That's got a beat to it! MoMa in SoMa! MoMa in SoMa! How come nobody's thought of that?"

"A lot of people have thought of that," Rosemary snarled.

"How's your head feeling, Will?" Laurel asked.

"Much better," he said. "I'm ready to host my show. I'm up for it!"

"That's great, honey," Rosemary said, snuggling against him as they walked. "This is your day. You enjoy it!"

By the time they arrived at the museum, the exhibit had been open for nearly half an hour, and a few people were already milling about.

An easel near the entrance door displayed a huge greeting placard that boasted a large photograph of William, dressed nattily in a black turtleneck sweater and light blue blazer. Alongside the photo, displayed in large type, was a brief explanation of the modern-surreal style he'd just introduced to the art scene. A bit of biographical information appeared below.

The showing was due to run a week, but William was only scheduled to be in attendance today, the first day, and again on the final day. The docent assigned to the room recognized him as soon as he entered and rushed over to greet him.

"Mr. Wozniak," she said excitedly, "so glad you could make it. Did you have any trouble finding us?"

William smiled warmly. "I've lived in the Bay Area a long time and visit all the art museums regularly," he said. "So no trouble at all."

William had rehearsed that line, and had constructed it carefully so as not to reveal that, in truth, he was a much more regular visitor to the museums that displayed more traditional art. He was especially fond of the Impressionist period. Modern works had never really appealed to him much, and he felt a bit strange now being considered a poster-boy for that movement.

"Here." The docent handed him a laminated identification badge attached to a lanyard for him to wear around his neck. "This will help people recognize you, and"—she chuckled sheepishly—"help them believe it's really you if you walk over to talk to them. Please just feel free to wander about and mingle. It's okay to strike up a conversation with someone if you see them looking at a specific work, but just bear in mind that not everyone is totally comfortable talking to a featured artist, so it's generally best to keep conversations short and move on."

"Okay," Rosemary said, "thanks for the tips. We'll let you know if we need anything else."

Within an hour, the exhibit was packed. Arthur and Laurel said they needed to sit down, so they excused themselves and went to the cafeteria to have lunch and drink some wine. William and Rosemary leisurely made the rounds—walking hand in hand and talking briefly to anyone who approached them, but making no effort to talk to anyone who didn't.

They were standing in a far corner when two women entered the exhibit, scanned the room, and then began walking directly toward them. Rosemary immediately recognized one of the women as Joyce Miller.

Joyce smiled and initiated brief hugs with both Rosemary and William. She then introduced her friend, Sybil Harrington, and polite handshakes were exchanged.

"Well, congratulations, William," Joyce said. "You've come a long way from teaching art at a senior home."

"I appreciate the uh, the uh . . . opportunity you gave me," William said.

Rosemary noticed that in addition to fumbling for words, her husband had suddenly started stammering. She found that odd.

"You're a big star now, William," Joyce said. "Just look at all this! It's amazing."

Rosemary flashed a smug grin.

Joyce glanced down at William and Rosemary's interlocked hands, then looked back up. "So, you two seem to be the happy couple again," she declared with a lilt of sarcasm.

Rosemary felt William stiffen, but her gaze was fixed on Joyce. Scowling, she said sharply, "What is *that* supposed to mean? Will and I have always been happy."

"Well, dear," Joyce purred, "while *you* were sleeping with the hunky dentist, adorable William here was shtupping *me*. So, I really wasn't certain how *any* of it would turn out. But I'm happy that you two are still together."

William attempted to say something but only a guttural, inchoate rasp emerged. Rosemary tightened her grip on his hand and took half a step forward—she would handle this.

"You're a pathetic bitch," she hissed at Joyce. "And by the way, you have lousy gums. You're going to have all kinds of awful problems down the line. Maybe try flossing once in a while." She tugged upon William's arm and led him away.

When they had found a brief refuge, William started to sputter something, but only a few incoherent syllables emerged.

Rosemary touched her finger to his lips and stopped him. "We'll talk about it later. You need to focus on the show now. It's not a problem. I love you."

At a few minutes past five, William and Rosemary said good-bye to the docent and found Arthur and Laurel in the cafeteria, and the four headed back to Sonoma.

They'd made a reservation at the Mexican place in Petaluma, which had become a frequent haunt for all of them. A full celebratory dinner would eventually ensue, but the first hour there was devoted to a procession of icy margaritas accompanied by baskets of tortilla chips served with bowls of salsa and guacamole. Repeated toasts heaped kudos upon William for producing such spectacular paintings, upon Arthur for realizing their worth and corralling a prestigious art dealer, and upon Rosemary for the wonderful food she cooked every night that kept the house going. So that Laurel wouldn't feel left out, William finally proposed one toast to her for "keeping Arthur happy" (which to him and Rosemary meant palliating the older man's potentially catastrophic insanity—at which she was surprisingly adept).

It wasn't until Arthur and Laurel both went off to use the restroom that Rosemary finally turned to William, grinned, and whispered impishly, "So, were you really sleeping with that bitch Joyce Miller?"

"Only one time," William said, a bit surprised by how effectively three margaritas had dampened the discomfort he would normally feel talking about it. "She kind of ambushed me in her office. She was my boss, you know? I kind of felt like I had to go along. But then she tried again, and I quit."

"So *that's* why you quit?" Rosemary chuckled.

"Well, that—and the commute, and a whole bunch of things. But yeah, mostly that."

"Well, we're both so much better off now." Rosemary pulled William's face toward hers and kissed him passionately.

"What about you?" William stammered as soon as their faces parted. "Were you . . ."

"I was, Will. But he was my boss, too—and that was before you and I reconnected. I would *never* cheat on you now, honey. I only want to be with *you*. I love you so much. And I'm so proud of you and your painting."

They picked up their drinks and toasted. When they put their drinks down, Rosemary pulled William to her again.

As she held him, she closed her eyes and marveled at how their knot of deceit had unlaced itself so effortlessly. It was actually a strange relief that he had cheated too—though she was grateful it had been just the one time.

At about that same moment, about thirty miles south of there, Joyce Miller and Sybil Harrington were poking their chopsticks at spicy Chinese entrées at House of Same in Mill Valley. Rather than just sipping on the hot tea that was their habit to consume with their meal, they'd ordered a bottle of sake, which was now nearly gone. That, along with the three pomegranate cosmopolitans they'd each enjoyed first at the dive bar, emboldened Sybil to blurt out the question she'd been stifling all evening.

"So, tell me, Joyce—at the museum today: were you planning that ambush, or did it just come out?"

Joyce gulped down a bit of sake and grinned. "You know, honey, on our way over there—the more I thought about how William walked out on me when he worked at the center, the more I did consider saying something. But honestly, by the time we got to the museum, I'd decided not to say a word—that is, until I saw the two of them holding hands, and Rosemary flashing that coy bitch smile that she's so damn good at."

CHAPTER 17

THE neurologist, Dr. Kumar Satchidananda, was reassuring and trustworthy. Or at least William found him to be so.

And he'd come highly recommended.

William's primary care doctor, whose office was just a few blocks from the small flat William and Rosemary had shared for so many years in San Francisco, knew William well. He had opted to remain her patient when they moved, despite the long drive down from Sonoma it entailed. When he'd gone to see her about his headaches and his difficulty remembering words, she'd found his symptoms troubling and immediately referred him to Dr. Satchidananda, insisting he was one of the best neurologists in Northern California.

Dr. Satchidananda had interviewed William at length, and then ordered an MRI and a battery of other tests. When the results came back, Dr. Satchidananda had consulted with a neuroradiologist and a neurosurgeon to help interpret them.

Now Dr. Satchidananda sat behind his desk. William and Rosemary were in the two comfortably upholstered guest-chairs facing him. The doctor was a short, portly man with a bald head and a thick white moustache. He spoke softly and had a soothing voice, his English accented heavily by his native Hindi dialect.

"Mr. and Mrs. Wozniak. How are you both today?"

"We're fine, thank you," Rosemary said. "We're very interested to hear how Will is doing."

"Yours is an interesting case, Mr. Wozniak."

"Interesting?" William asked, curious and concerned.

"Well, the results of the MRI and the tests themselves are quite straightforward. You have a tumor. It is in your left temporal lobe. It appears to be growing rather quickly. The imaging gave us a very good look at it, and it is *not* cancerous. That is very good news. But the tumor *is* causing you trouble. Luckily, it can be removed surgically. Quite cleanly. That would be the recommended course of treatment."

"And that accounts for his headaches?" Rosemary asked. "And his forgetting words?"

"Yes," Dr. Satchidananda said slowly. "But more—this is what makes the case so interesting—it appears that the tumor is also responsible for Mr. Wozniak's sudden change to a new style of art. It's rare to have an effect like this, but not unheard of."

"The tumor is causing me to paint the way I do?" William asked, his voice tinged with a hint of apprehension.

"For you to adopt a completely new style of painting—entirely foreign to you and without any prior intent to do so on your part—in the same time proximity as the appearance of the tumor . . . well, I really can't see any other explanation. As I said, it's not unheard of. I consulted with several other specialists on this. We are in complete agreement."

"So," Rosemary probed, "if you remove the tumor, he won't paint this way anymore?"

"He will, most likely, paint the way he did before."

"I don't want to paint the way I did before!" William exclaimed. "I don't want that at all."

"I understand that, Mr. Wozniak. This is troubling for you. But what you must understand is that the tumor is growing, and it presents a serious danger to you. Allowed to continue growing, your headaches, your fumbling for words, those will exacerbate. Other symptoms may also arise. But all that aside, eventually, the tumor will grow too large for the brain to handle."

"What does that mean?" Rosemary asked. "Too large for the brain to handle?"

"At that point, the tumor would be fatal."

"You mean Will could die?" she cried.

"Yes. Eventually. If left untreated. But please understand, that need not happen. Not at all. As I said, the tumor is operable—it can be removed. It is a straightforward procedure. The projected outcome from this sort of surgery is quite good."

"And then I'll be exactly like I was before?" William asked.

"Yes, if all goes as expected. Exactly as you were before."

There was silence. William pondered his next question.

"How long before it threatens my life?" he finally asked.

"Oh, it's difficult to assess something like that with great precision," the doctor said.

"Well, ballpark—I mean will I be dead in a week? A month?"

"No, no," Dr. Satchidananda assured him. "Not nearly so soon. I don't see it becoming a critical situation quite so quickly at all. You could probably last a year, maybe two, even more, perhaps, doing nothing. But we must be prudent, Mr. Wozniak. You cannot be reckless with something like this. It is a very serious thing. In your case, to be absolutely safe, I would certainly not wait any longer than six months, and even that is not the most prudent course. The sooner the better. The tumor grows every day. And bear in mind, the headaches and language issues—they will become very bad in the interim."

"Well, I definitely need to wait—at least a little while," William said.

"That's fine," the doctor replied. "But not too long. I think a wise thing for both of you to do immediately would be to have a consult with the neurosurgeon. You can do that now, even if you want to put the surgery itself off for a couple of months. That way, you can hear the surgeon's perspective and he can explain exactly what the surgery entails. You can then set a date for the procedure."

"Okay," Rosemary said. "That makes sense. Can you recommend a neurosurgeon?"

"Yes, certainly. In fact, I've been consulting on your case with Dr. Harold Yee. He works here in the hospital. He's a good friend, and a superb surgeon. He's won many awards. Nearly all my patients who've required surgery have used him, and they've all been very, very satisfied. I can put you in contact with some of those patients if you want to hear what they thought of him."

William gazed silently ahead—not because this news of a tumor had rendered him momentarily insensate but because he was thinking hard, attempting to conjure up a name he couldn't quite recall. He receded completely within himself, trying to retrieve that memory.

Very slowly, the rhythm of the name came to him—two syllables with the accent on the first, followed by three syllables, the accent on the first again. Gradually, a vowel and consonant sound manifested—but it wasn't the first name. Those sounds belonged somewhere in the middle.

Finally, like a serene explosion, the name popped, fully formed, into William's head. His head twitched slightly and his eyes widened for an instant.

"Doctor," he asked, "are you familiar with a neurosurgeon named Judith Feigenbaum?"

Rosemary turned toward William with a confused grimace on her face. "Who is that?" she demanded.

"Just a doctor I've heard of," he said. He looked back to Dr. Satchidananda. "Have you heard of her?"

For the first time since they'd entered his office, Dr. Satchidananda looked uncomfortable. He hesitated, and his tone suddenly grew less soothing and reassuring. "I have heard of her. Yes. Certainly, I have heard of her."

"Can I use her?" William asked.

The doctor was silent for a moment. "Well, yes, I suppose," he finally said, his voice raspy and wavering. "You could. But I haven't worked with her. You see, she's not associated with this hospital."

He sounded unconvincing.

"Do you recommend her?" Rosemary asked.

Dr. Satchidananda said nothing—he appeared to be carefully formulating his words. "She has an odd reputation," he finally, begrudgingly acknowledged.

"What do you mean, 'an odd reputation'?" Rosemary pressed.

"Um—how to say it, exactly? I mean, well, undoubtedly she is a brilliant and celebrated surgeon. And a writer of books. You can certainly trust the quality of her work. Yes—but that reputation I spoke of—you see . . . she can be difficult to communicate with . . . for some people. Other people do not have a problem with her. But as I said, some do."

"Will," Rosemary said, "go with Dr. Yee—the doctor he recommended. He sounds solid. This woman sounds weird."

William spoke softly. "This is *my brain* we're talking about, Rosemary. My life. I feel a connection to Dr. Feigenbaum. I want to use her."

"What do you mean, a connection?" Rosemary cried. "Have you met this woman?"

"No, I haven't met her. I've read some of her stuff. I've heard her talk on the radio."

"I think you should go with the doctor's recommendation," Rosemary insisted.

"No. I need to use Dr. Feigenbaum." He turned back to Dr. Satchidananda. "Can you set that up?"

The doctor had regained his composure as he listened to Rosemary and William discuss the matter. He leaned back in his chair now and said calmly, "I see no harm in having the two of you meet Dr. Feigenbaum. In fact, interviewing more than one surgeon can be a very reassuring thing to do. How about if I arrange consults with both Dr. Yee *and* Dr. Feigenbaum. Then you two can decide."

"Can we do *that*, Will?" Rosemary pleaded.

William had already made his decision. But he had been with Rosemary long enough to understand that consulting with both surgeons would be the most effective—and, more important, least contentious—means to settle on Dr. Feigenbaum.

"That makes perfect sense, honey," he said. "We'll talk to both of them."

The next day, during her lunch break at the dentist's office, Rosemary placed a phone call to Dr. Satchidananda's nurse, who informed her that an appointment with Dr. Harold Yee had been secured ten days hence. The appointment with Dr. Judith Feigenbaum would need to wait an additional week.

When Rosemary returned home a few hours later, she went directly to William's painting studio to let him know about the appointments. To her surprise, he wasn't there. Rags were strewn about, his paints were uncapped, and his brushes and palette appeared to have been hastily set down.

She began searching the house and calling to him. It wasn't until she finally made her way upstairs that she heard him answer. He was in the room at the end of the hall, which she'd recently outfitted as an office.

She was relieved to find him there. It had become her favorite room in the house—a place where she felt especially safe. It was the only spot that seemed to her to be theirs alone. Even their bedroom, which contained mostly furniture from their old San Francisco flat, also had a few of Arthur's pieces to help fill out the bigger space—and those objects still felt foreign to her.

But everything in this office was brand-new, purchased by Rosemary with the money William's paintings had provided. The large computer that now held his rapt attention sat upon an L-shaped desk with a long credenza built of African Blackwood. Rosemary loved that piece, and had carefully selected a chair to go with it, upholstered in lush black leather as well as a matching couch that sat across the room.

No one besides William and Rosemary used the space, and right now it was sparkling and pristinely clean; the housekeepers Rosemary had hired to come twice a week had been there earlier that day.

She gazed over William's shoulder at the webpage he was scrutinizing. She wasn't certain, but it seemed to be an article about Harpo Marx. Her features scrunched into a perplexed gape. "What on earth are you reading?"

William swiveled slowly in his chair and looked at her. His voice was subdued—his demeanor pensive. "Did you ever watch old Marx Brothers movies?"

"I think I saw one or two when I was little."

"Do you remember Harpo, the one who never spoke? There was always a scene where he played the harp?"

"Sort of."

"So," William said softly, "it turns out that he was actually a very dedicated and serious musician. He practiced the harp hours every day. When he got old, he got heart disease. His doctor told him that playing the harp was too taxing for him—he'd have to stop, or it would kill him. And Harpo tried. But he couldn't stand it. So he went back to practicing the harp for hours every day. He said life wasn't worth living otherwise."

Rosemary moved closer to him and laid a hand gently on his shoulder as he sat. "You didn't leave your painting and come all the way up here to google Harpo Marx, did you?" she asked quietly.

"No," he said, his voice now a halting whisper. "I started with cases of artists who had—um—um—what is it I have growing in my brain now?"

"A tumor," Rosemary said, her lips pursing sadly.

"Right. I was googling cases of artists with tumors. To see if removing them affected their work."

"And did you find any?"

"A few. Like the doctor said, it's rare—but it happens. There were two articles in particular that got to me—you know, the artists they wrote about. One was a painter. The other was a—um—oh—what do you call it—a guy who carves stone . . ."

"A sculptor."

"Right. They both decided to refuse the surgery. Take their chances. Their art was more important to them. It was the second guy, the, uh . . ."

"Sculptor?"

"Right. He was talking in the article about Harpo Marx. That's why I googled Harpo."

"Harpo was old," Rosemary whispered. "Were the other two artists young, like you?"

"Yes."

"And what happened to them—after they refused surgery?"

"I couldn't find that," William said, gazing up into her eyes. "They both said they'd keep working till they died. So I guess they either died, or they changed their mind. Nobody wrote about that. Nobody followed up. I guess it didn't matter to anybody."

William's head dipped and he buried it in Rosemary's breast. He began to sob. Soon his whole body was heaving.

"Oh baby," she said softly, cradling his head with her hands. "Don't even think like that. Please, baby, it's going to be all right. I'm going to take care of you."

Now she was crying too.

The conference room was located on the third floor of a large and somewhat intimidating University Medical Center annex located half an hour south of San Francisco. The room was small and drab, with bare white walls and no windows. Rosemary and William sat alone on two of six plastic chairs arranged around a narrow oval table.

They were waiting to talk to Dr. Judith Feigenbaum.

Their meeting with the first neurosurgeon, Dr. Yee, had taken place a week prior. He had presented himself in a pleasant and straightforward manner, displaying professionalism, high energy, and sincere geniality. As promised, he had indeed won a number of awards, some a result of positive patient feedback; the certificates and plaques attesting to those honors were displayed prominently about his office. He'd gone over William's procedure in great detail, including diagrams he'd sketched for them on the front of the manila folder holding his notes—and he talked reassuringly about the number of similar operations he'd performed.

Unlike Dr. Yee, who had greeted them promptly at the hour designated, Dr. Feigenbaum was already twenty minutes late.

"How long are we supposed to wait for this dingbat?" Rosemary whispered.

William shrugged. "Let's just be patient, and when she gets here, we'll see what she's like."

Rosemary sighed audibly.

A few moments later the door opened and the doctor, wearing a long white coat, entered. She did not say hello. Nor did she apologize for being late.

"William Wozniak?" she inquired, checking the documents in her hand as she did.

"Yes," William said, standing up. "And this is my wife, Rosemary."

Dr. Feigenbaum glanced at Rosemary but said nothing. William waited for the doctor to extend her hand in greeting, but she instead walked past both of them toward the other side of the table.

She was much taller than William had imagined, nearly his own height. He glanced down to see how high the heels of her shoes were. She was wearing flats.

She was very thin, almost gaunt. Her straight, reddish-brown hair was tied back in a severe pony tail. William noticed that her gait was unnaturally stiff and awkward.

She sat down.

"I've gone over the notes provided by your neurologist," she said. "The fact that you adopted a new style of painting is quite fascinating."

"I've heard your talks on the radio, and read a couple of your books," William said. "I know you've studied situations very much like this."

"Yes. I have. Did you read the episode about the man who'd been a carpenter, and after a brain concussion became a concert pianist and composer?"

"Yes, I remember that one."

"That comes to mind because it was similar—but still somewhat different. That was an unambiguous case of acquired savant syndrome, because the man had absolutely no musical ability prior to the accident. In your case, you were a painter already. The tumor just altered your style."

"And made me incredibly more, uh . . ."

"Productive," Rosemary interjected.

"Interesting," the doctor said. "So, when you paint, do you sink into a sort of creative trance now?"

"Exactly."

"But not before?"

"No."

"And you never fumbled for words before, or had headaches?"

"No."

"With your permission, William, after the surgery, I'd like to write about your case."

William smiled. "It would be an honor."

"Can we talk a little about the surgery?" Rosemary's tone conveyed annoyance and impatience.

"As the neurologist explained," the doctor said matter-of-factly, "I surgically remove the tumor. We utilize general anesthesia. For a man of William's age and general good health, we would not expect complications."

The couple waited a few moments for the doctor to continue. But nothing additional was forthcoming.

"Have you performed many of these sorts of operations?" Rosemary probed.

"More than I can count."

"I want to get back to the art," William insisted. "I need to be honest with you, Dr. Feigenbaum. I'm very hesitant to do the surgery at all; I don't want to go back to painting the way I did. People *like* my art now. *I* like my art now. I don't know if I could stand to go back. I want to put the surgery off as long as I can."

"William!" Rosemary cried. "Your life is at stake!"

Dr. Feigenbaum ignored Rosemary's comment and posed a question, calmly and logically, to William. "How did you paint before?"

"My work was literal. Uninspired. I wouldn't admit it to myself then—but it's obvious to me now. I don't want to go back to that. Do you know how painful that would be?"

"What exactly do you mean, *literal*?" the doctor asked.

"I mean I painted things precisely the way they looked. I didn't necessarily use models, but I painted everything realistically. Even if it was a creature I conjured up, it was composed of realistic parts. Nothing interpretive. There isn't anybody who's interested in that. Honestly, even *I* wouldn't be interested in it that now that I've been through this change."

Rosemary studied Dr. Feigenbaum's features, trying to gauge her reaction to William's anguish, but the doctor's face, like her voice, was impassive—Rosemary could discern no hint of concern or empathy. There appeared, in fact, to be no emotional constituent to the woman whatsoever.

Dr. Feigenbaum moved ahead as if conducting a legal deposition. "When you say you painted things *literally*, then I assume you were good at copying, be it from a model or a sketch, or even from memory."

"Yes," William exclaimed with an exuberance that Rosemary found strange and off-putting. "I was always excellent at that—almost photographic in every detail. Even in art school, people marveled at how I could duplicate anything I saw. One guy used to call me a human camera." William paused for an instant. "I don't think he meant it very kindly."

Dr. Feigenbaum fell silent for a long moment, apparently deep in thought. "William," she said finally, "your idea about deferring the surgery for as long as possible—to enable you to paint the way you do now, for just a bit more time—it is dangerous, and self-defeating. And not very smart at all. With every additional month, each of your symptoms will get worse. The headaches alone will eventually prevent you from working—your artistic trances won't be sufficiently powerful to stave them off any longer. And the operation will become more difficult as the tumor grows, more subject to negative complications. We can't have that."

Rosemary sat up straight in her chair, her mouth hanging slightly open, and gazed intently at Dr. Feigenbaum. "Thank you!" she exclaimed, her tone sharp and resolute. "I'm amazed—grateful, but amazed—that somebody is finally giving my husband the straight dope. Thank you! He needs that."

Dr. Feigenbaum glanced briefly at Rosemary. It was possible that the doctor offered the slightest hint of a nod of acknowledgment—but it could well have been something Rosemary merely imagined.

The doctor turned back to William. "You must stop producing any more commercial work, right now, William. Not another painting. Four months is the absolute maximum we can wait without risk. So for the next four months, you must compile a dictionary."

"A dictionary?"

"A dictionary of images," Dr. Feigenbaum said. "Of every object you can think of. Every person you know. Every animal. Every flower and piece of fruit. Include inanimate objects as well: furniture, buildings, cars, trucks, airplanes, boats, pieces of machinery, tools, utensils. Everything! Sketched and, to the extent possible, fully painted, in your current style. The tumor has granted you a manic capacity for work. Use it now. Work as if your life depends upon it."

William thought for a moment. "So I can copy the pieces later?"

"Yes, exactly. You will return to being the natural photographic mimic you were before. By compiling this dictionary, you'll be able to duplicate the way you paint now. You'll be able to form the components into full canvases. They won't necessarily flow together in the precise manner they do now—probably not—but I suspect that will be seen as normal artistic growth and change, not a loss of talent or style."

William leaped to his feet. "Yes! That will work. Yes! Thank you. I knew you'd have the answer!"

Despite her reluctance to acknowledge it, Rosemary found Dr. Feigenbaum's suggestion absolutely brilliant. On a metaphorical level, it was a sort of artistic Noah's Ark.

She gazed at William, who was still standing, his clenched fists hovering above his shoulders and pulsating victoriously—and she felt tremendous relief, fused indelibly with a profound sense of love.

She found it utterly bewildering, though, that no one aside from this bizarre and exasperating woman had been able to persuade her husband to embrace the surgery he so urgently needed to save his life. To enable him to embrace it not just intellectually but with the sort of visceral enthusiasm he'd need to buoy him psychologically through the anticipation, the trauma, the pain—and, eventually, the healing and rehabilitation.

Rosemary beamed. "Yes," she said softly. "That will work."

William was due at the hospital at 6:45 a.m.

They expected to hit traffic at some point during the long drive down from Sonoma, but the roads were clear and they arrived forty-five minutes early. Rosemary was tempted to get a coffee before heading to the admitting office—there was a Starbuck's kiosk in the hospital's lobby—but William had been on a strict fast for the past twelve hours, and she knew how much he'd love a latte right now. She didn't want him to have to watch her sip on one while he remained emptyhanded, so she forced her legs to keep moving and pass the kiosk by.

The admitting office was in the lobby, too. William and Rosemary provided their obligatory personal information and submitted copies of their living trust, medical power of attorney, and living will (documents Arthur had assisted them in procuring). William had named Rosemary as his decision maker if he became incapacitated, and he'd opted definitively to be allowed to die rather than sink into a vegetative state.

The woman at the admitting desk snapped a plastic identification bracelet securely around William's left wrist, then pointed them to the elevators that took them to the fifth-floor suite of operating rooms.

The young woman at the fifth-floor Surgery check-in desk greeted Rosemary and William with a warm smile.

"Hi," Rosemary said. "Checking in William Wozniak. We were told to be here at six forty-five for prep, with the surgery at eight thirty."

The young woman glanced at the wall clock. "Oh, you're way early. Great. No problem. You'll be right on time for the doctor and the nurses. They tell people to get here way before they need to—you know, because most people run late all the time. Let me take care of a few things, and I'll call you when I'm ready to check you in."

William thanked her, and he and Rosemary sat down together at the bank of chairs near the window. For a while they were the only people in the waiting room, but over the next fifteen minutes two other couples trickled in.

Rosemary could sense how nervous William was becoming. He said almost nothing. If she posed a question, he responded monosyllabically. He rocked constantly—forward and back—in his seat. She put her arm around him and held him. "You're going to be great," she whispered. "You have a good doctor, and a wife who loves you more than anything. You did a fantastic job on your image dictionary, so you'll be able to paint just like you did before."

The image dictionary had been a prodigious enterprise. William's work ethic had morphed from prolific to manic as he'd toiled on it over the past four months. He'd often worked eighteen or twenty hours a day. Rosemary could not be certain whether he'd actually be able to use those images as the basis for new canvases as he hoped, but she knew this: the act of producing the vast collection had kept his headaches at bay, and, more important, had kept him from sinking into a rut of obsessive fear and worry.

After a ten-minute wait, William and Rosemary were checked in, met by a nurse, and taken together into the OR suite. William's weight, temperature, and blood pressure were recorded, and then the nurse showed them to the prep room. Inside, there was a narrow bed on wheels with a couple of folded blankets, a thin cloth robe, and several packets of cleansing wipes.

"Are you doing okay, Mr. Wozniak?" the nurse asked. She was a short Asian woman who appeared to be in her forties.

"I guess so," William stammered.

"He's a little nervous," Rosemary added.

"That's completely normal," the nurse said. "You're doing fine, Mr. Wozniak. You're actually much calmer than most people when they're getting prepped. Your blood pressure was just a little high—that's expected."

"See, Will," Rosemary said. "You're doing really well."

"Okay," he said, his voice no more than a hoarse exhalation.

"Take your time," the nurse said. "I won't be back for fifteen or twenty minutes. Just get undressed and put on the robe. It ties in the back. But before you put the robe on, wipe down every part of your body, including your face and head, with the wipes. Dr. Feigenbaum is a stickler for cleanliness. She wants her patients absolutely germ-free."

"Are they going to shave my head?" William asked shakily.

"They'll position you and shave the section they need once you're under the anesthesia. It's easier on everybody that way."

"Okay."

William managed to get his clothes off, but he had a bit of trouble manipulating the wipes—his hands were trembling.

"Here, let me help you, baby," Rosemary said softly. She wiped him, gently and thoroughly. Then she helped him get the skimpy robe on, and covered him with the blankets when he got into the bed.

"How about we make a little video?" Rosemary asked.

"No, no." William shook his head. "I don't want anything posted about this."

"Not to post," Rosemary said, as she fetched her mobile phone from her purse. "Just for you and me. To look at, when this is all done, and you're better."

"All right," he mumbled.

Rosemary fiddled with the phone for a moment, then pointed it at his face. "Are you ready?"

"Okay."

"All right . . . go!"

William gazed at the phone for a moment, then began to speak softly and haltingly. "Well . . . here I am . . . I . . . uh . . . everyone tells me I'm going to get through this. I sure hope they're right. If they are . . . I guess I'll see you when it's done." He tried to form some more words, but no sounds manifested, and he began to cry. "If I don't make it," he finally stammered, "I want you to know, Rosemary, how much I love you . . . I really do." He started sobbing heavily. "Okay," he whispered, straining to get the words out and gesticulating anxiously with his hands. "That's all for now."

Rosemary stopped recording and put away the phone.

"I love you too, baby," she said, and teared up along with him. "I'll be here waiting when you come to. You'll do great. Don't worry. You'll do great. I know it. We'll be together again in a few hours." She squeezed his hand.

By the time the nurse returned, they had stopped crying, but William could feel that his eyes were a bit pink and puffy.

"I'm going to put your IV in now, Mr. Wozniak."

"Call me William."

"Okay, William. Good. This will just pinch a little as it goes in."

William turned away. The nurse was quick—he barely felt it enter his flesh.

"So, this is just a saline drip for now, but we'll be adding a sedative soon. The anesthesiologist is going to come in and talk to you first."

About ten minutes later, the anesthesiologist poked his head through the curtain. Rosemary thought he looked ridiculously young.

"Hi, William," he said. "I'm Dr. Ogawa. I'm going to be administering the anesthesia for your procedure today."

"Hi," William whispered.

"You look a little nervous," the doctor said.

William chuckled. "Yeah, you could say that."

"I'll add the sedative to the drip now. It won't put you to sleep, but it should relax you a little."

"Thanks."

As the doctor prepared the syringe, he said, "We expect this procedure to go very well. You should feel confident. People your age, in good health like you, do very well with both the anesthesia and the surgery. You're in good hands." He injected the sedative into the IV line. "Any questions?" he asked with an upbeat smile.

"I'm good," William mumbled.

"Thank you very much," Rosemary added.

"All right then. I'll see you in the operating room, William. You'll do fine."

With that, he was gone.

William grew calmer and quieter as the sedative took effect.

The nurse came in. "It's time to wheel you into the operating room, William. How are you feeling?"

"Okay."

"I love you, baby," Rosemary called as the nurse wheeled the bed out of the curtained area.

"I love you too," he said softly.

He watched the walls and the ceiling as he rolled through the prep area. When two heavy doors parted and he was wheeled into a smaller chamber, he knew the surgery would start soon. Despite the sedative, he began to panic.

Dr. Ogawa greeted him. "Hi again, William. We're almost ready."

The nurse helped William onto the operating table. It felt hard and cold. She secured a strap around his waist and another around his thighs. She placed his arms on padded arm-boards and attached those straps as well.

William lay on the table, taking in the monitors and machines around him. The light above him was particularly bright.

An empty, hollow shroud of terror seized his being.

What if these are my last moments? Right now. My last moments of consciousness in this life? I may die on this table. Never see Rosemary again. Not even be aware that I'm dying.

No!

I can't let them put me under when I'm in this state of mind. That won't be good for the surgery. I can't go under, terrified. I need to be positive going under. It will make a difference in how I respond. How I fight. Whether I live.

William tried desperately to cease all thoughts. He closed his eyes and tried focusing solely on his breath. He attempted to slow his inhalations and exhalations, and to experience every aspect of them fully. It was a meditation technique he'd read about once.

It helped a bit. Feeling encouraged, he concentrated even more intently upon his breath.

Then someone touched his chest. His eyes snapped open. It was Dr. Feigenbaum, leaning over him. She looked very tall. In her green scrubs, green surgical mask, and clear plastic head bonnet, she looked ominous and mysterious. Dominating. Commanding.

She leaned down a bit lower, her gloved hand still on his chest. He could swear that he saw her smile. The mask obscured it, but her cheekbones rose, her eyes narrowed, and her eyebrows twittered—almost imperceptibly, but he saw it. He had never seen her smile—not in photographs or in person.

"I'm going to take good care of you," she said, her voice assuming the same reassuring, nurturing timbre it radiated in her readings. "Just a few questions now. For protocol. Tell me your name."

"William Wozniak."

"When did you last eat or drink?"

"Over twelve hours ago."

"What organ will I be operating on?"

"My brain."

"All right, then, William. Begin counting backwards. Silently. From a hundred."

William started the count, but suddenly felt his penis bolt upright. The erection was stupendous—it pressed upward against the thin cloth of his robe like a wigwam's center pole—he could feel the smooth, flimsy cotton straining against it.

He thought he heard Dr. Feigenbaum start to speak—it sounded like the beginning of a sentence that he'd once heard her recite on the radio.

An instant later, the anesthetic sucked him into oblivion.

CHAPTER 18

*B*ERT was scrambling about the kitchen—packing food and seasonings into his cooler and a couple of tall shopping bags. He'd already made certain that his knives were tucked securely into their designated slots in his thick canvas knife case, which had been securely rolled shut.

It was late afternoon on a Saturday. Dag had spent most of the day at the Rotary Club, but Bert had just heard him come in the front door.

Dag stepped into the kitchen doorway.

"Hey," Bert said. His greeting was cheerful, but he was too busy and preoccupied to look up from his preparations.

"Looks like a big gig tonight," Dag observed. "What's the occasion?"

"It's Gina's birthday. Her husband's out of town—some extended business trip in Asia. Singapore, I think. So she made it a girls' night. She has five friends coming over, so six women altogether. I'll be cooking for a crowd." Bert looked up and chuckled. "She asked me to come over early—she has special instructions for the night. I have no idea what she has up her sleeve." He resumed loading the cooler. "That's why I'm crankin'; I really gotta get over there."

"Sounds like quite a gig. Ought to be a nice payday."

"Oh, yeah. Definitely. And Gina's always generous with a big tip on top of everything else. So I should have a nice contribution to the family kitty tomorrow morning."

"I always like that," Dag said with a smile. "Oh, by the way, something came up with some members at the Rotary Club today. I wanted to run it by you."

Dag's tone had changed. It was subtle, but Bertram picked up on it immediately—in the months they'd lived together, he had become keenly attuned to such small variations in Dag's intonation. Bert stopped what he was doing, gazed at him, and girded himself for the accusation that was surely forthcoming. "What's up, Dag?" he asked, his voice a weary monotone.

"Oh, a few people at the club today mentioned to me that they'd asked you to do a chef gig and you said you couldn't, you were all booked. Didn't offer them another night that week. You said it would be two or three weeks before you were freed up."

Bert glared at Dag for a few moments before responding. "So— you're saying that various people just came up to you and said this? Out of the blue. Just came up to you and said the same exact thing— that I declined a chef gig? That sounds hard to believe, Dag."

"Well . . . all right . . ." Dag fumbled for a moment before collecting his thoughts. "I heard it from one fellow. Then I started asking around. Either way, it's clear that it's been happening."

"So this is how you spend your day? Poking around the Rotary Club, trying to dig up shit on me?"

"Bertie, you're not booked every night. You're booked maybe two or three nights a week. Tops. You have openings. Why are you telling people you don't?"

"It's none of their fucking business if I do or don't. And frankly, it's not yours either."

"What the hell does *that* mean? This is your *job*, for God's sake. It's *work.*" Dag's voice grew shriller as he went on, "Believe me—*I'd* sure as hell like to work only two days a week! That would be fun, Bertie. But I wouldn't make a living! We're trying to be a household here—a family. So take some goddamn responsibility and act like an adult for once in your life. Go to work five nights a week and contribute to the house."

"I don't have time for your shit now, Dag. I'm due at Gina's. For a big fucking night where I'm going to work my ass off, cooking for six people, and then bring back a huge wad of cash. Maybe that'll make you happy. Nothing I do seems to make you happy anymore unless it involves a goddamn wad of cash. So, are you happy now?"

"Do I look happy?"

"Go fuck yourself, Dag."

Dag shook his head and muttered something under his breath as he stormed off to the bedroom.

Bert finished packing his gear and was gone.

Gina allowed the door to shield her as she let Bert into her apartment. When she closed it, he finally got a look at her. He could do nothing but stare—motionless, silent, and slack-jawed.

A silver-studded red leather corset hugged Gina's torso. Its garters clasped the tops of black fishnet stockings which reached high on her thighs, inches below a pair of crimson satin bikini panties. The heels on Gina's snug red leather boots looked to be six inches tall. A black leather choker cinched her neck—it was bejeweled with what appeared to be real diamonds.

She held a black riding crop, but didn't seem to be paying much attention to it at the moment.

"How do I look, sweetie?" Gina asked, after allowing Bert abundant viewing time.

"Well," Bert said hesitantly, "you look beautiful. But exactly what kind of party are you throwing here?"

"That's what I wanted to talk to you about, sweetie. Why I wanted you to come so early. I need your help to make it good."

"I don't understand. I'm here to cook, right?"

"Yes, to cook and serve. But I have a surprise. I got you help serving."

"Help?"

"Right. There are five women coming, and three of them are bringing slaves, to be your servers."

"Slaves?"

"Come on, sweetie. You're gay. You have to know what's going on here."

"I think you need to enlighten me, Gina."

"Well, first of all, for tonight, don't call me Gina. Call me ma'am, or Mistress."

"Ma'am?"

"As in yes ma'am, no ma'am. Like that."

Bert's head twitched conspicuously. "All right," he mumbled.

"It's a femme domme SM party!" Gina exclaimed, with a giggle. "All the ladies are dominatrices—or at least they were at one time."

"You too?" Bert asked incredulously.

"Yes, sweetie, that's how I made a living. I started in college to help with tuition, and just stuck with it. I did it for years. It's how I met my husband. He was a client." Gina paused and observed Bert's reaction. She laughed. "You have that look on your face like . . . *Oh! Now I understand.*"

Bert chuckled. "Yeah, I guess so."

"So, are you ready to make it a great party?"

"Sure. What do you want me to do besides cook?"

"Well, first off, just for tonight, don't act like my pal. Act like my slave."

"Your slave? Uh . . . okay . . . How does a slave act?"

"It's easy. You just obey. Don't make any small talk—with me or anybody else. It's 'yes ma'am' or 'no ma'am' or 'yes Mistress' . . . like that. And do your work."

"Okay. I can do that for tonight. That's no problem."

"Now these three guys who the women are bringing, they're all slaves, so they're all submissive to all the women, just like you will be tonight. But as the chef, you can very quietly tell them what to do to help you serve the food. And they can bus the table for you and that sort of thing. Just do it quietly."

"They're not eating?"

"No, only the women will eat. The guys'll eat when they get home." A mischievous grin seized her features. "If they behave."

"All right. I got it."

"Fantastic!" She clapped her hands. "And oh! I have a costume for you to wear tonight!"

"A costume?"

"Right. Let me get it."

Gina went to her bedroom, and came back with a black leather jock strap, a harness that looked a bit like a very skimpy black vest comprised of leather straps, and a wide leather neck collar equipped with a hasp and a padlock.

Bert gawked. "You want me to wear this stuff?"

"Yes, just this and nothing else, sweetie."

"Look, Gina . . ."

"Ma'am."

Bert took a long breath. "Okay—look, *ma'am*, I'm not sure I'm comfortable wearing this—all night—in front of a bunch of people."

"Sweetie, the women will all be dressed kinda like me. So they'll be in costumes too. And the guys, well . . . They'll be naked or in a harness. And they're all paunchy, middle-aged businessmen. You have a beautiful body. An athlete's body. I can tell, even through your clothes."

"Well, I did play baseball in college."

"And if you're supposed to be my slave, you've gotta look the part. Right? So, will you do it, sweetie? For me?" Gina looked at him pleadingly.

Bert gazed again at the jock strap, the harness, and the collar in Gina's hands. He looked down, and then back up. "All right. I'll do it. I'll go in the bedroom and change."

"Put the collar on so the lock's in the back," Gina advised as she handed over the items.

After he'd donned the outfit, Bert spent nearly a minute examining himself in the bedroom's full-length mirror. He had to acknowledge that he looked pretty hot. He imagined himself borrowing the outfit and making a meal at home for Dag—*that* would improve Dag's attitude, fast.

Bert returned to the living room.

"Oh, wow!" Gina howled. "What a hunk you are!" She eased closer to him and slowly ran the riding crop up and down his torso. "You make a beautiful slave!" She cocked her head and smiled coquettishly. "Oh, listen, sweetie, one other thing." She touched the square leather whacker at the tip of the crop lightly to Bert's lips. "I might playfully slap you with this now and then tonight, sweetie. Just for effect—not hard. Do you want to see how it feels?"

"Not especially," Bert said, chuckling. "But I suppose better now than later, in front of a bunch of people."

"The appropriate response is 'yes ma'am,'" she gently reminded him. Then she whacked him on the side of the arm.

"Whoa!" Bert said. Then he laughed. "It didn't actually hurt. But it definitely got my attention!"

"What a good slave!" Gina cooed.

Bert blushed.

Bert got to work on cocktails and dinner. From the kitchen, he observed the pattern once guests started arriving. Everyone entered the apartment in normal street clothes, with black satchels holding their costumes and toys. They changed in the bedroom and came back out fully in character.

The meal plan was elaborate. Bert spent most of the evening at the stove and the kitchen's prep counter. He'd come out every few minutes to politely ask if the ladies wanted more cocktails, or were ready for the next course.

About an hour into the evening, Gina screamed for a drink refill—her glass was sitting empty. The fact that he'd just served her a cocktail and she'd chugged it in mere moments did not mitigate her agitation. After he set the new one down in front of her, she slapped her riding crop smartly across his thigh. "Be more attentive, slave," she commanded.

Bert had to strain not to giggle. He held his lips tight, whispered, "Yes ma'am . . . sorry ma'am," and looked Gina in the eyes.

She grinned and nodded. "He's really a darling slave," she announced to her friends.

Bert's first course was cream of asparagus soup served with crisp crostini. He followed with a delicate insalata tricolore featuring fresh arugula, radicchio, and endive. He was tempted to explain to the group that the colors of the salad leaves (green, red, and white) mimicked those of the Italian flag, but he assumed it would be considered impudent for a slave to flaunt such knowledge, so he instead whispered it into Gina's ear when he refilled her glass of wine. She thanked him with a loving stroke on the rump, and he heard her proudly dispense that bit of food trivia to her fellow dominatrices a few minutes later as they munched.

He had whipped up an apple and Calvados sorbet and packed it into his small ice cream maker as soon as he'd arrived. It was perfect now, and he had the men serve small bowls to each of the women as a palate cleanser before the entrée.

Having the slaves at his disposal to help serve did make his job much easier, and enable him to focus more on the kitchen tasks.

The main course, comprised of veal piccata, scalloped potatoes, and roasted cauliflower, was much praised by the women, though Bert noticed that all congratulations for the fine cuisine were directed at Gina, as if her kitchen slave were just one more utensil at her disposal. It made him chuckle to listen, from the kitchen, to all the dining room banter—though he was careful to keep his laughter sufficiently subdued so as not to be heard.

He had assembled the tiramisu the day before, and had chilled it overnight. But Gina came into the kitchen and instructed him to wait before serving dessert. The ladies were full, she said, and they wanted a little time to play.

Bert didn't watch the proceedings closely—that would be inappropriate, he thought, and embarrassing for him—but he made sure that as he got started washing the monumental stack of pots, pans, and dishes already accumulated, he allowed himself quick, occasional glimpses of the goings-on. Each of the three men was tormented in some exuberantly playful and unique manner. One man was forced to his knees in front of an easy chair—then his mistress strapped his wrists to the chair's wooden armrests, and he was beaten on his naked rump with various paddles until the skin was bruised bright red. Another man was bound and gagged and had clothespins clamped onto his nipples, scrotum, and eventually any piece of available skin remaining on his legs and torso. The third man was made to lie on his back, upon a tarp that had been set down over the rug, and then remain still as paraffin candles, tipped downward, were waggled above him by three of the women. The hot wax that drizzled upon his body clearly caused him a good deal of pain, but also resulted in a surprisingly artistic and colorful design on his skin, which remained there as a memento for the duration of the evening.

Tiramisu and coffee followed. The three men served dessert in a remarkably sprightly manner. They displayed no ill effects whatsoever from their torturous ordeals; they in fact appeared energized by them.

As had been the case all evening, when the men weren't serving, each knelt silently on the floor beside the chair in which his mistress sat. They remained still as they watched the women sip and chat and laugh.

Bert poured shots for the six women from the bottle of fine limoncello he'd purchased for the occasion. He snuck a quick sip for himself, making certain to do so secretly—he was quite certain that such an offense, if detected, would merit some sort of dire, publicly administered punishment. After his intermittent witnessing of such roguery over the course of the evening, he had no appetite for any personal experience in that regard.

He brought the six glasses out, balanced elegantly on Gina's silver serving platter, and set one down before each of the women, serving Gina first. None of the ladies thanked him or even for a moment interrupted their incessant banter, but Gina did slip him a quick nod and wink.

After a second round of limoncello and another few minutes of conversation, the five guest dominatrices reluctantly acknowledged that it was probably time to leave. They thanked Gina profusely for a lovely evening, then went with their slaves into the bedroom to change back into normal attire.

Gina insisted that Bert prepare doggie bags with leftovers for all the ladies, and asked him to prepare three somewhat less copious bags for the men. She asked each of the women who'd brought a slave the same question as she was about to leave: "Was your boy sufficiently well behaved tonight to earn a doggie bag?"

Each of the of the women smiled and said, "Yes."

It took Bert another half-hour to finish cleaning the kitchen. He packed the dishwasher and got the cycle going, scrubbed the pots, pans, and baking dishes, wiped down the counters and sink, and packed his gear to take home.

He found Gina in the living room, relaxing on the loveseat. He was surprised that she hadn't yet changed out of her costume.

"Well," he said, "I think you threw a great party. I guess I'll put my clothes on and get going."

Gina smiled. "Oh, stay a little longer, sweetie," she said slowly. "I have one more thing I need."

Bert noticed that she was slurring. Between the cocktails he'd mixed, the wine he'd paired with each course, and the limoncello digestivo, she and the other women had consumed a colossal amount of alcohol. The persistent stimulation of her guests must have energized her before, but now that Gina had been sitting quietly for a while, the alcohol was making its effects quite perceptible.

"What do you need?" he asked.

"You look so hot. I want you to *do* me."

He thought she'd misspoken, due to being inebriated. "Sorry," he said. "I didn't get that."

"*Do* me!" she cried.

"What do you mean, *do* you?"

"Oh god, sweetie. *Do* me. Go for a muff dive."

Bert froze. He stared at her. She was nearly limp, half-reclined on the loveseat, a crooked smile on her face. "You want a blow job?"

"Yes. You got it. Good boy. Yes. That's what I want."

"I think you're drunk, Gina," he said softly. "Let's call it a night."

"You look sooo hot, sweetie—please, *do* me. I'll pay you an extra three hundred dollars. You'll still get the tip. This is on top of that."

"I'm gay!"

"You told me you've been with a few women. A long time ago. So you must be just at least a tiny bit *bi*."

"I did that because I thought that was what men were supposed to do. I didn't know who I was then."

"I'll give you four hundred." She smiled coquettishly. "My husband does very well. And he gives everything to me! Come on, sweetie. An extra four hundred on top of the tip."

"I'm just not into it, Gina."

"Damn it. I'm not asking you to get excited by it. I'm asking you to do it for *me*. Five hundred. Come on. You can't say no to that. Don't I look at least a little hot to you?"

Bert thought about the total he'd bring home with an extra five hundred dollars. How Dag would feel when he saw that.

He pondered it for a moment.

"If I do it, can I also borrow the costume I'm wearing? I think my boyfriend would get a real kick out of seeing me in it."

"It's a deal, sweetie! Five hundred, and you can *keep* the costume. My husband's gotten too fat for it anyway."

Gina unhooked her garters, yanked off her panties, pushed her hips to the very edge of the loveseat, and leaned all the way back. "I want to come at least five times," she said, laughing softly. "So kneel down and get comfy. Here"—she sat up and grabbed a pillow from the loveseat's corner—"put this under your knees, sweetie. You're gonna be down there a while."

Across the street, Central Park teemed with people. It was late morning.

Bert and Dag were lounging in their living room, each reading different parts of the Sunday *New York Times*. Dag was perusing the Business section, while Bert was engrossed with the Food pages. Aside from the occasional rustling of paper, the room had been silent for over an hour.

Bert had grown increasingly sullen and pensive in the week since he'd shared his cash bonanza from Gina's party. The earnings from that night had buoyed Dag's spirits for a day—but his fixation on finding a way to profit from the success of Will's paintings had rematerialized almost immediately. Bert was starting to feel trapped in the house with Dag, much as he'd felt trapped for years in the Scarsdale house with his father. But he saw no viable way out.

Even more troubling for him was his obsessive rumination about Gina's party, especially the oral sex he'd performed on her at the end of the night. He kept picturing himself kneeling in front of her—her hands clasped inexorably around the back of his head, pulling him tight against her.

In retrospect, he knew he should have refused to do it. He felt demeaned and exploited—but worse, he now believed that the whole slave persona Gina had coerced him into adopting for that evening was actually closer to how she truly viewed him than was the friendship and camaraderie he'd imagined prior to this ordeal.

The costume she had given him as part of his compensation now seemed to him tainted and repulsive. He'd thrown it in a drawer and hadn't touched it since. The fact that he even for a moment envisioned wearing it for sex with Dag was difficult now for him to reconcile with himself.

As he inattentively perused a recipe for Indonesian spring rolls, a tone signaling an incoming text chimed from the pocket of his jeans.

He put the paper down and pried out his phone. The text was from Rosemary.

"Holy shit!" he cried after taking quite a while to scrutinize the message.

"Is there a problem?" Dag asked.

"I had to read this text four times. I couldn't fucking believe it. It's from my sister-in-law. My brother just got home from brain surgery. Brain surgery! They cut a goddamn tumor out of his brain."

"Jesus!" Dag's eyes narrowed ever so slightly. "You should go out there, Bertie."

Bert's features tightened as he gazed incredulously at Dag. "What the fuck, Dag? My brother might be clinging to life by a thread, and you want me to go out there and sign a deal with him so you can make some money? What the fuck is wrong with you?"

"I didn't say go out to make a deal. For God's sake, Bertie, I'm not like that. I meant, go out there to be with them. To help them out. Mend some fences."

Bert sighed, inhaled deeply, and exhaled slowly. "Okay. Maybe I over-reacted. This news is upsetting, Dag. Sorry. Listen. I do want to see them. But I honestly don't think my father will let me in the house—even with all this going on with Will. My father's a lunatic, and he holds grudges forever. When I lived with him, he used to get drunk and talk about some asshole who stole a parking space from him, like, twenty years ago."

"Jesus."

"I think I'm gonna call Rosemary. Just to see what's going on."

"That's a good idea, Bertie."

Bert took a moment to gird himself for the call, then walked into the bedroom and closed the door.

As Dag sat alone on the sofa, he silently rehearsed phrases he could employ with Bert when they talked after the phone call—words that would display compassion regarding William's plight but would nonetheless keep preeminent in Bert's mind the necessity of snagging a piece of that huge financial portfolio.

A few minutes later, Bert returned and sat back down in the living room.

"So?" Dag asked.

"Well, I talked to Rosemary. She sounded okay."

"What's going on out there?"

"Will's home. Everyone from the hospital is telling them they think the surgery went well—but they'll know more in a week or so. For now, Will's mostly sleeping. The operation knocked the shit out of him. But he can walk to the bathroom and he's starting to eat a little, so that's good. When he's up more and starts having real conversations, they'll be able to assess his brain function better. But for now, they say it looks good."

"I guess that's the best you can expect right after surgery," Dag said. "Did you tell her you wanted to go out there?"

"Yeah. I did. Rosemary said she'd like that. She knows Arthur's against it, but she's gonna try to work on him—see what she can do."

"Well, that's a start. Listen. If you do get out there, Bertie—remember, your brother won't be thinking straight for a while—he'll need help making decisions. Arthur will try to bully him into God knows what. You can protect him, Bertie. Help him look out for his best interests."

Bert closed his eyes and leaned his head back. He said nothing.

CHAPTER 19

"**I**'D like to have dinner with everyone . . . at the table . . . tonight."

When he said it, William was in bed, tucked under the covers. His head was propped high on a pile of pillows. A perfectly straight incision, cleanly and precisely sutured, rose like a purplish-red centipede above the stubble growing on the left side of his head where he'd been shaved.

Rosemary had been sitting placidly on the chair near his side of the bed, keeping vigil. But when she heard him say this, her pixie-like features joyfully erupted—her eyes ballooned wide and an almost imperceptible gasp escaped her lips as they unfurled into a broad and exuberant smile.

William had been home nearly a week.

He'd spent four days in the hospital post-surgery. The nurses had been wonderfully attentive. He'd had sessions, each of those four days, with a physical therapist and an occupational therapist, and both had said he was way ahead of schedule. A speech therapist had paid him an initial visit but had said at the end of it that his speech was fine—she detected no loss of function whatsoever from the surgery, and explained to Rosemary that William was just too tired and sleepy to chat much at that point.

William insisted that Dr. Feigenbaum herself had paid him two brief visits while he was recovering in the hospital. But Rosemary had been by his side nearly constantly and had never seen her. She was convinced that William had conjured up those visits in his still-hazy imagination.

Since he'd been home, William had spent most of every day in bed. He slept many hours, and had just enough strength and focus while awake to watch comforting old westerns from the 1950s and 1960s on the cable channel that featured such vintage fare—which Rosemary found curious, because he'd never had much interest in television in general, and certainly not old cowboy shows, before now.

He was supposed to walk a few minutes every day to gradually build up his stamina, and Rosemary saw to it that he did. She'd taken a four-week leave from work to help see him through his recovery.

He'd been instructed to eat as much as he could keep down. His body's effort to regenerate was ravenous—it stole copious calories and nutrients from his bloodstream as it tried to slowly rebuild tissue and bone and restore strength and control to his muscles and nerve pathways. It left the rest of his body's needs wanting.

Even so, his stomach had at first refused to cooperate and ramp up his appetite. Thin soup and ice cream shakes were all he'd been able to tolerate. He'd graduated to peanut butter and jelly sandwiches just two days ago, and only yesterday had finally managed to eat something more substantial: chicken with mashed potatoes and carrots.

So, when he announced that he intended to somehow make his way downstairs and sit at the dinner table with Rosemary, Arthur, and Laurel that evening—Rosemary was astounded.

"That's wonderful, honey!" she exclaimed, her voice energetic and supportive. "Are you sure you feel up to getting down the stairs and sitting for an hour or more?"

"Oh . . . the stairs," he whispered. "I hadn't thought about the stairs." He looked hopefully at her. "But I can walk for ten minutes at a shot now. I did that this morning. So if you help me, I think I can make it down."

"And back up?"

"Yeah. Yeah, I think so. Back up. Right. I think I can. If we take it slow. Honestly, honey, I can't stand just lying here anymore. I'm ready to move around a little. I need to."

"Okay, baby. We'll make it work. The physical therapist predicted that you'd be joining the family for meals in a week or two, and you've been ahead of schedule on everything—so even though it's not quite a week, if you feel ready, we'll give it a try. Just be careful and take it really slow."

"Right. We'll take it slow."

"And don't even think about having a drink."

He chuckled. "Yeah, I know. Dr. Feigenbaum told me that. And the nurses. And the occupational therapist too. They all said no alcohol. Maybe not ever again, but certainly not for six months to a year."

"And you're okay with that, right? You'll be able to abstain if other people at the table are drinking? Your father's going to be drinking for sure. You have to be able to stay away from it. Alcohol is a poison to your brain right now, so you really have to."

He smiled. "I actually have no taste for alcohol at all, honey. Not a bit. Just the thought of it is kind of repulsive."

"Good! Keep that thought."

That evening, Rosemary suggested that a robe and slippers would be more than adequate for his first dining room appearance, but William insisted that she help him don jeans and a sweater. And a pair of sneakers, with thick white socks. She agreed, saying that that the sneakers would give him better traction on the stairs, but for

William it was more about the fact that he knew the clothing would be a real boost to his morale.

He made it down the stairs without a stumble. He held the banister tightly with one hand while Rosemary supported the other and he settled firmly on each step with both feet and paused a moment before attempting the next.

A huge smile permeated his face when he finally stood safely on the ground floor. He felt a part of things again.

Laurel and Arthur were in the living room, having cocktails, when William made his triumphant landing. Laurel struggled to her feet and applauded.

Arthur, too, rose from his leather recliner, drink in hand. He ambled over to the staircase and slapped William gently on the back. "Good job, son!" he said. "You'll be painting again in no time. And I want you to know, the stocks I invested your earnings in are doing great." He started to take a sip of his drink, then stopped and added, "I would have helped you down the steps myself, but you know, my hip still isn't all there—I have enough trouble getting up and down myself."

William heard Rosemary stifle a snort. He allowed himself a faint grin, then walked slowly into the living room and sat down.

"Just get comfortable, honey," Rosemary said. "I'll make you something to drink."

Rosemary had anticipated this moment—William's resumption of evening rituals, particularly cocktail hour in the living room before dinner, a rite Laurel had championed and eventually made stick. She knew he would need something to drink that tasted good, and had enough complexity to enable him to savor it leisurely. She'd scoured the internet and accumulated half-a-dozen enticing non-alcoholic cocktails.

Her inaugural salvo tonight was a virgin white lady, a luscious concoction that was designed to be made of egg whites mixed with grapefruit and lemon juices, elderflower cordial, and simple syrup. But she feared that raw egg whites would be too risky for William as he recuperated—and she didn't want to heat the egg, because that would change the drink's consistency. So she'd delved into vegan websites for a substitute and discovered a substance called aquafaba, which was nothing more than the liquid in which canned garbanzo beans were packed. She'd learned that many bartenders actually used aquafaba in place of egg whites as a matter of course, in part because it was safer but more so because it was superior in flavor and aroma.

She presented the drink to William in a martini glass garnished with a narrow ribbon of lemon rind she'd tied into a bow.

He loved it.

She'd made one for herself as well. It was delicious.

Everyone toasted to William's health, and settled in for conversation.

Rosemary periodically checked on the food she had cooking in the kitchen over the next hour.

But she kept an even closer eye on Arthur.

She was carefully monitoring his drinking. He'd finished his first martini, and Laurel had poured him another. It was here, during that second cocktail, that Rosemary planned to target precisely the right moment to pose her question. She had observed by now that every night, about halfway through his second drink, Arthur reached a noticeably mellow state. But it was short-lived. By the time he finished that round, he was already transitioning into unruly belligerence.

He was now about a third of the way through his cocktail. She dared not wait any longer.

"I spoke to Bertram the other day," she said, seizing upon a lull in the conversation.

"Bertram?" Laurel asked.

"Will's younger brother," Rosemary replied. "He's very concerned about Will's recovery. He'd like to help if he can."

Arthur placed his drink down onto its coaster with a resounding clink and leaned forward in his chair. He remained silent, but his interest was clearly piqued.

"You know," Laurel said, "you could certainly use some help around here."

"Yes, I could," Rosemary agreed. "Bert would like to come out and stay a while. I think that would be nice. And he could help with the cooking, especially. I understand he's quite gifted at that."

"I don't want him out here," Arthur said.

"Why not?" Laurel asked, shooting a glance his way.

"This is *my* house." Arthur said, his tone becoming defensive. "He's not coming out here. That's it. End of discussion." He picked up his martini and took a hearty swig—as if for emphasis.

"You haven't answered my question, Arthur," Laurel said. "I asked you why not."

"It's none of your business."

"It certainly is, and I want to know. Why don't you want him here?"

Arthur put his drink down and tightened his lips. His eyes narrowed; he took a long, pensive breath. "He's a fag," he finally muttered.

Laurel's features screwed themselves into a horrified scowl. "What did you just say?"

"I *said* he's a *fag.*"

Laurel turned her body fully in Arthur's direction. "I can't believe what you just called your son," she said sharply. "And I can't believe you're forbidding him to come into this house and help take care of his brother."

"Well, believe it, 'cause he's damn well not coming here."

Laurel stood up and took two steps toward Arthur. Her girth, coupled with her growing anger, made her presence formidable. She clenched one hand into a fist and rested it on her ample hip. Her other hand shot out and pointed itself menacingly in Arthur's face. "You listen to me, Arthur Wozniak. If you expect to have a woman sleeping in your bedroom with you tonight, you'll let your son visit."

"Jesus, Laurel. You're getting all dramatic."

"I sure as hell am. I am *not* going to be with a man who won't let his own son stay in this house because of who he loves. So make up your mind, Arthur Wozniak. Do you want me here or not? Because I'll leave right now—don't think I won't. And I promise, you'll never see me again."

Arthur's jaw grew slack. He took another huge gulp of his cocktail and gazed at Laurel. "Jesus. What the hell is such a big deal? For God's sake, all you people out here in California are crazy."

"What's your answer?" Laurel demanded.

Arthur put his drink down and sighed. "All right. He can come."

"And stay here?" Laurel pressed. "Here, in this house?"

Arthur inhaled slowly and reluctantly through clenched teeth. He expelled the breath with an audible hiss. "All right. He can stay in the house."

"Thank you, Arthur," Laurel said. She walked over, slowly leaned down, and gave him a quick kiss on the forehead. Then she returned to her chair.

As Laurel sat down, Rosemary arose, her face beaming. She jumped in excitement and clapped her hands a few times, her fingers pointed upward in an almost prayer-like pose. "Oh, I'm so happy," she cried. "This is great! I'm going to go call Bert right now." She ran into the kitchen.

Arthur held up his martini glass. "Hey, Laurel," he said morosely, "can you get me another one of these? I really need it."

William took a sip of his virgin white lady, then leaned back in his easy chair, smirking. It seemed to him that he'd chosen exactly the right night to return to the dinner table.

The place was small—just ten tables packed close together, with four narrow hardwood chairs crammed tightly between the legs of each one. The decorations hanging from the bare walls were kitschy knockoffs of pre-Columbian figures and masks.

But it was open all night, and the food was authentic and good. The beer list featured brews from all over Central and South America. The menu, however, was scrupulously Colombian.

At this hour, a few minutes before midnight, most of the diners were cooks whose restaurant shifts were finally over and who appreciated the well-prepared, hearty dishes.

Miguel and Bert were both halfway through their second bottles of Dos Equis. The beers were served with a wedge of lime jammed into the bottle's spout.

"You know," Miguel said, "I was kinda surprised when you called me yesterday. I mean—we call each other to pass off the occasional gig, but turning over all your clients to me? I wasn't expecting that, man."

"Well, at least for now," Bert said.

"Yeah. Either way, I appreciate it, man."

"It's not that many people, really. They're a nice bunch, though. I'm sure you'll take good care of them."

"If I can't cover them all, I know people who can," Miguel assured him. "And I'm really sorry about your brother. I hope he does all right."

"Thanks, I appreciate that."

Their food arrived, delivered by a young, athletic-looking Colombian man at whom Bert stared a bit longer than was appropriate. Set down before Bert was a platter of assorted empanadas—pork, chicken, and seafood—served with a spicy ají picante dipping sauce.

Miguel's choice was a steaming bowl of sancocho de cola soup. The broth was rich and shimmering, garnished with cilantro leaves. The deep-sided white square bowl that held the soup was packed with a corncob, a large hunk of oxtail on the bone, and hulking slabs of potato, plantain, and yucca.

"Damn this is good!" Bert exclaimed as he munched. "This place was a terrific choice."

"Yeah, I come here sometimes after a long night cooking. If Connie's over at her mom's, you know?" Miguel gingerly picked the corncob out of the bowl, then gnawed off a mouthful of juicy yellow kernels. He slurped a couple of additional spoonfuls of the broth as he chewed and quickly scanned the sheet of paper with the names, addresses, and phone numbers of Bert's clients. "So, anything special about any of these folks I should know?"

"Well"—Bert chuckled—"Gina's on the list. What you want to do about her is up to you. I gotta tell you though, you were damn right about her. She turned out to be a bitch. Honestly, I wouldn't cook for her again."

"Wow! What happened? She was your favorite there for a while."

"Yeah, well, I'd rather not get into too much about that. I'll just tell you that what you said about her wanting me sexually—that was totally right. But—you know, the thing with her—it was like I was just someone she could pay to do it. That's bullshit, man."

"Yeah, I saw through her. Gotta say, though, she pays well—and the gigs can be kinda fun. For *me*, I mean. She's not into *me* that way. So we'll see. Maybe I'll take a gig, if she'll have me." He gouged the potato with his spoon and popped a scoop of it into his mouth. "When are you telling your clients that you're leaving?"

"Tomorrow." Bert gulped down some beer. "I just wanted to make sure you and me were squared away on this before I let them know."

"So, man—the big question: when are you coming back?"

"That's the thing . . . I don't really know. Could be a few weeks—a couple of months—could be longer. Hell—maybe I won't come back at all."

"You and Dag not doing so good?"

"No, we're not." Bert took a bite of the chicken empanada and chewed it pensively before saying, "You know, it's complicated with him. Dag really helped me. He kinda took me under his wing and helped me come out. Nobody else was there for me like that. Jesus, I might never have come out without him. I know that sounds ridiculous—I mean, gay marriage is legal now, and it seems like everybody comes out before they even get to high school these days. But I kinda missed out on that whole thing. I'm a little older and—I don't know—I just really was never sure." He drank some more beer. "It was hard for me, Miguel. Dag helped with that. I feel like maybe I owe him."

Miguel offered Bert the slightest hint of a smile. "You don't owe him shit, man. He wanted you. You're a good-looking guy. An old guy like him doesn't get someone like you very often—so he got something out of it too. Now you gotta live your own life."

"Thanks, Miguel. I think you're right."

"So what are you gonna tell him?"

"Yeah, that's gonna be hard. I think I'm just going to say I'll be gone a few weeks. Leave it at that for now. I mean, that's a lot easier, and then if I do decide to come back I can just come back—you know, no hard feelings, nothing to explain. But if I decide to stay out there—assuming there's a way I can make a living—then it'll be easier to just tell him that from there."

"Makes sense, man. I wish you luck. You said it was Sonoma, right? North of San Francisco?"

"Right. Sonoma."

"I got a cousin who lives out there now. In Sonoma. Good guy. You should look him up. He does some cooking—and now he's trying to get a catering business going. His name is Davey, I'll let him know you might call. Okay?"

"Yeah, that'd be great, Miguel. It would be nice to know some other people out there."

CHAPTER 20

*A*CCESSING Sonoma County's small airport, just north of Santa Rosa, would have meant taking connecting flights on small planes. Bert chose instead to fly nonstop from New York to San Francisco and pick up a rental car there.

Rosemary had described the drive from San Francisco's airport to the house in Sonoma as about an hour and a half long, and very pretty. Bert thought that being on the road and getting a feel for the area was a good idea. He'd never been to California.

Having the car also gave him options. If things did not go well and he needed to find alternative lodgings on short notice, a car would enable him to get out quickly. It also now afforded him time alone—valuable time to quiet his rampaging fears and brace himself for the inevitable encounter with his father. Rosemary had told him that Arthur had a girlfriend now, a woman named Laurel who William thought looked somewhat like their deceased mother. Bert wondered whether that woman's influence had possibly softened his father's demeanor.

SFO, and its nearby rental car hub, sat twelve miles south of San Francisco. From there he headed north on Highway 101, which seemed to him to be a typical freeway until he reached San Francisco's Market Street, about two miles southwest of downtown—from that point up to the city's northernmost tip, Highway 101 was all city streets. That surprised Bert quite a bit. He'd pictured California as a land of super-highways. But when he thought more about it, he realized that was probably more the case for Los Angeles. San Francisco was evidently a very different animal.

Highway 101 resumed its rightful freeway identity just prior to ushering him over the Golden Gate Bridge, and continued that way through picturesque Marin and into Sonoma County.

When he exited the freeway, he drove slowly, following narrow roads that wound through vineyards and forests. He finally reached the turnoff that led to the circuitous driveway up to his father's house.

But he balked and drove past it.

He wasn't ready.

By the time the text message came through to his phone, he had declined that same driveway turnoff three more times, and was cruising aimlessly along a dirt road that circled a pond. He glanced at the phone, lying on the seat beside him. The text was from Rosemary.

Bert pulled over to read it.

She was asking if he was okay—the airline's website, she said, showed that his plane had landed over three hours ago—and saying that she hoped he wasn't lost or injured.

Bert took a long deep breath. He texted back that he was almost there.

He pulled in just a few minutes later. Rosemary was standing in front of the house, and when she saw him she smiled exuberantly, clapped her hands, and jumped up onto her toes. She yelled to William through the open front door, and he and Laurel came out to join her.

Bert emerged from his vehicle sporting a hesitant, sheepish grin. Rosemary ran to him and hugged him enthusiastically. William ambled over and waited his turn behind her.

Laurel stood a few feet back. She had never met Bert. She watched closely as the two brothers approached each other, smiled warmly, and hugged. She found the contrast between them fascinating.

Will was just a bit taller than Bert, but Will's leisurely, round-shouldered slouch rendered the two nearly identical in height. The similarities ended there: Will was gentle and doughy, with an easygoing bearing and relaxed manner, whereas Bert was lean, athletic-looking, and, at least for the moment, possessed of what Laurel read as a caged, turbulent vigor.

The brothers' hug lingered, and grew more emotional and fervent. Soon Rosemary joined them, embracing both men tightly, her head barely reaching to their shoulders.

"Oh, I have to fetch Arthur," Laurel exclaimed, touched by the affectionate moment. "He needs to be part of this!"

She walked quickly into the house and found Arthur gazing at the scene through a window. "Get out there and hug your sons!" she cried.

"I don't think so," he mumbled.

"You're going out there *right now!*" Laurel yanked him by the arm and dragged him outside, depositing him just on the outskirts of the group hug. But when he stood and did nothing, she shoved him into the cluster between his two boys (on the opposite side from that which Rosemary had chosen), pressed her considerable torso powerfully against Arthur's back, grabbed each of the brothers' shoulders, and pulled hard, effectively sandwiching Arthur inescapably between herself and the ardent mass embrace.

Arthur was a good deal shorter than his two sons, so nobody could see the expression on his face. But had they been able to, they would have seen that his features, in contrast to the broad smiles all around him, were puckered into a mortified grimace, and his shoulders squeezed tightly upwards, as if to form a sanctuary inside which he could conceal his head.

Rosemary led Bert up the stairs to one of the unoccupied bedrooms. Bert carried his two heavy suitcases, managing them effortlessly. Rosemary helped with his small carry-on satchel. Laurel lagged a bit behind, lugging a briefcase that held Bert's laptop, his tablet, and a few cookbooks.

Down in the living room, William was resting, a bit exhausted from all the hugging and milling about.

Arthur had skulked off to the small cottage next door.

When Bert entered the spare room his face froze and he nearly gasped. All of the old furniture that had been in his bedroom in the Scarsdale house was right there in front of him, laid out almost identically to how he'd had it for years.

"Wow," he said. "This bed, and the nightstand and all—it's like déjà vu. Kinda spooky."

"Is it okay?" Rosemary asked in a concerned tone. "It's the only spare room we have that's fully furnished."

Bert chuckled. "I slept on this bed for, like, thirty years. I can sleep on it another few weeks. No worries. Really. I'm fine." He set his suitcases down. "Hey, I'll unpack first—but after, is it okay if I take a quick shower? I'm kinda grungy from the flight."

"Sure," Rosemary said. "Let me show you where your bathroom is. You'll have it all to yourself. I put fresh towels out."

He grabbed his toiletry case and followed her.

When they reached the bathroom, she added, "Oh, one more thing—we have a cat. Her name is Molly. You won't see her much, but if you do, don't be startled."

"This is great," he said. Thanks for everything."

About an hour and a half later, Bert ambled downstairs. He had on a clean shirt, and his hair was still slightly wet. He found everyone in the living room.

"Ah," Laurel chirped. "Welcome. Just in time for cocktail hour!"

"I could use a cocktail!" Bert said with a smile. Now that he had a moment to observe Laurel closely, he realized she *did* bear an eerie resemblance to his late mother—the way she looked when he was young.

Bert sat down in an easy chair next to the loveseat that William and Rosemary were sharing.

Laurel walked over. "Your father and I are drinking manhattans. May I get you one? I mixed a whole pitcher!"

"Sure," Bert said. "Thanks."

As Laurel went into the kitchen, Bert smiled at Rosemary. "And what are you and Will drinking?"

"Oh, Will's off alcohol for a while," she explained. "It's a post-surgery precaution. So, I'm supporting him by doing it too. I actually feel good taking a little break."

"Well, what you have there looks interesting," he said. "We should compare notes some time on non-alcoholic cocktails. I have a couple of clients who don't drink, so I've built up a little repertoire."

"I have a repertoire too!" Rosemary replied with an enthusiastic grin. "That will be fun. So, are you all settled in?"

"Yeah. Thanks. The shower felt good."

"How was the flight?" William asked.

"Oh, it was fine. But I want to hear about you. How's my big brother doing since his brain operation?"

"I'm coming along well," William said. "Really well."

"I'm glad to hear that. So, tell me—what was the surgery like?"

William smiled and closed his eyes for a moment. "You know, after all the prep, and then lying on the table waiting for the anesthesia to kick in, and all the worrying before that—what I remember most is the moment I woke up."

"When you woke up, you mean after the surgery was done?" Bert asked.

"Right. When it was all done. So, I was alone there. All by myself in this tiny bed in the recovery room. It had a curtain around it and nobody was there, because they didn't expect me to come out of it so fast. So, I woke up, and at first, I was really confused—you know, it took me a few seconds to figure out where I was. But then it was, like, this totally joyful moment. I'm lying there, alone, thinking—*I made it! I'm alive! I made it through!*—you know, because honestly—I didn't want to think too much about it before the surgery—but there was a part of me that really didn't think I'd make it." William smiled, then leaned over and put his arm around Rosemary and kissed her lightly on the cheek. "Then, a few minutes later, the nurse came in, and when she saw I was awake, she brought Rosemary in right away."

"Yes, it was quite a moment," Rosemary said, beaming. "I'll never forget it. Seeing him. Awake. And smiling."

Laurel returned from the kitchen with a manhattan in a chilled stemmed glass, garnished with two brandied cherries. She handed it to Bert, then walked back to join Arthur.

"Thank you," Bert said, then extended his glass toward William and Rosemary. "To good health."

As Bert took his first sip, he noticed Laurel sidling back toward him. She leaned down close to his ear. "Come over and toast with your dad and me too," she whispered.

Bert turned and looked at Arthur. He was sitting in the opposite corner of the room, hunched and sullen. He clutched his drink as if he feared that someone would snatch it from him.

"He, uh, doesn't look like he wants company," Bert stammered softly.

"Oh, you leave him to me. He needs to start talking to his son again. Come on."

Bert followed Laurel over and stood in front of Arthur, who was still huddled on his black leather recliner, cradling his manhattan. Laurel picked up her cocktail from the coaster upon which she'd set it and proposed a toast.

"To new beginnings," she proclaimed animatedly. She clinked glasses with Bert and Arthur.

Bert slowly extended his glass in his father's direction. Arthur stared down at the floor and made no gesture to reciprocate.

"Have a toast with your son, Arthur," Laurel said petulantly. "We talked about this."

Arthur reluctantly clinked glasses with Bert, and immediately looked away.

"Well, it's a start," Laurel said with a sigh. She and Bert walked back across the room to where William and Rosemary were sitting.

"I'll keep working on him," Laurel said with a wink. "We'll wear him down."

Rosemary sneered. "I wish you the best of luck with that," she muttered sardonically. She leaned over and kissed William lightly on the mouth, then stood up and gave Bert a quick kiss too. "Well, you guys keep chatting. I'm going to start dinner."

"We hear Bert's a great chef," Laurel chimed in. "How about we put *him* to work tonight?"

"Oh, no!" Rosemary said. "He just got here. He must be tired. I'll cook dinner."

A broad smile spread across Bert's features. "I love cooking, Rosemary. There really isn't much I love doing more. I'd really enjoy cooking with you."

Rosemary glanced at Laurel and sighed. "Well, then," she said, "I guess we're a team tonight! Come on."

The two of them walked together into the kitchen. When they got to the work area, Rosemary said, "If you had déjà vu with your bedroom, you're going to have it all over again—big time—in here with the pots and pans and dishware."

"Oh god!" Bert said. "It's like seeing old friends. The living room's the same too. I think I'm over the shock now, though." He had a quick laugh. "So, what's on the menu for tonight?"

"Well, I thought a nice, earthy Italian dinner would be a good choice for the family reunion. A big salad with goat cheese and a balsamic vinaigrette. Some garlic bread. A side of creamed spinach. And I have this recipe I'm dying to try—it's spaghetti and meatballs but you make the meatballs out of eggplant, zucchini, and breadcrumbs—you know, with a nice tomato sauce, and lots of fresh grated cheese, I don't think even Arthur will miss the meat. And I bought some top-shelf gelato and biscotti for dessert."

"That sounds wonderful!" Bert cried. "You know, I've actually made veggie balls just like the ones you're talking about a few times. It works better if you add a little egg, to bind it. Is that okay?"

"Yes!" Rosemary said excitedly. "The recipe I have calls for egg too."

"Great, let's get to it."

By the end of an hour, the salad was tossed, the dressing was mixed, and the veggie balls and marinara sauce were off to a good start.

"You know," Bert said, "you cook here every night. Why don't you take a break and spend some time with Will? I got this."

"Really? Are you sure?"

"I came out here to help you, didn't I?"

"Oh, you're so sweet! Thank you. Thank you." Rosemary hugged Bert and went back out into the living room. She found Laurel alone, glancing through a magazine and sipping on her cocktail.

"Where's Will and Arthur?" Rosemary asked.

"Oh, Arthur took Will out to his office to look at investment stuff. Here, sit down." Laurel patted the area next to her on the couch. "You and I can chat for a while. Some girl talk."

Rosemary would rather have been in the kitchen, cooking with Bert. But she saw no way to squirm out of Laurel's invitation. So she sat down.

"I realize you haven't been drinking alcohol so you can be in solidarity with Will, dear—and that's so sweet—but it's just you and me here for a while, so can I pour you a manhattan? I have a glass chilled already, in the freezer."

"Actually, I think I *could* use one," Rosemary said.

"Groovy!" Laurel exclaimed, and was back quickly with Rosemary's drink. She sat down and the two women toasted.

"So, what have you been thinking and feeling lately?" Laurel asked. "There's so much happening."

Rosemary lifted her drink and took a few uncharacteristically huge swallows. She noticed Laurel leaning toward her, clearly intent upon inducing a heartfelt and introspective response. Rosemary didn't want to bare herself that way, so she opted to talk about Laurel instead—a bit of verbal jiu jitsu, she thought. "I really want to thank you, Laurel. You're sweet to welcome Bert like you have. And the way you keep on Arthur—you know, not letting him get away with shit—I can't tell you how much that helps. And how good at it you are."

Rosemary felt very satisfied with her deflection. She took another gulp of her manhattan.

"Well, thanks," Laurel said with a giggle, "but I have an advantage nobody else has: I have something Arthur wants. He really wants to be with me. He doesn't want me to leave."

"That *does* give you leverage," Rosemary agreed, and took another sip.

"You've probably noticed that Arthur has a thing for big women," Laurel said. "So this is very different for me. It's not just that he tolerates my size because he likes me as a person. I mean, he likes me as a person—I guess. But my body is the primary draw. I've been big all my life, and I've never once experienced that kind of attraction. I can't tell you how wonderful it feels."

"I'm sure it does," Rosemary said.

"I know Arthur can be difficult. And there's a limit to what I'll put up with, and that's when you see me put my foot down. But, you know—it's a give and take. I'm grateful to have a man too."

Rosemary gazed at Laurel for a few moments and said nothing. Laurel suddenly looked more real—the lines on her face, the subtle asymmetry of her cheeks. Rosemary had never looked closely enough to notice those things before. "Well, you certainly have your hands full now," she said. "Arthur's thing with Bert is bad—and it seems pretty well entrenched."

"Like I said, we'll wear him down."

"I'll help where I can," Rosemary said.

Laurel held up her empty glass. "I'm going to get another. Can I top off yours?"

Rosemary smiled and took a couple of big gulps, leaving her glass just about a quarter full. "Absolutely."

When Laurel returned with their refreshed drinks, she said, "So, tell me—how's Will doing? I mean *really*. He seems to be coming along so well. I just want to be sure."

Rosemary sipped on her manhattan and thought about Laurel's question before saying, "I think, physically, he's really doing well. I wonder, though, about his thought process—I mean—what has all this done to him, emotionally and psychologically?"

"And what do you think?"

"You know, he hasn't started painting yet. He says he needs more energy. But I think he's also scared, worried about what's going to happen when he starts up again. He has no idea what the canvases will look like. That has to be terrifying."

"He seems so calm and happy, though," Laurel said.

"That's just it!" Rosemary cried. "That's exactly it. Calm and happy. I mean—he was mellow before, but he's even more so now." She took a few more sips of her cocktail, then glanced around to be sure nobody was nearby before leaning in toward Laurel and whispering, "And I have to say, he's not quite as sharp—I mean, verbally and intellectually—as he was. Maybe that'll all come back. Maybe not. But he's so damn sweet. Like, he appreciates just being alive and being with *me*. I hope he doesn't lose that. In a way, I'd rather have that—I mean, if I had to choose."

"I don't think he'll lose that," Laurel said. "I've seen it too. It seems very real—very, like, intrinsic to who he is now. I don't think he'll lose it."

The two women were quiet for a time, nursing their drinks. Then Laurel blurted out, "You didn't like me at first, Rosemary. I know that. Did you think I was too chatty?"

Rosemary was nonplussed by the directness of the question. "Well . . ." was the best she could do in the way of a flustered reply.

"See, that's my work head," Laurel said. "I'm driving around with people. Trying to keep their attention on the properties. On getting to a decision. I don't make any money unless they come to a decision—and I've learned that lulls in the conversation aren't good, Rosemary. They lead to a loss of interest. It's kind of like being a radio deejay. You know, no white space allowed. Silence on the radio is like death—they fire a deejay for that." Laurel sipped on her drink. "It takes me a while to get comfortable enough with someone I like to finally slow down. I'm sorry if I was a bit much." She laughed and held up her manhattan. "This helps a whole lot."

Rosemary put down her drink, hugged Laurel, and gave her a kiss on the cheek.

"Thank you for explaining that," she said. "Thank you."

The two women were still drinking and chatting when Bert came in from the kitchen and announced that dinner was ready. Laurel walked out to the cottage to fetch William and Arthur, while Rosemary went back into the kitchen with Bert to start serving.

CHAPTER 21

*O*N Bert's third night in town, William felt exhausted. He opted to skip dinner and sleep through to the next morning. He assured Bert and Rosemary that he was enjoying Bert's visit very much—it just had taken a bit more out of him than he expected.

Without William, nobody felt like cooking that night, so they called the little Mexican place in Petaluma and ordered a bunch of food to-go. Rosemary and Bert drove over to pick it up.

Bert thought the food was delicious. The way it was spiced and prepared gave him some new ideas he was anxious to incorporate into his own Mexican-style dishes. And though he'd only spent a few minutes in the restaurant while picking up the food, he'd found the atmosphere there enchanting.

So, a week later, when he finally worked up the gumption to call Miguel's cousin Davey, he suggested they meet there for lunch.

As he pulled into the restaurant's parking lot, he saw Davey standing in front of the entrance. They'd texted headshots the night before so they would recognize each other.

It was a warm day. Davey was in a snug black polo shirt and jeans and was just above average height—but wiry and lithe, like a soccer player or a bicyclist.

Bert parked and hurried over. "Hi, I'm Bert Wozniak," he said, extending his hand. "It's nice to meet you."

"Davey Reyes. Good to meet you, too." Davey grinned warmly as the two men shook hands. "Miguel was right. He said you were a tall guy. Nice-looking. Said you played a sport in college—but he couldn't remember which one."

"Yeah. Baseball. I was a pitcher."

"Nice. I played tennis. Had a winning record. Singles and doubles."

Bert thought back to his college days. "You know"—he smiled wistfully—"I always wanted to try tennis. But it was a summer sport, and it competed with baseball, so I never really had an opportunity."

"Well, maybe one of these days you and I can go out to the courts together. I'll show you the strokes. A guy like you could pick 'em up pretty quick, I think."

"I might actually take you up on that," Bert said. "Are you hungry? This place has really good food. I've only had takeout, but I've been meaning to come."

"Yeah. Let's give it a try."

Inside the restaurant, they got started with a pitcher of sangria, along with chips and guacamole, to share.

"So, you're Miguel's cousin?" Bert asked.

Davey put his drink down and laughed. "We're not cousins! Hell, he's Puerto Rican and I'm Mexican."

"What?" Bert cried with a hearty chuckle and incredulous shake of his head. "He kept calling you his cousin."

"Yeah, he does that. See, I spent some time in New York City. It was a few years ago. Me and Miguel cooked at the same restaurants, and we hung out a fair amount. Which was interesting, cause he's straight, and I'm gay, and that doesn't always go well, but he was really cool. So it was nice. But the thing was, he'd tell everybody we were cousins. We used to laugh about that. I always told him that he only said that so people wouldn't think he was gay."

Bert smiled. "Did he deny it?"

Davey was still laughing. "Not really."

"Well, Miguel always seemed totally cool with me being gay too. He's a good guy." Bert took a healthy swallow of sangria and leaned in toward Davey. "Just between you and me though, he can be a little bit of a hothead. We had a couple of run-ins, you know. But we worked it all out."

Davey put down his glass. His polite laughter had morphed now into heaving guffaws that seemed uncontrollable. "A hothead? You think?" He raised his right hand and pointed at Bert for emphasis. "I've seen him go off about the tiniest little thing—like a madman! But then, you know, he gets over it. He really never holds a grudge."

The waitress brought a plate of enchiladas and a plate of quesadillas. She glanced at the men, as if to ask who got what.

"Just put them in the middle of the table, please," Davey said. "We're sharing everything today."

"Oh, okay," she said, smiling. "Then I'll be right back with a couple of extra plates."

When the two small plates were set down, Bert and Davey each took an enchilada and a wedge of quesadilla and dug in.

"So," Davey asked, "how are things going for you since you got here? Miguel told me a little about your family. Your dad sounds like a real piece of work."

"Oh, he's that and more," Bert said. "I kind of zinged him, though. The very first night I got there he didn't realize that I had cooked most of the dinner. He was going on and on about how good the food was and what a great cook my sister-in-law is—you know, trying to show me that he really didn't need me around anymore—until we sprang it on him that I'd done most of the cooking that night."

"How did he take that?"

Bert chuckled. "He just kinda rolled up into an angry ball and wanted to burst. And for the longest time he wouldn't say anything. Then his girlfriend finally got him to admit that I was a good cook too. She knows how to pull his strings. I've been there a week and a half now—and I've seen her do her thing with him. She's impressive. She might actually make it possible for me to stay out here a while. Maybe for good. I don't know."

Davey grabbed another wedge of quesadilla. "Wow. The food here is terrific. Thanks for turning me on to this place. I live less than half an hour away, but I never tried it."

Bert drank some more sangria. "So, are you seeing anybody?"

"No," Davey replied. "I just went through a breakup a couple of months ago, actually. You?"

Bert finished the sangria in his glass and poured himself another. He topped off Davey's glass too. "I guess technically I'm still living with a guy. Dag. He's back in New York."

"Miguel mentioned him. Said you two were having problems."

"Yeah. Quite a few. The more I'm out here, the more I don't think I'm going back."

"What kind of problems were you guys having?"

"I just don't think we belong together. He's a lot older than me. And picky about so many things. Prissy—that's the word—prissy. And really into money. Always acting important." Bert swirled his sangria. "You know, I was doing personal chef gigs back there—but I don't think Dag ever really respected that as a job. He would have been a lot happier if I was selling real estate. God, I hate real estate."

"That reminds me of this word I came across the other day," Davey said. "I do this thing online every morning—learn a new word a day. A couple of days ago it was one I really liked. It summed up so much that you could say in a single word. *Cockalorum*. Have you heard of that word?"

Bert snickered. "Cockalorum? No. But it sure sounds interesting. What the hell does it mean?"

"A self-important little man. You know, a guy who prances around like a rooster—a cock. Cockalorum."

Bert laughed and reached for the last wedge of quesadilla. "Yup. That's him exactly."

There was silence for a short while as the men finished the food on their plates. Then Davey looked up. "You know, like I said, I live close by. You want to come over and hang out a while?"

Bert grinned. "I'd like that very much."

Davey's house was small, really more like a bungalow. There were two steps up to a wooden porch with a couple of rocking chairs. From there, the door to the house led directly into the kitchen and eating area. Behind that was a modest living room, and then a sort of narrow vestibule bordered by two little bedrooms and a bathroom.

"Cute place," Bert said. "Do you own it?"

"No, I rent it. I think there's this one guy who owns, like, every house on the block. They're all pretty much the same. It's a nice neighborhood, though. Good folks. A lot of younger people. Chefs. Musicians. Artists. I like it here."

Bert sat down on the living room couch.

Davey went into the top drawer of a small desk and pulled out a joint. "Do you smoke?"

"Sure, now and then," Bert said.

Davey lit the joint and sat down next to him on the couch. They each had a couple of hits.

The pot was strong. Bert leaned back and glanced around the room. "Having a place like this all to yourself—it's so nice."

"It really isn't much," Davey said. "Sometimes I'm embarrassed to bring people here. It's kinda small."

"I've never had my own place," Bert said. "Not once in my life. When I was a kid I lived with my parents; then with just my father, after my mother died—that went on for years; and the last six months or so I've been living in Manhattan with Dag, in his place. Now that I'm out here, I'm living with my family again." Bert bowed his head and felt his eyes begin to tear up. He blinked hard and took a deep breath to reset. "I'll tell you, this place looks like a little castle to me."

Davey leaned over and brought his face close to Bert's. Bert closed the gap and their lips touched. Their kisses became passionate. Davey unbuttoned Bert's shirt and pulled off his own.

Their ardor escalated quickly.

Davey took Bert's hand and led him to the bedroom. They both stripped naked, still kissing, and leaped into the double bed. After a bit more kissing and rolling about, Davey deftly curled and reversed his body's orientation, and the two men began simultaneously pleasuring each other orally.

That continued for quite a while as the intensity built. Then, with a loud scream, Davey orgasmed. He closed his eyes, and his body relaxed blissfully. Bert withdrew, and waited a few moments for Davey to perk up. When Davey opened his eyes and smiled, Bert's strong hands gently positioned Davey onto his knees.

"The lube's in the top drawer," Davey said, pointing to the small nightstand next to the bed. Bert's long arm could reach it with just a slight lean and stretch.

Bert mounted Davey from behind and noticed immediately how relaxed and receptive he was. Bert thought about all the times he and Dag had done it—how tight Dag always was to start, how he needed to be gently coaxed and cajoled with incremental forays.

Bert was soon pumping with uninhibited passion. His movements were ecstatic and instinctual—devoid of conscious thought. He hadn't experienced this sort of mind state since the first few times with Dag, when everything was still new.

He lost track of how long it went on, and was a bit shocked when his orgasm suddenly engulfed him—he hadn't felt it coming until the last moment. He roared gutturally as he ejaculated, then dismounted—more as if he were gently melting away in exhaustion than pulling out.

He was about to lie down, thinking the session had ended, when he noticed to his surprise that Davey was hard again. He became unnerved when he felt Davey's hands positioning him for anal penetration.

He tensed, uncertain of what to do. A spasm of momentary panic seized him. Finally he closed his eyes and whispered, "Hold up. I'm sorry—you're not going to believe this—but I'm a virgin down there."

Davey paused and rubbed Bert gently on the lower back. "That's okay, no judgment. Is it because you don't like it?"

Bert slowly rolled over onto his back and propped his upper body up on his elbows so he could look at Davey as they spoke. "Well," he said haltingly, "you're actually only the second guy I've ever been with. I know I'm almost forty, and that's crazy. But I didn't come out for a long time. I had a lot of trouble accepting who I was."

"A lot of people do, Bert. That's okay. You seem to be doing just fine now."

"Thanks." Bert flushed, fumbling for the right words. "Um—see— Dag's the only guy I've ever been with—and he never wanted to be top. He only wanted to bottom. I don't know why."

"Yeah," Davey said. "The passive receptor. I've known guys like that. For me, it gets a little old to always do it one way."

"Honestly, though," Bert stammered, "I'm not even sure I could do it if we tried. My anus is small. It's a long story. A congenital thing."

Davey smiled and stroked Bert's thigh gently. "You want another hit?" he asked. "Let me go get the joint from the living room."

He climbed off the bed but was back in just a moment. The joint was lit and he was in the midst of a long drag as he walked back into the bedroom. He handed it to Bert, who took a couple of short puffs. Then he cuddled up next to Bert and kissed him. "Do you mind if I have a look?" he asked.

"You mean at my . . ."

"Yeah."

"Okay," Bert said hesitantly. "Don't expect much." He maneuvered onto all fours.

Davey sat up in the bed and brought his face close to Bert's buttocks. He probed very gently around Bert's anus and gingerly tested the tips of the sphincter muscles inside. "Yeah, it's a little small, but really not that bad," he said softly and reassuringly. "You want to get to a point where you can do it—right?"

"If I can, absolutely."

"I'm sure you can. Listen. We'll take it real slow. Part of it is you learning to relax, and part of it is just getting the muscles and skin to gradually stretch out. How about I try it with just one finger, and a lot of lube?"

Bert nodded. "Sure, go ahead."

Davey slathered his finger with as much of the jelly as he could pile on and very slowly maneuvered it in—first just the very tip, then gently working up to the first knuckle, then the second, and finally, after several minutes, his whole finger, lightly sliding it in and out with a comfortable, predictable rhythm.

Bert started to relax. "Wow, that feels good," he said, his voice resonating as much with relief as with pleasure.

Davey gently withdrew his finger and grabbed a couple of tissues to wipe his finger off. "That's enough for today."

The two men lay down next to each other and looked into one another's eyes.

"So, I did okay?" Bert asked.

"You did great. You really relaxed, and everything opened up. Next time, we'll see if, after a little work, I can get two fingers in. We'll get there." Davey squeezed his arm. "It may take a few weeks. But I'm sure we'll get there."

"I want to see you again, soon," Bert said.

"Absolutely," Davey agreed with a huge grin and a hug. "Maybe the day after tomorrow?"

"Sure!" Bert said. "But it's better for me if we do it during the day, like this, if that's okay with you. I'm kind of committed to help cook dinner for my family every night."

Davey nodded in agreement. "Days are actually much better for me too. My cooking gigs are all at night."

"And you said you're doing some catering gigs too, right?"

"Yeah—that's the business I'm really trying to get going. That's kinda my dream. The gigs vary—I do book stuff on Sunday afternoons now and then, but most of them are at night."

"Daytime the day after tomorrow it is, then," Bert said, smiling, before leaning in for a kiss.

The nurse noted William's weight and blood pressure. He then led Rosemary and William to the small conference room where William's follow-up meeting with Dr. Feigenbaum was scheduled.

They were surprised to see the doctor already sitting in the room when they entered.

Brief hellos were exchanged as they sat down.

Rosemary noticed immediately that the doctor appeared some-what less dour, and a good deal more comfortable, than she had when they'd all met prior to Will's surgery.

Dr. Feigenbaum rose and walked over to take a look at Will's scalp. She pulled back the hair that had started to grow, and her fingers gently prodded the area. "You're healing beautifully," she observed before returning to her seat.

"That's great to hear," Rosemary said.

"And how are you feeling, William?" Dr. Feigenbaum asked.

"Good, I think," William said. "I'm still tired a lot. But I can get around pretty well now." He smiled. "I'm very grateful for everything you've done."

"How are your thought processes?"

William looked quizzically at Rosemary. "What do you think, honey?"

Rosemary hesitated and cocked her head gently as she looked at Will—lovingly, but a bit sadly—then turned to the doctor. "Overall, I think he's doing fine," she said. "But he's not quite as sharp or quick as he was." She looked back to William. "I have to just tell her the truth, baby, I'm sorry."

"It's the truth," William said softly. "I see it, too."

Dr. Feigenbaum pursed her lips. Her words emerged slowly and thoughtfully.

"That's not uncommon, William. It may improve. Your mind may very well return to the way it was before."

"But it may not?" Rosemary pressed.

"It's impossible to know." Dr. Feigenbaum shifted in her chair to sit more upright. "I wish I could say. It's just something that has to play out. It's only been a few weeks. As the healing progresses, we'll continue to observe. It can take quite a bit of time. Months. Sometimes even a couple of years."

Rosemary studied the doctor's features as she listened. It was subtle, but it seemed to her that there was more emotion in the doctor's face and voice than she had ever before detected.

William turned to Rosemary. "Maybe it will improve," he said. "We'll have to wait and see, honey."

His tone was measured and calm. Rosemary detected a hint of quiet optimism that roused her spirits.

"Have you tried painting yet, William?" the doctor asked.

"No," he whispered, looking down. "I'm still very tired, Dr. Feigenbaum."

"And perhaps a little afraid?"

He nodded. "A little."

"Give it time," Dr. Feigenbaum said. "I'll be curious to know how it turns out—when you're ready, of course."

William hesitated for a moment, then tentatively said, "Do you remember, Doctor, when you asked me if you could write about my case? And I said yes. So, I was wondering . . . have you started doing that?"

The barest trace of a smile materialized on Dr. Feigenbaum's lips. "Oh no, William," she said. "I *will* write about your case—in time. It is indeed a fascinating one, and I'm looking forward to chronicling it. But your journey is far from over. There is so much that is yet to happen; so much that you will undoubtedly discover about yourself. New neural pathways will replace old ones. New perspectives will develop. I can't possibly write about it yet. The more I know you, William, the more I am convinced that for you—there is still so much to come. And I want to record every bit of it."

CHAPTER 22

*I*T had become a nightly ritual: Rosemary and Bert prepared dinner together in the kitchen while William lounged in the living room, sipping on drinks, with Arthur and Laurel.

Rosemary and Bert had indeed pooled their knowledge regarding non-alcoholic cocktails, and William was provided with wonderful concoctions to nurse each evening. Tonight he was drinking a Donn's Virgin Sacrifice, an alluring blend of grapefruit and lime juices mixed with two syrups—one concocted from unfiltered honey and water, the other from pulverized allspice berries, sugar, and water. The drink was garnished with a stick of cinnamon and a slice of apple.

While they cooked, Rosemary and Bert indulged in cocktails too—theirs with alcohol. It led to probing conversations and much laughter as they put together their spectacular presentations.

This evening they were sharing a small pitcher of top-shelf side-cars—Cognac and Cointreau were the featured reagents. Rosemary still felt a twinge of guilt about returning to alcohol while William had to abstain—but he himself had encouraged her to do so, and he *was* out of sight in another room while she drank with Bert, so she regularly convinced herself it was okay.

Tonight, Rosemary and Bert were experimenting with a cuisine with which neither had much experience: they were creating, from scratch, a vast array of Lebanese mezze. These appetizer plates, along with fresh pita bread, would be shared by everyone. Several cook-books sat open on the counter as Bert and Rosemary busied them-selves creating hummus, babaghanoush, dolmas, tabbouleh, tzatziki, and falafel. There would also be an enormous Greek salad, topped with sharp, salty, sheep's milk feta cheese. And for dessert they were baking Lebanese baklawa, similar to Greek baklava but soaked in an orange blossom and rose water syrup rather than honey.

Their cutting boards were just a few feet apart as they worked.

"So, you've been back at the dentist's office for a couple of weeks now," Bert said as he loaded garbanzo beans into the blender to start the hummus. "I guess that's going well."

"I didn't miss it as much as I thought I would," Rosemary said as she sliced up cucumbers and tomatoes for the salad. "Maybe I'm just getting tired of cleaning teeth after all these years. And the bending over all the time—my back can't take it like it used to. I don't know. While I'm there all day, I'm mostly looking forward to coming home and cooking with *you*! This is really fun."

"Yeah, it is. I love cooking with you too, Rosemary."

Bert opened a jar of tahini and added some to the blender. Rosemary grabbed a red onion for the salad.

"So, you've been seeing a lot of Davey," she said. "You seem to really like him."

The tips of Bert's ears reddened slightly. "He's a great guy. I love spending time with him."

"I know he's been trying to get a catering business going. Has he found customers?"

"More and more. It's really taking off. I've helped him with a few of the big orders. Maybe you'd like to come help too sometime. Especially if the dentist's office is getting old."

Rosemary stopped peeling the onion and thought about what Bert had just proposed. "I've really never considered making a change like that," she said. "Wow. Now you've got me thinking."

"You love cooking."

"I do," she said, her mind racing. "Maybe I could try to help now and then—on weekends, to start. I wouldn't want to give up my regular job unless the catering became a steady thing."

"Well, you're in luck," Bert said with a chuckle. "Davey kind of overbooked himself for this weekend. He has three gigs and he's really excited about them, and I said I'd come over to his place to help. He's afraid even with two people it's still too much work. Do you want to give us a hand?"

Rosemary took a deep breath. This was coming at her faster than she expected. "Um, uh, okay," she stammered. "You're sure I'm good enough to work with two professionals like you guys?"

"You're way good enough. I told Davey about you. You're just as good as I am, and that's what I said."

"Wow. That's quite a compliment. Thank you." She pondered it just another moment, to be certain. "All right! I'll do it!" she cried. She put down her knife, clapped her hands, and jumped up and down, a huge grin stretched across her face. "This sounds like fun. Does he have a big kitchen?"

"No, it's pretty small, actually. We'll be cramped but we can make it work."

"Why don't you have him come over here? This kitchen is enormous. There are three workstations, an island, tons of counter space . . ."

"That would be so great. Thanks, Rosemary. Davey's going to be really excited."

Every surface in the expansive kitchen of the Sonoma house was laden with bowls and plates arrayed with delicious concoctions.

Dirty pots and pans were piled high in the sink, while others sat on the stove heating yet more food. Cookbooks with pages stained by multicolored sauces and juices sat open upon chairs and on the corners of cutting boards.

The aromas were seductive.

It was undoubtedly those beguiling aromas that lured Arthur and Laurel directly to the kitchen when they entered the house. They'd just returned from a leisurely Saturday morning drive, replete with a couple of stops for wine tasting. Laurel had some houses to show later in the day—but those properties were local, so she had plenty of time to frolic prior to going out.

They found Rosemary and Bert hard at work, along with a young man they didn't recognize.

"Who's this?" Arthur demanded.

"Well, good morning to you too, Arthur," Rosemary squawked derisively. Her tone grew considerably warmer as she wished Laurel a good morning as well.

"This all looks quite delicious!" Laurel said.

"I asked who this is!" Arthur cried, his voice a bit louder and more insistent.

"This is Bert's friend Davey," Rosemary said.

"What?" Arthur's face began to turn a shade of crimson.

With an emphatic series of audible footsteps, Laurel positioned herself directly in front of Arthur, effectively blocking him from the rest of the room. Her hands rose to rest menacingly on her hips. "Arthur," she warned, "you be nice!" Her tone was assertive, her enunciation impeccably exaggerated.

"But—"

"Arthur!" she repeated with authority. "You be nice to everyone in this room. I'm not in the mood to argue. Got it?"

Arthur emitted a soft, guttural snarl before muttering, "All right."

As Laurel stepped back to her position at Arthur's side, Rosemary said, "Davey is a caterer. We're helping him with a huge gig."

"Rosemary and I are making money off this," Bert added.

"Money? Really?" Arthur said, suddenly interested.

"Well," Laurel proclaimed, "money or not, whoever gets to eat all this stuff is really lucky. It looks fantastic."

Arthur had regained his composure. He kept his head down but strolled about, sniffing the plates and bowls. "Laurel's right, everything looks and smells damn good," he said. He raised his head and glared at Rosemary. "Jesus, Rosemary, I own this damn kitchen. Don't I get to taste anything?"

Rosemary's face reddened and her neck muscles tightened. Her rage was about to detonate when Arthur surprised her by concluding his coarsely stated demand with a playful smirk and wink. She relaxed, returned a sardonic smile, and dug out a handful of teaspoons and salad forks, which she handed to Laurel. "You two can taste whatever you want," she said, "just use a clean utensil for everything."

"Actually," Davey said, "we'd like to know what you think."

"I don't recognize anything," Arthur complained as he began to taste. "What the hell is all this stuff?"

"Just taste it, and then we'll tell you," Rosemary said.

Arthur and Laurel spent several minutes walking from item to item, taking small tastes of each. There was lots of masticating and swallowing, mixed with an occasional monosyllabic utterance of delight.

Finally, Arthur looked up. "This stuff is fantastic! Everything! Jesus! The three of you should be a full-time catering company!"

"It's all vegan," Davey announced.

Arthur's features screwed themselves into an incredulous scowl. "What?" he bellowed.

"I agree," Laurel said. "That's hard to believe."

"This is something I wanted to do from the start," Davey said, "to make us stand out from the other caterers. We can do the regular stuff, but we can also do vegetarian, vegan, pescatarian, gluten-free, that kind of thing."

"And you know how to do all that?" Arthur asked.

"Between the three of us we know a lot," Davey said. "But vegan is especially challenging. We have three gigs this weekend, and the biggest, by far, is this vegan wedding. It's an outdoor affair, fifty people, totally vegan. Not many caterers can do that kind of thing—I mean, really do it right. I've been experimenting with vegan food for months now, and I've gotten pretty good at it. It's really creative, and very different in technique. You have to use the blender a lot—you're creating your own nut-milks, and purées, and sauces. We have more to learn. But I think this meal came out really good."

"You know the other night when Rosemary and I made Lebanese mezze for you guys?" Bert said. "Most of it was actually vegan too—not because we were trying to be vegan, just because that's the way the dishes are done traditionally. And Davey's right, Rosemary and I were at the blender all night."

"Well," Arthur said, his voice uncharacteristically enthusiastic, "I love it, and I'm Mr. Carnivore! You three are amazing. You should definitely be in business."

"That's nice of you to say," Davey replied, "but it's going to take a long time to grow. A business like this—if you want to go full bore—you need a good chunk of start-up capital; you have to have something to live off while you build your customer base. I've been working and saving, but it's going to take a while."

"If you can make food like this," Arthur said, "and the three of you are in—I'll finance you."

Davey's mouth dropped open. "For real?"

"Believe me," Bert said, "he can do it."

"I'll have my lawyer draw up some papers," Arthur said. "Standard stuff. Then we can negotiate the fine print and the numbers. Basically, it'll be a loan—I'll be a silent partner, and I'll take a little chunk of the profit every month, then one day you'll buy me out."

"That sounds great," Davey said.

"We're in business, people!" Arthur exclaimed as he walked over and shook the hands of the three chefs.

It was not lost on Bert that it was the first time he had shaken his father's hand in a very long time.

As Arthur turned to leave the room, Laurel rested a palm on his shoulder. "You know," she said, "if they keep on serving vegan food here in the house, I'm going to lose some weight."

Arthur turned abruptly and pointed his finger threateningly at Laurel. "Don't you lose too much!" he barked. "I like my women cushy."

His remark engendered laughter that persisted long after the couple exited the kitchen.

CHAPTER 23

ROSEMARY was at work at the dentist's office.

Laurel had driven down to San Francisco to show houses.

Arthur was sequestered in his cottage, researching companies for investments.

Bert and Davey were spending the day hiking at Mount Tamalpais State Park.

Which left William sitting motionless, alone in his painting studio, endeavoring desperately to fortify his resolve. It was finally time to try to paint.

He had repeatedly made excuses and put it off. At least now, with everyone out of the house, he could have a go at it alone, with no danger of anyone seeing what he'd done.

He was fairly convinced that it was going to be a disaster.

He'd chosen a few pictures from the surreal dictionary he'd so painstakingly compiled. Now, using them as a starting point, he began to paint.

He labored for over two hours, copying the dictionary entries and trying to fuse them into a reasonably harmonized gestalt.

What he produced, though, looked wooden and discordant.

Over and over he tried to integrate the pieces into a meaningful whole, trying every technique he could muster. But everything he attempted just made it worse. In the end, it looked to him as if some feral child had broken into the cottage of a painter, torn shreds from the canvases he found, plopped the fragments onto the floor, splashed paint haphazardly on top of the pile, and allowed the result to congeal into a hideous, motley fiasco.

William stepped back and stared at it. He began to tremble. Then to cry. What started as modest tears soon morphed into hysterical sobs. He collapsed to the floor and lay curled like a fetus, weeping uncontrollably for a quarter of an hour, until his tear ducts could produce nothing more.

He lifted his head and screamed to the empty house, "What's the point? What's the fucking point?"

The volume of his voice modulated to a morose whisper as he continued, "I can't paint anymore. And I'm not smart like I used to be. That's not coming back. Nothing's coming back. I'm nothing. I'm no one. There's no point in any of this anymore."

William leaped to his feet. He grabbed a jackknife that was sitting among his paintbrushes, yanked it open, and slashed to slivers the canvas he'd just completed.

He then gazed at the open jackknife in his hand, its blade thick with oozing paint. It was a very sharp knife. He shifted his glance to his forearms, exposed beneath his rolled-up sleeves. Unmoving, he studied his flesh for a very long time.

He pictured blood spurting from his arms. Pooling on the floor. Draining all the wretched life from his body.

He recalled reading once that the right way to do it was lengthwise, along the arms. Not across them.

Suddenly he threw his head back and began hyperventilating. These thoughts terrified him—paralyzed him. The fact that he was considering taking his own life—that his imaginings were so visceral, so real, so immediate—inspired a terror he had never experienced before. Suicide was something he'd never remotely contemplated.

What the hell was going on?

He clenched his teeth and tried to slow his breathing.

It was at that exact moment that a blinding flash of light emanated from behind his eyes and filled the room around him.

His breathing became slow and steady. The muscles of his face and body relaxed. A pervasive sense of peace, happiness, and love engulfed his entire being.

He opened his eyes wide—and it was as if a heavy gauze had been peeled away from them. Everything looked clear and crisp. The energy around him was palpable and immediate; it enveloped him, sheltered him in its immensity.

A grand realization seized his mind with a fundamental, all-encompassing, non-rational power. He suddenly understood that he was a tiny part of an enormous, intricate, timeless, infinite entity. Everything that ever was or would ever be was within him. A tangible eternal love emanated from its essence—its power was dazzling.

He'd been blocked by ambition, self-obsession, a preoccupation with how people saw him. He understood, finally, that he just needed to love. To accept. To appreciate. To be a tiny part of a greater whole.

William raced to the corner of his studio and pulled out a large canvas he had primed with gesso months earlier. He set it upon his largest easel and—working manically—covered the entire canvas with a spectacular array of light, composed of every color of the spectrum. The manner in which he employed his pigments somehow empowered them to generate their own mystical luminescence as they blended together.

Then he painted a collection of surreal objects from the dictionary he'd meticulously compiled, but now rather than trying to artificially connect them he scattered them about the canvas atop that blinding spiritual light and added disembodied waves of water, seemingly without source but cascading perpetually amidst the objects—animals, trees, planets, asteroids, and balls of fire. In the center he painted an array of flowers—radiating light as they unfurled, glistening in brilliant hues—being pollinated by giant, cherubic bees whose fleecy yellow fuzz melted into the petals of the blossoms around them.

It was massive, beautiful, and overwhelming.

Rosemary found William sitting on a chair in his studio, staring across the room at his creation.

Molly, who hadn't been spotted for days, was curled serenely in his lap.

Rosemary noticed the cat first and was about to comment about how strange it was to see her sitting peacefully like that—but then she glimpsed the massive painting on the other side of the room, and her head jerked around and her body spun to face it.

"Oh my god!" she screamed, her mouth opened in astonishment. She scanned the canvas, over and over, struggling to catch her breath. "This is amazing, Will! Just amazing. My god—so different, yet with bits of the old. So powerful. Jesus, Will, you're going to be a celebrity . . . *Again!*"

He looked up from his chair and, stroking the back of Molly's head, said gently, "That really doesn't matter anymore. If it happens, that's nice. But I don't need it. *We* don't need it. We don't need to be famous or clever, Rosemary. We just need to love each other. We're part of something that we can't really ever understand. It's infinite. And it's eternal. And as much as anyone tries to wrap their head around all that—they can't. But all of that is in our love—all of it—at every moment."

Until that instant Rosemary had felt sorry for him—for his loss of intellectual acuity, for the things his surgery had changed about his brain. Suddenly, she no longer did.

He was going to be seen now as an even greater painter in this new style—a genius.

But that wasn't the reason.

What they already had really *was* all that mattered. And although much of what William had just said didn't seem to make any rational sense, he'd nonetheless convinced her—on a level that she could feel viscerally, though not cerebrally—that all those things he insisted were contained in their love actually were.

Bert and Rosemary were in the kitchen, cooking a vegan Ethiopian dinner for the family.

Arthur and Laurel had been sipping drinks in the living room for quite a while when William, who had been napping, finally joined them. He found a tall Cloudy Tokyo—green tea, coconut milk, and coconut soda—waiting for him, chilling on ice, white and frothy.

Greetings were exchanged, and William sat down.

"Oh, Arthur," Laurel said with excitement. "Have you seen Will's newest painting? It's remarkable."

"I saw it yesterday," Arthur said. "It's great. I emailed a photo of it to my guy in New York. He loved it too. Said it's the best thing Will's done yet." He turned to William. "You heard him say that, right?"

William smiled and nodded.

"As soon as William gets a few more paintings like that together, my guy's gonna work him up a new online gallery show. He's going to be hotter than he ever was."

Bert and Rosemary called everyone into the dining room, where the first course had just been laid out on the table.

They sat down and started eating.

"The food is great, as usual," Arthur said, gulping manically. "How's our catering business going?"

"Excellent," Bert said. "We're drumming up new clients all the time."

"I submitted my notice at the dentist's office," Rosemary said. "I told them I'll be leaving in four weeks. I think by then there'll be enough customers for me to start cooking full time."

"Very good," Arthur said.

Laurel put her fork down. "Now, Arthur, there's something *else* that's good that you need to tell everybody."

Arthur looked at her oddly.

"You know," Laurel said. "We talked about it. How you're proud of your boys. Come on. You promised."

Arthur groaned. "Oh, all right." He swallowed the enormous mouthful he'd been chewing. "I have to admit," he said in a hoarse whisper, "I never really thought painting or cooking were ways to make a living. But you're both making money now. And you're both doing good. So yeah, I'm proud of you both." He turned back to Laurel. "Okay? I said it."

"That's good, Arthur," Laurel said. "Now tell them about the will."

"Jesus, I'm trying to eat, here."

"Arthur," Laurel demanded, "tell them about the will!"

"Oh, all right. Jesus. So, I had my will redone. I'm splitting everything three ways."

"Three ways?" Rosemary asked.

"That's right," he said. "A third to Laurel, a third to William, and a third to Bertram." Arthur chuckled. "What the hell. I'll be dead. Why should I care?"

"Well, that's very kind of you," Rosemary said. "And very fair, I think. But your will's not going to matter at all for a very long time. You have lots of good years ahead of you, Arthur—you're not going anywhere soon."

Laurel grinned wickedly. "Hell," she said, "if being ornery keeps a person alive, he's going to live forever."

Everybody laughed. Even Arthur could not refrain—he wound up laughing harder than anyone, and had to prop his hand on the table to keep himself upright in his chair.

In New York City, on the fifteenth floor of his office building, Dag Ødegaard was alone in the men's room. He was standing in front of a urinal, zipping up his pants, when the IT guy who habitually tormented him strolled in and said—loud enough so that his affected tenor echoed off the tiled walls and ceiling—"Oh, girlfriend, someone had asparagus for lunch again."

"Jesus Christ!" Dag screeched as he flushed. "You're such a schmuck. Can't you just keep your goddamn mouth shut?"

"Why must you be such a shrill old queen?" the IT guy trilled as he sashayed closer. "Can't you just laugh at yourself now and then?"

"Go to hell."

"You know what you need, girlfriend? You need to be soundly and longly fucked."

"Oh yeah?" Dag screamed, his face red now, his cadence apoplectic. "That's the answer to all my problems, huh? What's your solution to that one? You gonna come over to my apartment and do it tonight, you asshole?"

The IT guy smiled archly. "Actually, I'd love to. I've had my eye on you for a while now."

Dag's brow furrowed and his eyes ballooned, as he gazed up,

dumbfounded, at the younger man. "What? You *like* me? You sure have a hell of a strange way of showing it."

The IT guy laughed. "You're probably right," he said. "Sorry if I've been obnoxious. It's kind of my curse in life. My name's Barney, by the way."

"I'm Dag."

The men shook hands.

Barney stepped a bit closer, leaned down, and softened his voice. "How about this, Dag? Tonight, after I fuck you very soundly, if you have anything decent in your fridge, I'll whip us up some supper. I'm pretty good around the kitchen, you know."

ACKNOWLEDGMENTS

MANY thanks to Lauren Wise, Brooke Warner, and the entire publishing team at SparkPress for their tireless efforts on the book's behalf; to Krissa Lagos for enhancing the novel with a diligent and artistic copyedit; to Megan Hannum for a meticulous proofread; to Julie Metz for an eye-catching cover design; to Rachel Hutchings of Books Forward, a publicist who, at every turn, made me feel that the book was as important to her as it was to me; to Elysse Wagner of Books Forward, whose charm and expertise made everything she touched easier; to Madeleine Jones, Ken Jakobs, Michael Rose, Carla Damron, David Jenkins, Glenn German, Michael Miller, and Michael J. Coffino for their kind and rousing endorsements; and most of all to my beautiful wife Sandy, my eternal soulmate, whose love enriches every moment of my life.

ABOUT THE AUTHOR

© Nancy Warner

*R*OBERT *S*TEVEN *G*OLDSTEIN retired from his job as a healthcare information executive at age fifty-six and has been writing novels ever since. His first novel, *The Swami Deheftner,* about problems that ensue when ancient magic and mysticism manifest in the twenty-first century, has developed a small cult following in India. His second novel, *Enemy Queen,* an erotic thriller set in a North Carolina college town, was published in 2020, and was a finalist in the category of cross genre fiction for the International Book Awards. His third novel, *Cat's Whisker,* published in 2021, probes the perceived rift between science and spirituality; an excerpt from *Cat's Whisker,* entitled "An Old Dog," was featured in the fall 2018 edition of the literary journal *Leaping Clear. Will's Surreal Period* is his fourth novel. Robert lives in San Francisco with Sandy, his wife of thirty-three years, and Cali, a fearless, lovable Akita/cattle dog. Robert has practiced yoga, meditation, and vegetarianism for more than fifty years.

SELECTED TITLES FROM SPARKPRESS

SparkPress is an independent boutique publisher delivering high-quality, entertaining, and engaging content that enhances readers' lives, with a special focus on female-driven work. www.gosparkpress.com

Attachments: A Novel, Jeff Arch, $16.95, 9781684630813
What happens when the mistakes we make in the past don't stay in the past? When no amount of running from the things we've done can keep them from catching up to us? When everything depends on what we do next?

Enemy Queen: A Novel, Robert Steven Goldstein, $16.95, 978-1-68463-026-4
A woman initiates passionate sexual encounters with two articulate but bumbling and crass middle-aged men, but what she demands in return soon becomes untenable. A short time later she goes missing, prompting the county sheriff to open a murder investigation.

That's Not a Thing: A Novel, Jacqueline Friedland. $16.95, 978-1-68463-030-1
When a recently engaged Manhattanite learns that her first great love has been diagnosed with ALS, she is faced with the impossible decision of whether a few final months with her ex might be worth risking her entire future. A fast-paced emotional journey that explores whether it's possible to be equally in love with two men at once.

Rooville: A Novel, Julie Long. $17, 978-1-940716-60-2
Intent on a simpler life, Owen Martin returns to his Iowa hometown. What he finds is a changed town, one that's just as complicated as the world he's left behind.

Ways of Leaving: A Novel, Grant Jarrett. $16.95, 978-1-940716-41-
Chase Stoller's life is crumbling. He just lost his job, his wife Jennifer has filed for divorce, and now his brother Aaron wants him to return to Pennsylvania and help care for their ailing father. But Chase's greatest challenge comes when his sister attempts to end her life.

ABOUT SPARKPRESS

SparkPress is an independent, hybrid imprint focused on merging the best of the traditional publishing model with new and innovative strategies. We deliver high-quality, entertaining, and engaging content that enhances readers' lives. We are proud to bring to market a list of *New York Times* best-selling, award-winning, and debut authors who represent a wide array of genres, as well as our established, industry-wide reputation for creative, results-driven success in working with authors. SparkPress, a BookSparks imprint, is a division of SparkPoint Studio LLC.

Learn more at GoSparkPress.com